# The Ark Ranch

# The Ark Ranch

Barclay Franklin

# THE ARK RANCH

iUniverse books may be ordered through booksellers or by contacting:

iUniverse
1663 Liberty Drive
Bloomington, IN 47403
www.iuniverse.com
1-800-Authors (1-800-288-4677)

Because of the dynamic nature of the Internet, any web addresses or links contained in this book may have changed since publication and may no longer be valid. The views expressed in this work are solely those of the author and do not necessarily reflect the views of the publisher, and the publisher hereby disclaims any responsibility for them.

Any people depicted in stock imagery provided by Thinkstock are models, and such images are being used for illustrative purposes only. Certain stock imagery © Thinkstock.

ISBN: 978-1-5320-0625-8 (sc)
ISBN: 978-1-5320-0626-5 (e)

Library of Congress Control Number: 2016914201

Print information available on the last page.

iUniverse rev. date: 08/27/2016

# *Acknowlegments*

I would like to thank Phil and Rose Shivel for allowing me to take pictures of their goats for the cover of my book.

# *Chapter One*

Several years passed since the Blackburns had moved to their ranch in Chino Valley. Andy was in high school. Alli was in sixth grade and Kade and Abby had a new set of twins, Kory Alan and Kathy Amber.

"Hey, wife, you'll never guess what happened today," Kade said, sitting down at the dinner table.

"I don't have time for guessing games. Kory has another earache and spent most of the day crying."

"Okay, I'll wait for a more auspicious time to give you my news. Since it looks like we'll be here for the foreseeable future, I think we should name our ranch. Who wants to suggest a name for it?"

Andy piped up, "We should call it the Goat Ranch, since we have produced so many."

Alli chimed in. "We have horses, too, and I think they'd be sad if we named it for only the goats."

"We have lots of pairs of things on this ranch. Mama and I are a pair, Andy and Alli are a pair, Kory and Kathy are a real pair, being twins. We started off with two goats, two horses a couple of hens, too. What do all those pairs suggest to you?"

"You're never satisfied with having just one thing at a time?" Abby said.

Kade gave her a grin. "No, that wasn't what I was thinking about. What Biblical figure collected two of each thing?"

"Are you talking about Noah?" Andy asked. Andy was the only one acquainted with Biblical stories, since he'd attended those play days in the basement of the church when he was younger.

"I was talking about Noah. He gathered up two of each animal and his sons and their wives, so I was going to suggest calling our place the **ARK RANCH** as we have two of about everything on our ranch, too.

"Are you expecting a flood, Kade?" Abby asked.

"Are you going to build a real ark, Dad?" Andy asked.

"Nope, to both questions. Almost every other ranch in this valley has a name, and some of them have a brand, too. Just got to thinking we might as well name our place and develop a brand to go with it."

"I thought you hated the smell of burning flesh. You told me it upset your stomach when Dad asked you to help him brand his calves."

"I wasn't interested in branding anything, just having a brand on the sign for our ranch."

At that point, Kory started crying again. "Let me have him, Abby. Finish your dinner. Kade picked up his six-month-old son and took him upstairs. "Hey, little man, what's with those ears of yours? I remember how bad an earache hurts. I read that using a hair dryer on it sometimes helps."

Kade picked up Abby's dryer and turned it on. Let it get warm then directed the warm air onto Kory's ear. After a half hour, the hot air seemed to have relieved the pain and Kory fell asleep. Abby came up to spell Kade so he could eat. She was amazed to find Kory sound asleep in his crib.

"How did you manage that?" she asked. "No matter what I did, he cried every half hour all day long. Go eat while he's quiet."

Kade followed her back down the stairs and sat down again in front of his plate.

"Let me nuke it in the microwave, Kade. It's surely cold by now."

"It's fine, Abby. Rest while you can. I'll get up with our new son if he cries in the night. I know how hard it is to cope when you've had no sleep."

"But you need to work tomorrow."

"No, I have the next week off."

"Was that what you wanted to tell me before dinner."

"No, but I'll tell you my news in the morning, after you've had a good night's rest. I'll clean up after dinner and Alli, Andy and I will do the dishes, too. Go take a nice warm shower and crawl into bed. Get some shut-eye."

After the 10 p.m. news, Kory was still deep into dreamland, so Kade took a shower and got into bed without waking Abby. *She must be exhausted,* he thought, *if she didn't even stir when I climbed into bed. We may need to get some of those tubes put in Kory's ears. That's about the fourth time he's had problems and it's not good to keep plying him with antibiotics.*

Kade got up once in the night to give Kory a bottle when he cried. His son went right back to sleep after a diaper change. He fed Kathy, too, and changed her as well. When he returned to his own bed, Abby didn't stir, letting him know his assessment of her exhausted state was probably right on the money.

In the morning, it was a different story. He was still sleeping when she kissed his ear. "Ummm," he said. "You haven't done that to me in a long time."

"I know, and I'm sorry, Kade. Those twins just wear me to a frazzle. What was your news? I appreciate you letting me sleep, but I'm awake now, so spill it, partner."

"You think your friend, Marcie, would be willing to come and mind our children for a weekend?"

"Yes, I know she'd be willing. She needs the money she'd earn, for next fall's classes at the college."

"Ask her for the last weekend in July, then. We'll be going to Phoenix for a relaxing weekend."

"Why? Not that a weekend away from here doesn't sound like heaven on earth, but you've never invited *me* to go to Phoenix with you."

"You're referring to the weekend I spent with Corrine down there?"

"I don't want to fight with you this morning, Kade. Not after you were so nice to me last night, but yes, I was referring to that weekend you spent with her in Phoenix."

"Shall I rent a room at the Biltmore? Same room? We could swim in the pool. I could wear my Speedo. I'd even pose naked for you if you want to sketch me," he teased.

"Why are you going to Phoenix? There are places much closer to have a weekend getaway."

"I agree, but the Arizona Journalist's annual meeting is being held in Phoenix this summer. I'd prefer it if they held it in Flagstaff . . . much cooler up there, but it wasn't my place to decide the location."

"You didn't go to it before. Why now?"

"Don't think I'll tell you. Let it be a surprise. Are you going with me or not?"

"Yes. It's likely the only time in the next 20 years we can get away from all the kids."

"Are you regretting indulging in the sex that led to the twins? I think I'll take care of a small matter before we head to Phoenix, so we won't be overcrowding the ark by having more."

"No, I don't regret having sex with you that led to the twins. If both of them would stay healthy at the same time . . ."

"I'm sorry, Ab. You should have let me know how much strain you were under."

"So you could do what, Kade? Stay home from work to help me out? All those twos this ranch contains—I couldn't possibly sustain all the feed and care for them on my salary. I know you have to go to work."

"Yep, I do. In the evenings, however, I could do more to help out around the place. Then you wouldn't be sitting up with your bookkeeping duties until midnight."

"You do help out around the house. You often do the dishes, start a load of laundry, and you always feed the stock."

"I think it would be good for us to get away from all the chores inherent in this place. Maybe a couple of times a year we'll just take off and spend some time by ourselves."

"Is it some special occasion?"

"You'll just have to wait and see. Buy you a pretty dress to wear to the meeting—something cool and summery. Shoes to match, and maybe a shawl to wear, too, since they tend to crank up the AC in Phoenix in the summertime. Don't want you down with an earache like Kory."

"Can we afford all those items?"

Kade got out of bed and picked up his pants. Handed Abby $400. "Will that cover a dress and shoes?" he asked.

"Where did you get all that money?"

"I got a substantial raise at the paper, due to me being elected . . . but that will have to wait until we go to the meeting. I'm not going to tell you about it now."

"How did you get Kory to sleep all through the night?"

"He didn't sleep all through it. He cried about 3 a.m. I fed him a bottle and changed him. He went right back to sleep."

"I never heard him cry."

"I know. You were dead to the world. I gave Kathy a bottle, too."

Summer came on with a vengeance. In Abby's closet hung a summery sundress with matching shoes taking up space on the shoe rack. Kade still hadn't said why he was determined to go to the Journalist's meeting, but he'd approved of what she planned to wear.

Abby was tempted to call Ms. Dean and ask what the occasion entailed, but after all Kade's tales about his strong-willed boss, she was reluctant to phone up Dean with her question.

Finally the weekend arrived. Marcie had jumped at the chance to mind the children. Not that Alli or Andy needed adult supervision, but the twins certainly did. Abby left both her and Kade's cell phone numbers and posted the number for the twin's doctor in case any of them got sick. Andy had passed his driver's test in May, and he volunteered to go to the store for anything they wanted to eat.

"No rodding around after dark," Kade warned Andy. "I need you here in the house after six or seven, to keep everyone safe—since you are my only karate black-belt child."

"I'll be good, Dad. Can't leave all these girls to their own devices. With you gone, I'll be their tough protector."

"No running your girlfriend into your bed so you can spend the night protecting her, too."

"D-a-a-d!" Andy protested, drawing the word out. "Molly and I don't have that kind of relationship."

"You don't? How come after every date, you come home with your lips all dry and cracked. You have to be doing some serious swapping of spit for them to look like they've been through the Boer War."

"Don't you trust me, Dad?"

"Sure, I trust you. Take care to maintain my trust in you. If you ever lose my trust you'll rue the day."

Driving the old truck he'd had for years, Kade and Abby headed for Phoenix. He'd reserved a room at the Biltmore—not the one he'd shared with Corrine, but one on the same floor. He'd packed his Speedo, too. When Abby saw that going into his suitcase, she'd pulled out her bikini and packed it in her bag.

"The only thing different about this trip—as opposed to the one I took with your mother—this time I cleaned out the truck. Got rid of all the loose hay, the pebbles and the dirt that gets tracked in. That's how much more I appreciate your company than hers."

Abby gave him a look. "Yes, and I left my sketch pad and paints at home, too, so as not to remind you what you're missing this trip. I won't be asking you to take off your Speedo so I can sketch you, either."

"You may want to voice that request. It led to a pretty hot tumble in the bed."

"Just what we need. Another set of twins."

"No more kids, Abby. I took care of that problem back in May. We can enjoy a hot tumble without worrying about increasing our family."

"You took care of the problem? How? I think I'd know if you'd done something permanent. You'd have been sore if you'd been clipped."

"Remember that week I was in San Diego to cover the story about the how the state of California was trying to shut down those Orca shows where that whale drowned its handler? Remember I told you and Ms. Dean I wanted an extra week to follow up on the changes they were making to Sea World policies?"

"Yes, I thought at the time you were just trying to avoid all those midnight feedings for the twins. Having yourself a short vacation at my expense."

Kade grinned. "Yep, I was having a short vacation, but it wasn't a very pleasant one. I *was* sore. Remember how, when I got home, we went a whole six weeks with no sex?"

"I thought that was because I was so mad at you for deserting me while I was trying to nurse both twins."

"I had to wait six weeks to be tested, so I just let your simmering anger work to my advantage. Since then, I haven't resorted to a condom, because the test was clear."

"I wondered about that. I thought you were beginning to feel your age and wanted another couple of kids before you couldn't keep it up without Viagra."

Kade laughed so hard at that statement, he almost ran off the highway. "Sweetheart, you're so delectable in bed, I'll be ninety before I might need some of those pills to make love to you."

That earned him another spate of rolling eyes from Abby.

"You don't believe me, sweetheart? I love the way you look. I love having sex with you. You are delectable in bed."

"That's why you strayed so often? Because you loved making love to me?"

Kade sighed. *Should I tell her? Ruin my tough-guy image?* He reached over and caught her hand in his.

"I might look like a tough Army Ranger to the outside, but I'm soft as a marshmallow inside, especially when it comes to you or our children. If you'll recall, the only times I strayed was when you were so angry with me—you delivered some very painful statements to me— that's what drove me into someone else's arms.

"Straying was my form of revenge on you, pure and simple. My way to cope with how much your words hurt me. I couldn't keep up my tough façade, not if I'd taken to mooning around or crying. I wanted you to hurt as much as I was hurting, and that was the one method I knew would hurt you."

"Really, Kade?"

"Think about it, Abby. The only time my sense of revenge was not in play was on my trip to Phoenix with Corrine. All the other times, you'd either said something that hurt me—like threatening to file for divorce—or you left me behind in Flagstaff when you went to spend Thanksgiving at the ranch—telling me I wasn't welcome to join in."

"I may just have to revise my whole outlook where you're concerned."

"I think we're over those various humps in our marriage now. I haven't felt the need to hurt you in a long time—about as long as you've stopped wounding me with your words."

"I never realized . . ."

"Yeah, I know. That was part of what made it so painful. You never realized how some of the words you were flinging in my direction cut me to the core. You only saw the tough guy, not the softer one inside."

"I'm sorry for missing the softer side of you."

"Doesn't matter anymore. We've settled into being a comfortable, old married couple now."

They eventually arrived at the Biltmore and were shown up to their room. "The pool is warm. Want to go for a swim?" he asked.

"I don't know. I should have gotten a full suit. Not sure I want all my stretch marks on display."

"You earned them all honestly. Put on your suit and I'll give you a tee shirt to cover up with. I'm kind of nervous about tomorrow night, so a few laps might uncoil some of the kinks in me."

"Would it help you to talk about the meeting? Do you have a part in it?"

"Yes, a big part, but I'm not going to let you wheedle my part in it out of me."

"There's a shop on the basement floor of this hotel. Give me an hour and I'll go to the pool with you."

"You're going to get a full suit? Need more money? I kind of like you in the bikini, Abby."

"I have money, Kade. I'll be back in a little bit."

She disappeared out the door and he turned on the TV to wait. When she came back, she'd had her hair clipped very short. She looked like a gamine.

"Whoa! Wife. What prompted you to get a pixie cut?"

"It's too hot down here and this kind of cut will let me swim with you and not be all stressed out about the meeting tomorrow night. I won't need to spend hours on my hair—either here or at home. I think it's a liberating cut. You don't like it?"

"I do like it. Might take a bit of time to get used to seeing you in it, but I think it suits you."

Abby got on her bikini and pulled his tee shirt over it, and they went to the pool. Unlike Corinne, Abby swam laps alongside Kade. She was a strong swimmer. After 25 laps, they both got out to lie in the sun and dry off a bit.

"I see you watching all the broads," Abby said, as Kade's eyes roved around the pool.

"Just comparing them to you. None of them have anything on you, sweetheart. In fact, with all those deep, dark tans, I bet they'll die of skin cancer shortly."

"Yeah, like I could compete with them with all those stretch marks on my belly."

Kade stood up and lifted Abby from her chaise lounge. He took off her tee and sat down with her on his lap. "Woman," he said, tracing the marks, "those stretch marks signify the family you've provided me with. Because I love all four of our children, I also love those stretch marks. They're badges of honor, just like my Medal of Honor. There's not a tanned bimbo at this pool I'd trade you for."

"Then why do you keep ogling them?"

"Doesn't mean I don't appreciate a fine female form. I can appreciate their form, but not like I appreciate what you've given me in the form of four wonderful children."

"Let's go back to the room. I don't want skin cancer and I can't abide all those svelte beauties laughing at my stretch marks either."

Kade shook his head. "They're probably wishing some of them had the same marks. Must be a very vapid life to have noting to do but lie about at the side of a pool. Bet they wished they had kids to give some meaning to their lives."

Abby got up and grabbed the tee back, sliding it over her bikini before starting on the long march back to the hotel. Kade draped an arm around her shoulders, giving her a squeeze. With that arm around her, he felt her cringe each time she passed the lounge where one of the svelte women was arrayed. It didn't help matters that a couple of them whistled low at his physique.

"You want to take dinner at the restaurant or eat up here in our room?" he asked.

"Eat here. Here, none of the women will be whistling at you."

"Okay. What do you want?"

"How about a dose of rat poison?"

"Abby!"

"No matter where we go, Kade, the women have their eyes all over you. They all want to take you to bed. I should have stayed home . . . so you could *enjoy* them . . . in the fullest sense of the word."

Kade stretched out on the bed and folded his hands beneath his head. "You aren't exactly helping my stress levels about tomorrow's ceremony."

"I heard what they did. All those wolf whistles."

"You think I can control what they do?"

"No. But I think if I weren't here, you'd be taking one or two up on their offers."

"Really?"

"Yes, really. They all admire that tough exterior you display—those abs and long muscular arms and legs. You should have been the one wearing the tee shirt, not me. But you don't choose to cover yourself up, do you? You like their admiration."

He ordered dinner for both of them, calling down for room service. Took care to ask for any dressings to be put into a separate container, not put on the food, because he knew she preferred her food that way. While he waited for the order to come up, he stood at the window, looking out.

When the bellhop knocked, he paid for the food and gave the young man a good tip, too. He set the containers on the table under the window and removed the tops.

"Come eat while it's hot," he said.

Abby slid into the chair across from him. "I've managed to hurt you inside again, haven't I?"

Kade shrugged. "Are you ever going to get over the thought I'm just looking for another excuse to cheat on you?"

"I wish you were fat and bald and ugly to boot. Then . . ."

"You'd feel more confident of my love for you?"

"Yes. When temptation crops up on every path you take, it calls up all those times when you succumbed to temptation. We can't even go for a relaxing swim without you getting whistles."

After that, Kade ate and attempted no other conversation. When it came time for bed, he indicated she should sleep in the left double while he took the right one.

In the middle of the night, she slid into bed next to him and kissed his ear. "I'm sorry, Kade. I don't know why I say those things to you. I've hurt you again, and I really don't want to keep doing that. It's just when women come on to you it revs up all those old memories."

"I share in some of the blame for those memories, so . . . I don't know what more I can do to assure you that I'm past taking any other woman up on her offers. I can't help their offers, their comments, or their whistles. I'm perfectly content with you as my wife, sexual partner and mother of our children. Could you manage to let that statement pop into your brain first from now on? Use it to displace all those other memories?"

"I'll try. I think I'll start going to a gym and get as buff as you are. Maybe then you'd have eyes for only me."

"Not sure I want to make love to a woman with six-pack abs. I like the softer you under me."

"Even if it gave me more confidence to have abs like that? Can you teach me what you do—or did—to get yours?"

"Sure. You want me to teach you the whole Army regimen, or just the ones for your abs? Most soldiers spend a long six months trying to get in shape. I guess you could sign up for a tour of duty and do the boot-camp training."

Abby chuckled at that thought.

"I only love you," he said. "Even when I tumbled into bed with other women, I never deluded myself I was in love with them. My cheating only involved the physical act of sex. Neither my head nor my heart was into loving them."

"How do I know you don't feel the same about me?"

"If you don't know by now how I feel about you, there's nothing I can say that will convince you. Sometimes you just have to take things on faith—not proof. I'm still married to you. I'm still trying to do nice things for you. I tell you in a hundred ways a month, that I love you. Show you as often, too."

"I grew up with parents who loved me when it was convenient. Other times, their agendas counted more than I did. I guess that makes me fearful that some day your agenda will overtake your love and . . ."

"Isn't going to happen, Abby. I'm in this marriage for the long haul, no matter what it takes. I don't only love you when it's convenient. I love you 24/7. Can you plant that thought in your head and get past doubting me?"

"Can you make love to me? That's what usually allays all those fears in me."

"Sure."

Kade made love to her gently, in the way she loved best, then pulled her over to cuddle her. "I swear on a stack of Bibles, you're the only woman I love."

"You aren't a religious man, Kade, so that promise rings false."

"No, I'm not religious. Let's try this, then. I swear on the grave of my mother, you're the only woman I love. I would never swear on her grave if I were intent on telling you a lie. I loved Mom. It's one of my greatest sorrows that she died while I was overseas and I never got to say goodbye to her."

"I'm more likely to believe you when you swear on her grave, Kade."

"Good. Can we have no more doubts about my fidelity to you from this point on? I'm not going to take up with anyone other than you—not sexually or physically or in any other manner."

They slept late the next morning, then went down for breakfast. Kade avoided the booth where he'd once sat across from Corinne eating two steaks and double all the other items, too.

"Are you still nervous about tonight?" she asked.

"Yeah, a bit. It's put me off eating a big breakfast. I'm just having tea and an English muffin with some scrambled eggs. What do you want?"

"I'll have what you're having but add in a couple of links of sausage for me."

He gave the waitress both orders. She gave him a huge smile and a wink. Abby caught both of those. She sat shaking her head. "Even turning in our order earns you a wink and a smile."

"Did I respond to either thing? Did I jump up and ask her for her number and what time she'd be available for sex? Do you realize how far you blow their responses to me out of proportion?"

"I'm not going to say another word to you about those matters."

"Good, my ears could use a reprieve for the rest of this weekend."

"What should we do with the rest of the day?" Abby asked.

"If we had the kids along, I'd vote for a tour of the zoo. Since we left the kids at home, is there a movie you'd like to see?"

"No, I can't think of any. We should go see Mom's new exhibit at the Heard Museum."

"Wouldn't that dredge up more doubts about my . . ?"

"No, I promise you I won't think about that if we go to see her paintings."

"Okay. I'm game if you are."

After breakfast they got into his truck and he navigated the streets to the museum from memory. He held open the door for her to enter and he picked her up a brochure of the paintings that were currently hung. "Looks like one of the side rooms are where her portraits are displayed," he said, taking her arm to find the room.

"She really is a good artist," Abby said. "Oh, look, there's one of you hanging among the Hopis and Navajos."

"Guess I should be glad she left my pants on in that one. I don't think the Heard welcomes that kind of art—I don't know if they even hang *women* portrayed in the nude."

"Can we tour all the displays to see if that's true?"

"Only if you don't accuse me of ogling the nude females . . . if they have some."

They spent most of the afternoon walking from room to room, checking out the art displayed. When it came to four, Kade suggested they return to the hotel to have time to shower and get dressed for the journalist's dinner, which was to be held before the ceremonies.

"Okay, though with this much shorter haircut, I won't need an hour to do something with it."

"Will wonders never cease? I might actually get to stand in front of the mirror and tie my tie before I have to sprint for the elevator."

"I've never taken that long to do something with my hair."

She caught his grin reflected in the glass door of the museum. "Well I haven't!" she protested. "Name me one time when you were late for a function because I took too much time to arrange my hair."

"I think discretion is the better part of valor in this instance, so I won't mention how I almost didn't arrive at Dutch Kline's wedding in time to serve as his best man."

"You can't blame that on me. It was you in the shower for 45 minutes that afternoon. I don't think you wanted to stand up for him, since he was one of the soldiers who often took Major Richards' side in those days."

"Like the armory dance, it was another of those times when someone thought it would look real classy to have a Medal of Honor recipient stand up for him. Don't think he'd have asked me, save for his future wife's insistence. She wanted to set just the right tone for her upper-class friends. You remember she asked me to wear the medal, don't you?"

"Yes, I recall that episode."

# *Chapter Two*

They arrived at the banquet hall and Kade found their seats at the table, which were delineated by their pin-on nametags. Their seats were but a couple of yards from the edge of the stage.

"At least we won't need to stand on our chairs to see what's occurring up on the stage tonight," he said, pulling out her chair to let Abby sit down. "You really enhance that dress. You look very nice. Want a drink?"

"Yes, some white wine would be nice."

"Coming right up."

Kade made his way to the bar. When he got there, someone called his name.

"Well, if it isn't Kade Blackburn, the cop puncher."

"Hola, Mr. Scott. I think you still owe me a day's pay. Have you come to this function in hopes to catch up with me and pay what you owe me?"

"I'd like to know how you merited and invitation to this function. Are you working as a reporter again? Who's your boss?"

"I'm working in Prescott for Ms. Dean."

"The bitch that can't seem to hang onto any reporters for long."

"I've been there for four or five years now, so she's hung onto me for a long time."

"You're working there for that long only because you couldn't find a job at a respectable paper. Second-rate paper. Second-rate editor. Follows that she'd hire a second-rate reporter."

"You should come and meet my wife. You're one of the reasons I married her. After you fired me, I got a job with her father, Owen Watkins, and fell in love with his daughter, Abby."

"No thanks. I'd prefer not to associate publicly with such a disreputable character. You might get into another bar fight and I'd likely end up in the middle of the slugging match. I prefer to maintain my nose and eyes in their original color—not have them all bruised and bloody."

"What do you consider those natural colors to be, sir? Brown for your nose, for always having it totally up someone's ass, and green for your eyes because they're full of envy for other editors who put out papers far superior to yours?"

"I'm up for an award tonight, Blackburn, so I think it's your eyes that will shortly turn green with envy."

"We'll see who's more envious once the evening comes to a close, Scott."

"What took you so long?" Abby asked when he finally returned with her wine.

"Ran into Mr. Scott, the editor who fired me after the dustup at Boler's Bar. He says he's up for an award tonight. I can hardly wait to see what award they're bestowing on him. Clown of the year, maybe."

They ate dinner. Abby scraped off the gravy from her cut of meat, causing Kade to grin at her. Twice more, he got her another flute of wine before the awards ceremony began in earnest.

"You're not drinking?" she asked, when he didn't arrive with a glass of anything for himself after hitting the bar.

"Can't. I'd better be able to control both my mind and my tongue tonight. Not sure if I lubricated my tongue with several drinks I'd be able to do that. Mr. Scott already thinks I might get into another fight in the bar here."

"Not even one drink?"

"Not tonight. I need to function as your designated driver, since this is your third one."

"Do you begrudge me a couple of drinks?"

"No, ma'am. You deserve to relax and enjoy the evening. You were still sober enough to scrape the gravy off your meat—like you always do—so I don't think I'll have to haul you out from under the table anytime soon."

When the tables had been cleared, the master of ceremonies vaulted up onto the stage and grabbed up a microphone.

"Ladies, gentlemen, editors, reporters, and photographers welcome to the 15th annual Arizona Journalist's Association Awards Program. There are several categories in which awards will be made. We didn't list winners in the program, so as not to give any of you advanced notice, but after all the awards have been handed out, a complete list of the winners will be available in the lobby.

"The first award for best sports photo goes to Mike Clanahan, of the Arizona Republic. I understand he laid on his belly in the end zone to capture it, risking being aerated like sod by the players' cleats."

Mike danced up the aisle, buoyed by a few drinks, to claim his prize.

"That's why I'm not drinking," Kade whispered to Abby, as Mike stumbled up the two stairs to the stage.

"The next award goes to Tom Scott from Payson for his human interest story about the Apache family displaced by last summer's forest fire."

Scott's chest visibly swelled as he made for the stage. He managed to catch Kade's eye and gave him a gloating grin. "See?" he mouthed to Blackburn.

Several more awards were dispensed, before the MC called Ms. Dean to the stage. She took the mike from him and launched into her speech.

"As most of you know, I have trouble hanging onto reporters at my paper. I usually haunt all the university graduations in Arizona, always hoping to find a decent journalism grad to hire. About seven years ago, I attended the graduation ceremonies in Flagstaff. At that graduation, I took note of a young man who'd graduated magna cum laude. I was also impressed by his speech. In it he promised to listen to the common man as closely as he listened to the more affluent. He also promised to tell the truth in his articles, no matter whose toes he stepped on, or who tried to bribe him not to tell the truth.

"I attempted to approach him after the ceremonies were over, but he was surrounded by a cadre of well-wishers, so I decided it was not the time to offer him a job. Imagine my surprise when he showed up in my office almost a year later, looking for employment. That young man remains my best reporter. I think my paper could survive if he were my *only* employee. That's why, when the call for nominations for this function appeared on my computer, I had no dilemma about whom to nominate. His coverage of the Yarnell Hill fire was what won him this state award.

"Not only did he interview the wives and children of the firemen who died, he did it in so compassionate a manner that several of the wives called me up to thank me for sending him out to do the interviews. They said he was polite, quiet, and never overstepped the bounds of decency with those who were mourning their losses.

"In addition, he held the feet of Yavapai County and Prescott City officials to the fire when they declined to pay benefits to some of the surviving families, claiming the part-time firefighters of the Hotshot crew didn't deserve any compensation. With them, Kade was neither polite nor quiet and he definitely stepped on some toes, hard and often, as several of my recorded calls of complaint will attest to.

"Without further ado, I'd like to invite, Kade Andrew Blackburn, to the stage. Kade is this year's winner of the Arizona top-reporter award. Kade, come up and say a few words."

Kade got up slowly and walked to the stairs. He climbed both of them deliberately, without a stumble. He gave Ms. Dean a hug and kissed her cheek, then took the microphone from her hand.

"I am truly honored to be this august group's choice for the state's top journalism award for 2013. If you'll bear with me, I'd like to thank a few people who made it possible for me to receive it.

"First, I'd like to thank Mr. Scott, editor of the Payson paper, for firing me. Next, I'd like to thank Owen Watkins for giving me a job on his ranch. Third, I'd like to thank Major Richards of the Flagstaff Army recruitment office who provided me with three months in solitary confinement, a period during which I decided for certain I wanted to write for a living.

"When I mustered out of the Army for the second time, I applied for a job with Ms. Dean, who sent me out on lots of assignments. Working under her guidance, allowed me to perfect my skills at reporting. Ms. Dean is a tough boss to work for, but, given my not-so-always-spotless background, I sincerely thank her for giving me the chance to work for her paper . . . and for her nomination of me for this award, too.

"Through all the storms and trials in my life, I've had very strong anchors in the persons of my wife and children. With apologies for the use of a song's cliché, my wife, Abby, has truly been the wind beneath my wings. My four children, Andy, Alli, Kory and Kathy, have given me so much joy that I can't imagine where I might have ended up without them. Likely still in a cell someplace.

"As for my interviews with the survivors of the Hill fire, I never held much truck with jamming a microphone in faces to get into the raw emotions of those who were hurting. I kept in mind how I'd like someone to interview my wife and children were such a tragedy to befall me. I tried to understand their sorrows and their angers, both. A few of my tears often joined the ones they were shedding. That's about the extent of the comments I'd like to make, but I invite any questions you have at this time."

A woman rose from one of the tables. "You spoke of your less-than-spotless background. What did you mean by that?"

"After one stint in the Army, where I was sent to Iraq, I worked for the paper in Payson. Mr. Scott was the editor. He sent me to cover the weekend's festivities in Camp Verde during their annual parade and celebration of Ft. Verde Days. I got into a scuffle in Boler's Bar one evening and was sent to jail for socking a local policeman. Mr. Scott made the trip down from Payson to fire me as I sat in my cell. After I was released, I took a job at a Camp Verde ranch and married the owner's daughter. When I thought her father was going to fire me, I re-upped in the Army to have a job so I could support my wife and our new son.

"I landed in Flagstaff, interviewing recruits for the Army at the Army's recruitment center, while I also was taking classes in journalism at the university.

"Major Richards was my commanding officer. We seldom saw eye-to-eye. He brought me up on insubordination charges before a panel of Army officers. I got to spend the last three months of my enlistment in solitary confinement. Being unable to write or call my wife and son for three months was the hardest thing I ever did. My separation from them was what finally convinced me to straighten up and try to do better.

"This award you've bestowed on me tonight, indicates I might be doing better—at least I choose to regard it as a symbol of trying hard to be a credit to journalism and my family. Thanks again for this award. It will occupy a honored place beside the other award I'm also proud to have been given."

"What other award were you given?" another woman asked.

"This miniature gold typewriter will sit on the same shelf as the display case containing my . . ." He let the sentence drift away, shaking his head, not willing to say what the other award entailed.

". . . his Medal of Honor," Abby said, completing his sentence, knowing how much Kade was reluctant to discuss his other award. "He got that for saving Joe Biden's life in Afghanistan."

"Ah, you're *that* soldier," the woman said.

"I am, indeed, though I don't like to dwell on that episode—or discuss it either."

"Good thing your wife doesn't suffer a similar reticence."

Kade chuckled. "Nope, she doesn't. Not only is my wife often the wind beneath my wings, she also occasionally functions like a tornado who lifts my small accomplishments to dizzying heights." He shot Abby a wink and grinned down at her. "I'm glad she's proud of me, now. There were a few times in our married life when she wasn't so enthralled with my behavior—but that's another topic I'd rather not discuss."

"You've whetted our curiosity, Mr. Blackburn."

He shook his head again. "It's really not open for discussion, ma'am. However, I'm writing a novel in my spare moments. When it's published you may want to read it. It may partly satisfy your curiosity."

"Is it a tell-all novel?"

"Some of it is based on my experiences. Of course, even reading it, you'll never discern what parts are based on those experiences, and which parts fall into the area of pure fiction."

"What's the name of your book?" another woman asked.

"It's as yet untitled. Looks like dessert is about to be served, so I'll stop yakking and let you all enjoy your pie. Thanks again for the honor you've given me this evening."

He sat down next to Abby as a big slab of lemon meringue pie landed in front of him. He picked up his fork to indulge in it.

"Now I'm a tornado? You think I'm trying to destroy you when I say why I'm proud of you?"

"Eat your pie, sweetheart. Let's not give those women another reason to wonder how enthralled you are with me."

"Could you ever get any award without bringing up that kind of thing—alluding to the times when . . ?"

"Several people know about some of those rough times in my life. To gloss over them—or not mention them—would leave me open to a raft questions about my supposed honesty. They'd be saying, 'Kade has the reputation for telling the truth about all the journalistic issues, but he's less honest about his personal issues.'

"Remember, a long time ago, I told you if you were honest about your shortcomings—if you admitted to them in your head—it tended to blunt what others said about you? Made their denigrating comments less painful?"

"I don't mind you admitting to your—our—rough patches in your head, Kade, I'd just prefer you not to share those patches with a room full of total strangers."

"If my honesty makes you uncomfortable, I'll stop talking about our patches."

"Thank God for small favors," Abby sighed in relief.

Kade closed his mouth and didn't say another word. Several people stopped by their table to congratulate him. He acknowledged their words with a smile and a nod, but no words accompanied those gestures.

Abby was glad when most of the journalists departed. "See you bright and early on Monday, Kade?" Ms. Dean asked.

"Yes, ma'am."

"I expected you to ask for a week off to celebrate," Dean said.

"No, I'll be in at the usual hour," he said, giving Abby a lukewarm smile.

They returned to the hotel. Kade had remained a silent Sam since being lectured by Abby. Their drive back to the Biltmore was very quiet.

"Will we leave early in the morning?" she asked. "What time?"

"Nine." Single word.

"Are we eating here before we leave? What time do I need to set the alarm for?"

"Yes. Seven?"

"If you aren't going to give me any more than monosyllables, I'll set the alarm for 7:45. If you aren't going to talk to me, you should be able to eat quickly."

"Okay."

The tension in the truck on the way north to Chino Valley was like a fog swirling around on a damp, cold morning. He maintained his one-word answers to her questions. The longer the silence went on, the angrier she got. When they pulled into the ranch, she went inside, slamming the front door after her. Left him to bring in all the bags, pay the sitter, and take her home, too.

"You didn't have a good time?" Alli asked. "Why are you mad?"

"Your saint of a father can't seem to keep his mouth shut about personal issues. He always wants to share things better left untold. He frankly embarrasses me when he gets on his honesty kick in public. He couldn't just get his award. He had to tell about being fired by the Payson editor, how he'd spent time in a cell in Camp Verde, and about his three months in a cell in Texas, too."

"Mom, I think it's good he acknowledges his faults. Why does it embarrass you? They're his faults, not yours."

"Because then people are looking at me, wondering why I'd married such a flawed man. Smirking at me for being so gullible as to wed him."

Alli shook her head. "Dad is our dad. He's always taken care to be honest with us about many issues. He's always talked openly about his faults—I think in the hope he could persuade us not to make the same ones he made. I don't know why you find his honesty so onerous."

"I doubt you'll understand until you get married. Then you may begin to have more sympathy for what he puts me through."

Kade returned, putting an end to any further discussion between Alli and Abby. Alli knew he'd go out to feed around five, and she intended to ask him what the problem was when he fed the goats, horses and hens.

# *Chapter Three*

"Mama is mad at you," Alli said. "I'd like to know why."

"What business is it of yours?" Kade said, in no humor to discuss what had occurred.

"When she's mad at you, we all suffer."

"Mama is mad because I alluded to my weekend in the Camp Verde jail, my three months in the Texas stockade at the awards ceremony. She told me she wished I'd stop talking about my rough patches. So I have."

"Aren't there other topics you could converse with her about?"

"I'm sure there are. We could discuss the weather ad nauseam. We could talk about finances or religion or politics. I can do that with many of my acquaintances. Your mother is the only one I can discuss the rough patches with, because she understands what motivated me. Now, she's practically told me I can't mention those more personal items—at least in public."

"Instead of trying to pry into your mother's and my personal life, how about if you set the table and get the twin's hands washed for dinner. I picked up a bucket of chicken on my way home from dropping off your babysitter."

"Dad, you do realize you've just done to me what Mama did to you, don't you? Shut me down."

"Alli, it's not something I can get into with you. For most of your questions, I try to answer them honestly, but I can't do that about the current disagreement between me, and your mama, without perhaps altering your love for one or both of us. Let it go and I'll try to re-establish a better relationship with Mama tonight, so the rest of you don't need to suffer."

"Thanks, Dad. One of those lurking fears, when you're mad at each other, is— you'll file for a divorce and leave us a divided family. One week with Mama, and the next one with you."

"I'm not leaving our marriage, Pumpkin, so you don't need to worry about any divided families. I'm too poor, with feeding all these critters, to even think about filing for divorce."

"Good, cause we all love you both—equally."

"I know, and thanks for your concern. You'll maybe understand more of the stresses inherent in a marriage when you get married yourself."

"That's almost exactly what Mama said."

Kade had to chuckle at Alli's comment that Abby had voiced the same thought.

"Most times, marriage is a wonderful thing, Alli, like receiving a dozen red roses. Occasionally, marriage manages to prick you like the thorns left on the stems of roses do. Makes you bleed a bit at times. The secret is to remember the beauty and the good smell of the roses. Concentrate on those items, not on the thorns or the bleeding.

"This weekend, with your mama, I forgot to think of the good smells and beauty. I was heavy into bleeding and managed to grow a few thorns of my own to prick her with. I need to remember the good memories of our marriage, not the few times we've had serious problems. I will endeavor to make things right with your mama later tonight."

When Kade crawled into bed, Abby turned her back on him. "Hey, wife, it upsets the family when we are angry at each other. Alli trailed me to the barn to inform me I'd better make things right with you."

"So you're going to apologize for the silent treatment, but only because it upsets Alli?"

Kade sighed heavily. "I don't like it when you're mad at me, either. I just don't understand why you so desire everyone's good opinion of you—total strangers' good opinions of you. Why does it matter so much to you? You have my total approval of the way you are, so why do you place such value in what others think?"

"I'd like those others to have a good opinion of you, too. When you tell them about spending time in various cells around the country, I can see their opinions about you begin to slide lower. You've overcome a lot of adversity, Kade, so why allude to those down periods at every opportunity? I'm proud of how you've become such a good, upstanding citizen, and I'd rather you didn't keep bringing up those times when . . ."

"When I wasn't such a good upstanding citizen? Because I've spent time in a cell or two, that diminishes me in your eyes, too?"

"Well, yes. It's hard to be proud of you when I think of those times."

"Let me understand you. You wish I hadn't had some of those experiences? You don't think they had a hand in bettering what I've lately become? Let me assure you, Abby, those three months in solitary are largely responsible for me deciding to straighten out my life and do right by my family. Instead of being ashamed of me for being in a cell or two, I'd think you'd realize those experiences have only added to my desire to be a good upstanding citizen."

At her raised eyebrows, he said, "It's not like they detract from what I am currently. They definitely added to my resolve to do better."

"Those times you spent in jail tend to make you into a common criminal in most people's minds. That's not how others see those episodes, Kade. They don't see them in a positive light."

"Guess not, if someone like you is willing to look down your nose at me when I mention those episodes. Gives you a feeling of superiority to know I've fallen off the tracks a couple of times, does it?"

"I knew you wouldn't understand my feelings."

"No . . . doubt I'll ever understand why you feel that way. I'd prefer not to have you remain angry with me, though. I'm willing to promise you I won't ever mention my previous transgressions in public again, if you'll get over being angry with me."

"Thank you. If you can stick to that promise, I won't have a reason to get angry with you."

"Okay. My life previous to this moment is a closed book, never to be referred to again. Can we indulge in some sex to seal the deal?"

Abby gave him a grin. "Why is that the only thing you think seals our deals?"

"You are rather delicious in bed, wife. It helps me to supplant my anger if we have some hot-and-heavy sex. Makes me think of all the good reasons I married you, not dwell on those few negatives. I prefer the look and the smell of the roses . . . most of our life together has been like roses . . . than to keep thinking of the few times when we both resorted to using the thorns of those roses to draw blood."

"Why don't you use flowery language like that in the columns you write for the paper?"

Kade laughed. "Wouldn't want Ms. Dean to think I was into wooing her with my columns."

"Is that why she's kept you on for all these years? Like Mom, she has designs on you, too?"

"She's told me a few times that she values me because I'm like eye-candy to her. I believe she retains me because she likes looking at males who keep themselves in good physical shape. Most of the other reporters have a paunch from sitting around all day, staring at their computers, or stuffing their faces with donuts at morning breaks, and taking long lunches where alcohol is as important as food."

"Have you encouraged her in that way of thinking?"

"Other than keeping up with my Army exercise regimen? No."

They made love to seal the deal. Abby was also glad Kade had not abandoned his Army exercise regimen. He was her eye-candy as well.

"Friends again?" he asked, pulling her close to cuddle her. "Will it be smiles, not snarls, at breakfast?"

"Yes. Can't have Alli all upset or she'll blow those AIMS tests scheduled for this week."

"AIMS tests?"

"I think the acronym stands for Arizona Implement or Instrument to Measure Success. In certain grades all students take those standardized tests."

"In other words, they regurgitate answers, which they've never examined or thought critically about before . . . or after . . . the tests?"

"It's to see how the teachers are doing—or delineate how the school is doing as far as teaching goes."

"Maybe I'll run for the school board. It's one thing to choose the right answer on a test from four or five choices, and another to have to write an essay explaining what you know about the subject in depth."

"When would you have time for another interest?"

"Where my children are concerned, I'd make time. I don't hold much truck with rote memorization. I like the Socratic method of instruction because students have to think to give an answer. If more people were acquainted with thinking, we'd never have gotten into the war in Iraq. Bush and Cheney would not have been able to convince us there were weapons of mass destruction in that country."

"And you wouldn't have witnessed the woman and her children being shot?"

Kade went into his silent mode again for several minutes. "I believe that's one of those incidents I'm not allowed to refer to anymore. I am only permitted to look forward, not back."

"Kade . . ."

"Nope, sweetheart. You can't have it both ways. If you want to be proud of me—not ashamed of me for all those rough patches in my life—I have to delete all those parts from my memory . . . forget all the incidents that shaped me into the man I am today. You aren't allowed to ask me about anything that occurred outside of the present day. Maybe not even the events that occurred more than 12 hours ago."

"I just hate it when you take me so literally. It's like you're Andy at age six and you . . ."

". . . I'm writing a novel in my head? Literally writing it in my head? Transcribing it directly on my brain?" he asked, laughing at how Andy interpreted his statement about writing a novel in his head.

"The difference being, sweetheart, once I explained how I was writing in my head by just thinking how the story should go, Andy got it. No matter how often I explain to you why you don't need to worry about the opinions of others, you still don't seem to get the point."

"Now you're calling me stupid—less adept at taking your meanings than Andy was at six?"

"There's no possible answer to that question which won't get me into greater Dutch with you. No matter what I say, you'd still be snarling, not smiling, at breakfast. I suggest we get some sleep. Maybe with a few hours of shuteye, thinking about having sex with you, I, at least, can smile across the table at you in the morning."

Abby got out of bed. Kade watched her go over to the dresser and open her jewelry box. She slipped off the heart with the cowboy hat—one she'd never taken off in all the days since he'd given it to her—and stuffed it in the box.

It filled him with regret that he'd offended her so deeply she'd consider taking off the heart. "Abby . . ." he started to say, before she cut him off.

"No, Kade. If you intend to erase all your previous memories, I'm entitled to erase a few of mine, too."

He left for the paper before breakfast. Sat down at his desk and checked what he'd been working on before the award's ceremony. It no longer, in his present mood, held his interest, so he deleted the dozen paragraphs from his computer. It wasn't long before Ms. Dean arrived.

"You're already hard at work?" she quizzed. "You want to assure yourself you'll win the same award next year?"

"No. Can I talk to you in private?"

"Of course, Kade. Give me a minute to clean off my desk and I'll be ready to see you."

He nodded.

It was closer to ten minutes when she invited him into her office and closed the door. "You look at all sixes and sevens this morning, Kade. What's wrong?"

"Forget my request to speak to you. I'm not supposed to discuss the rough patches in my life anymore, so I'll just go back to work."

"I saw the look of dismay on Abby's face when you told how you'd been in jail on more than one occasion. She looked like she wanted to shove a gag in your mouth."

Kade nodded. "I've never understood her deep-seated need for approval from strangers. Her parents didn't give her much attention growing up. They largely went their own way without regard to her. Her goats seemed to give her more love than her mom and dad did."

"She spent time trying to win the approval of others because approval of her was lacking from her parents? I can well understand that need. I suffer from the same need."

"You?" he asked. "You never struck me as being . . ."

"Why do you think I never kept reporters around for long, Kade?"

"Because you were a tough boss and they resented taking orders from a woman?"

"No, I often fired them when I suspected they were coming close to seeing me as a woman in need of their approval. I viewed that as a reversal of our roles, so I fired them before they could come any closer to the truth. My parents were of the absentee variety, too. Nothing I did impressed them. You need to be infinitely patient with your wife, Kade. It's a deep-seated malady she suffers from. I imagine you had a better childhood experience. Put yourself in her shoes and know how devastating it is to not matter to anyone. That's why she wants—tries to garner—the approval of others."

"Does that mean you're about to fire me, now that I know . . ?"

"No, Kade. I'm not about to fire you. You, at least, seem sensitive enough to be worried about your wife's need for approval. I would hope you'd have the same sensitivity in regards to my need for the same approval—not use that need as a weapon against me."

"I've got enough problems on my own plate without taking up a cudgel against you. What do you suggest I do, to get back into Abby's good graces? I've suggested she list all her good points, to see she has many more of them than bad points. I've always felt if you were honest about your shortcomings, then when others pointed them out to you, it stung less."

"She didn't take you up on your offer?"

"No. I got her a ledger and gave her time to list her points, both for and against her self-image, but she never sat down to do it. I even told her 'know thyself, and then the slings and arrows of others cannot wound you.'"

"I feel like that's how you approach life, Kade. You seem very well acquainted with both the positive and negative sides of you, so you don't really care what others think, do you?"

"Except for my relationship with Abby—no, I don't care what others think. With her, though, I admit to being totally at sea in that regard. I'm never sure exactly what she thinks of me."

"Your current difficulty with her gives you a bit of empathy with what she feels, doesn't it? When you're never sure if she likes you, or if she doesn't, it fosters the same need in you for her approval, doesn't it?"

Kade narrowed his eyes and thought about Dean's statements, carefully. Finally he nodded his head. "I begin to see an opening in the clouds that obscured the sun this morning. Thanks for your insight into my problem. I'll get out of your hair now and go back to work."

"Take the rest of the day off, Kade. You've earned it. Go home and make peace with your wife, or I will be forced to fire you."

Abby was out scratching goat ears when he arrived at the Ark Ranch. It brought to the fore the feeling that he hadn't given her as much support as she needed, if she were again seeking love from her goats.

"Hey," he said, kneeling in the dirt beside her. She turned away so he wouldn't see her tears. "What are you doing home?" she asked.

"I felt we had some unsettled business between us, so I took the afternoon off in hopes we could settle it."

"How?" she asked.

"I know I'm often fairly dense when it comes to a woman's emotions—doubly so when it comes to yours. When you took off the hat-heart last night—that gave me a real insight into how much you were hurt by some of the things I said—both last night and at the award's ceremony. Let's go sit on the swing and I'll try to heal the current rift."

She gave the goats' ears more scratches, using the time, he supposed, to weigh whether he or them gave her more unconditional love. Finally she rose and laid her hand in his. He retreated to the porch, and sat down on the swing, pulling her down onto his lap. Shaded by the roses that twined up the arbor behind the swing, he thought about their smell and how often his thorns had frequently made Abby bleed.

"First and foremost, I'm sorry if I indicated in some way, that you aren't intelligent enough to understand me like Andy did at six . . . once

I'd explained things to him. You often understand me all too well, even when I don't offer you any explanation for my behavior.

"You aren't stupid, Abby, and it was wrong of me to let you think I believed that about you. I marvel at how well you intuit things, especially feelings. I don't have that ability, or I wouldn't be sitting here with you trying to explain away how much I know I've hurt you. Your husband is a lot denser than you are.

"I know you need the approval of others, and it was mean of me to make light of that need in you. If I'd have had to endure your childhood, I'd very likely be possessed of the same need for approval. Fortunately, I had two parents who doted on me, so I never developed a need for anyone else's approval. Can you forgive me for being so unsympathetic?"

"I know you think me pathetic to need approval from others—but you don't understand what it's like to grow up with no positive feedback—ever."

"During our marriage, haven't I given you lots of positive feedback? Why do you still feel so needy?"

"Yes, Kade, you've been very good at reinforcing my positive self-image. Thank you for making an effort to do that on lots of occasions."

"Making an effort? You weren't convinced I really meant my praise of you?"

"You often grin at me when you tell me stuff like that. It makes it hard for me to believe you—take you seriously."

"I'm sorry, Abby. I do mean my praise of you. I can't think of another woman who is as loving, as smart, who takes as good a care of me, and our children. You are a whiz at keeping books—and that's not just my opinion—I've heard others lavish the same praise on you."

"What brought all this on, Kade. Does it have anything to do with me taking off the heart you gave me last night?"

"Yes, I'll admit that sorely pinched my conscience. In all the years since I gave you the heart, you've never once removed it. But that wasn't what prompted me to come home and try to make amends with you."

"Then what did?"

"Would you be willing to accept my statement as truth if I said it was my deep and abiding love for you that brought me home?"

"Not sex?" Abby asked, teasing him. "I could sooner believe it was sex."

When Kade looked upset by her teasing, she grabbed both his ears and kissed him hard. "I know you love me, Kade Andrew Blackburn. You just have a funny way of showing it sometimes. You're forgiven for making me feel bad yesterday and last night."

He pressed her head against his chest. "Listen," he said, "it's finally beating in a regular rhythm again. It gets all out of sync when you're upset with me. Please, Abby, when you're upset by something I've said or done, tell me right away. I don't mean to hurt you on purpose, it's just hard for me to understand—when you have all of our family's approval—why do you need more than that to feel worthwhile?"

"I'm going to try to content myself with only Blackburn love from now on."

"Good. We all do love and value you, you know. Maybe we don't often voice that out loud, but it underlies everything we feel or do in our family—totally underlies what we feel about you."

"I'm going up and get the heart to wear again."

"I'm coming up with you."

"For sex?"

"No! Would you please get past the idea that I only came home for sex?"

In the bedroom, he took the heart's chain from her hands. He kissed the heart before fastening it around her neck again. "Now you have both a symbol . . . and a sweet kiss representing my love for you . . . dangling between your breasts. I'd appreciate it if you never took it off again."

Abby tried undoing the buttons of his shirt.

"Stop that! I didn't come home for sex. I only came home to apologize for hurting you."

"You've done an adequate job of that, but does that preclude having sex? We have an hour until the bus lets our kids off at the gate. The twins are still asleep."

Kade tried to suppress his grin, but failed miserably. "Okay, but that really *wasn't* the reason I came home."

Alli came marching up the stairs just as Kade buttoned his pants and tucked in his shirt. "We're home, Mom," she announced. "Why is Dad's truck home? Did he get fired? Where is he?"

"None of your damn business, daughter."

"Oh," she giggled. "You came home for sex to make Mama smile again?"

Kade rolled his eyes at Abby. "Damn cheeky kid," he whispered. "And I didn't come home for sex!" he shouted at the closed door.

"Then why is it taking you so long to come out of the bedroom?" Alli asked. "Can't manage to get your zipper up?"

Kade, now fully clothed, with the bed made, and with Abby scooting to the bathroom to take a shower, yanked the door open to confront his oldest daughter. "My sakes, you're one nosy Rosie this afternoon. If sex is the only thing on your mind these days, I may have to take you down to the farrier's place and get him to forge you a chastity belt."

"You were having sex with Mama, weren't you?"

"Yes, but that's all I intend to say about the matter."

"Is she in a better humor now? She was certainly not over her anger at breakfast."

"I think I can affirm her humor is back on track this afternoon."

"And yours is on the mend as well?"

"Yes, Dr. Phil. At least I think so. Don't you have some homework to do?"

Kade waited for Abby to get dressed. As they started down the stairs, he could hear Alli apprising Andy that their parents had engaged in sex and all was now copasetic between them again.

Abby broke into silent giggles, muffling her amusement behind a hand pressed tight to her lips. "Seems our furtive activities have been discovered," she whispered. "It'll be all over school tomorrow."

"Not if I have anything to say about the matter," he groused. "Everyone get cleaned up and then get your butts in the van. We're going to an upscale restaurant to eat tonight. We'll be picking up your grandparents on the way, so everyone put on something decent to wear."

"Not sweats?" Abby teased.

"If I'm not allowed to speak about those times, you're not permitted to refer to those incidents, either. Call your parents and tell them we'll be by at six to take them to the Manzanita Inn. That will give me sufficient time to climb into my tux."

"Your black suit will do just fine."

"And your award's dress will be appropriate, too. Let's make sure the kids are all spotless. I need to be sure the place is open on Monday. I'll take care of the twins. You convince Alli and Andy that jeans aren't de rigueur for such a dining experience."

He called and found the restaurant was open, so Abby called her parents. Kade had both twins bathed and dressed in a flash. He then climbed into his suit and let Abby tie his tie.

"Get in the van," he ordered, buckling the twins into their car seats. "Fasten your seat belts. Andy and Alli, if I hear one word out of you about Mama's and my afternoon activities, I'll ground you both for two months. Understand?"

"Yes, father," Alli said, stifling a giggle. Andy had the decency to look embarrassed, before he also agreed to keep silent.

They arrived at the Watkins Ranch at a few minutes past six. Owen and Corrine were sitting in rockers on the front porch.

"Alli, Andy, get in the far back seats so your grandparents can sit in ones that are easier to get into and out of."

The kids both grumbled, but they got into the rearmost seats. Kade slid open the side door and helped Corrine into the van. He was about to assist Owen, too, when the old man jerked his arm away. "I think I'm capable of getting into your van on my own," he snapped. "At least you had sense enough to look decent this time around."

"It's a dumb bunny who never learns from previous lessons."

"That's exactly why I have as little truck with you as I can. You are a very dumb bunny."

"Dad, could we just enjoy dinner without all the nasty comments?"

"Sure, Abby. For you I'll go out of my way to be pleasant with this dumb bunny. Did you bring a wad of money, or are you picking us up because you expect we'll pay for all the dinners?"

"I have money, sir. Enough of a wad so everyone can order what he or she likes."

They were shown into the restaurant. Highchairs were provided for the twins. Andy sat between his grandfather and his father. Kade imagined he'd chosen that seat because Andy wanted to protect him. His son had not forgotten how nasty Owen could be to his father.

"Relax, Andy. He's not going to embarrass himself in this restaurant," Kade told his son.

Andy leaned over to whisper, "Yeah, you're probably right. He tends to keep his nasty side under wraps in places like this. That didn't keep him from unloading on you in the van, though. Why on earth do you invite him to go out with us? He's as toxic as the ruined Fukushima nuclear plant."

"To provide you with life lessons. You need to learn how to handle unpleasant people. I never learned that lesson early in life, and it got me into a few difficulties. I tended to shoot from the hip at the first sign of trouble."

"I still think that's the better way. You're honest, at least. Not like Granddad, who puts on a veneer of polish when it's called for, but dumps his manners as soon as he knows no one is around to see his coarser side."

"Mom, Dad," Abby said, "Kade won the top prize in Phoenix last weekend. He claimed the 'top reporter' at the press ceremonies Saturday night. They gave him the gold typewriter for being the top-dog reporter in the state."

"Operative word being 'dog' in that statement," Owen said.

"**Grandpa!**" Andy said, turning on Owen.

Kade laid his hand on Andy's shoulder and said softly. "Son, I'm still in Army-fighting shape. I really don't need you to take up with him for me. I can manage to mount my own defense if it comes to that . . . though I appreciate your willingness to jump into the fray."

"Then why don't you invite him outside and mop up the parking lot with him?" Andy replied. "He makes me so angry!"

"Calm yourself. He just makes statements like that to rile me. If neither of us gets riled, it takes a lot of wind out of his sails. Understand?"

"I should just ignore him?"

"You got it, son. He loves to provoke our ire in a place where he knows we can do little about it. Don't rise to the challenges he lays out. Just give him a smile, like what he said is of no consequence to you—or me."

Andy finally relaxed. He gave his father a wink, letting Kade know he understood the rules of the game his father had laid out concerning Grandpa Owen.

Dinner arrived and everyone fell to eating. Corrine kept glancing at Kade with undisguised longing. Abby noticed her glances and frowned in Kade's direction. He cupped his hands beside his eyes like he was wearing horse blinders and didn't notice her frequent glances. That sent Abby into a spate of giggles and she choked on the mouthful of water she'd just swallowed.

"You okay, wife?" Kade asked. "Need me to do the Heimlich?"

"No. The water just went down my Sunday throat, and it's not Sunday, now."

"Grandma, when we got home from school today . . ." Alli started to say, ". . . Mom and Dad were up in their bedroom . . ." She glanced at her father and immediately shut her mouth. "I almost forgot, Dad. I'm sorry," she said, hoping not to be grounded for a month or more.

"No harm done," he said, "since you remembered my warning in time."

"What would you be warning her not to discuss, Kade?" Corrine asked.

"If I warned her not to discuss something, Corrine, why would you surmise I'd be willing to discuss the same issue with you? I'm **not** willing to discuss it."

Andy was wearing a grin about as wide as the barn door at the Ark, knowing what Alli was about to divulge.

"Looking at your son, Kade, I'd be willing to guess it was something related to sex. When they got home from school, were you going at it hot and heavy with Abby?"

"Most likely, consummate lecher that he is," Owen contributed. "Celebrating your Phoenix victory with a roll in the hay, were you?"

"Might be construed as a bit of a victory celebration, because I was still flying high about the honor conferred on me last Saturday. But it didn't involve sex," he lied.

"I knew it. Nothing like a meaningless award to inflate your ego to the max," Owen said.

"Our conversation wasn't only about the award. Between my job at the paper and all the chores at the ranch, I don't often find the opportunity to sit down and discuss things quietly with Abby. When I get the chance, I often invite her to the bedroom, and lock the door. Then we lie down on the bed and talk about all the stuff I never get to discuss in private with her, since with four kids, some of them are always listening at one keyhole or another."

He winked at Andy and Alli, so they'd know he was teasing. "Who wants what for dessert?" He asked. "They make some awesome pecan pie here, along with a chocolate concoction that's to die for."

When the waitress arrived at their table, Kade ordered two small bowls of vanilla ice cream for the twins, then let the older siblings choose what they wanted from the tray with desserts on it. Both Alli and Andy got the chocolate dessert. Abby said she didn't have room for one more bite. Owen and Corrine opted for the pecan pie, and Kade indicated he wanted a slice of the carrot cake.

"Did the twins get enough to eat?" Corrine asked. "All they had were mashed potatoes with gravy, some green beans and the ice cream."

"They don't have molars big enough to tuck into porterhouse steaks quite yet," Kade said, laughing inside about the time he'd eaten two of them on his trip to Phoenix with Corrine. "If they're still hungry when we get home, I'll feed them some pureed stuff from the Gerber's line."

"Let me pay for Corrine's and my dinner," Owen offered.

"No, sir. When I invite quests to dinner, it's with the full understanding I'm picking up the bill."

"You got a bonus, too, in addition to the award?" Owen asked. "How much?"

"That's another subject I'm not willing to discuss. Ms. Dean was happy enough to give me a nice bonus, but I'm not going to divulge how generous she was. At the same time she dispensed some information to me, which I think—in the long run—will be more valuable to me than the money."

Abby frowned, asking silently with her knitted brows what information she'd given Kade.

"I'll reserve our discussion of that issue for another bedroom conference, later this week," he teased.

They let the Watkins off at their ranch, before they headed for Chino Valley. Both twins fell asleep before they hit I-17.

"Dad, Andy and I know you were having sex with Mama when we got home from school. Why did you lie and say you weren't?"

"If you were indulging in a like activity—and I warn you'd better not be doing so until you're well over the age of 21—would you like me to talk about your relationship with your boyfriend or husband with your grandparents?"

"Good grief, no!"

"Then perhaps you'll understand why I didn't want to talk about it with them, either."

Alli looked confused when he glanced at her face in the rear view mirror.

"Some things are just family stuff and not to be talked about outside the family—like when Mama showed me how she nursed Alli?" Andy asked.

"You got it, son. Every family has a raft of family secrets that they guard with care, because others might not understand them. It's what makes us such a close family—those family secrets cement us together like glue. If we were to broadcast them to the four winds, they'd lose the ability to weld us together. When we tell others our secrets, that allows them to be insiders in our family and weakens the bond the six of us share."

"Like the time I broke Mama's favorite bud vase and you took the blame, Daddy? You lied that time, too," Alli said.

"That's one example. What if I'd told your teacher and your friends what you'd done? Word would have gotten back to Mama and she'd be disappointed in you, so I said I'd knocked it off the mantle, so she wouldn't be mad at you. Didn't my lie make you feel closer to me?"

"Yes. I was really relieved Mama was mad at you, not me."

"That's what I mean about the glue that holds us together as a family."

"When we get home, Kade, first I'm going to wash your mouth out with soap because you lied to me. Then you'll have to sit in the corner for five hours, facing the wall. That's my punishment for the kids when they lie to me. The same punishment for you will be part of the glue that also cements our family together."

"Really, wife?"

"Yes, really, Kade. Alli might join you in that punishment as well—for not having spoken up at the time—for letting you take the blame."

"Looks like we might be sharing the same corner, Alli. It'll give us at least five hours to forge even stronger family ties."

The twins were still asleep when they got home, so Kade put on their pajamas and placed them in their cribs. On his return to the kitchen, Abby said, "Ready to serve your punishment for lying? Call Alli. She needs to come suffer the same fate."

"Ah, Abby. Take out your ire on me, but leave Alli out of the equation. Hers was a lie of omission, not one of commission, so it wasn't a lie in the true sense of the word."

"I still want her to see that I'm consistent when anyone lies to me. **Alli!**"

Alli appeared at the doorway. "Mama, it happened so long ago, do you really need to . . ?"

"I do. Bend over sink, Kade and open your mouth."

He followed her directions. She wet the soap cake and used it to thoroughly wash his mouth out. He gagged a couple of times in the manner he'd heard the kids gag, though, truth told, he was hard pressed not to erupt in laughter.

"Alli, set a chair in the corner for your father to sit in. You can't get up until I say you can—long about midnight should cover those five hours you owe me for your lies."

Alli reluctantly dragged over a chair and faced it into the corner. When he sat down in it, she burst into tears. "It isn't fair, Dad. I was the one who broke the vase and I should have to sit here, not you."

"You have school tomorrow. I'm off this week. I was the one that told Mama the lie, not you, so go to bed and get to sleep." He pulled her close to hug her and confided, "That soap tastes horrible. Almost lost my dinner when she washed my mouth with it. I'd suggest always telling your mama the truth. I sure intend not to lie to her again. YUCK!"

That statement finally elicited a small smile from Alli. "Scoot up to bed. I'd just as soon none of my children witnessed the rest of my punishment. Do you think Mama will let me read a book for the next five hours?"

"No, she won't. She says we have to stare at the corner and think about the consequences of lying to her."

"If you don't go to bed, Alli, and stop chatting with your father, he'll still be sitting here when breakfast comes around tomorrow."

"Can you let him have a book to read, Mama?"

"No, Alli. His punishment for lying will be the same as yours. No books, no TV, no iPod, nothing. Fairness is another of those glues that holds our family together."

# *Chapter Four*

"Your time is up now, Kade," Abby announced on the far side of midnight. "You may not need to report in for work, but you still need to feed all the residents of this Ark in the morning."

"I may have to *lie* in bed and let you cover the chores tomorrow morning."

"You didn't feel I should mete out the same punishment to you as I do to the kids when they lie to me?"

"I'm not complaining. Consistency is important for kids."

"You didn't enjoy the soap in your mouth, did you?"

"No, you're right. Almost lost my dinner at one point."

Abby erupted in laughter.

"Rubbing salt in my earlier wounds?" he asked. "Go on up to bed. I'll lock up and be there shortly."

"What did you learn from Ms. Dean that you think will be more valuable to you than money?" Abby asked, when he finally arrived in their bedroom to get undressed.

"It's beyond the 12-hour rule, and since I'm not allowed to revisit past events, per my promise, I can't tell you what she said to me."

"You are the most maddening man ever foisted off on the earth," she screeched. "Don't tell me then, see if I care!"

"You're angry again? You're the one who told me I wasn't allowed look backwards. I'm just trying to follow your suggestions to the letter." He had a hard time controlling his urge to laugh as she continued to fume.

She sat up and tried to unfasten the heart-hat necklace again.

"No you don't," he said grabbing both her hands. "I keep my promises to you better than you keep yours to me. Were you telling me a lie when you said you wouldn't take the necklace off again? We may have to return to the kitchen so I can soap your mouth. I'd be tempted to do it, but that means I'd get no sleep, from having to keep my eye on you as you sat in the chair for the next five hours."

"I purely hate you, Kade Andrew Blackburn!"

He did spill over into laughter at that point. "I suppose that rules out any hope I had for one of those hot-and-heavy sexual encounters."

"Yes, definitely. Go to sleep. I want nothing to do with you. Not tonight, or maybe for another six months."

He pulled her close and kissed her hard. One hand dragged up her nightgown. He used the same hand to massage her breasts, before he trailed it lower to massage other areas. When she started to breathe in ragged gasps, he moved to cover her and slid into her, having already produced a fine erection. He went at it hard until she finally succumbed to his efforts.

"Six months is a long time to go without what just occurred, wife. Sure you want that long a hiatus between sexual encounters? With me?"

"I could last six months without any more of that," she affirmed.

"Really?"

"Yes. Maybe I'll look up Alan White and see if he'd be interested in providing me with what you just did. I could ignore you for a year if *he* was interested."

Kade inclined his head in her direction, bothered by the thought she'd seriously consider contacting White. Doubly bothered by how fast that thought had sprung into her head.

"You'd really consider an affair with Alan?" he asked.

"Why not? Maybe you're having one with Ms. Dean, since you admitted what she'd given you was more valuable than money."

Again Kade erupted in laughter. "She gave me some sound advice—not sex, sweetheart."

"You're not inclined to divulge what she told you, are you?"

"I promised her I wouldn't voice what she said around, and I tend to honor my promises better than you honor yours."

Abby was still on the prod at breakfast. Kade made short work of his cereal, then plopped both twins in their double stroller and went out to feed. Alli and Andy were waiting at the end of the lane for the school bus. He waved and they waved back.

"See goats, Daddy," Kory said.

"No, ride horses," Kathy said.

"When did you guys start talking? I must be spending too many hours at work to have missed that turning point." As he fed the animals, he continued to be amazed they'd started voicing their thoughts. Doubly confounded that he'd missed the event when it first occurred.

Once feeding chores were done and he'd turned on the sprinklers to water the garden, he returned to the house. The twins went directly to their room, to find items to play with. Abby was nursing a cup of coffee at the kitchen table.

"When did the twins begin talking?" he asked.

"I believe it happened longer than 12 hours ago, so I'm not permitted to tell you when they started putting words together."

"Okay. I guess I deserved that response from you this morning."

He made a cup of tea and settled opposite her at the table. "Abby . . ."

"What, Kade? Another apology is in the offing?"

"Not from me, though I thought you might want to offer me one today."

"For what?"

"You'd really consider taking up with Alan White? Sexually?"

"Ah . . . that's what finally got through to you. Is your ego in tatters that I'd consider a relationship with him? He, at least, doesn't play games with me the way you do."

Kade got up abruptly. Slammed his half-full teacup in the sink and went back out to hoe weeds in the garden. Abby sat still for a long time before deciding she'd better make some attempt to mollify his feelings. She got out the container of iced tea from the refrigerator and poured him a tall glass. Grabbing her sunglasses from the counter, she went out to the garden.

"Kade, I brought you some iced tea. Come sit down on the swing and drink a glass."

He laid down the hoe without saying a word and trailed her back to the porch. He sat down and accepted the glass from her hand. Drained it in less than 20 seconds. Abby wasn't certain if it was his hoeing efforts, the heat of the day, or the heat of his anger that left him so parched.

"You were really thirsty," she said.

"Yes. I need to get back to my hoeing."

"I'm sorry for what I said to you this morning and last night," she told him.

"Apology accepted," he said without any degree of inflection in his voice. He got up to go out to the garden again.

"Kade . . ."

He shook his head. "I don't think you can recall your threat—to take up with Alan again—that easily from my mind. I'm having a hard time forgetting—how that solution so quickly leapt into your brain."

"But . . ."

"Do you want a divorce?" he asked. "You'd be free to take up with White then."

"No, I don't want a divorce. It's just that you frustrate me so often—that's why I mentioned Alan. He was like a slobbering puppy, always trying to get on my good side. You, in contrast, don't ever seem to **want** to be on my good side. You work hard at making me angry most of the time."

"If I'm such a burr under your saddle pad, I'll move into the loft in the barn—treat our current relationship like a trial separation. I'd eat at your table to keep the kids from discerning we've separated, but I'd spend all the hours when they weren't around, in the barn."

"They aren't stupid, Kade. They'd know in a minute we're on the outs."

"Then tell me what you expect from me."

"I expect a greater amount of consideration from you. When I ask you to tell me something, I'd like you to tell me, not give me a bunch of crap about the 12-hour rule."

"You want me to be like a slobbering puppy, always trying to get on your good side?"

"That would be a pleasant reversal of the way you often treat me."

"Fine. I'll attempt to stay on your good side. You may want to lay in a good supply of Milk Bones to remind me to treat you with consideration. Now, I really do need to hoe the garden."

Abby returned to the kitchen, unsure of where things stood between them. She watched him hoe and knew his anger was fueling the speed with which he plied his hoe. At four, once the kids were home, he returned to the house they shared. He gave her a hug and brushed her lips with a soft kiss, but she wasn't fooled by his outward display of affection. *That was for the benefit of our children,* she thought.

Abby produced dinner from her crock-pot as Kade quizzed the older two about their day at school.

"I'm getting a B in algebra," Andy announced. "I missed an A by two points."

"You couldn't have volunteered for some extra work to raise your grade to an A?"

"I don't like math at all, Daddy," Alli contributed. "Girls don't seem to be good at math—just like boys aren't good at Language Arts."

"I was always pretty fair at Language Arts," he told her. "I got an A in almost all my classes in that subject. Probably what landed me the reporter's job."

"More milk, Daddy?" Kathy asked, holding up her plastic cup.

"How do you ask?" Kade said. "I need to hear you say 'please' before I'm willing to fill up your cup."

"I no say peas. I don't want peas. I want milk."

"Sorry, without you telling me 'please,' I'm not going to fill up your cup."

"Kade, I think she's telling you she doesn't like peas, those little green vegetables," Abby said. "She never liked them as a baby. I could feed her green beans until the cows came home, but she didn't ever want to eat peas."

"Not peas, Kathy. 'Please' is the word you say when you want someone to do something nice for you. After they do what you ask, then you say 'thank you.'"

"Oh," Kathy said. "Will you peas fill my cup with milk?"

"I'd be happy to fill it with milk." He got up and opened the refrigerator and poured a cup of milk for her. "Now what do you say?" he asked.

"Tenk you."

When supper was over, Kade volunteered to bathe the twins. Alli and Andy went to their rooms to tackle homework. Once the twins were in their pajamas, he sat down in his recliner to read to them. He chose a book about a farm where most of the pictures had vegetables on the pages.

"What's this one?" he asked.

Kory said, "Corn! Like we feed chickens. This one is tomato. This one is slerry."

"Celery," Kade corrected. "What's this one, Kathy?"

"Please?"

"Nope, this vegetable is a pea, one of those things you don't like to eat. It sounds a lot like that word you should use when you ask someone to do you a favor. These are peas, but the favor word is please. Puh-lease is different from peas, the vegetable," he said, drawing the word out to let her hear the difference in the sound of both.

"Read dog book, Daddy," Kathy said. "I don't like begible books."

"How do you ask?" Kade said.

"Puh-lease read dog book now," she said.

"All right. The one about the dog with the rough, red tongue that goes in and out? Where is your tongue? Can you point to your tongue?"

Kathy stuck out her tongue and touched the tip of it.

"Good job, Kathy. Kory where is your ear?"

"Here and here," his son said, "two ears."

"You guys are so smart. Where are your knees?" Kade continued to ask them to point out body parts, most of which they knew.

"This is my pee-pee," Kory said, pulling his tiny penis out of his pajama bottoms. "Kathy doesn't have a pee-pee."

"Oh, no? Then how does she wet her diaper? She has a pee-pee, but it doesn't stick out like yours."

"Kade," Abby admonished from the kitchen. "It's too soon for anatomy lessons."

"Yes, ma'am. Let's go get in bed. If you go right to sleep, I'll let you help me feed the chickens in the morning."

"Chickens like corn," Kory announced.

"Yep, son, they do indeed. They also like grubs and worms. In the morning let's see if we can find some worms or grubs and you'll see they like those things even more than corn."

As soon as the twins were settled, he came into the kitchen to do the dishes. Abby was working on the books for one of the companies she had a contract with.

"Let those go, Kade. I can do them in the morning."

"I'd rather do them now before all the food sticks like cement to their surfaces. Why don't you take your books to the office if you want some privacy? It's a lot quieter to work on them there. Must be hard to keep your mind on the figures with the radio blasting away."

"I prefer to work here. You could turn the radio down a bit."

Kade snapped the radio off and drew a sink full of hot water, into which he piled the dishes.

"You didn't need to turn it off, just down."

Kade shrugged. "It's fine. I'll just hum in my head."

"Is that akin to writing in your head?" she teased. "Do you have a few guitars inside your cranium along with all those sheets of paper and a pencil?"

"I'd tell you 'smart ass,' but I'm trying hard to be more considerate of you, so I won't say that."

When the kitchen was shipshape, Kade again sat in his recliner. He picked up a magazine and read, waiting for Abby to finish her bookkeeping.

"If you're tired, go up to bed," she told him. "I should join you in about another half hour."

"Okay," he said.

He was asleep when she crawled into bed, but he stirred enough to wrap an arm around her. "All done?" he mumbled.

"Yes. Kade . . ."

"What?" he asked.

"I'd still like to know what Ms. Dean told you."

He was quiet a long time and she thought he wasn't ever going to tell her what his boss had said. She rolled over, putting her back in his direction as a silent protest over his refusal to divulge what Dean had told him.

"Her lecture followed the awards ceremony," he began softly. "She'd evidently caught . . . seen . . . that you were less than pleased about my references to the various cells I'd spent time in.

"I said you seemed to have this basic need for approval from total strangers. She said she suffered from the same need. At first I didn't believe her. She's a tough cookie and doesn't hesitate to confront anyone. Then she told me the reason she so often fired reporters was because when they came close to discovering that she needed lots of approval from them, it was like a reversal of their roles, so she fired them rather than have them discover her neediness for sure."

"How dare you discuss our personal life with your boss, Kade? I don't appreciate being the . . ."

He got out of bed. "I'll be in the barn's loft," he said.

"Fine!" she said. "You can talk to the chickens who roost up there. At least they won't be cackling about my shortcomings in any kind of language others will understand."

He didn't come in for breakfast. When she checked for his truck, it was gone. She supposed he'd gone in early to work.

"Daddy said feed chickens. Give corn and crumbs," Kory said.

"Not crumbs, Kory, grubs," Abby corrected.

"Where is Daddy?" Kathy asked.

"Maybe he got called in to work at an early hour," Abby said, fully knowing he was off that week. She spent the rest of the time, while feeding the twins breakfast, wondering if he'd even come home for dinner.

"What are grubs, Mama?" Kory asked.

"They're little worms that curl into a ball. After you finish your eggs we could see if we could find one or two for the chickens," she said, shuddering because she hated to touch anything like that. Kade was the one who didn't recoil from handling such critters.

It struck her then how much the twins would miss out on if she and Kade separated. For years, Alli and Andy had enjoyed his innate ability to teach them about the things she hated to be confronted by. The twins had just recently arrived at the age where they could understand what he was willing to teach them.

After breakfast, she took a shovel out of the barn, ignoring her strong desire to climb to the loft to see where he'd gone. Along the fencerow where the horses stood, she turned over pile after pile of horse manure that had eddied around the posts.

"Oh, here's a grub," she said, brushing away the dry manure to expose the worm. "See how it curls into a ball when you touch it," she said, using her fingernail to make it curl.

"Can I hold it? Does it bite?" Kory asked.

"I don't think it bites, but maybe we should just carry it on the shovel over to where the chickens are. Or we could get a can and find more grubs, so all the chickens could have some to eat."

"Get can, Mama. Find more grubs," Kory encouraged.

She located a can that Kade used to scoop out sweet feed for the horses. She took up her shovel and attacked another pile of manure. This pile had six grubs in it. She was trying to brush away the manure so as not to fill the can with that, rather than the grubs, when a hand reached past her and picked the grubs out of the shovel, depositing them in the can.

"Go back to the house," Kade said. "I can see you don't enjoy grub hunting."

It didn't take another word of encouragement for her to abandon that duty to her husband. From the porch, she watched as he let the twins each hold a grub. The laughter of Kory and Kathy drifted on the afternoon breeze to where she sat.

"Daddy, get worms, too," Kory reminded him.

"We'd need something from your mama's cupboards to catch some worms," Abby heard him say. "Brush off your hands and let's see if she has what we need to catch worms."

He gave her the coldest look when he arrived at where she sat on the porch. "Do you have any mustard—not the wet kind, the dry sort?"

"I think so. It'll be on the top shelf if I do."

"Stay outside, because your shoes are full of horse crap, and we don't want to mess up Mama's floors," he said, toeing off his boots before going inside. "Found some," he said, coming out again with a small dropper bottle full of yellow liquid. He sat beside Abby on the swing to put on his boots again. "Okay, this time we have to look for little hills in the grass. Since you're both so short, I bet you find some before I do."

The twins bolted from the porch as Kade stooped down to show them the hills he'd referred to. "This is a hole where a worm lives. We have to put some of this stuff into the hole and the worm will come right out."

"Is it like magic? That stuff?" Kory asked.

"Nope. Mustard makes the worm's skin itch, so it comes out of the hole to try to wash away the itching powder. Watch!"

Kade dribbled a bit of the mustard into the hole and before he could get up from his stoop, the worm appeared. Kory picked it up. "Take him over to the fountain and rinse him off so he quits itching," Kade instructed.

"I make worm come out hole, Daddy?"

"Of course, Kathy. Just one squeezer full does the trick."

She put some liquid in another hole and shortly the worm appeared. Without a moment's hesitation, she pulled his tail free of the hole and marched off to rinse the earthworm off.

After another dozen worms and grubs resided in the can, Kade said it was time to feed the chickens. Abby went in to begin dinner, amazed at how Kathy had pulled the worms free.

"Dinner is ready," Abby called over the laughter of all four kids. Andy and Alli were watching Kory and Kathy feed the grubs and worms to the chickens, to loud peals of laughter. "Okay," she heard Kade say, "It's time for dinner. You both need to scrub your hands very well, so you won't be eating grubs and worm slime for dinner. For the second time, Abby shuddered.

There was no hug or soft kiss as he entered the kitchen that night. He glanced briefly at her, as if to ask if he'd be welcome to sit with them for dinner.

"Long as you wash the grub and worm slime off your hands, too," she said, making an attempt to lighten the mood.

Dinner was a long, quiet affair. Kade, having spent the afternoon with the kids, didn't engage them in any extra conversation. After the older kids went up to do homework, he bathed the twins and read to them. Tucked them into bed with a kiss.

He returned to the kitchen to do the dishes. Abby already had her books spread out on the table. She'd turned on the radio to a classical station. He turned it off.

"Kade, you don't have to turn it off. That's not a bunch of rap music, just classical tunes. They don't bother me."

He made no attempt to turn the radio on again. He collected the dishes into the steamy water and began to scrub them clean. On impulse, she jumped up and grabbed a dishtowel to dry them.

"Work on the books," he said, uninviting her to join him for household chores.

"I want to help with the dishes," she said.

"I can do the dishes—both wash and dry—but I'm not good at bookkeeping."

"You are, however, amazing at locating grubs and worms. How do you stand to touch them? Or get the twins to touch them?"

"I make it into a game. They're so busy competing with each other, they don't stop to consider what they're holding onto."

"After the dishes are done, I'd like to talk to you."

"Hasn't it all been said, time after time, Abby? How will another session of talk change anything?"

"I just realized something this afternoon, Kade."

He shrugged. "Doubt your realization will change anything, either."

"You aren't willing to meet me halfway?"

"If I thought there was any chance of a 50/50 discussion with you, I'd be there with bells on. No matter what I say or do, it's apparent you aren't happy in this marriage."

"That's not true, Kade. I value my relationship with you."

He rolled his eyes at her, letting her know he didn't believe her. "Once upon a time, when your papa was dead set against me having anything at all to do with you, you maybe valued my relationship with you. Now, without those strongly opposing forces, you can't seem to remember those feelings . . . you seem to have forgotten to value me.

"Maybe it's like soldiers in war—when we're all scared of dying, we love all the other men like brothers, but once the hostilities are over, we go our separate ways and don't care if we ever see each other again. That's kind of the way I feel now, like you don't care if you ever see me again."

"You couldn't be more mistaken, Kade. Come and sit outside on the swing with me."

He hung up the dishrag and emptied the dishwater. Followed her out the door. Sat on the lawn chair, not beside her on the swing. Waited for her to let him know the direction her chat would take.

"Kade, I would agree, that I felt the need to side with you more when everyone seemed to be arrayed against us. Here on the Ark things are less stressful, so I've stopped feeling I need to stand up for you—to protect and defend you. We've settled into a rather comfortable lifestyle now, and perhaps, from our former days when we had to fight everybody to remain a couple, we now can't seem to get over those Hatfield/McCoy tendencies—only now we're battling each other."

He nodded, agreeing silently with her analysis of their current state.

"What made me mindful of your worth to this family was the laughter of all four children this afternoon. Andy and Alli have had your attention and your teachings for long enough that their twigs are bent in the right direction. Kory and Kathy still have a lot to learn that only you can teach them."

"So, my worth to this family lies only in what I can teach the twins?"

"No, Kade. You're worth a lot to me, as well. When you're gone from the ranch, I don't sleep well. I'm scared. Each creak in the house is like a threat to me. No one understands me as well as you do. My fears, my phobias, my needs."

"Most of the time I don't understand you at all, as all our infighting testifies to, on a daily basis. I had a really tough time understanding why you'd bring Alan White into our discussion so quickly, because you were mad at me for something else. When I'm upset with you, do I throw Corrine in your face?"

"No, in fairness, you haven't done that."

"Again, I ask, what do you expect of me, Abby? It doesn't seem like I can tease you anymore. I feel like I'm walking on eggshells with you. I make a single statement and you jump all over me."

"I'm truly sorry, Kade, for the way I've been acting. I have no right to censor your thoughts or what you choose to tell others about those rough patches in your life. I will endeavor not to do that to you anymore. I know I've hurt you on more than one occasion, so when you seek advice from others, I have no right to complain.

"It's just that I believe our private lives should be kept private—at least between the two of us. I don't enjoy being the recipient of gossip or speculation on every street corner. I'd prefer it if the butcher wasn't asking me if I'd had a fight with you when I order a roast for dinner. He seems to think that's my way of making up with you."

For the first time all evening, Kade's lips curved into a smile. He finally nodded. "Okay, I agree that our family problems should remain within the family. I apologize for asking Ms. Dean for her advice, but it was just so hard for me to understand why you were so upset about my talk in Phoenix."

He got up from his chair and joined her on the swing. "I can't imagine my life without you in it. I was scared you wanted a divorce and didn't have the courage to say it out loud. When I'm scared, I tend to go all cold and hard, which is exactly the opposite of the way I need to act to get back in your good graces."

"Neither of us is faultless in that respect, Kade. I spent all afternoon wondering what the kids and I would do if you moved out on a permanent basis. I couldn't contemplate my life without you in it either.

"Can we agree to talk about what bothers us in the future without getting all hot and angry and defensive?" she asked.

"Stop acting like the Hatfields and McCoys? Bury the various hatchets and stop taking potshots at each other?"

"Yes, I'm willing if you are, Kade."

"All right, I'm also willing to call a truce. Please, tell me if you're upset and why you're upset. I promise not to let things fester inside me either, without letting you know why I'm angry. Shall we have a special time each day when we retreat to a private place and discuss our differences?"

"That sounds like a sound plan, Kade. Eleven each night, lets drink some chamomile tea so we can each go to bed with some understanding between us, and a clear conscience. I don't want to fight with you anymore."

"Nor I with you. It's almost eleven. Break out the tea, and let's talk."

# *Chapter Five*

"Your boss really needs everyone's approval, like I do?" Abby asked.

"I guess so. She never struck me as someone needy for the good will of others. She's one tough lady, so I never imagined she was anything like you."

"You've been after me for years now to list my good and bad points, so I know you were cognizant of my need for approval. You seem very attuned to my needs. Why did you miss her need for the same thing?"

"I guess because I never saw her on her knees scratching goat ears. She just never struck me as the type to desire anything from anyone. Surprised the hell out of me when she told me why she so often fired reporters."

"Will she be firing you, now you know about her need for approval?"

"I sincerely hope not. She told me at the end of our discussion she didn't believe I was the type to hold her need for approval over her head, like she feared others would. I guess because I've never indicated I thought I could do a better job of putting out the paper, than she does, she doesn't consider me a threat to her position."

"Now that you know her secret, do you think your attitude will change?"

He shook his head, "No. I don't have any desire to run the paper. I'm happy with my reporter's job. It gives me time to spend with you and our children, not suffer from weekly headaches trying to produce those papers."

"Your turn to ask a question," Abby said.

"I'd still like to know why White's name came up so fast when we were sparring. I didn't think you liked him—at least that was my initial impression. Now I'm not sure how you regard him. Is he your ace in the hole? Someone you drag out when you feel like you're at a disadvantage?"

"No, Kade. You get so far under my skin when we argue, I feel the need to burrow into your insecurities on occasion."

He cracked a smile. "Alan White is one of my insecurities?"

"If your reaction to my mention of him was any indication of that, I guess he still is. If you'll recall, right after I said that, you asked me if I wanted a divorce."

"Okay, I'll admit when you mentioned taking up with him, that hit me like a sucker's punch—that you'd consider falling into bed with White—just because we'd had an argument."

She reached over and took his hand in hers. "Let's have an understanding here, Mr. Blackburn. You satisfy me so well in bed and in all the other ways when we come together, too, I would have to be senile to entertain Alan in that manner. Just to look at you when you get undressed, sends my heartbeats into overdrive."

"I understand that feeling, Abby. Naked, you definitely kick up my heart rhythm, as well."

"Except for when you asked me if I wanted a divorce, I never had the feeling—even when we fought—that you didn't love me," she told him.

"That's because I've never stopped loving you—even when we fought. Yes, it kind of rocked my personal boat when you said you'd consider sleeping with Alan, but even then, I didn't stop loving you. I was just concerned you'd perhaps stopped loving me."

"Never, Kade. I think if we can keep to our 11 p.m. discussions and not let things build up or get out of hand, like they have in the past, we can mellow out enough as a couple to be married well into our old age, with no more major issues standing between us."

"I'd like that, too. I don't enjoy going ten rounds with you every night."

"Shall we seal the deal with some sex?" she asked.

"Nope, not tonight. I would sincerely like you to believe I came willingly to this first meeting—not because I hoped it would lead to sex."

"If it did lead to that conclusion, though, you wouldn't be complaining about the outcome?"

A second grin split his face. "No, you wouldn't hear a word of complaint out of me."

Abby got up and put both cups in the sink. "While I rinse these out, why don't you draw us a nice warm bath. Seems a shame to have such an enormous bathtub when we seldom share it."

"Yes, ma'am. One hot Roman bath coming up."

When she arrived at the door to their private bathroom, she saw he'd filled the tub almost to overflowing. He had shed his clothes and was sitting on the edge of the tub. She doffed her clothes. He held out his hand to her and she took it as he steadied her descent into the water. Once she was immersed up to her ears, he eased in behind her, urging her to lie against those six-pack abs.

"Lying on you like this is like lying on a washboard," she said. "I would have believed by now, you'd be softer. None of what you eat seems to fatten you up. I have a few extra pounds on me, but you never gain any weight."

"We could reverse positions—let me lie on you for a change. I like lying on soft bodies, as Joe Biden would be quick to tell you."

"So much has happened since you saved his life. I can't imagine how all those years flew by without me being aware of them."

"Yes, but you only need to look at the children to be aware of all that's transpired. Every day, I look at them and marvel how each one has enriched my life with you."

"Kory wanted me to look for worms and crumbs this morning."

"Crumbs?"

"That's what he thought you'd said when you said grubs."

"Like Kathy didn't want peas when I told her told her to ask me please for some milk?"

"I'm surprised you haven't had them marching, shouting, 'K-dens, Let, Rye,' yet."

"Life seemed a bit easier with only one child to contend with. Sometimes I'm afraid I'm not devoting enough attention to the rest of them."

"It was definitely easier with only one, though, I'd be reluctant to part with the other three now."

Kade moved over so he was lying on his side with her facing him. "You're still the girl I first married, Abby. You may have a few more stretch marks and you're a bit softer than when we wed, but in all the ways that count, you're still the woman I fell in love with and seriously wanted to court."

"It's kind of you to tell me that, but one glance in the full-length mirror gives me a different view of myself."

"We may have to climb out of the tub and go back to the table for more tea and discussion, if you refuse to believe me when I say you're still same—still the same beautiful woman I was lucky enough to marry in haste—so I could keep my promise to your father."

"Did you ever regret the speed of our marriage?"

"No! I never regretted our hurry-up marriage. All the years since have been like a dream to me—a very satisfying dream."

"I agree, Kade."

He kissed her softly. "Thanks, for always being there, Abby, through the good times and the bad ones. You have always given me your total support. I am the man I am today, largely because of you. Haven't been in a cell in years—not since you took me in hand."

"Stop, or you'll make me cry. The water is getting cold. Let's dry off and go to bed."

He got out of the tub first to support her departure from it, wrapping a thick towel around her and gently rubbing her dry with it. She caught his hand and stepped back from him so she could see him in his entirety. "Get those six-pack abs into our bed, Kade Andrew Blackburn, and prepare to be loved like you haven't been loved in months."

"We're not having sex. I just want to hold you close and kiss you. We'll seal the deal we struck tonight on some other evening."

"We'll see," came her enigmatic reply.

# *Chapter Six*

He smiled at her across the table the next morning. "Did you sleep well?" he asked.

"Better than I have in the last few days," she told him. "I think we may have hit on something good. Whether it was the chamomile tea or the cessation of hostilities, it was a very restful night."

"Good."

The following Monday, Kade went back to work at the paper. He'd enjoyed his time at home with Abby and the kids, but he missed his job, too. Ms. Dean followed him to his cubicle. "Kade, can you come to my office?"

"Yes, ma'am," he said rising from his chair. "You have a hot assignment?"

"No. Things have been very quiet in the past week. How do you know it promises to be dullsville when you ask for a week off? You seem to have some psychic powers in regards to how slow it will be."

Kade laughed. "No, I don't have any psychic powers pertaining to the work load. Just now and again I feel the need to reconnect with my family and do some of those 'honey do' chores that pile up at the ranch. Garden is growing great, now that I've subdued the weeds. Rented a tractor and used the gannon behind it to clean out the goat and horse runs. Next fall, I'll put the dried manure on the garden."

"Things are better with your wife?"

"Yes, ma'am." He didn't elaborate further.

When they both arrived at Dean's office, a woman he'd never seen before was sitting across the desk from Dean's usual chair. Dean took her seat and motioned for Kade to take one next to the strange woman.

"Diana Gardner, please meet my best reporter, Kade Blackburn."

He half rose from his chair to shake her outstretched hand. "Ma'am." he said, nodding to her.

"Ma'am?" she questioned. "You make me sound like an old lady."

"Sorry. I spent so many years in the Army, I tend to revert to those forms of address out of habit."

"I've hired Ms. Diana Gardner, Kade, so when you want to take a week off, maybe I'll have someone on board who can cover the articles as well as you do."

"Welcome aboard, Ms. Gardner."

"Diana is also a laude graduate, of the U of A. Kade is a magna cum laude grad of NAU. He carried a 4.0 average in all his classes."

"I'm impressed. I only managed a summa cum laude. I had a 3.8 GPA."

"That's still well above the average. My wife graduated with the same GPA in bookkeeping. I have a great deal of respect for her, as she managed that grade-point average while dealing with our children and me. It's not as easy for women to excel, given the time restraints involved in raising children—or contending with me," he said, giving Dean a wink.

"Well, I'm not married, nor do I have any children, so I don't have any excuse for not maintaining a 4.0 GPA."

"My statement about my wife shouldn't have been interpreted as a condemnation of your 3.8. I only maintained my 4.0 because I was forced into it. If I'd gotten any B-type grades, I'd have lost my Army stipend."

"Kade, would you be willing to take Diana under your wing? Show her the ropes? Let her go out with you to cover stories until she learns her way around Prescott, and the paper's procedures."

"Of course, ma'am. It'll be my distinct pleasure to acquaint her with the town and how the paper works."

"Good. I knew I could count on you. There's a problem on the front burner at the community college. Seems like the people on the east side of the mountains don't think they're getting their fair share of classes from the taxes they pay into the college. A couple of the popular programs in the Verde Valley have been moved to our side—nursing for sure, and they've decided not to fund the Sedona film-making classes, either. People are hot on the Verde side. One of the board members has already resigned in protest."

"Start on this side, or go talk to the disgruntled members over the hill?" Kade asked.

"Most of the fireworks and hot tempers are on the other side of Mingus. I'd suggest you begin on that side."

"Okay. I should take a few moments and sweep the dirt, manure and gravel out of my truck if I'm going to take Ms. Gardner with me. Doubt she wants to assume the role of a 'farmer's sidekick' this early on in her reporter's career."

Ms. Dean laughed. "Kade, in addition to being in the Army—serving one tour in Iraq and part of one in Afghanistan—Mr. Blackburn is also an ex-bull rider, a cattle-punching cowboy, a Medal of Honor winner and is currently a staunch family man and a dedicated farmer."

"I'm not put off by a bit of dirt and gravel, Mr. Blackburn—kind of goes with the territory in Arizona. Long as there's a space for my laptop in your vehicle, you don't need to clean it out for me."

"All right, then. Let me grab my notebook and my recorder and I'll meet you at the front door. We can either take the scenic route over the mountain, or go by the Cherry Road. Depends if you tend to get carsick or not."

"Long as I sit in the front seat, I should be fine."

The two of them were soon on the way. Kade took 89A over Mingus Mountain and down through Jerome to reach the Verde Valley. Once there, they went to the home of the board member who'd resigned. They knocked on his door and when he opened the wooden one, they presented their credentials through the still-locked screen. As soon as he understood who they were and what they wanted, he let them in and provided them with some cold lemonade.

"Sir, would you mind if I recorded your point of view?" Kade asked. "I'm slow at taking notes, and if I have you on tape, I can be certain to quote you accurately."

"Of course you can record me. I certainly hope you'll quote me accurately."

"Thank you, sir. My sidekick is new to the Prescott paper, but I've been led to believe she's very fast on the keyboard of her laptop. May she set it up on the table in the dining room?"

"Sure. Let's all sit at the table. I'll be less likely to spill my lemonade if we do. I tend to get hot under the collar discussing that issue, and I wave my hands a lot, too."

As soon as Diana and Kade had their equipment in place, Hamilton launched into his spiel. "We pay a goodly sum of money to support the college on this side of the hill, yet it seems like the programs that most benefit us here, the board intends on moving them to Chino Valley or Prescott Valley. We have a big medical center right here in Cottonwood, but they want all the nursing students to trek across the mountain to take nursing classes in Prescott. Some of the students don't have reliable transportation, nor should women be asked to drive home after classes in the dark. If they had a flat or other problems with their vehicle, they'd be at the mercy of anyone who came along."

"Do you have the figures denoting what this area pays into the college in taxes, sir? How does what the eastern side pays, translate into the percentage of classes on this side, compared to the number of classes on the Prescott side?"

"I certainly do. You'll notice, via this sheet, we don't have the commensurate number of classes to reflect the percentage of taxes we pay in. Plus, that campus in Prescott has dorms for students. We started off on this side with buildings resembling Quonset huts. They've been improved over the years, but we have yet to have any dorms."

"Does either campus need dorms, sir?" Kade asked.

"I don't believe so. Most community colleges make due with classrooms, not dorms. Most students commute to community-college classes, not stay on campus."

Kade continued to ask questions and got rather heated replies. When the afternoon grew late, Blackburn thanked the gentleman profusely, handed over his contact card in case the former board member thought of something else, gathered up his recorder and prepared to leave.

"I'd like to see what you write before it's published," the man said. "It's not that I don't trust you both . . ."

Kade grinned, "But you don't know us from Adam and Eve, so you'd like the chance to see what we're going to put out for the public's edification before it hits the streets. Do you have an e-mail address? I'll forward the exact copy to you, once our editor approves it."

"Yes, it's aHamilton@gmail.com."

"I'll see you get a copy of the article, sir. May take a day or two to send it, but I promise you'll have it in hand in time to correct anything that doesn't seem kosher to you."

"Coming from the Prescott side, you don't have an negative agenda in mind, do you?"

"No, sir, I don't. I'll report honestly what you've conveyed to me. I'm not going to skew the article to make the Prescott side's opinions come out smelling like a rose."

"You don't seem like the other reporters I've talked to. Most of them seemed to have made up their minds about the issue before they even asked me for my side of it."

"I'm not going to do that to you, sir. I have no axe to grind in this case."

"Well, thank you for your approach, then. It's nice to work with two people who are so mannerly."

"We'll be in touch, sir."

"Were you in the service? You keep saying 'sir' like you had been."

"I served one stint in Iraq and part of a second stint in Afghanistan. However, long before my military career, my father insisted that good manners required saying 'sir' and 'ma'am' when you spoke to anyone even a day older than I was."

"His lessons will continue to serve you well. Too many young folks these days have no concept of good manners. I'm not a prude, but some of the language coming out of their faces makes even me blush."

"I'm years younger than you, sir, but their language makes me blush, too."

"Do you have children?"

"I have four, sir. They also have good manners, at least the older two do. The twins are a bit young for . . . no, that's not true. Even the twins ask 'please' when they want something, and say, 'tenk you' when you supply what they ask for."

"Tenk you?" he asked.

"The twins are only two, sir. In fact I had to tell my female twin there was a difference between 'please' and 'peas.' She asked for a glass of milk one night at dinner and I said she had to ask me to 'please' get her some milk. She protested loudly. 'I no want peas. I no like peas. I no say peas. I want *milk*, Daddy.'"

Hamilton burst out laughing. "You have a good sense of humor, too, Mr. Blackburn."

"Afternoon, sir. Look for the article to show up about Wednesday or Thursday on your computer."

They got back in Kade's truck, and started for Prescott. "That was very well done, Mr. Blackburn. You had him eating out of your hand, due to your manners."

"I've found listening to what people say, instead of interrupting them with all kinds of questions, works well. A little prompt now and then if they go off topic, but I think it's best not to browbeat anyone if you want them to open up to you. I was hoping you'd jump in with a question or two from the female angle—especially when he said it wasn't safe for the students from this side to drive late at night to get home after classes."

"His age is showing. Women aren't petrified to drive after dark in these times. We all have cell phones, so it's probably good I didn't tell him my thoughts on the matter."

"You can change a tire?"

"Of course I can. Probably better than you can, seeing you're missing a couple of fingers."

Kade could hardly contain his grin at her comment. "Want to go mano-a-mano some time to see who can change a tire faster?"

"I keep thinking I've seen you someplace before. It's like a word that's on the tip of your tongue, but you can't quite come up with it. I've never been this far north in Arizona, so I don't think I've ever met you before, but still . . ."

"Did you watch television in Tucson?"

"Yes, as often as I had completed my class requirements—my homework and studies."

"Did you see the Medal of Honor ceremony a few years back for the soldier that saved Joe Biden's life?"

"Ms. Dean said you had one of those medals. You actually saved Biden's life? I didn't see the ceremony, so I don't think that's why you look familiar."

"Don't know, then, where our paths might have crossed."

"I'm going to lose sleep until I figure it out."

The next day, Kade was busy typing up his article, when Diana leaned over the divider of his cubicle. "Can we compare what we each write up on our interview? I'd like to know if I'm in the ballpark with my version."

"I fully intended to share what I write and I want to see what you've written, too. In fact, we should both send what we write to Mr. Hamilton and let him decide which one he likes best, or if he wants to combine them."

"I wouldn't presume to suggest such a thing, Mr. Blackburn. You're Ms. Dean's star reporter."

"You didn't suggest it, Ms. Gardner. I did."

"If we're going to work together, could you please call me, Diana?"

"Long as you call me Kade, I will."

"Okay, we'll share our articles with Mr. Hamilton. Are you going to get all squirrelly if he likes mine more than yours?"

"No, ma'am. He'll like what he likes and it makes no difference which version he prefers. I don't have a jealous bone in my body."

"How do you manage to type so fast with those missing fingers?" she asked.

"Years of practice, I guess. It was hard at first, especially when trying to hit the shift key for those right-handed capital letters, but it was adapt or be slower than Moses, so I adapted."

"I think you are a most amazing man, Mr. . . .uh, Kade."

"Tenk you!" he said, giving her a broad grin.

"Your daughter really let you know she didn't want any 'peas' when you asked her to say 'please' for the milk she wanted?"

"Guess my enunciation left something to be desired. My wife assured me Kathy never liked peas, even as a baby."

"I'll let you be so you can finish your article. This is my e-mail address," she handed him a note card. "Send yours when it's completed. That way, if mine is horrid, I can hide my red face inside my cubicle until mine is repaired."

"Have some faith in your reporting skills, Diana. I'm sure your report will be better than mine. Women tend to be more intuitive."

# *Chapter Seven*

Kade finished his article first and sent it to Diana's e-mail box. He knew she was still in her cubicle, and he began to worry when he didn't hear a word out of her.

"You okay, over there?" he finally asked.

"I'm fine," she said in a rather subdued tone of voice.

"Well? When are you sending your article to me?"

"Probably never."

"C'mon, Diana. That's not the right attitude."

"It's time to quit. I'll send you mine in the morning, after I've had time to think about it for a bit."

"Okay. See you tomorrow, then."

Kade was in early, but Diana didn't arrive before him. He sat down at his computer and found she'd sent him her article. He read through it, nodding at the parts he thought were good. He finally printed it out on paper, so he could tell her where she needed to improve it.

"You're awfully quiet over there," she said. "Is it truly that ghastly?"

"No, there are lots of parts that I consider superior to what I wrote. Let's grab a cup of coffee and discuss yours and mine."

In the coffee room, they sat side-by-side. "You do know, don't you, that you need to answer who, what, where, when and how questions in the first couple of paragraphs? If there's a hot item that takes precedence over our softer piece, all the other paragraphs might get cut, so you need to put the meat of the article in the first couple of them."

"I know that, but Hamilton said so much, how do you cram it all into two paragraphs?"

"It's not often easy. I very much liked what you said about the women when they're required to travel to Prescott to attend classes. I'd like to take my first couple of paragraphs, before including what you wrote about how women are more self-sufficient now. We can always hope that nothing of greater importance comes up to reduce what we've written."

"Go ahead, put our pieces together in the way you think is best," she told him. "You have mine on your screen—so knit them together."

"No hard feelings about me giving you advice? I don't have a total lock on correct procedures, I've just had my articles cut often enough to know you'd best put the most important things in the first two paragraphs."

"You're Ms. Dean's star reporter, so feel free to give me lots of advice. Oh, and I know where I recognized you from, now. When I can't decide what line to take in articles I write, I often put the problem in my head right before I go to sleep. Without fail, about 4 a.m. the approach I should take pops up in my mind.

"Last night, I put the problem of where I'd seen you, prior to being hired here, in my head. At that early pre-dawn hour, I remembered. Either you are displayed—in a portrait—at the Heard Museum in Phoenix, or you have a twin someplace."

He nodded, looking mostly unhappy because she'd discovered that portrait.

"It really is you? Watkins paints mostly tribal members, Navajos, Hopis. How did you manage to get painted and displayed among the Native Americans? Are you part Indian?"

"No. Corrine Watkins is my mother-in-law. She was always after me to pose for her. She called me her 'perfect' male model."

"Under that shirt you really look like that? If you do, I envy your wife."

Kade gave Diana a sharp look before he stood up and placed his cup in the sink of the coffee room. "I'd better try to knit our separate articles together, so we can get Ms. Dean's approval and Hamilton's, too. I'll send the combined one to you for additional input before I send them to both entities for their approvals."

His voice had taken on a hard edge and Diana wasn't sure if she'd offended him by asking him about his criticism of her article, or over the painting.

"Are you angry with me?" she asked.

He sat down again opposite her and leaned across the table in her direction. When he answered her question, he kept his voice low and devoid of the anger that roiled inside him.

"I think the paper's offices are not a place to discuss what you saw in the Heard. I definitely believe your statement that you 'envy my wife' was *totally uncalled for*. I'd prefer it, if we are destined to work together, you leave all references to my physical person or my personal life out of your observations."

"I'm sorry Kade. I didn't mean to offend you. Why are you so upset? I'd think you'd be damn proud of that portrait. You're one hot dude."

"That's not the only one Corrine painted of me. The other one got me into a lot of trouble in the Army recruitment center in Flagstaff. That's why I didn't appreciate your comment. Those portraits seem to make women think I'm available for their sexual needs. I can assure you, *I'm **not** available!*" he said, his voice rising.

Startled by his outburst, she recoiled, so he softened his tone to explain.

"I'm happily married. I have four children, so any hint that females are hitting on me . . . well, I'd just prefer not to have anyone referencing those paintings, including you."

"You thought I was hitting on you?"

"You envy my wife? I'm one hot dude? Weren't you?"

"I assure you I have no sexual interest in you."

"All right, I'll accept your assertion. Sorry if I misinterpreted your twin statements . . . it's just I've so often heard other women make the same comments."

He returned to his cubicle and welded his words in the article to hers. Sent the combined product to her email. Waited for her comments.

"It's fine, Kade," she said, leaning over the wall between her compartment and his. Her enthusiasm was definitely lacking.

"If there's something you aren't happy with, spit it out."

"Well . . . I'm not entirely satisfied, because you left out my statement that women aren't exactly the helpless creatures they once were in regard to driving. I know you want to make the point we shouldn't be required to drive clear to Prescott for classes when we've previously had nursing classes right there in the Verde Valley, but couldn't you state that without letting on women are afraid to drive after dark?"

"Sure, I'll delete that if it bothers you."

He highlighted the couple of sentences and deleted them both. "Suit you better?" he asked over the divider between them.

"Yes, that more closely approximates what I think. Why do you believe women shouldn't be on the roads after dark?"

"I read a lot of police reports. There was a woman who lived in Lake Montezuma who worked the evening shift at the Medical Center in Cottonwood. She got off at 11 p.m. She had car problems on the Cornville Road. She was a sitting duck for the guy who offered to help her—before he raped her."

"You think a man would be any less vulnerable?"

"Most men don't choose to rape men."

"No, but he could have demanded the guy's credit cards and money, so men aren't entirely free of vulnerability."

"Are we agreed? It should go to Ms. Dean and Mr. Hamilton now?"

"Yes, I think it's as good as it's going to get."

"What else do you think needs to be changed?"

"The summation for the entire article. Shouldn't you include the highlights in the summation? And your hook or lead doesn't grab me hard, either."

"You now have the entire article on your screen. Change it to suit yourself. Send it to Ms. Dean and Hamilton."

"You don't want to okay my changes?"

"No, ma'am. If we continue to debate this article, it will be 2017 before it gets into the paper."

"Now you're mad?"

"Only dogs get mad—when they do, they froth at the mouth and become aggressive. You'll notice I'm not frothing at the mouth and I have no desire to bite you on the leg, either. Send your version, I'm not going to waste any more time on it."

"But if Dean and Hamilton reject it, you're going to say, 'I told you so,' aren't you?"

"I'm not going to say a word. If you'd rather not take my advice, then I guess you'll have to satisfy yourself with Ms. Dean's critiques."

The article disappeared from his screen. He supposed she'd tinkered with it and forwarded it to their boss. He saved his version to a thumb drive and left for lunch. When he returned, Dean was in Diana's cubicle giving her some of the same thoughts he'd expressed, about putting the meat into the first couple of paragraphs. Kade sat down and started on an article about a crooked policeman. It was impossible to close his ears to Dean's critique of what Diana had sent her, and he knew he was about to get a stern lecture for letting her submit her version after Dean had asked him to take the cub reporter under his wing.

"Mr. Blackburn," Dean said, coming around the corner into his cubicle.

"Yes, ma'am?"

"Have you forgotten all my lectures about what to put into an article?" she queried.

"No, ma'am," he said, knowing Diana was listening to his lecture, too.

"Then why isn't the meat in the first two stanzas of this report?"

He wasn't willing to let the blame fall totally on Diana's shoulders, so he said, "We had a brief discussion on what was needed. Hamilton is a very talkative guy. Diana felt my lead wasn't strong enough, and I hadn't summed up the highlights at the end, either. I realized she was probably correct, so . . . ."

"So you let her send me her version? Kowtowing to a cub reporter demonstrates your idea of being kind and mannerly?"

"If you'll remember, Ms. Dean, you trampled hard on a few of my articles when you first hired me. Couple of those times, I decided I wasn't cut out for this job, when you upbraided me roundly and soundly.

"I came to this job with a pretty tough hide, due to my years in the Army. I was well acquainted with being yelled at. With Ms. Gardiner lacking any Army experience, I decided not to trample on her first effort as I wasn't sure how tough her hide was."

"You're here to teach her the ropes, not coddle her. Where is your version of the article?" Dean asked.

"On thumb drive, #15."

"Send it to me. Sometimes I wish you weren't quite so kind or mannerly. When I put someone new under your tutelage, you'd better step up to the plate. You're here to teach her. If you aren't up to the job, I'll take over. Do you understand me, Blackburn?"

"Yes, ma'am."

When Dean retired to her office to read Kade's version of the article, he heard sobbing coming from Diana's cubicle.

"Hey," he said, coming into her area. "We all get our chance to take some lumps from Ms. Dean. Don't let her discourage you. You'll catch on soon enough."

"It's not her lecture about my article that upset me. It's the way she took after you, when you were just trying to be kind. Why did you take the blame for what was my fault?"

"I'm still possessed of that tough hide, Diana. Wasn't sure you had the same."

"Still . . ." She shook her head. "You're such a nice guy, I felt bad for her dressing down of you—it should have accrued to me."

Kade pulled her up and hugged her, pressing her teary face into his shoulder. "Shhh—it's nothing to be upset about—at least not to the point of tears."

"That's twice I've upset you today," she mumbled into his chest. "Maybe I should quit."

"***Don't you dare!***" he said. "I'll never get any time off if you do. For my sanity, please abandon the idea of quitting. We'll work on it and soon you'll be the second-star reporter at this publication. We're going to work on making your hide tougher, too."

"You don't have a tough hide—a muscular one, maybe, but not a tough one. And you definitely have a soft heart. You could have heaped all of the blame on me, but you didn't. You shared the blame. Not many men are willing to do that."

"You don't seem to have a very good impression of men in general. Something must have soured you on them. Not only am I going to teach you the basics of writing a sound article that will stand up to Dean's scrutiny, but I'm going to endeavor to change your mind about men, too."

"Thanks for being so kind to me, Kade."

"Okay. Now get busy. Revise the article again, in case Dean rejects my version, too. Send it to both of us when you complete it. Don't worry if she feels the need to assault my ears a second time. It's not as if I haven't heard her screech before."

Diana smiled for the first time all day. "You really are a very sweet guy, Kade. I think if . . . uh . . . you've already definitely upgraded my impression of men in general just by your comportment this afternoon. I just knew you were going to blame everything on me. You didn't, and I'm enormously grateful."

"All those compliments are getting in the way of your revisions. If you feel the need to thank me, do it by revising your article per Dean's and my suggestions. A good article will function as the best form of thanks from you—to both of us."

"Okay. I'm on it."

Before the quitting hour arrived, she'd revised the article again, winning his and Dean's approval of the final version. Mr. Hamilton added his praise once Diana sent him the article, too.

"Good job, Diana," Kade told her as she walked to her vehicle. "I knew you had it in you, so no more talk about quitting, okay? See you tomorrow."

She nodded and blew him a kiss before she got into her car. He gave her a crisp salute in return.

# *Chapter Eight*

On his way back to his ranch, he debated if she had blown him the kiss because she was so grateful he'd not thrown her to the wolves—in the form of their alpha-male leader—Ms. Dean.

That her gesture might imply a deepening regard for him troubled Kade. He hoped it was the former, not the latter reason, as he knew he would find it hard to work with her if she entertained the idea of establishing a more personal relationship with him.

*It's another one of those touchy issues to discuss with Abby at eleven tonight. Better do so before she comes to the paper to invite me to lunch and finds Diana draped all over me.*

He was still shaking his head when he got home and he went directly to the barn to feed the stock.

"You have a hard day, Dad?" Alli asked him. "Is your neck stiff?"

"No more than usual after spending all day hunched over my computer. What's for dinner?"

"Mom said it was pork roast with candied yams and green beans. Grandma and Grandpa came over and they're staying for dinner, too."

"I'm only going to get one slice of the roast, and one yam?"

"I think Mom made plenty."

"Good, I'm starved. Has your grandpa been running me down all afternoon?"

"He had some few things to say. Said he went to Prescott to pay his taxes and saw you driving around with a strange woman in your truck."

"Ms. Dean hired a new reporter. She sent us off to the Verde Valley to cover the hubbub about the college moving a lot of the classes to the

Prescott side. It was just a work assignment. I'm supposed to teach Ms. Gardner the ropes and acquaint her with the areas we cover—familiarize her with the streets in Prescott—but I'll bet Owen is going to make a federal case out of seeing me driving around with her."

"He already has."

"You're pretty observant. What's your mama's frame of mind about him seeing me with another woman in the truck?"

"She burned her hand on the unit while cooking the beans, so if I had to choose a frame of mind for her, I'd say she was a bit distracted and maybe a tad upset, too."

"You need to study psychology in college, Alli—maybe go into social work. Not much escapes you, does it?"

"It's not hard to decipher either you or Mom. You're both as easy to read as a large-print book. Though in the last few days, both of you seemed less stressed. I was hoping that positive outlook would continue."

"It's a real shame you have to live with such stressed-out parents, Alli," he said, giving her a grin. "When you're older no doubt you're going to blame both of us for those permanent wrinkles in your brow, the wrinkles generated from worrying about your mother and father almost 24/7."

"What wrinkles? Do I really have wrinkles?" she asked, dismayed.

"Nope, and if you don't want to develop them, I suggest you stop worrying about Mom and me. We're fine—at least we were until Owen stirred up some doubts in your mama. Help me dispense sweet feed to the horses, so I can sit down at the table before your grandpa eats everything in sight."

"Okay, Dad."

Kade caught Abby by the hand in the kitchen. "Alli said you burned your hand. Is it okay? Let me see it, please."

She turned her hand over and there were fat blisters on two of her fingers. "You don't usually manage to fry your hand along with our dinner. Turn off everything and come upstairs with me. I need to remove the fluid from your blisters and put some antibiotic cream on them."

"I'm okay, Kade. Mom and Dad showed up unexpectedly. If I turn off the oven, dinner will be very late."

"Let them wait, since they didn't have an invitation. I'm going to insist on treating your burns before you come down with an infection."

Before she could protest again, he picked her up bodily and marched up to their bedroom. He closed and locked the door and dragged her into the bathroom. Made her sit on the lid of the toilet while he carefully washed her blistered hand. Getting out a needle, he sterilized it in a flame from his lighter, before he poked a piece of white thread through its eye.

He drew the needle through the blister, letting the thread absorb the fluid inside it. He repeated the entire procedure for the second blister, then smeared on some Neosporin ointment and covered both blisters with a Band-Aid. "I'd kiss your fingers all better, but I don't want to contaminate them again. I'll just kiss your lips, instead."

He pulled her to him and gave her a very sexy kiss."

"Dad said he saw you and a strange wo . . ."

"Save it for our 11 p.m. chat. I'll tell you then why I had her in my truck."

Owen tried to pry information out of Kade during dinner. "I was on my way to Prescott. You were inching through Jerome's tourist traffic when we passed on that narrow street where the speed limit is only 15 miles per hour. At first, I didn't think it was you, but it was definitely your truck. You were so busy chatting up that attractive woman who was with you in the front seat, I doubt you realized we'd passed each other."

"You're right, I didn't realize we'd passed each other."

"Who was that woman?" Watkins asked.

"I don't believe that's any of your business, Owen. I certainly don't intend to be grilled about the matter over dinner. I spent a long hard day doing my job—went in to work at seven and I only got home at six—so if it's okay with you, I'd like to eat my supper, not be interrogated by you—at least not until I can assuage my hunger."

Kade gave Alli a wink. She covered her smile, at his sharp reply to her grandfather, behind a napkin. "Please pass me those yams, daughter. I'm purely starving by this point. I'll take a nice thick slice of the pork roast, too."

"You didn't get lunch?" Corrine asked.

"Kade probably didn't have time to stop for lunch . . . not if he was shacked up all afternoon with that woman I saw in his truck," Owen said.

"Owen," Kade warned. "I don't believe we discuss topics like that at the Blackburn dinner table. While the twins are too young to grasp your insinuations, my older children are not. If you persist in making comments like that, I'll be glad to escort you out to your vehicle and you can go on your way."

"This is Abby's home as well, so I doubt your threat has any validity. Are you going to let him toss us out before we finish eating, daughter?"

"Kade is right, Dad. You shouldn't be talking about those topics in front of any of our four children."

"You're not curious? He must have you brainwashed if you're willing to let the matter slide. He hasn't been the most faithful of partners . . ."

Kade got up from his chair at the head of the table. "You're both leaving. ***Now!***"

"Like hell, Kade. You can't throw us out."

Kade pried Owen up from his chair with one hand on the back of Owen's collar and the other grasping his thick leather belt. "Andy, go open the front door. Corrine, you can either follow your husband out to his vehicle, or I can come back for you and show you to the same exit in the same manner I'm using on him."

"Would you?" she asked. "It's been forever since you laid a hand on me. Come back for me. I've missed your touches."

Kade saw his wife's eyes grow cold at Corrine's comment. She got out of her chair and was around the table in four steps. Abby grabbed her mother's arm and marched her out the door, which Andy was holding open wide.

"Get in your car, Owen, and don't come back unless I invite you to do so. No, Corrine, get in on that side. I've got my hands full of your no-account husband and I have no wish at all to lay my hands on you," he said, mocking her previous statement.

Owen threw gravel to the four winds as he exited the drive of the Ark Ranch. Kade put his arm around Abby, and together they went back to the dining room. On the way, Andy raised one hand and garnered a 'high-fives' gesture from his father. "Good for you, Dad," he whispered. "You finally stood up for yourself."

"I doubt we've seen the last of them." With that comment, Kade sat down again at the head of the table and loaded his plate with Abby's dinner. "Your mother is such a good cook. I'm very glad our guests have departed. Leaves a lot more on the platter and in the various bowls for me to eat," he said, trying to restore some normalcy and humor to their household. "I think I should treat Mama to a banana split later in the week."

"Only Mama?" Alli asked. "I like those splits, too."

"We'll all go, then. Is Friday okay with you, wife? Don't fix much for dinner that night, if we're going to indulge in a banana split."

"Friday sounds good to me, Kade."

"Dinner at the Chicken Shack before we hit DQ or Sonic for our splits? That way Mama doesn't need to cook at all. All in favor raise a hand."

The twins saw all the older arms waving in the air, so both of them added two arms apiece to the vote. "Looks like we have a *super* majority in favor of the plan," Kade said. "I'll come home at four to feed the denizens of the farm. You all be ready to leave by 5:30."

By eleven, all four children were in dreamland. Abby brewed some chamomile tea and took her seat at the small table in the kitchen.

"Before you get all exercised over your father's comments, Ms. Dean has hired another first-rate reporter—also a cum laude graduate—from the U of A in Tucson, this time. She asked me to take Ms. Gardner under my wing and show her the ropes. Apprise her of the haunts and streets in Prescott where most of the news occurs."

"Then why were you in Jerome?"

"Today, she sent us over to interview the college-board member who resigned over the brouhaha about the classes being curtailed or moved from the Verde side of the mountain to the Prescott side."

"Why were you so late getting home?"

"When we got back to the office, we each wrote up our separate reports on the interview. Ms. Gardner got some suggestions from me on how the report should go. She had some ideas that were contrary to mine. We went around and around on how the report should be written. When I finally got tired of revising it, I invited her to send her version to Dean. That earned both of us a rather strident lecture from the boss—her for not putting the important facts in the first couple of paragraphs—and me for not insisting she write in my style, since I'm supposed to be mentoring her."

"How old is she?"

"I don't know. I didn't ask. I'd suppose in her late twenties or early thirties, since she did the undergrad scene and went on to grad school."

"Is she pretty?"

He grinned and shook his head. "No, not particularly. She'll never make the grade as a movie star, but she's not the ugliest woman I ever saw, either. Average looks, I guess."

"Did she express any feelings for you? Most of the women you spend time with, fall in love with you sooner or later."

"She thanked me for not blaming her entirely for the version she sent to Ms. Dean. I could have said, since she disagreed with me on the wording, it was all her fault, but I didn't think that was fair."

"But it was her version. Why not let her take the blame?"

"I remembered my first days on the job, when Dean reamed me a new asshole about every other day. While I had the advantage of a fairly tough hide, from being yelled at frequently by Army officers, Dean's tirades often made me question if I'd made the correct career choice.

"Ms. Gardner—I knew she hadn't any similar Army experiences. Didn't think she'd developed the thick hide I came equipped with when I started, so rather than lump the disaster of the article totally on her, I offered to share the blame. Dean yelled at both of us, equally."

"What are we going to do about my parents?"

"What would you like me to do? Apologize? Invite them back for dinner? I'd rather let sleeping dogs lie. I don't appreciate your father's comments, especially in front of the children. Alli is well aware of the significant differences that often plague our marriage. She's worried that one of our battles will result in a divorce and they'd all be forced to spend one week with you and the next one with me."

Abby shrugged. "They are my parents, Kade. I think you had every right to react like you did, but when you respond like you did tonight, it puts me in a very uncomfortable position."

"What are you trying to say, wife? I was justified in sending them on their way, but you wish I hadn't done so?"

"You can't learn to ignore his comments?"

"Like you were willing to ignore your mother's invitation that I come back and lay my hands on her, too?"

Abby started to grin. "She never misses an opportunity to have you hug her, does she? Yes, I was furious that she continues to want your sexual attentions. I guess we'll just have to see how it all works out."

"I don't want them calling you or upsetting you, Abby. I'll get a restraining order against both of them if that happens."

"I guess it was good you'd finally had your fill of my father's insinuations. He does upset me when he starts in on you. He had me half believing you were cheating on me again. Said you'd gone over the mountain so fewer folks would realize you were having another affair."

"Hey, wife. Don't let him drive a wedge between us. I'm not having any affairs with anyone but you."

"In my heart, I know that, Kade. It's just my mind that has a hard time believing in you, especially when someone tells me they've seen you out with another female."

"Your father knows how to create those doubts in you. It's always the same song he sings.

'I saw Kade with another woman today.
He certainly wasn't trying to hold her at bay.
He wrapped her in his arms and gave her a sexy kiss.
Must be hard to be married to a handsome male like this.

You'll know for sure he's cheating on you again,
If you start getting calls at midnight, when
No matter how much you beg and cry,
The caller hangs up without even saying goodbye.'"

By the time he'd sung her both verses of his contemporary poem, she was laughing.

"I didn't know you were a poet," Abby said.

"I am a poet, and my feet show it—they're long fellows," he said, giving her that old saw. "Could we go to bed now that I've again assured you I have no interest in any women but you?"

"Kade?" Dean called out to him on his morning arrival.

"Yes, ma'am?"

"A rancher just called to say two of his race horses just died. He called the vet to see if the doctor could give him a reason why they were dead. The vet asked if he'd changed feed or anything. Rancher said he'd begun feeding local hay, because it was cheaper than the alfalfa they ship in from the southern farms.

"The vet attributed the horses' deaths to the hay baled in Chino Valley. Seems they have an infestation of blister beetles out your way. When a horse eats one of those beetles in the hay, it causes the horse severe gastric pain and he or she dies 90% of the time, usually after struggling with a gut-twisting colic for hours. Take Diana and interview the rancher and the vet, both. We need to warn others about the problem."

"All right. I don't feed my horses or goats hay baled in that area as I'd heard of problems with those beetles before."

As soon as Diana showed up for work, he said, "Hey, partner, we have just been handed an assignment in my neck of the woods. Get your laptop and come with me."

"Is it going to be another assignment where we both get our butts kicked? This time, I'd appreciate it if you didn't try to cover for me."

"You're still on that kick? This assignment deals with dead horses, due to blister beetles in the hay. Tell me you aren't going to break into sobs if the rancher has yet to bury them."

Diana gave him a glare. "I think I can handle a dead horse just fine."

"Meet you out at my truck in a couple of minutes, then."

"What are blister beetles?" she asked as they headed north.

"There are several beetles that contain a substance, called cantharidin, that can poison horses—or other creatures—that eat alfalfa hay. The beetles swarm in the hay when it's cut and left to dry in the field. They get baled up in the hay."

"How do you know so much about those beetles?"

"I've heard other tales about hay from Chino Valley that contains those beetles. Others have lost horses, too. It's why I don't feed hay from there to my stock."

"You live in Chino Valley?"

"Yes. In fact we'll go right past my ranch on the way to talk to the rancher who lost his horses."

He pointed out the ranch as they passed it. "The Ark Ranch?" she asked. "Where did you get that name?"

"Mostly pairs of animals inhabit our ranch. We've gathered up pairs of lots of critters."

"Oh," she said, making the connection. "Like Noah gathered up pairs to put onto his ark before the flood?"

"Exactly. Once we do our interviews, I'll stop at the ranch and you can meet my wife and kids—maybe I can entice Abby to provide us with lunch. We had a big pork roast for dinner last night. Didn't think there'd be much left as Abby's parents showed up to eat with us. But once I tossed Abby's father and mother off the ranch, that left a lot more roast to make sandwiches from today."

"You tossed them off the ranch? Why?"

"Yeah, I gave them both the bum's rush. Neither of them have ever had much use for me . . . no, that's wrong. Abby's father, Owen Watkins, hates the fact I married his daughter, so he spends most of his time running me down. I don't mind when he tries to do that one-on-one with me, but I resent it when he sets in to belittle me in front of our children . . ."

"Her mother does likewise?"

"Nope. She **never** runs me down," he said with a grin. "I'm her favorite poster boy."

"Then why did you toss her off the ranch, too? Watkins? Wait a minute. Corrine Watkins?" she asked as if she'd made another connection. "Ah, she's the artist, isn't she? The one who said you were her perfect male model?"

"Yes. She's a good artist, but she has a hard time keeping her hands to herself in regard to me. Here's the vet's office. We need to talk to him before we visit the ranch where the horses died."

"Damn shame," the vet told them. "Paul Greene had a couple of good prospects in those horses. He was planning to run them at Turf Paradise when they turned five. He's not one of those trainers with stars in his eyes. He didn't want to put his stock on the track before their bones matured enough to stand up to the strain. He was content to wait—not that it makes any difference now."

"That's the same agent as you find in Spanish fly, isn't it?" Kade asked. "The aphrodisiac?"

"Cantharitin, yes. Same agent, only it's a different species of beetle. It irritates the urinary system in the case of Spanish fly. Guess it makes men hot to trot when all that blood rushes in down there, though I'd warn against its use. Might end up the same as those horses."

"Did you do an autopsy?" Kade asked.

"No, but I did a flake-by-flake inspection of the bale Greene had fed from the previous evening. Didn't take long to find several beetles in the hay. I based my final diagnosis on the fact I could demonstrate blister beetles in the hay."

"Thank you for your information, sir. After we interview the rancher who lost his horses, we intend to write up an article warning others to be aware of the danger inherent in Chino Valley alfalfa."

"Greene is very upset about his loss. It might be good to leave a longer period before you interview him."

"We'll be gentle with him in our questions, sir. I have no intention to upset him further, but we need to get the word out about the beetles."

"Let me call him and see if he's amenable to talking to the press."

The vet put in a call to Greene and asked how he'd feel about talking to a couple of reporters. When he hung up, he said, "Greene also would like to get the word out about the dangers in feeding hay from here. He asked you to meet him at the stable area, as his wife is still crying over the loss of their horses, and he'd rather you didn't upset her more."

"We won't do that, sir. I have horses, so I understand how hard it must be to lose one."

"Good, keep that thought in mind as you ask your questions."

They met Paul Greene at his stables. He was sitting on a bale of stall straw, but stood up as they pulled into the area. "May I see your credentials?" he asked. Kade and Diana both fished their press cards out of their wallets.

"Ordinarily, I would have turned Doc down when he asked me if it was allowable to send you out to talk to me, but I feel a pressing need to spare anyone else in the area the sorrow that comes with losing a horse or two. Lots of 4-H kids live around here and I think they'd react with the same feelings as my wife—should their horses die."

"We understood from the vet, that she's still very upset, so we'd prefer to talk to you alone and get the warning out to others about the dangers lying in bales of Chino Valley's alfalfa."

"Yes, she's still upset. Rocking Roy was her favorite. His mother died six weeks after giving birth to him and she bottle raised him from that point on. Roy was like her child, in essence. I think you can relate to how hard it might be to lose a child—and why she's still so upset."

"I can relate, sir. I have four children and I'd be devastated if I lost any of them. What was the other horse's name?"

"Valentino Red."

"Both were being groomed for the track?"

"Yes. Both showed some promise on the oval that lies behind the stables. Course, I wasn't in any hurry to send them south to the track in Phoenix. Too many send three-year-olds to the track only to have them end up lame because their bones are still in the process of getting stronger."

"Good for you, Mr. Greene," Diana said. "How many other horses do you have on this place?"

"I've got a stallion, and eight brood mares. War Chestnut throws some good colts. He came off the track about four years ago, having won just short of half a million during his racing career. The mares I picked up from the tracks, too, because they also had racing bred into them, though most of them earned in the low thousands, not millions."

"I always heard it was the dam who made the difference in the colts, not the sire," Diana said.

"I believe it takes both sets of parents to produce a good colt," Greene said. "War Chestnut is the commonality in this equation. That he continually produces good-quality racing colts, regardless of the mare he inseminates, I tend to think it's the sire that makes the difference in my stable."

"What happened to the dead horses?" Diana asked.

"We buried them over close to those trees."

"Anything else you'd like to tell us about?" Kade asked.

"I just want a big spread on the front page to warn others about the danger."

"Pictures tend to grab a reader's attention. Mind pulling out a couple of your mares, or your stallion so we can take a picture to put on the front page?"

"I'll get War Chestnut. He's the stallion, after all. He's very impressive, both in size and color. Will the photo be in color? He's named War Chestnut, because he's a chestnut color."

"Yes, we can take a color photo," Kade assured him.

While Greene went to put the stallion on halter, Diana said, "You'd think the mares had no part in producing those colts he's so proud of. Colts, only? No fillies? I think we're dealing with a male, horse chauvinist."

"A comma, not a dash between male and horse, in your last statement?"

She had to think about that question for a couple of seconds. "Yes, definitely."

"You might want to scrub that look from your face before he comes back with his stallion. Your lack-luster impression of males includes the four-legged variety?"

"That's twice you've alluded to my attitude about males. When I get to know you better, maybe I'll tell you why I think males are not God's gift to the world—either the two-legged or four-legged variety, and there are dashes between those words, too, not commas."

"Unlike my mother-in-law, who admits I'm her favorite male model—I should abandon all hope of being your favorite reporter-type male model?" he teased.

"Men and their egos are just insufferable. They never believe a woman can accomplish anything close to the male's attainments."

"You might want to discuss that with me when you stop making your $0.77 compared to my $1.00 in wages."

As they started down the road toward Prescott, Diana wore a big grin. "What did Corrine pay you to pose for her?" she asked. "Did you earn more than a female model would?"

"I didn't earn a damn cent. Just took a lot of grief for being included in the book. You've seen it? Her book?" he asked.

"When you mentioned your mother-in-law, I remembered I had her book in one of the boxes I'd yet to unpack. I bought it in Tucson. It was all the rage among the art students there. I dug it out and looked through it. You were in the book, the only man with a recognizable face and a body to die for. After I scoped out your portrait—you really are very well endowed—I had even more envy for your wife. Must be a memorable experience having you make love to her."

She noted his frown had returned in spades. Kade sailed past his ranch without slowing. In fact, he seemed to go even faster.

"Hey, weren't you going to stop at the ranch, introduce me to your wife, and build both of us a sandwich?"

"I don't think that's such a good idea. Not after your recent comments. A lot of women seem to come on to me. I have no control over that, but I choose not to subject Abby to their salivating. She's very aware of . . ."

"Of other women's admiration of you?"

"Yes. I'd prefer it if you don't attempt to pry into my private life or make any more comments like you just voiced. I don't want you to be friends with my wife, so I'm not going to introduce you to her. I'm willing to stop and buy you lunch somewhere. It just won't be at the family ranch."

"You're mad . . . uh . . . angry again, aren't you?"

"You'll notice I haven't asked you questions about why you take such a dim view of men. It's none of my business. Just as my sexual relationships with Abby are none of yours."

"Well, shut my mouth."

"That'd be a good thing to do, right about now."

"You want to know why I don't have much regard for men? You just demonstrated the reason. First you blow hot, then you blow cold. I think you're going to be a wonderful mentor for my first baby steps into journalism. You seemed so warm and encouraging at first.

"Twice now, your brow's knotted up and you scowl at me like I'm some sort of ogre. I don't know you well enough yet to avoid the minefields of your personal existence. Forgive me for admiring your very sexy body—and it is a very sexy body—in the book. I won't ask you another question about the portrait, though, believe me, I have plenty of questions I'd like to ask."

"Like what?" he said.

"No. You've made it perfectly clear that you don't want any relationship with me—not even a mutual friendship—just one where everything outside the journalistic story we're covering is off limits. I thought you were a kind and considerate guy. Guess I'll have to revise my first image of you."

Kade drove to a Mexican restaurant just a block off the Courthouse Square. He parked the truck and went around to open her door. When he tried to take her elbow, she yanked it free. He tucked both his hands in his back pockets. Didn't offer to open the door of the restaurant for her. Didn't offer to pull out her chair, either.

"Have you eaten here before? What do you recommend?" she asked, offering him a bit of balm to assuage his obviously wounded male pride.

"It's all good. I like their shredded-beef chimichangas, but it's entirely up to you to choose what you want."

"Are we going to be at loggerheads for the rest of the year?" Diana asked.

"I honestly don't know. If you want some sort of deeper relationship with me—if you continue to envy my wife—we likely *will* be at loggerheads."

"Kade, you can't help it if women are attracted to you. Look around this restaurant. What do you see? Bald men. Men with a paunch. Men slouched over their plates. Men with stupid grins on their faces."

"So?"

"You are a handsome man with a full head of dark black hair. I know from the portrait that under your shirt there's a six-pack of abs. You have a military bearing, and your grin is anything but stupid. You're what every woman in existence desires. Not many attain their desires, but faced with a prime example of maleness, you cause all of us to dream. I don't intend to apologize for being attracted to you."

His frown was back. "It's those attractions that have caused me innumerable problems in my marriage." He didn't elaborate as the waiter came to take their orders.

Kade let Diana order what she wanted. Ordinarily he'd have asked her for her preference and given both their orders to the waiter, but after she'd spurned his assistance alighting from his truck, he wasn't about to suggest that a male should order for them both. While she might admire his military bearing, his abs, and his head of hair, he felt she definitely didn't want him to usurp any of her female independence.

"Would you entertain a couple of questions about Corrine's portrait of you?" she asked.

"How would I know unless you ask them?"

"Okay. I'll take a chance and hope you aren't about to toss your glass of ice water all over me. All the other faces are blurred. Yours is not. Why?"

"We'd had a lengthy discussion about the fact that few nude males showed up in paintings over the millennia. When Corrine told me she planned to bridge the gap in her book in that respect, I agreed it needed bridging. Nude females over the ages didn't insist they be unrecognizable due to poorly rendered faces, so I thought it only fair that men didn't hide behind anonymity either. While I understood the Native American's reluctance to be thus recognized, I had no tribal reason to want my face blurred."

"You came to rue that decision after the book came out?"

"No, not so far as the art work goes. I'm rather proud to be the only male in the book that is captured in entirety. I felt my decision helped to bridge the gap without looking like it was a tentative step on my behalf."

"You said it caused you a lot of problems. How?"

"I was assigned to the recruitment center to enlist young men into the Army. A woman ran into me with her car and broke my wrist. Made it hard to type up stuff, so I was assigned a female soldier from the steno pool to type reports.

"Corrine, angry about my unwillingness to pose for her again, left a copy of her book on Corporal Smith's desk. My portrait was book marked, and after she saw it, Smith found it hard to work with me."

"The little inked-in image in the corner is drawn to scale?" Diana asked.

Her question elicited the first smile from Kade since they'd sat down. "Yes, I believe it is," he said.

Their food arrived and it put an end to any conversation. Over a refill of cola and tea, he suggested they both write up their articles about the beetles in the hay separately then compare what they'd written, before combining both viewpoints into one whole article. She agreed that might be best.

Kade was willing to pay the bill for both meals, but Diana insisted on going Dutch. "I know you make more money per hour than I do, but I refuse to let you spend your *extra* wealth on my food."

That comment earned her a second grin from him. "Good. Leaves more in my wallet for Friday's dinner out with my family. If I'd had to pay for your meal, I might not get my banana split Friday night."

"You can be so pleasant when you choose to be that way, Kade. Why don't you choose to be that way all the time?"

"I don't appreciate females coming on to me. I love my wife and our children. If you can steer clear of personal issues with me, we'll get along just fine. I'll respect you more as a journalist—not as a female Blackburn groupie. I don't want anyone idolizing me for a single aspect of my personal self—not the hair, the military bearing, the abs, and certainly not for the length of my . . . drawn to scale or not."

He opened the door for her, but declined to help her into the truck.

# *Chapter Nine*

Two days later, Abby showed up at the paper, having left Alli and Andy in charge of the twins.

"Hello, wife, what brings you to town?"

"I needed a screen to use as a sifter. Every afternoon, Kory and Kathy want me to dig up grubs for the chickens. They want to pour mustard water in those holes, too, but I drew the line at that. I don't mind gathering up a can of grubs for them to feed to the chickens, but worms are too slimy." She visibly shuddered.

"Did you find what you needed?" he asked.

"Yes, it has mesh wide enough for the dry manure to go through, but not the grubs."

"Hey, while you're here, I'd like to introduce you to my partner in crime," he said, knowing Diana was probably listening in and wondering about a woman who hunted up grubs for chickens. Putting an arm around her waist, he went around the corner to 's cubicle.

"Diana, this my wife, Abby Watkins Blackburn. Abby, this is our newest reporter, Diana Gardner."

"I'm so happy to meet you, finally. Kade says you're doing well in this new job," Abby told her.

"I'm happy to meet you, as well. Every time I hear a long lull in Kade's typing, I stand up and look over the wall between his space and mine, to find him staring at the pictures of you and the children lining his desk. I have to remind him often that the news doesn't write itself."

"You'll get fired some day for all your woolgathering," Abby said, giving him an elbow to the ribs.

"It's just—sometimes I feel the need to be better grounded. Much of the news is so bad or depressing that it helps me to stare for a minute or two at what's good and real and pleasant. Those photos lining my desk have the same effect on me as licking into a banana split."

"Idiot," Abby said, smiling up at him. "Have you had lunch? Could you skip out for a quick one?"

"Let me ask the boss."

Kade went off to consult with Ms. Dean about lunch.

"Abby, that husband of yours surely loves you to pieces," Diana said. "Seldom an hour goes past that he doesn't say something nice about you or the children."

"Yes, things seem to be getting better and better between us—especially since we moved to the ranch. Before we moved, I always had the feeling he didn't think he'd provided well enough for us. Now, he seems more content."

"The boss says I can take a couple of hours for lunch. She told me that after I said I'd bring her back a banana split."

"Kade Blackburn, don't you dare return without two of those concoctions," Diana informed him.

"Do you want to come to lunch with us?" Abby asked.

Standing behind his wife, Kade shook his head 'no' in a barely perceptible manner. She understood his reluctance to foster a friendship between them.

"No, thanks. Someone has to remain on post to churn out the news for the day. Take as long as you like, because I'm here to cover the big events while you're gone, Kade. I think I may even be able to mumble my way to the police station now, due to your excellent directions."

"The map—I'll leave you the map in case you get lost," he teased.

"It's only men who are too stubborn to ask directions when they're lost. We women don't have the same reluctance, so I'm going to be fine without the map."

"Okay," he said. "We'll send out the search dogs if you don't return from a hot scoop by six this evening."

He returned about 1:30 in the afternoon, with two banana splits in plastic containers. He left one with Dean in her office and toted the other one to Diana's cubicle.

"Your wife isn't exactly how I pictured her," Diana said. "She's not the same woman as portrayed in the pictures on your desk."

Kade's brow wrinkled in a frown, not understanding what Gardner was alluding to. Diana went on to explain her comment.

"In those pictures, she looks like a woman of the world. In person, she seems a bit earthier. Not so much the sophisticated wife I imagined her to be."

Kade considered her comment for a long moment. "Abby was raised on a ranch," he said in her defense. "She can ride a horse, brand a calf, drive mules pulling a chuck wagon and cook up a decent meal for cattle drovers. She may not be very sophisticated or worldly, but she suits me just fine, since I'm not very sophisticated, either."

"I'd have thought you'd choose a woman who complimented your achievements better. You must be smart, since you graduated at the top of your class in journalism. Yet you chose to marry a woman who needs a sieve with which to collect grubs."

Kade burst out laughing. "You can't imagine Abby in a Dior gown— only in bib overalls, collecting grubs for the chickens? Let me assure you, when she gets all gussied up, you'd have a hard time telling her apart from the females pictured in **Elle Magazine**. My wife is no slouch when it comes to . . . ah, hell, Diana, I don't need to defend my wife to you."

"But you're one of the better-looking males on earth."

"Yes, so you've said several times. I believe Abby's one of the prettiest women on this planet. She's both educated and has practical knowledge as well. You may think you're miles above her in sophistication, but I doubt you could harness a mule team or cook a filling meal over a campfire."

"Why would any woman aspire to do either of those things?"

"What exactly do you think women should aspire to?" he asked.

Diana numbered off five points on her fingers of one hand. "One, she should always dress well. Two, she should enhance her husband's ambitions by being refined enough to fit in with his co-workers. Three, she should be well spoken and up on current topics of interest. Four, she should have exquisite manners, and five, she should always endeavor to look her best—be pretty—and she should also be good in bed."

Kade considered those points for more than a few minutes. He grew angrier the longer he thought about Diana's points. Debating whether to defend his wife or just let go of the whole issue, he decided his wife deserved his 'white knight' defense, so he rode in to defend her.

"Abby does dress well for special occasions. For the state award at the journalism meeting, she looked elegant in her sundress. Just because she wore bib overalls to lunch today, doesn't mean she's ignorant of the proper attire for important occasions.

"She does fit in with me and my co-workers—in far more scenarios than you can imagine. She's equally at home with my journalism co-workers as she is with the drovers on a cattle drive. As for being well spoken, she can converse with those widely divergent groups with ease. She has the ability to connect with each of them.

"As to her manners, they are superior to yours, I think. She'd never belittle you, as I feel you've denigrated her. She has a much kinder heart in that regard. As for her being good in bed—there's no question about that point. She satisfies me in a thousand ways, as our many children give mute testimony to."

"Yes, it must be such a thrill to make love to a woman who spends part of her days raking grubs out of manure to feed to the chickens. I can only hope she showers after those activities."

It dawned on Kade at that point, Diana was jealous of his close relationship with Abby—wished she were the one in bed with him.

"This conversation is over. I have work to do," he told her, turning the corner to go back and sit in his cubicle. He opened his center drawer and smiled at the picture of Abby in her overalls. It was his favorite shot of her, the one he kept hidden, because of all the pictures of his wife, it was the one that best encompassed all their years together. Their good times and bad times, the rough-and-tumble times—the struggles, the joys.

*Yes, ma'am, wife, you stand head-and-shoulders above Diana, no matter what you wear. I could have searched a lifetime and not found anyone who fit so well with me—not among my co-workers, or the cattle drovers, or in bed. How dare she suggest you don't measure up to me? If she knew the truth of the matter, you're so far above me in so many ways . . . I'm surprised you don't suffer from altitude nosebleeds.*

He closed the drawer, and returned to typing up a news item he'd covered that morning. Just before the quitting hour, Diana sat down in his cubicle.

"Kade . . ."

He looked up from his computer screen. Said, "Yes?" in a less-than-cordial tone.

"I hope you weren't upset by what I said about your wife. She just wasn't what I imagined her to be. I really believed a man like you would have wed a more urbane woman."

"I married the woman I've loved since I saw her kneeling among her goats. Unlike all those super-sophisticated women, I knew Abby was a woman who needed love and would value the man who provided it."

"Why did kneeling among goats sell you on marrying her?"

"Conversations over breakfast at the ranch house, where she lived, led me to believe the goats were the only ones on the ranch that loved her unconditionally. Her parents seemed to go their own directions without concern for Abby. I wanted to fill that role with Abby—give her my love unconditionally. Suppose you could chalk it up to the white-knight gene in me."

"You also had a need to be needed? That doesn't fit with my idea of you, either. You seem very self-sufficient."

"She's had that unconditional love from me, ever since I recognized that need in her. She's forgiven me several times for my errors in judgment. She stuck with me through all the rough times—and there were some very rough periods we've weathered together."

"No, my wife might not be very urbane, but I know one of those urbane, super- sophisticated women would have long since divorced me. Those urbane types wouldn't have needed the same unconditional love that Abby counts on from me. It's just nice to know Abby needs my love . . . as many more-jaded women wouldn't."

"You don't think she holds you back?"

Kade shook his head. "No, far from it. She's always the first to speak about my small accomplishments. I'm reluctant to blow my own horn in those instances, but Abby has no such reluctance. I find it much easier to speak about her successes, than my own."

"It's a mutual admiration society?"

"Yes."

"Well, I hope my earlier comments don't curtail our burgeoning relationship."

"Burgeoning relationship?" he asked. "I don't think we have one of those."

"Kade, I admire you enormously. You have to know how I feel about you. I'd like to have a better relationship with you. I don't want us to be enemies over my few casual remarks about your wife."

"I suspect you'd also like to have an intimate relationship with me—as have several other women of my acquaintance. Am I reading you correctly? Is that what you meant when you've said on several occasions that you 'envy my wife'?"

"Rumor has it, you've indulged in a few of those extra-marital liaisons before."

"Go home, Diana. This conversation is at an end. I'm not going to indulge in any liaisons with you."

"Why not? It's not like you have scruples against it, if the rumors are true. Once in my life I'd like to experience sex with such a well-equipped male."

"Then I suggest you find one—outside this office—because I have no interest in you in that way."

"Are you saying you do have an interest in me, just not a sexual interest?" gave him a smile that suggested she didn't believe him.

"That's right. I'm interested in seeing you become a top-notch reporter—nothing more. If this line of . . . if it doesn't cease, I'll have to speak to Ms. Dean about your harassment."

"Oh, that's rich. I don't think Ms. Dean will believe I'm harassing you, as it's usually the man who's harassing a woman, not the other way around."

"Go back to work, Ms. Gardner. I don't think you can count on me mentoring you from this point on, either."

"Expect she'll be calling you into her office, then, since she suggested you teach me the ropes. She's going to kick your butt again if you refuse to follow her orders."

"I'll take my chances. Please, *get out of my cubicle!*"

Diana arose and went back to her side. Kade heard her on the phone to Ms. Dean, complaining he wasn't willing to mentor her anymore. Taking his jacket, he slipped out the back door and left for home. Knew he'd need to talk to Abby about Diana's desires for an intimate relationship with him over their chamomile-tea session at eleven.

# *Chapter Ten*

"You're upset about something, Kade. Tell me what has your brow all wrinkled up."

He closed his eyes and reached across the table to take her hands in his. "You know how much I love you, don't you?"

"Yes, Kade. I'm well aware of the depth of your love for me."

"There's a problem at work."

"Diana? I have the feeling she . . ."

He shook his head at how perceptive his wife was. "Yes, today she wondered why I'd married such an earthy woman."

"She thinks I'm a country bumpkin because I showed up in my jeans and talked about grubs?"

He nodded.

"She's putting herself forward as the type of woman you should have married, isn't she?

Again he nodded.

"I knew, just from the envious look on her face, that she'd like it better if you belonged to her."

"What is it about me that makes all the females want me to enter into an intimate relationship with them?"

"That's what she suggested?"

"Yes, in no uncertain terms."

"Well, Kade, you can't help it that you are a prime specimen of maleness. You project an aura of sexiness. You put most males to shame with your bearing and your finely sculptured physique. That's why women come on to you."

"I don't mean to project any auras like that."

"It's not possible for you to do otherwise. Do you intend to take her up on her invitation?"

"Of course not. How could you even ask me that?"

"Because, husband mine, if you don't disabuse her of her wishes, she'll be on your case for months. Your brow will have permanent creases."

"How am I supposed to disabuse her of her desire to have sex with me?"

Abby smiled. "By having sex with her, of course. After that one time, you will indicate she's not so hot in bed, and you prefer my lovemaking to anything she's offering. She'll be so angry you've spurned her, she'll turn her attentions to someone else."

He could hardly believe she'd said that. "You're inviting me to have sex with Diana?"

"I realized, after one of your statements . . . once when we had a fight . . . that you *are* capable of separating the physical act of sex from the emotional side of sex. With me, you give me everything—the emotional side, your body, your mind, your soul and your heart are all involved to the max. Could you give her just the physical side?"

"You know I don't give anyone but you that kind of love. For the others, it's only ever been a physical release, not one with my emotions involved."

"I know, Kade. Take her up on her invitation. Then, turn your back on her. Let her know she doesn't measure up, because you felt nothing more than a physical release. Tell her you felt no emotions in your heart or head during the experience, so you'd as soon not repeat such a disappointing liaison."

"You think that's all it would take?"

"I'm pretty sure her ego would be crushed. She evidently thinks she's more attractive than I am. If you indicate she's not, I'm pretty sure she'll hate you from that point on."

"I still don't feel right about cheating . . ."

"But you *won't be cheating* on me, Kade. I know the difference now. It took me years to realize the difference between the types of love you're capable of dispensing. I know you love me in the fullest sense—heart, mind and body. The physical side is just—How do the guys put it? Getting your rocks off?"

He had to laugh. "Maybe Diana is right in her statement you're an earthy girl. No sophisticated, urbane woman I've ever run across would put a physical release in those terms. Yes, I can get my rocks off without feeling anything for my sexual partner. Only with you, does the physical release have far deeper meanings."

"What's this I hear?" Ms. Dean yelled as soon as he came in the door early the next morning. "You're refusing to mentor Diana?"

"Yes, ma'am."

"That's not an option, Kade. She doesn't yet have your grasp on how to write up reports yet."

"Then perhaps **you** should kick her butt like you kicked mine until your lessons sank into my cerebral cortex. You're a pretty effective teacher."

"Flattery will get you nowhere, Kade. I don't have time to mentor Diana, so I suggest you get on with that chore. Otherwise, I might be forced to reconsider your value to me."

"You'd fire me?"

"I would. Does that change your mind about mentoring Ms. Gardner?"

"I guess it does. Can't pay my mortgage without a job."

"I'd suggest you offer her your apology and straighten out your differences first thing this morning."

"Yes, ma'am."

When Diana arrived at eight, Kade had been at work for an hour. He shut off his computer and went around the corner into her cubicle. He pulled out a chair and sat on it backwards, resting his crossed arms on the back of it.

"You're here because Dean let you know not mentoring me is not an option?"

He didn't give her a response, just a cold stare. Finally he said, "Yes, Dean told me it's not an option not to mentor you, but let's have an understanding. I'm not going to tolerate any more personal comments from you. You will not discuss my wife, my children, my lifestyle, or anything else like that with me. From this point on, it's going to be strictly a conversation about the business of news reporting.

"You can ask me about the articles you write up, but that's all you can ask me about. I have no desire to have an intimate relationship with you. Is that clear?"

"I believe your wife . . . your grub-hunting wife . . . suspected you might have some feelings for me. She gave you your marching orders last night, didn't she?"

Marching orders reminded Kade of Abby leaning out into the aisle at his graduation ceremony and whispering, "K-dens, Let, Rye," as he passed her seat. He had to smile at the memory.

"I'm right, aren't I? Your smile gives you away."

"No, she didn't give me any marching orders in regard to you, but she offered up a few suggestions."

"Ones that you'd better adhere to, or she'll . . ."

"Abby doesn't make threats like that. In fact, what she suggested surprised me so much I found it hard to sleep last night."

He had, in fact, tossed and turned after their discussion, until Abby hugged him close and said, "I trust you, Kade. I know you'd never hurt me by getting involved with her to any emotional extent. I've accepted the fact your mind, heart and soul belong to me, so give her a taste of your body, while withholding your mind, heart and soul."

"You're sure you're okay with that?"

"I am."

"*I'm* not comfortable with what you suggested, Abby."

"I know, love. That's why I'm not worried if you engage in sex with Diana. I know you belong to me. Took me a long time to figure it out, though you often told me your encounters with Mom only took a physical form. Can't you see I've evolved since those times? I now trust you completely."

"What did she suggest?" Diana asked.

"I can't tell you, not here in the office. I'd be open to coming past your place to discuss it there, as I prefer not to mix work with pleasure," he said, emphasizing 'pleasure' slightly. "Abby and the kids are going to Camp Verde for dinner with my in-laws. I'm never invited there. How are you at cooking?"

"Let's go out to eat, then we can go back to my place. I'd love to be seen on the arm of such a good-looking stud. Might provoke other men to take more interest in me."

"Fine. Any place you prefer to dine?"

"The steakhouse on the Cherry Road is a good place to eat."

"All right. We both drive our separate vehicles, or you want to ride with me?"

"How about you ride with me? After our discussion, I'll drop you back at the office. That way, you won't need to sweep out the dirt and manure from your truck."

"Okay."

Dean intruded on their plans at that point. "Diana, I need you to go to the courthouse. Attorney General Horne will be up for his depositional hearing at one with the county prosecutor, over the issue of his campaign finances."

"Shouldn't you send Kade? That's an important story and he's better at picking out the meat of stories than I am."

"No time like the present to learn. I understand the Governor might also be in attendance. You won't be allowed into the depositional meeting, but perhaps you can interview the governor, so take your voice-activated recorder. You don't need to let her know you're using it."

"Isn't that illegal?" Kade asked.

"Diana, as a new reporter, will want to get the facts down pat, so I don't think it's illegal to assure our readers she's done that by recording the conversation."

"She'd be smart to let the governor know she's recording it—using the recorder because she wants to get the facts right."

"Who appointed you to make my paper's decisions, Mr. Blackburn? If Diana says she's recording their conversation, the governor isn't going to say anything off the cuff."

Kade shrugged and went back to his computer. As soon as Diana left for the courthouse, he called Abby. "I may be very late getting home tonight. I told Diana you and the kids were going to Camp Verde for supper, so I invited her out to dinner. Depending how things go after dinner . . ."

"You might be getting your rocks off?" Abby asked, before breaking into laughter. "I just wish I could be a fly on the wall when it happens, Kade. I won't be upset if you spend the night with her. If you do, call me in the morning and let me know how it went. If you come home to crawl in bed with me later tonight, do me a favor and shower first. I'd rather not smell her overpowering cologne on my favorite guy."

"Last chance to change your mind, wife."

"I still trust you."

"I'll definitely shower before I crawl in bed with you. I'll need to wash off all the guilt I'll have, before I lie down with my favorite girl."

"If you come home early enough, make love to me. That way, maybe those guilty feelings will all get erased."

"Count on it, Abby."

At six, he got into her car for the ride to the steakhouse. "Your vehicle is definitely cleaner than mine," he said, making idle conversation.

"That's because I've never rooted up a grub in my lifetime," Diana said, smiling at him.

"Don't knock it until you try it," he said. "Those chickens purely love those grubs. I do believe their egg production goes up the more grubs they eat."

Diana insisted on paying the bill at the end of their dinner. Kade protested he'd like to pay his share, but she wouldn't hear of it.

*I suspect you want me to feel obligated, so I'll be more open to repaying the dinner charge in other ways. If you only knew what's about to transpire— you'd let me pay for both our dinners.*

She drove to her apartment, located in a new and prosperous part of Prescott.

"We're here," she announced, taking his arm as they approached the front door.

"Can I get you something to drink?" she asked, when he sat down at her table.

"Have any chamomile tea? I'd rather not drink anything full of caffeine this close to crawling into bed."

"You're planning to crawl into bed?" she asked. "Here?"

"Isn't that what you wanted? Me to take you to bed?"

Kade had a hard time keeping the grin off his face as her eyes widened in surprise.

"I'm not prepared . . . unless you are. I don't keep anything on hand for protection."

"I'm not infected with anything, and I've had a vasectomy, so I don't think you'll need anything in the way of protection."

"This is so sudden. What changed your mind?"

"You did. You dropped enough hints about sexual liaisons, I began to wonder what you'd be like in bed. I'm always more inclined to bed a woman who's impressed with my physical attributes."

"Um, Kade . . ."

"If you've changed your mind, you can always drop me off at the paper."

"I haven't changed my mind. How do you want to proceed?"

"Proceed? You aren't one of those closet virgins, are you? Do I have to mentor you in the subject of sex, too?" At the look on her face, he realized she might well be one of those. "I'm out of here, Diana. I'm not going to bust your cherry and leave you all sore. You might have told me."

"No, don't go, Kade, please? It won't be my first time—just my first time to have sex with a stud like you. The others didn't look anything like your portrait."

"You're sure?"

"Yes. I'll just go and slip into something more comfortable."

"No, don't. Part of what turns me on is being able to divest you of your clothes. Lead me to the bedroom, Diana. I want to undress you, then, you can do the same for me. After we're naked, I find a nice warm shower enhances the sexual experience."

She rose and took him by the hand. In the bedroom, she said, "I'd prefer to undress you first."

"Okay. I have no objections."

When he had no clothes on, she said, "Wow! I guess Watkins' sketch told no lies."

"I remember telling you before, she'd drawn the little figure to scale."

"You had relationships with her after she drew you?"

"Yes, but that's over now."

"Why?"

"She isn't as good in the sack as my wife. I'd rather not waste time on inferior females. Are you ready to let me undress you?"

"I guess."

"If you have reservations, I'll put my clothes on and leave."

Diana raised her hands in resignation. Kade unbuttoned her blouse and removed it. He peeled the straps of her slip down over her shoulders. "Kick off your shoes," he instructed.

When she'd complied with that direction, he unfastened the button of her skirt. He ran the skirt's zipper down. Grasping her outfit on either side, he slid it down over her hips, leaving only her bra and panties intact. He reached behind to unfasten the hooks of her bra and when it dropped free, she covered both breasts with her arms.

*That's definitely a defensive move*, he thought. He knelt and removed her panties. "Now, how about we take that shower?" he asked.

She opened the door to a good-sized shower stall and turned on the water, adjusting it to a shade warmer than medium. Kade ran his hand under the spray and commented, "You're trying to chill my ardor? Cold water tends to deflate it." He turned down the cold and upped the hot water. "Now that's more like it," he said, shoving her under the hot water."

"It's too hot for me, Kade," said, reaching for the cold water faucet.

"You'll get used to it," he said, trapping her hands in his.

After 20 minutes, her skin had taken on a pale, lobster-red shade. Kade shut off the water and stepped out of the shower. He grabbed a towel and rubbed her briskly, drying her off first, before he dried himself.

He picked her up and made for the bed.

"Wait!" she cried. "You're so big down there. I need to get my jar of Vaseline from the bathroom.

"Really? I think with a little foreplay, you'll produce enough lubrication that you'll accommodate my size just fine. I'd rather not wade through a mountain of petroleum jelly to reach nirvana tonight."

She stretched out on the bed, and he began to touch and tease her erogenous zones. Occasionally, he ran a finger inside her to test her wetness.

"You ready?" he asked, as he positioned himself to enter her. Raising her hips, he drove into her. He chose to ignore her blood-curdling scream, but he resisted his immediate desire to set up a punishing rhythm. "Let me know when you want me to continue," he told her.

"My God, Kade, that hurt so badly I'm not sure I *want* you to continue."

"You've got me all hot and bothered now, so as soon as you adjust to my size, I'd really like to complete the deed. I need to get my rocks off."

He waited five minutes then began to rock gently inside her. Didn't take long for him to explode, but he kept up his rocking, waiting for her climax.

"Kade, please, it burns so much. Can you withdraw now?"

"But you haven't . . ."

"I don't care. Get off me. ***Now!***"

He withdrew and sat on the edge of the bed. Used a corner of the sheet to clean his ejaculate off.

"As a lover, Diana, you sure don't measure up to my needs. I sometimes enjoy sex with Abby three or four times in succession. Even the first time we had sex—and she was definitely a virgin—she never indicated I was too big or too rough on her. ***She*** never asked me to get off her before we both reached our respective climaxes."

Diana glared at him and yanked the sheet up to cover her nakedness.

"You're kind of a dud in bed, Diana. I didn't enjoy what just occurred."

Diana began to sob loudly. "I thought . . ." she hiccupped, "I believed . . ."

"Believed what, Diana? You believed you outclassed my grub-hunting wife? You decided once I'd slept with you, I'd abandon my wife and family to take up with you? You may be more refined than my wife, but I really prefer a less-refined woman. I definitely prefer my *earthy* wife . . . the one who always manages to accommodate my sexual needs without voicing a litany of complaints."

"***Get out of here!***" she screamed.

"I can't. You drove, remember?"

"There's a phone in the kitchen. Call yourself a cab."

"Yes, ma'am."

He dressed quickly and called a cab to take him back to the paper. Leaning in the doorway to her bedroom, he said, "See you at work in the morning, then. Does tonight mean you won't be asking me again for any more sexual liaisons? You really don't cut the mustard as the kind of woman I enjoy having sex with."

Her answer was an alarm clock hurled in his direction. "Don't ever speak to me again."

"That's going to be hard, seeing as Ms. Dean expects me to mentor you."

"I'm going to change that directive in the morning."

"But if you don't want me to mentor you, she might take it in mind to fire me."

"Believe me, after tonight, I'd welcome that outcome."

"Night, Diana. Pleasant dreams."

A wide grin split his face as he went whistling down the hall to the front door. He was still grinning when the taxi driver rolled up. Kade gave him directions back to the paper's parking lot, where his truck sat.

Once inside the truck, he called the ranch. "Hey, wife, expect me in about 30 minutes. I didn't get all of my rocks off with Diana, so maybe you'd be in the humor to let me do that with you, after my shower."

"I'll wait up for your arrival, Kade."

*How did Abby know taking Diana up on her offer would squelch all her ardor in my direction? Wife, you aren't as refined a woman as I could have married, but you sure are a very smart, accommodating one. I wouldn't trade you for all the gold in the universe. You accommodate my size just fine while making love. You accommodate my foibles without screaming in my ear. You've never thrown an alarm clock at me, either. Abby, you're just a more than perfect match for this imperfect male specimen. Other women may admire my physique, but none of them will ever get to share what I share with you.*

# *Chapter Eleven*

Abby met him at the front door and pulled him to the kitchen where she put on the kettle to make chamomile tea. "Before you're allowed to get the rest of your rocks off, you have to tell me what happened with Diana."

"My rocks are pretty sore from being denied a complete release. What say we have sex before we come back down for an explanation of what occurred? Turn off the kettle."

"Okay, we can go out on the porch and I'll try to relieve your aching rocks. Put the swing's cushion on the floor. Use that."

"You don't want me to take a shower first?" he teased. "Wash off her smell?"

"No. The roses on the arbor will block out all of the perfume she wears."

There were no screams when Kade drove into Abby. The only sounds evident that evening, were the soft hoots of an owl sitting in the tree next to the porch. Abby matched his ardor, rising to meet his strokes until they both spilled over the edge.

"Feel better?" she asked, as he pulled her up into his arms to hug her. "Much."

"Come drink some tea and tell me all about it," Abby invited.

"We went out to dinner, then went back to her house. She drove, leaving me with no transportation. We talked a bit, before she asked me what I wanted to drink. I told her tea, as it was too close to bedtime for anything containing caffeine.

"She asked if I intended to go to bed at her place."

"I told her I thought that was her intention when she kept telling me she envied you. We undressed each other. She commented on the size of me, and wanted to get the Vaseline out of the bathroom to grease the skids. Told her, after foreplay she should have enough lubrication, as I didn't appreciate having to work my way through a lot of petroleum jelly."

Abby reached across and took his hand in hers. "Did you finally get around to the actual deed?"

"Yep. When I thought she was wet enough, I raised her hips and drove into her full length. I didn't move for a bit, but when the old rocks started singing to me, I set up a rhythm. My less-than-complete ejaculation must have burned the inside of her vagina. She ordered me to get off her at that point.

"I told her she might be more sophisticated than you, but she was a real dud in bed. I said I hoped our experience would put an end to her intimate comments at work. I got dressed and after one more of my disparaging comments, she flung her alarm clock at me. Told me to call a cab, so I did that."

"You didn't ever get to that nirvana place fully?"

"Nope. And neither did she. It was a total bust as far as an intimate relationship went. She no longer wants me to mentor her, either. I said Dean might fire me if she didn't want me to mentor her anymore. Diana said, 'Nothing would give me greater pleasure.' So, I think any of those desires she harbored for me are now completely dead, buried in a shallow grave—about as shallow as my dick is long."

"Oh, Kade. I just hope I can keep a straight face if I run into her again. You didn't tell her I was in on the plot, did you?"

"No, ma'am. But thank you for suggesting I take her on. Doubt I'll have to fend her off again at the paper. Are you up for a repeat upstairs? After I take my shower?"

"Always, Kade."

"Go on up. I'll lock up and be right there."

The next morning Diana avoided all contact with him. Each time he caught her eye, he smiled, while she glowered back at him.

After twice observing the frequent time-wasting undercurrents sloshing between Diana and him, Dean yelled, "Blackburn, in my office, immediately!"

He shut down the story he was working on, got out of his chair, and trailed his boss to her office.

"What the hell is going on between you and Diana?" she asked, slamming her door shut after he'd come through it. "You need to explain why you can't seem to spend two hours together without some sort of angry tension arising. I can't afford both of you wasting time like that. I'm trying to put out a paper."

"You know the day Abby came to invite me to lunch? The day I brought you the banana split?"

"Yes, but if you hope that small gift is going to prevent me from raking you over the coals about your treatment of Diana, forget it."

Giving her a grin, he said, "I entertained no such hope, Ms. Dean."

"What's going on between you two? I can't have this rampant animosity continue. She'll never learn the ropes if you don't mentor her."

"She suggested I not do that again?" he asked, laughing inwardly this time.

"Yes. I'd like an explanation, Mr. Blackburn. Why is she refusing to let you mentor her this morning?"

"Um-m-m. I don't know for sure why *she's* upset. I can only give you the reasons why *I* was upset."

"You were upset at her over something she said? Something about your wife?"

"Yes. After Abby showed up, Diana made some disparaging remarks about her mode of dress—the bib overalls. Suggested I should have chosen my wife more carefully. Married someone more 'urbane,' I believe she said.

"I got the feeling she'd like it if I divorced Abby and took up with her. In fact, on two or three occasions, she's said she 'envied my wife.' I believe that indicated she wished I was crawling into bed with her, not Abby."

"I don't believe that for a moment. She hates you, if our conversation this morning is any indication of her feelings for you."

"I had a discussion with my wife about how to effectively curtail Diana's suggestions we engage in a more intimate relationship. Abby suggested I take her up on her offer."

His boss's eyes widened. "Did you?" Dean asked.

He hesitated, not wanting to lay out the previous evening's scenario in its entirety.

"Well, did you?" she asked again.

"Yes. That's what's stuck in her craw this morning. I had sex with Diana last night. I then let her know our liaison was less than satisfactory to me. Told her she was a real dud in bed."

"I fail to understand what prompted you to consider such a liaison. I know how much you love your wife. How could you cheat on her with Diana?"

"I never cheat on Abby. She knows I love her completely—with my body, heart, mind and soul. She has recently come to understand . . . when I have sex with other than my wife . . . and I've been guilty of that a few times since I married her . . . it only involves a physical release. Neither my heart nor my mind nor my soul is ever involved in those instances."

"If Diana wanted you to have sex with her, and she got to enjoy that, why is she so upset this morning?"

"I thought she was . . ." he shrugged, " . . . ready. I'm fairly well endowed, physically. I don't think she was ready enough. She said it hurt and begged me to get off her. That's when I told her she was a dud in bed."

Dean closed her eyes, imagining the scene. "Kade, you never struck me as a man, who could deliver such a cruel comment."

"Maybe you don't know me as well as you think you do, if you believe I'm incapable of a remark like that. I hoped to put an end to her invitations, because they annoy the hell out of me. I shouldn't have to put up with invitations like that at work."

"No, I agree. Work is not a place for anyone to be hitting on someone daily, at least not sexually."

"Since my method seems to have worked—I think she hates me now—therefore, I can't feel any real remorse from my less-than-gentlemanly comment."

"She does hate you, now, if our previous conversation is any indication."

"I really didn't appreciate Diana's comments about my 'earthy' wife. I am certainly tired of her telling me she *envies my wife.* The only way to disabuse some women of their sexual desires is to have sex with them and let them know they don't measure up. Seems to have worked in Diana's case. She wants nothing to do with me this morning. If looks could kill, I'd already be six-feet under."

Dean rose from her chair and went to the door. Bellowed out, "Diana, get in here!"

She was reluctant to enter Dean's office when she saw Kade sitting there, but Dean held the door open and said, "Take a seat."

Kade moved his chair over a foot or two until he was sitting at the corner of Dean's desk, leaving about four feet between his chair and Diana's.

"Kade has explained why you refuse to let him mentor you anymore, Diana."

Her eyes held pure malevolence when she glanced in his direction. "You explained **what?**" she asked. "Surely not what occurred last night . . ."

"Yes, that."

"Everything?" she cried. "How could you do that to me?"

"Because you need to learn that this office—any office—is not an arena in which to practice your invitations to engage in sexual intimacies with a co-worker."

"I never . . ."

"It sounds to me like you did, Diana," Dean said. "From now on, you will permit Kade to mentor you, but only in regards to journalism. There will be no invitations to engage in activities other than journalism."

"So you swallowed **his** story? You believed **his** version—hook, line and sinker? He was the one who invited me out for dinner. He was the one who told me he only wanted tea at my apartment, because he wouldn't be able to sleep if he drank caffeine. Until then, it was just an innocuous dinner with a co-worker . . . until he suggested going to bed with me.

"First he scalded me in the shower, then he wouldn't permit me to use any form of lubrication. He was like a bull. Gave me no time to adjust to his size. It hurt so much, I asked him to quit, but he didn't until . . . it was really more like a rape than . . ."

"No, Diana, you can't lay that charge on me. It was consensual sex, until you realized . . ."

"Realized what? That you were like a bull in rut?"

"Enough, both of you. Kade, return to your workstation. I'll be taking over Diana's mentoring for the foreseeable future."

"Thank you, ma'am." He got up, gave Dean a crisp military salute, and left the office. Returned to his cubicle and pulled up the story he'd been working on.

Diana also soon returned to her computer. He could hear her sniffling like she was crying. He ignored her many muttered, "*Bastard!*" comments.

By the time it came to quit, he'd felt the need to open his desk drawer several times to look at his favorite photo of Abby. After one of those times, he felt a prick of conscience about laying out what had happened with Diana to Dean. He sent Diana a short apology via e-mail. She answered it with a string of symbols— #%&*@!!!— indicating she didn't intend to accept his apology. He made no further attempts to mollify her anger.

He was glad to return to the ranch. Everyone there seemed glad to see him. It lifted his spirits when both the twins and all the goats kept butting his legs, in order to merit his undivided attention.

Finally, he swung the twins up to carry them to the house for dinner.

"Alli, take the twins up and wash their hands for dinner. Andy, go feed the horses, I was so busy trying to fend off the goats, I forgot to feed the horses."

He sat down beside Abby and pulled her into an embrace. "What's got you down, this afternoon, wife?"

"Diana called me this afternoon, from her cell phone. "Told me she was going to charge you with raping her. Sounded like she was in some kind of a tunnel when she called."

"She was likely in the women's restroom. It's a narrow, two-stall room where anything that's said seems to echo like you were in a tunnel."

"How do *you* know what the sounds in the **women's** restroom are like?"

"I've resorted to using it a couple of times when the guys doing up the paper's weekly printings are using the men's room. When they're in there, they lock the outer door. If nature calls, it's either use the female's restroom or I'd have to come home to change my boxers."

"What if she files those rape charges against you?"

"Might have to spend a few more hours in a cell," he told her with a grin. "This time, at least, I think I can afford to hire a legal beagle to defend me. I don't want you to worry about it. When she thinks about having me explain my night with her in open court, I do believe she'll trash the rape charge."

"Why?"

"She'd be embarrassed. Both of us frequent the police station to dredge up news about local crime. I think that will make it hard for her to admit in court, to what occurred that evening, in front of the cops at the station who'd be called to testify."

"Oh, Kade. I should have kept my mouth closed, not egged you on to give her what she wanted."

"Sweetheart, you knew what it would take to make her stop lusting after me, so no remorse is allowed on your part, now. She's just mad because I told her she was a dud as a lover. Pretty soon, her rational mind will overcome her anger and she'll drop the rape charge."

"What if she doesn't?"

"We'll deal with it then. In the meantime, I don't believe you're going to see my brow all wrinkled up like yours is. Quit worrying, will you? What's for dinner?"

"I was too upset to make anything."

"Okay, I'll take over that chore for tonight."

He went to the kitchen and checked cupboards. Pulled out two fat cans of chili, along with a box of saltine crackers. He made a salad, and noted that they had ice cream, bananas, chocolate sauce and crushed pineapple in a can. *Enough to rustle up my own version of some banana splits,* he thought. *There's even some diced walnuts residing in the cupboard's baking supplies. We aren't going to go hungry tonight, nor will we need to go out to a restaurant.*

He called them to dinner at seven. Put bibs on the twins to prevent the chili from staining their tee shirts. He sat down in his chair at the head of the table, with Abby on his right. "Eat up," he said. "I'll make banana splits for those that eat their dinners."

"Mom makes better chili than this hog slop you made," Andy said.

"Andy, how dare you tell your father that?" Abby protested.

"Well, you do. This canned chili is so far inferior to what you make, it's almost inedible."

Kade gave Andy a raised eyebrow and said, "Son, you just talked yourself out of dessert. No banana split for you."

"Why didn't you cook chili, Mom?" Alli asked. "All day, you sat on the couch looking worried, but made no attempt to fix dinner."

"You're treading on dangerous ground as well, daughter," Kade admonished her. "I was worried there'd not be enough bananas for all the splits, but now I'm beginning to believe there'll be plenty. Later, I'll give you an explanation why Mama didn't fix dinner, Alli," he continued, indicating he didn't intend to get into the subject in depth, now. As she continued to give him her quizzical look, he gave his daughter the much-shortened version.

"A woman at the paper accused me of something. Your mother was worried I was about to be arrested. That's all I intend to say about the matter, but if the police show up at our door to haul me off, both you older children will take over as many of my usual chores as you can. I don't want you to slight your homework, but maybe you can feed for me, and help your mama with the twins."

"Accused you of what?" Alli asked.

"I told you that's all I intend to say about the matter over dinner. Eat this inferior chili so you'll have the strength to feed the critters twice a day if I'm in jail."

He kept his grin in place to let them know it was no big deal about Diana's charges.

"Dad?" Alli asked again.

"Not now, Curious George," Kade said.

"I think we have the right to know the reason, if you're going to be arrested."

"If I am, your mother will be happy to explain the circumstances."

"Kade, don't lay that explanation off on me."

"Okay, after the twins are fast asleep, we'll have a family conference and I'll explain."

He never got to explain. Right after he'd fixed six banana splits, the police showed up at his door. They invited him out on the porch to read him the charges. Chose to extend him that courtesy in deference to his children. They cuffed his wrists behind his back and placed him in the rear of their squad car for the trip back to Prescott.

About eleven that night, he was released on his own recognizance. He called Andy to come in and pick him up.

When he arrived home, he asked, "I never got to eat my banana split. Who ate my dessert? You, Andy?"

"I put your split in the freezer, Kade. Andy, it's late. Go get into bed or you'll never get up for school in the morning."

As Andy headed up the stairs, Kade asked, "You really saved my split in the freezer? What if I'd been jailed for months?"

"Yes, I saved it for you—for as long as it took you to return."

"You're the best wife I ever married," he said, hauling the split out of the freezer. The bananas were hard as a rock, so he let it sit on the table for several minutes before he licked into it. Abby put on the kettle to make tea.

"Why did they let you go?"

He shrugged. "Guess it was because they believed my side of it. I enjoy a pretty good reputation—both as a man and as a reporter—for telling the truth. The detective in charge of the case, who'd interviewed her, said Diana was very evasive, which led him to believe she **wasn't** telling him the truth."

"Will it go to trial?" Abby asked, still worried.

"You know as much about that as I do. We'll just have to see how it develops."

"I'm glad you got to come home."

"Me, too. Every time one of those cell doors slams shut behind me, I go back mentally to those three months in solitary when I couldn't talk to you or Andy. The nightmares rev up again—it's like a subtle form of PTSD."

"Are you under house arrest?"

"No. I can't leave the state. Not that I planned to go anywhere, but I don't enjoy being restricted that way. What if a hot story takes place in California, Utah, Texas or New Mexico? Dean would have to send Diana to cover it, and she'd never get the tale right in her flawed-style of reportage."

"I think the whole mess could be remedied by firing Diana."

"Might be 'yours truly' Dean decides is expendable."

"I don't see it that way. She seems to like you."

"Probably depends on whom she thinks is more of a burr under her saddle pad."

"You know, if the situation at the paper proves to be untenable, I'd be willing to move again, Kade."

"Let's hope it doesn't come to that. Thanks for saving my split for me, but it's been a rather long day, so I'm going to take a shower and go to bed. Join me?"

"Sure."

# *Chapter Twelve*

Silence prevailed at work, especially between Diana's and Kade's areas. Dean was frequently in Diana's cubicle advising her on the proper method to write up a story or an interview. A few times, he'd heard Diana ask Dean why she never climbed on Kade's stories.

"Because he's learned to do his writing, to my exacting standards," she informed Gardner. "It didn't take him very long to learn my methods, either."

Kade had to smile. Dean's statement indicated she wished Diana would learn her methods quickly, too. "Kade?" Dean called over the divider between his cubicle and Diana's. "I'm sending you Diana's write-up about the court interview with Governor Brewer. Whip it into shape, will you?"

"Yes, ma'am," he said softly, knowing how much it probably galled Diana to have him edit her attempt.

In ten minutes, he'd sent the repaired copy back to Diana's screen.

"See," Dean said, "he's put all the important stuff in the first three paragraphs. I wish you'd learn to do the same."

"The *entire* report seemed important to me. I hate having it capsulated in the first two paragraphs like nothing else counts. It sounds so cut-and-dried to do it like Blackburn does it. Shows no flair. No individualism. Every report he writes sounds just like every other one printed up under his byline. I'd like to have my pieces reflect me—not be a copy of Blackburn's efforts."

"Then I suggest you write short stories or novels to reflect your style," Dean suggested. "The paper's news articles are not the place for that. They are important for the information they dispense, thus the major items of each article had better occur in the first couple of paragraphs.

"Eventually, you may earn a personal column with your photo at the top, where you can write in whatever style you choose, but the hard-news columns will be written in the style Mr. Blackburn has just sent to your computer. I suggest you print it off and use it as a template for your columns."

"Perhaps I'd rather work for a different paper—one that lets me exhibit more of my style right from the start."

"That could be arranged Ms. Gardner. As long as you work for this paper, however, you will write your articles in Kade's style of reporting."

Dean went back to her office, slamming her door in frustration.

"I hear you gloating over there, Blackburn. Your columns **are completely and totally boring** in my opinion."

He shut down what he'd been working on before he'd been required to edit her column. He got up and went around the divider to her cubicle. Again pulled out her extra chair and sat down backwards on it.

"I want you to know I didn't enjoy what just occurred. I hate being asked to edit what you write. You have a point. All the paper's columns do sound like carbon copies. Like you, I also wish I could insert a little bit of my personality into mine."

"I don't believe you, Kade. I think you hate me and relish every opportunity to point out the error of my ways. Took you less than ten minutes to trash what I'd written."

"We seem to have gotten off on the wrong foot, initially, Diana. I don't hate you, nor do I think you're a bad writer. Wish you'd been here when *I* got hired on. Dean kicked my butt so often and so hard, it was painful to sit down at the computer and try to do it her way.

"You know that old adage, don't you?" he asked. "'The boss may not always be right, but he or she is always the boss.' Don't keep banging your head on that same thick stone Dean wall. Learn to do it Dean's way and save your considerable writing talents for other endeavors."

"Like what? There aren't any opportunities for that, working for her."

"Doesn't preclude you from writing essays or articles for magazines, does it? You do have a computer at home, I presume. Give flight to your flair for writing on that one, not here."

"Is that what you do?" asked.

"Definitely. I've completed one novel and have started a second."

"When do you find the time to devote to a novel?"

"The first one I wrote in my head while I was in solitary confinement for three months in Texas. It was what allowed me to remain mostly sane throughout all those weeks of sensory deprivation. For three months, no one was allowed to speak to me.

"Worse, I had no contact with anything that might have stimulated me. I was confined in a cell with blank white walls—not even permitted a pencil to scratch off the days on those walls. No windows, either. No views of nature or the changing weather. No eye contact with another human being, save for my eight hours on the job."

"I didn't realize you'd . . ."

"I know. I don't like to talk about those dark times. When you filed rape charges against me, and they shut me in another cell, it dredged up all those previous memories. That's when I started the second novel. Only got a few paragraphs written in my head between dinner, when they arrested me, and 11 p.m., when they turned me loose."

"Have you published the first one, yet?"

"No. It languishes in the bottom drawer of my desk. I think it's a pretty good read, but I believe if it got published, I could be arrested for defamation of several people who are thinly disguised as characters in the novel. I haven't attempted to interest any editors or publishers because I hate the sound of cell doors slamming shut behind me."

"Kade, I'd like to apologize for filing those charges. I didn't know you'd spent time in solitary."

"Can we start over? I'd like to help you develop your reporting style, so it meets Dean's idea of a good column. Are you willing to let the past be the past and . . ?"

"For the first time since that awful night, I'm now inclined to accept your offer."

"Good. As for what I said, that night . . . if I could retract my statements about your abilities in bed, I would. Even Dean admonished me for making such crude statements about your performance.

"She said, 'Kade, you never struck me as a male who could make such a cruel comment.' And it was cruel. I tried to apologize via the computer, but when you sent me back a string of symbols, like those indicating swear words in the comics, I decided I'd better cool it with you after that."

"So you didn't really think I was that terrible in bed?"

"No. I pushed the issue because I'd hoped my comments would dissuade you from . . ."

"Indulging those fantasies in my head about what it would be like to have you make love to me?"

"Yes. I really do love my wife and our family. I don't entertain any serious thoughts about liaisons with other women anymore—haven't sought out another woman for sex in the last few years—not since we moved to the ranch. I have indulged in a few of those liaisons in the past, but I'm not open to them now."

"Then, I don't understand why you chose to indulge in such a liaison with me, Kade."

"It was a real error in judgment on my part. I just thought . . . if I gave you what you seemed to want from me . . . then told you I didn't enjoy what occurred . . . that would put a stop to . . ."

". . . my wishing for a more intimate relationship with you?"

He nodded. "I sincerely regret the clumsiness of the method I chose to dissuade you. There are few women who can accommodate my size without complaint."

"Abby, even as a virgin, could?"

"I guess. She never complained."

"Thank you for telling me all of this stuff."

"I'm sorry for everything—for hurting you physically and mentally, too. Friends again?" he asked, sticking out his hand.

She caught his hand and shook it solemnly twice. "Okay, Mr. Blackburn, tell me how you choose what to put in those top two paragraphs."

"Write out everything in your own style. Choose a strong lead, by underlining it with a red pencil. Underline the next most-important facts in orange. Do the third ones in yellow. You do know the red, orange, yellow, green, blue, purple prism sequence, don't you? What you've underlined in the first three colors constitute the first two paragraphs. You can fill in with the cooler-colored underlined parts depending on how much space you're allowed to fill."

"That's what you do?" she asked, giving him a dubious look.

"Come around the corner and I'll show you it's what I do."

She followed him to his desk and stood as he sat in his chair and opened his file-storage drawer. He pulled out several folders to lie on his desk. The reports the folders contained all looked like a kindergartener's first attempt at coloring.

"I have an extra set of colored pencils, if you'd like to adopt my method," he said. He rooted in his left-hand drawer and pulled out a box of them. Gave her a grin before saying, "You can use them, but please replace them in the next day or two. My other set is worn down close to the nubs, and I can't continued to churn out those *completely and totally boring columns* if I run out of colored pencils."

"I'll be sure to replace them during my lunch hour. Thanks, Kade. I guess you really aren't such a bastard after all."

After she began to use his color-coded system, her columns improved. Even Dean was pleased with Diana's progress, as she was with the obvious decrease of hostilities between the pair. Diana sent Kade all her columns before she forwarded them to Dean. It doubled his workload, but he didn't feel so overburdened that he felt it necessary to complain. Truth be told, he also appreciated the downturn in their rancorous dealings.

Abby noticed his much-improved demeanor at the ranch, too.

"What has you wreathed in that wide grin, Kade? For the last few days, you've been smiling up a storm."

"Things are going better at work. I gave Diana a few pointers and some pencils to use on her columns. Since then, her work has improved and Ms. Dean seems happier with both of us. Less tension all the way around."

"You also apologized to Diana, didn't you? Told her you were sorry for what occurred in her bedroom that night."

His grin grew even wider. "I doubt I could clip my toenails without you knowing I had done so. I can't keep any secrets from you. You're always onto me, even before I say a word. Yes, I told her I was sorry for what happened that night."

"Now she feels it's okay to continue her pursuit of you?"

"No. We're back to being friends, nothing more."

"We'll see how long that lasts."

"You know, Alli once told me, 'You and Mom are easier to read than large-print books.' Am I like that—so easy to read? Is that how you always know what's going on with me?"

"You are fairly easy to read, Kade. You tend to wear your heart on your sleeve. I know when you're upset, and when the problem that has upset you is resolved, I know that, too. I knew it went against your grain to tell Diana she didn't measure up in bed. It bothered you to tell her that, didn't it?"

"Did you discuss that night with my boss? She said pretty much the same thing. Dean said, 'I can't believe you'd make such a cruel remark to a woman, Kade.' Have you taken to calling the Boss up to discuss your concerns over my furrowed brows?"

"No. What goes on at your job, I'm more than willing to let you deal with those problems. I worry, of course, when your brow looks rumpled up like a tilled field for days on end, but before I'd consider calling Ms. Dean, I'd discuss that call with you, first."

"I'd appreciate that courtesy. I think nothing would undercut Dean's confidence in me more than having a meddling wife calling her every time my brow was puckered up."

"Now my concern for you has morphed into me being a meddling wife?" Abby asked with some heat.

"Since you haven't called her . . . at least to my knowledge . . . I have no reason to suspect you of being a meddling wife," he said, before breaking into chuckles. "Oh, Abby, you are such a gem, though you tend to have a hair trigger and are quick to bristle up over some of my comments."

"You should be glad I'm not holding an actual gun when you make some of those snide comments, or you might just find out how much of a hair trigger I really have."

She pointed her finger at him and mimicked pulling the trigger. He responded by pulling her into a warm embrace and kissing her softly. "I'd be more likely to believe you'd shoot me for my insurance money," he teased.

"Ha! You earn more at the paper than I'd ever claim from your insurance policy."

"Maybe I should up the value of my policy, then," he said, another furrow rumpling up his forehead. "I wouldn't want you to have to work full-time until the twins were in school, at least."

"Kade, you can't continue to take on all the cares of the world."

Work went along smoothly for several months, then Dean hired a young kid just out of college to be her third reporter. He'd also graduated from the university in Flagstaff. When Dean introduced Fred Rossman to Kade, Fred refused to shake Kade's extended hand.

"You're the guy all my professors held up as *the* one to emulate. I never felt I was being graded on my own merits, just in relationship to your sterling performances—in all my classes. I don't choose to shake your hand, Mr. Perfection, because during my student career, I genuinely came to hate you."

Kade shrugged and rose from his chair. "I guess I can go back to what I was working on, then, Ms. Dean. I'd appreciate it if you didn't assign me to mentor Mr. Rossman, either."

"Sit down again, Kade," she ordered. He sat, and she continued. "Mr. Rossman, I think you owe Kade an apology. Just because you failed to measure up to his high standards in school, is no reason to hate him or refuse to shake his hand."

"Do you know what it's like to have him thrown up in your face on a daily basis? Most of my professors touted his accomplishments during every class. 'Mr. Blackburn got perfect scores. Mr. Blackburn was working full time, he had a family and still managed perfect scores on all his quizzes. Mr. Blackburn graduated magna cum laude.' I've had a belly full of Mr. Blackburn's accomplishments, so you'll forgive me if I don't want to be bosom buddies with him."

"It's nice to know you're still so highly regarded at the university, Kade," Dean said. "Obviously Mr. Rossman won't enjoy the same regard ten years down the road after his graduation."

"It is nice to know they appreciated all my hard work, but I can understand Mr. Rossman's reluctance to shake my hand. I believe I would have hated my classes if I'd been too dense to get those top-notch grades, too."

"Too dense? Are you calling me stupid, Mr. Blackburn?"

"No, sir. By your own admission, you failed to achieve a 4.0 GPA. I don't have to call you names, sir. You've already admitted you fell far below me in regard to grades."

"I'm inviting you outside to apprise you I'm just as smart as you are. Maybe after I blacken both your eyes, you'll see me in a different light."

"I don't think you want to engage Kade in a fight," Dean told Fred.

"Why not? He might be good at studying, but I think he'll be like a creampuff in a fight."

Kade glanced at Dean and grinned. She knew he was always in top physical shape, so she shot him a nod, telling him she had no objection to a few fisticuffs.

"Meet you in back of the printing-press doorway in ten minutes. You may want to take off your shirt. Looks like an expensive one, so you probably would hate it to be covered in blood," Kade advised.

"Like that's going to happen," Fred retorted hotly. "You might want to take off your shirt for the same reason."

"I planned to," Kade said, giving Dean another grin. He then touched his fist to his heart and said, "We who are about to die, salute you," in the fashion that gladiators saluted Nero.

"I draw the line at loosing the lions," Dean said.

"Ah, shucks," Kade complained. "The lions would make the fight so much more interesting. More even, too."

Fred left for his office to doff his shirt.

"Don't hurt him too badly," Dean said. "Maybe it's you I should be concerned over. He's ten to twelve years your junior. He may make up for his lack of smarts by his stamina."

Kade shook his head. "I don't think you need to worry about me."

Ten minutes later, Kade, sans his long-sleeved white shirt, showed up out in the alley behind the printing-press room in his undershirt. "Are there going to be any rules attached to this scuffle?" Kade asked.

"Yeah," Fred said. "The last man standing gets the best reporter's cubicle. I plan to have yours, Mr. Blackburn. It has a better view and it's right next to that sexy broad, Ms. Gardner, too."

"Okay, I agree to those terms. Hit me with your best argument, then."

Fred sprang into action, connecting with a roundhouse punch that split Kade's lower lip. That was the last punch Fred managed to launch that did any damage. Kade sidestepped the next punch and Fred ended up with an arm pinioned up behind his back and Kade's arm wrapped around his throat, effectively shutting off his ability to breathe.

Kade continued to hold Fred tight that way, until Fred's knees buckled and he passed out. He then allowed Rossman to fall face-first into the mud at his feet. He reached down and pulled Fred out of the mud puddle, carried him inside and set him at his desk.

"Is he okay?" Dean asked, worried. "He looks really pale."

"He'll be just fine," Kade assured her. "He's breathing again, at least. Had to remind myself not to deliver the coup de gràce, per my Army training. His throat is going to be tender for a day or two, but there'll be no permanent damage."

"It was smart of you to wear your undershirt to the fight. Otherwise, he might have had second thoughts, once he saw your six-pack abs," Diana said.

"Okay guys, the fun is over—get back to work," Dean yelled to all the printers who'd assembled to watch the scuffle.

She went back to work, as well, glad that no one had been seriously hurt. She was surprised when she heard sirens stop outside the paper's office an hour later.

Two policemen approached her desk. "Where's Blackburn?" they asked.

"In his cubicle, I imagine. Is there a problem?"

"Some guy named Rossman is charging Blackburn with assault. Wants him arrested. Invite Blackburn to your office, along with the guy making the accusations."

Dean keyed her phone to connect with both men's cubicles. "Kade and Fred, your presence is requested in my office. Pronto!"

Kade showed up first and was surprised to see two officers. Fred finally arrived and shouted, "***Arrest him! He damn near broke my neck.***" He threw open the collar of his shirt to display the bruises on his neck.

"Wait just a minute, Fred. You're the one who challenged Kade to a fight—not the other way around. It's not fair to drag in the authorities just because you lost the battle."

"Maybe you'd better explain, Ms. Dean," the burly policeman said.

"Fred invited Kade to fight him out in the alley. I think he thought Kade, being older, wouldn't have the stamina to outlast him. Fred threw the first punch. Show him your lip, Kade," Dean said.

Kade rolled his lip down. It showed a bruise and a small cut inside where Fred's punch had driven the lip against Kade's teeth.

"When Fred tried to punch Blackburn again, Kade caught Fred in a hold with an arm up behind his back and Kade wrapped his other arm around Fred's throat. Fred eventually passed out. Kade picked him out of the mud puddle, where he'd fallen, and set him in his chair in his cubicle."

"You must have had a real strangle hold on his neck if he passed out," the cop said to Kade.

"My Army training kicked in once he threw his second punch. He's lucky I didn't kill him. I spent two tours, one in Iraq and one in Afghanistan. There's a bit of residual PTSD that I still suffer from. Once someone chooses to fight me, it's kind of hard to remember I'm back in the USA, not over there. My first instinct is to dispense with the combatant forthwith—by maintaining my chokehold until he expires. Fortunately, I remembered I'm currently a civilian . . . in time to prevent that sort of ending."

"You heard him. He wanted to kill me. I insist you arrest him."

"C'mon, Mac. The way I see it, you started the fight, and therefore you have no cause to complain because you lost in the end. I believe Blackburn has the right to defend himself.

"But . . . but . . ." Fred complained. "He tried to kill me."

"I realize he's capable of doing that, because I also served in Iraq and had the same kind of training. Since he stopped in time, there's nothing I can hold him on. I think you're very lucky he *didn't kill you*."

"So you're just going to let him go?" Fred asked.

"Yes, I am. And it would be good not to rile him up or take him on, physically, again. Sometimes in the midst of one of those PTSD fogs you think you're back on the battlefield. Fortunately, for you, he remembered not to break your neck this time."

Fred stormed out of Dean's office. Kade reached out a hand to shake the cop's mitt. "Thanks for your understanding, sir. Where were you stationed?"

"Kirkuk. You?"

"North of Basra for the most part. Qandahar in Afghanistan."

"Well, Blackburn, I sure am glad you didn't carry your Army hand-to-hand combat training to its natural conclusion. I'd have had to charge you with murder in that case."

"Yes, I don't currently have legality on my side, like you do, sir. Being still in uniform, gives you privileges I no longer enjoy."

"Try hard to remember that, Blackburn. If you served with honor in both Iraq and Afghanistan, it would be best not to tarnish that honor by following through with your training to its natural conclusion. Though in that asshole's case . . . sorry, Ms. Dean, I didn't mean to use that kind of language."

Kade had a hard time suppressing his grin, because it was evident to him the cop had reconnoitered Dean's frown correctly, and made a quick apology for his comment.

"I'm inclined to agree with you, Officer Sawyer. Rossman is an asshole. One I intend to send packing forthwith."

"Well, I guess I'd better get back to the station. Keep cool, Blackburn."

"Yes, sir. My thanks again for not arresting me."

Dean called Rossman into her office late on the next afternoon, and fired him. Kade felt bad for the rookie because jobs currently were at a premium. He also realized had Dean kept him on, the recently engendered tranquility of the office would be sorely disrupted. Working on a hot story, Kade put the whole episode out of his mind to devote his entire concentration to the article he was writing up.

He finished the article he'd been working just before time to quit. He got Dean's approval of the article and left the office feeling up. Climbed into his truck and headed for his ranch, anticipating a good dinner, some time with his wife and children, and the ever-present chore of feeding the animals.

Not five miles down the road toward home, a dark sedan passed several cars to cut in behind him. It dogged his back bumper for several miles. Wary that Fred might be even angrier over his firing than he was over Kade's grades, Kade pulled the loaded hunting rifle out of it's position across the back window of the truck. When he put on his turn signal to turn into his lane, the car continued up the way north, so he relaxed.

He'd just alighted from the truck when the same car turned into his driveway. Several shots followed, one of which hit Kade in the upper thigh. Leveling the hunting rifle, Kade made his one shot count, before he succumbed to the pain in his leg. As he crumpled to the ground, his last conscious thought was how glad he was that no members of his family were out by the barn waiting for him that afternoon.

He awoke to the sound of sirens. Abby was kneeling next to him and had placed a tourniquet around his thigh, very close to his groin. She was also pressing down on several sterile pads trying to suppress the small amount of bleeding that continued to flow from his wound.

"Are you and the kids okay?" he mumbled.

"Yes, we're fine," she assured him.

"Thank the powers you all weren't out in the barnyard waiting for me to come home." He shuddered at the thought.

The county sheriff's officers arrived first, minutes ahead of the ambulance. Abby tried to stop them from questioning Kade before the EMTs arrived.

"What's your name?" one deputy asked.

"His name is Kade Andrew Blackburn," Abby answered for him. "He just got out of his truck when I heard at least four shots. They came from that car over there," she said gesturing to the dark sedan.

"You always get out of your truck carrying a hunting rifle?" one deputy asked.

"I do when someone risks life and limb to pass several cars, then dives into the right lane right behind me, and continues to dog my back bumper for several miles."

"Someone have it in for you?"

"Maybe," Kade said. "A fellow reporter at the Prescott paper got fired today over an ongoing dispute with me. If you check the driver of the sedan, I think you'll find his name is Fred Rossman."

"Be hard to establish his identity, as he's dead."

"Maybe he has a driver's license if you can't ask him directly."

"You work for the paper, too?"

"Yes, sir."

"What was the nature of your dispute with him?"

"Wasn't my dispute—it was his. He attended the same university I went to, and he seemed to resent my 4.0 grade-point average. Said his professors were always touting my grades as those the rest of the journalism students should aspire to emulate. He even challenged me to go a round with him earlier in the day yesterday. When he lost the argument, he called the Prescott police and told them I'd tried to kill him."

"Did you?"

"If I'd tried to kill him, he'd have died yesterday morning."

"Martinez, put in a call to the Prescott precinct and get their take on the fight the previous morning."

The ambulance arrived at that point, so the questioning deputy went to check the dead driver for his identification, while the EMTs evaluated Kade's wound. They loosened Abby's tourniquet and the loosening started a fresh flow of blood.

"The bullet hit a bleeder for sure, sir. Good thing the shot didn't pass through the femoral artery, or you'd probably be dead," the tech said, re-establishing the tourniquet to quell the bleeding. He spoke to the other two EMTs. "Load him up carefully and we'll run lights and sirens to the hospital in Prescott."

"I'll be right behind you, Kade," Abby said, "unless the county guys have more questions."

"Tell them to talk to Ms. Dean. Only she knows what Fred's attitude was after she fired him. I don't know why he felt his firing was my fault. If he had a bone to pick, surely it would have been with her, not me."

"Don't worry about any of that now. Just get your leg fixed."

"Have Andy feed the animals. I don't feel up to the chore tonight."

They loaded him in the ambulance and took off for the hospital. As they pushed his gurney into the ER, he looked up to find Ms. Dean sitting there in the waiting room.

"Kade . . ." came her anguished cry. "I couldn't believe Officer Murphy when he said you'd been shot. I'm so sorry . . ."

"Hey, Boss, it's not your fault."

"But it is. I hired him. I fired him, too. That's what must have set him off."

"No, ma'am. If it hadn't been that, it'd been for some other reason. Do me a favor. Please stay with Abby until I'm assigned my room after surgery. She's on her way into the hospital. Should be here shortly. She's kind of upset."

"Kade, it goes without saying. I have no intention of leaving your wife alone."

"Thanks, boss."

They wheeled him into a different sort of cubicle. Hooked him up to a few monitors and had the lab tech draw some blood for various tests and a possible transfusion. When the ER doctor wanted to cut his pants off, Kade protested.

"No, don't cut them. Help me stand up and you can help me remove them in the normal way. All my stuff is in the pockets, so I'd prefer you hand the pants to my boss in the waiting room, or my wife if she's arrived."

"You can't stand up, sir."

"*Hell I can't!*" Kade said, jumping off the gurney. He unfastened his belt, the button of his pants and ran the zipper down. He danced on his good leg while the nurse pulled the pants off his bad one, then he leaned back against the gurney as she pulled his britches from the good leg. **"*Don't ever tell me I can't do something, sir!*"** he shouted. "*That's like waving a red flag in front of a bull—this bull-headed guy, anyhow.* Ma'am can you see my boss or my wife gets those trousers?" he asked the nurse.

"If you'll get back on the gurney, I will," she said giving him a grin.

Kade climbed back on the gurney. "Thank, you, ma'am. I appreciate your kindness."

The doctor was busy making arrangement for a surgical suite. Kade overheard him say, "I think he's lost so much blood he's irrational. I don't know his crit, yet. The lab hasn't called me back with that."

Kade lay back, shaking his head. "I'm nowhere close to being irrational, Doc. I just don't appreciate anyone telling me I can't do something. I'm so rational, I'm now going to apologize for my outburst—I'm sincerely apologizing to you."

"Okay, Mr. Blackburn. You'll be heading up to surgery. They'll take out the bullet still lodged in your thigh and hopefully they can repair the bleeder, too. I'm not used to shot men being that determined to shed their pants. Most of them are meek as lambs when they arrive here—mostly because they're afraid they're about to die."

"I served in both Iraq and Afghanistan. I long ago got over my fear of dying. Maybe because I have no fear of death, that's why I'm not lamb meek, though I'll attempt to be docile as a lamb from this point on," he said, giving the doc a grin.

"You're running on pure anger? Most men that injured would be unable to stand on a leg like your wounded one. Yet you stood on it and used it to climb back on the gurney, too.

"I'm mad as hell he managed to wing me, before I took him out. I'm not usually that slow on the draw. Anger creates a lot of adrenaline. Men filled with adrenaline have lifted and removed cars from atop a run-over child, so why does it surprise you I could remove my pants? They don't weigh nearly as much as a car."

"Ah, you come equipped with a sense of humor, too."

"Before they haul me up to surgery, would it be possible to speak to my wife for a moment?"

"If I say 'no' are you going to get up and walk out into the waiting room in your boxers?"

"Not if you allow her into this room."

"It's not usual to allow visitations in here, but that look in your eye tells me I'd better bend the rules in your case, or you will be hobbling out to the waiting room."

"I don't hobble, sir. Yes, bend your rules. I need to tell my wife something important."

Abby was shown into his cubicle. He reached up and grabbed her ear. Directed it close to his mouth, then whispered, "I love you. I did up my life insurance. Should be enough to sustain you until the twins are in school, should anything happen to me in surgery. If I survive that, you'd better prepare for me to be underfoot a week or two as I recover. Prepare for a lot of sex, too, as I hear that makes recovery go better."

Abby burst out laughing. "Kade, you idiot!"

"Do me a favor, wife? Ms. Dean seems to think what happened was mostly her fault. I don't believe that. Hope you can convince her it had nothing to do with her firing Fred. He was just unbalanced to begin with. If it hadn't been that reason, it'd been another. Tell her for me, and you, that she's not to blame."

The OR crew arrived at that point. They tried to lift him to the OR gurney, but Kade was having none of that treatment. Once more he stood up. He grabbed Abby and kissed her hard. "That's the best anesthesia ever invented," he said. "Rather than contaminate the operating room, let my wife take off my underpants and shirt. She's really adept at removing those items—she gets lots of practice removing them every night in bed."

He raised his arms and Abby pulled off his undershirt. She then wiggled his shorts down to his ankles. He stepped out of them. "Thanks, wife. This place feels a lot more like home to me now."

After Abby left the room, the ER doctor said, "For a moment there, I thought you were going to ask all of us to leave the cubicle so you could have sex with her once more before surgery."

"The thought did occur, but seeing as you'd bent the rules once, I didn't feel I could ask you to bend them far enough to accommodate that sort of situation."

"We're going to clean you up before I get the OR guys to take you up. That'll save them some time. Clark, get in here and while he's still standing, you and I are going to scrub him, head to toe."

"Do you think that's wise, Dr. O'Bannion? What if he falls over?"

"Are you going to fall over, Blackburn?"

"No, sir. I have no intention of falling over."

"Fill a basin with warm water and antiseptic liquid, Clark. You wash his back side and I'll do his front."

"I'd like to do his front side, sir. I think I'll be gentler around the wound than you'd be."

"You just want unfettered views of his considerable scenery, Clark."

"You might be right, sir. He does seem to possess some magnificent scenery."

"Flip a coin, you two. My wife's anesthesia is wearing off, and the pain is increasing in intensity, so get on with your car wash. I'm closing my windows so you can go to town."

He closed his eyes. "That way, I won't know who's scrubbing which side. That, in turn, will likely prevent my antenna from rising enough to bring in those New York radio stations."

"It's a shame the OR docs will have to give you real anesthesia," O'Bannion said. "They'll miss out on your wry sense of humor and all your hilarious comments, too."

Kade could tell, by the gentleness of Clark's touch she'd prevailed in her request to wash his front side. She started with his face and sponged lower and lower. She concentrated on washing the blood out of the whorls on his testicles, before tackling the fronts of his legs and feet.

"I think it's risen enough that I'm getting clear reception from the BBC in England now," Kade teased. "I enjoyed both the thoroughness and the gentleness of your scrubbings, ma'am."

"I've never seen Clark blush before," O'Bannion said. "If you'd open your eyes, you'd see a really good blush on her now."

"I have no intention of opening my eyes. Where's the OR gurney? Let me climb on it and throw a sheet over me. Let's get this show on the road."

"It's right behind you, Mr. Blackburn."

He took six steps to his rear, and climbed aboard the gurney, still with his eyes closed. Felt the sheet settle over him. "Thanks, guys and gals, for all your tender care. Hope to see you on the flip side."

# *Chapter Thirteen*

It was dark when Kade awoke. His thigh felt like someone was using a jackhammer on it. A nurse sat beside his bed in recovery.

"Aah, you're awake," she said. "How do you feel?"

"Sore," he said.

"I can give you something for pain."

He shook his head in the negative direction.

"There's really no reason to suffer, Mr. Blackburn."

"I could use a urinal."

"You won't need one, sir. You have an indwelling catheter. Any discomfort you feel in your bladder likely comes from the small balloon they inflate to hold the catheter in place."

"I'm awake, now. So yank it out . . . please."

"I can't do that until your doctor comes by and gives me an order to do so. But perhaps I can adjust the catheter down there to give you less of a pull on your bladder."

From experience she knew most men hated someone else fiddling around with their private parts. She'd found asking some questions to divert their thoughts from what she was doing in the area, made them less uncomfortable. "How did you lose the fingers on your left hand?"

"Incoming ordinance in Afghanistan."

"Were you in the Army or in the Marines?"

He winced as she moved the catheter. "Army," he said. "Damn that hurts. It's like my bladder is on fire."

"I'll check with Dr. Phillips. You might be one of those rare individuals who has a sensitivity to latex."

He dozed intermittently for most of the night, then sat up and took an open-handed swing at whomever was probing his very tender thigh that roughly.

"***Damn!***" the one doing the probing swore. "Does he have a load of painkillers on?" the doctor asked the nurse. "If so, I suggest you cut way back. My ear is ringing from his blow."

"He doesn't have any painkillers aboard, sir. He refused to let me give him some."

Kade opened his eyes and took in the redness of the doctor's ear. "Sorry for the slap, sir. You were putting a lot of pressure on a very tender area, and I reacted to that without thinking through my actions."

"Do you always react that violently?"

"Sometimes. I was thoroughly schooled in hand-to-hand combat by the Army. When someone starts in touching me . . . before letting me know he or she intends to touch me . . . the old Army training kicks in. I tend to hit first and save my questions for later."

"I'll remember that in the future. Your nurse says you're experiencing some bladder pain."

"I am, sir. Now that there's no danger of me contaminating the OR by pissing all over everything, can you tell her to yank out the catheter?"

"I'd prefer to leave it in for another day or two."

"As retribution for the slap I just gave you?" Kade asked.

"No, I don't think you're up to making three or four trips to the restroom quite yet."

"If I can demonstrate my ability to do that, will you let her remove it?"

"You can't possibly get to the restroom this morning."

"Want to bet?" he asked. He swung his legs over the edge of the bed, stood up, and marched off toward what he assumed was the john. *K-dens, Let, Rye.* Andy's words echoed in his head as he kept up his rapid pace. Though it hurt to march, he made it to the door and opened it, proving he was capable of getting to the restroom.

"Get back in bed, Mr. Blackburn. You aren't allowed to be up on that leg yet. You'll be lucky if you don't throw a clot, which could kill you."

"If you don't allow her to yank the catheter, I think death would come as a relief. My bladder is burning like the fires of hell."

"Sir, he might be one of those people who's allergic to latex," the nurse said.

"Okay, Mr. Blackburn, I'll allow her to remove it, but only on the provision you don't get out of bed again. Please use a urinal." He turned to the nurse, "I'll also prescribe him some Pyridium to be taken three times a day, following his meals," he said. "If you try to get out of bed again, I'll be forced to use restraints on you."

After she pulled the catheter and gave him two Pyridium doses, the fire in his lower abdomen finally began to ease off.

"Next time you use the urinal, I'm going to send part of your urine to the lab, just to assure myself that all that irritation you felt wasn't because of a UTI—a urinary-tract infection. The medication you're taking turns your urine a bright orange. I don't want you to be alarmed about that."

He grinned up at her. "You were afraid I'd slap you in the ear, too, if I became alarmed?"

"Dr. Feldheim is none too gentle with his exams. It amused me when you sat up to make a solid connection between your hand and his ear. I had to put my palm over my mouth to keep from shouting, 'Good for you!' or laughing like a hyena."

"What's your name?" he asked.

"Alberta Spence," she replied. "Why do you want to know my name? Were you planning to add my name to your little black book since I took pity on your bladder?"

"My wife trashed my little black book once I married her. Wiped out years of me asking females for their names. Wouldn't do me any good to start a new one with your name in it. She'd just trash that one, too."

"I can believe that. She looks like a female that brooks no nonsense from the man she loves."

"She was here? You met her?" Kade asked. "When?"

"I did. She stopped in for a brief moment before you came totally up from the anesthesia. You don't remember her kissing you?"

"Nope. Nothing must have registered in my foggy state."

"I don't think that's true. Afterward, you were far more agitated. Despite the tube in your bladder, you had a pretty fair approximation of an erection going on, too."

Kade grinned even wider. "That's my usual reaction when she kisses me."

Alberta did laugh then. "You must love her a lot."

"I do, ma'am. We've weathered some really tough times. She's stuck with me through thick and thin."

"I think I know why, Mr. Blackburn. Not many men . . ."

"Yeah," he said, knowing where she was going. ". . . are as well-equipped. But that's not the only reason she's stayed with me. We have four children that neither of us would ever contemplate parting with."

There was a knock at his door, curtailing any more conversation. Alberta went to open the door, after plumping up his pillows and folding the sheet neatly under his armpits.

"I'm Deputy Hathaway. I need to talk to Mr. Blackburn."

"Kade, is it okay to let him in? I don't want you to become agitated to the point you rip some stitches loose."

"Let him in, Ms. Spence. He's just doing his job. Doubt he'll be punching on my sore spots like the good doctor. I don't think I'll have an excuse to slap his ear."

"You hit your doctor?"

"I did, sir. He was probing my wound none too gently and I was still half-asleep. In my semi-conscious state, I sat up and connected my hand to his ear."

"Let's discuss your killing of Mr. Rossman. Why did you haul the rifle out of its rack?"

"I was suspicious when Fred's car passed a whole line of vehicles, and pulled in directly behind me. I wasn't going any faster than the rest of the traffic, so why didn't he pass me, too? He had a clear road ahead of me. That's what first alerted me that perhaps something was up.

"Then, he dogged my rear bumper, like he wished he could send me into a ditch."

"You didn't know what kind of car Rossman drove, initially?"

"No, sir. I'd seen a similar car in the paper's parking lot, but I'd never seen him get into it or out of it. Could have belonged to any of the regular employees, or the printing crew that comes in to work the presses three times a week."

"Why did you take the gun out of your truck once you got home?"

"I couldn't shake the feeling that something was seriously amiss. Before I could convince myself I was being paranoid, the same car turned down my lane and he opened fire."

"That's when you returned fire?"

"Yes, sir."

"Though you were wounded, you managed to kill him with one shot? I find that hard to believe. Are you sure you didn't shoot him first, before he squeezed off his shots?"

"It was only after the bullet tore into my thigh, I raised the rifle and pulled the trigger."

"Again, with all the pain the wound must have generated, how did you manage a perfect shot?"

"I'm an Army trained combatant, sir. I've spent months on the firing range. I spent two tours in the Middle East, too. When your life often hangs on your accuracy, you tend to make the first shot count."

"You aimed for his head or his heart?"

"His heart, sir. That area was perfectly outlined by the upper edge of the steering wheel and the center section, which contained the air bag. It was like shooting at the rifle-range targets—same black lines designating the kill area, only they were a bit thicker lines this time—making my job easier, essentially."

"You have no regrets about wiping out a life?"

"No, sir. None. All I could think about was having the guy reload, and my family pouring out into the barnyard to see what all the shots were about. I knew I had to kill him to keep my children, wife and animals safe. They are safe, so I don't have any regrets."

"You couldn't have just wounded him?"

"I knew I was bleeding heavily. If I'd only wounded him, and then passed out, what was to prevent him from finishing me off and maybe killing my family, too?"

"His widow has filed wrongful-death papers against you. You're not to leave this state. As soon as you're dismissed from medical care, you'll be fitted with a tracking anklet and you'll be required to notify us every time you leave the house or your place of employment."

"He was married?" Kade asked. "Any children?"

"No, no kids, but he was recently married, so his widow is understandably upset."

"I don't think he mentioned that on his employment application. You may want to ask Ms. Dean about the application. Could be she's claiming to be his widow to inherit his life insurance."

"I will check with Ms. Dean, Mr. Blackburn. I appreciate your candid answers."

After he left, Alberta said, "I'm betting Dr. Feldheim is glad you weren't packing a gun this morning. You don't strike me as someone who doesn't harbor at least a few regrets over killing another human being."

"You'd be wrong to think that way, Ms. Spence. Army training tends to nullify those sorts of regrets. Not many soldiers are plagued with regrets when they kill enemy combatants. Those who do harbor regrets are quickly washed out of the combat brigades. In a stiff fire fight, you can't afford to have soldiers sitting next to you who are debating whether it's right or wrong to shoot someone."

"Doesn't the Army have some conscientious objectors in its ranks?"

"Yes, but mostly they get trained as medics or become assistants to those who function as priests, rabbis, or ministers. If their conscience objects to killing they get to minister to the men who are wounded or dying. After a few months of seeing all that carnage, they often have a change of heart and request to be transferred to a squad bent on wiping the enemy out."

"Were you one of those kinds? One of the guys who had a change of heart?"

"No. I felt about my Army compatriots the same way I feel about my wife and children. If their lives were threatened, I had no qualms about killing as many of our enemies as possible. Fetch me the urinal, please, so I can pee in bright orange."

She collected his urinal from the bathroom, folded down his sheet and tried to lift his penis to direct it into the urinal.

"I think I can manage it from here," he protested.

"I just want to get a pure specimen for a culture. Surely a man who feels no regret about killing a human being—alleging that's his honor-bound duty—is not about to turn all embarrassed when a nurse tries to do *her* duty to the best of her abilities."

Kade raised both of his hands and folded them behind his head. "Carry on, Nurse Spence," he said.

"I just don't want to contaminate the specimen by touching your penis to the edge of the urinal."

The grin he gave her told her he didn't believe her explanation. "Might be easier to just get a ruler or a tape measure than to try and use the width between the tip of your thumb and small finger to ascertain the size of my unit."

"Don't be gross, Mr. Blackburn."

"Sorry," he apologized. "I thought Nurse Clark, from the ER squad, might have put you up to measuring it."

Her blush gave him the impression he'd hit the nail on its head.

"Uh . . . er . . ." she stammered, ". . . she did kind of hint she'd like to know the size of your package—fully erect."

"I have no objection to you taking a couple of measurements. Flaccid, it's about six inches long. Never measured it during the aroused state, as when it achieves that length, it's usually buried up to its hilt in my wife.

"With all your attempts to prevent contamination of the urine specimen, I'm sure it will manage a fully aroused state that you can measure, seeing as I have no wife here to bury my erection in."

"Are you always that brutally honest?" she asked as his erection grew and hardened in her hand.

"What's the percentage in lying about stuff? So many women come on to me, I long ago learned not to be reticent about discussing sex with them."

"I'm not going to measure you. If Clark wants to know the size of it, she can measure it herself."

"Give her a call. If she's on duty, she might be able to spare a few minutes to satisfy her curiosity."

"Not before you produce a urine specimen I can send to the lab."

"You're ready to collect it?"

"Yes."

He let fly with a good stream of urine, which nearly filled the urinal. "Enough?" he asked.

"More than enough. I think your bladder must rival the size of your other parts."

She bore the urinal into the restroom where she filled a sterile cup with some of the contents. She left him alone to bear the specimen to the lab. While she was gone, Clark came into his room. "I understand from Alberta that you're willing to let me . . ."

"She stopped to call you on her way to the lab?"

"No we passed in the hall and she whispered . . ."

"It's going to take a little hand jazz to re-establish my full erection. It kind of faded after I gave my urine up to the lab to be tested."

Clark didn't hesitate. She reached under the sheet and soon had it standing tall again. She then produced a tape measure from her uniform pocket and measured both its length and its circumference.

"Just a millimeter or two short of nine inches in length. Slightly less than three inches around at the base."

"Nice to know its true dimensions. Do you measure and compare measurements on all your male ER patients?"

"Hell, no. I used to work in the prostate-surgery ward. We were often asked by the patients to stimulate them to see if they could maintain an erection following surgery. That's when I began to be interested in size and length. Never measured anyone as big as you—not in all the years I worked in that ward.

"When you stood up so your wife could peel off your underwear, I just knew I had to chart your dimensions. You might be a candidate for Ripley's Believe It Or Not."

"I'd as soon you didn't submit my dimensions to them. I don't think my wife would like her favorite implement showing up in the record books. She already hates how many women come on to me."

"I can see why they do. I've never seen a man of your age in such good physical shape—all over—not just down there. But I'd better get back to the ER."

"Okay. Nice to see you again."

The day he was scheduled to leave the hospital, a deputy fastened a monitoring device to his right ankle and explained its use.

"When you leave the house, call in to let us know you're leaving and where you're going."

"Even if I just go to the barn to feed the horses and goats?" Kade asked.

"Yes, even then. When you return to the house, call again and let us know you're back inside. The calls will let us silence the alarm encased in the device. Call us when you get to work and when you leave, too."

"I make lots of trips to cover news. I have to call every time?"

"Yes."

Giving the deputy a grin, Kade said, "You're soon going to be sick of hearing from me."

"There will be dire consequences—up to, and including, being jailed—if you forget to let us know your whereabouts at all times. Do you understand?"

"Yes. What if I honestly forget to call you? Sometimes I'm so involved in a story, I . . ."

"Doubt you'll forget more than once. The consequences of forgetting tend to get harsher and harsher, so try hard to remember to call us."

"Okay, you've made your point."

Abby, who'd come to bring him home, asked a question. "Can he take it off when he goes to bed?"

"No, ma'am. Not without a key."

"Does it contain a microphone? I'd hate all the deputies to be sitting around at the station laughing because they're listening in while Kade and I make love."

"The device doesn't have any microphones, ma'am."

"Then how do you track his comings and goings?" she asked.

"It contains a GPS device we can track."

"Oh. Well, that's a relief. If he decides to romance some other woman, at least I know how I can track him down."

The deputy dissolved in laughter. "So even if his case is resolved in his favor, you'd opt to keep the bracelet on his leg?"

"You betchum, Red Ryder. My husband is so good looking, half the women in the county are into shining him on."

"How's your recovery going, Blackburn?" the deputy asked, after hauling up from the bedside chair.

"Well, sir. I'm sure it will get even better once I get home to my family."

"Just remember to call, sir, each and every time."

"I will. Thanks for your professionalism and courtesy this afternoon. I'll call in soon as we get home."

Once inside the ranch house, Kade made the obligatory call. "I'm home," he announced. "About five I need to feed the stock. I'll call on both sides of that chore."

"You'll hate all this rigmarole, won't you?" Abby asked.

"Damn right. It's like having one's mother standing right behind you. You can't even let loose with a good fart with her behind you."

"They said there was no microphone in that anklet, so I doubt anyone will hear you farting," she teased. "I thought you loved your mother."

"I did," he said. "But that doesn't mean I appreciated her sticking her nose into everything I did. She used to come in to wake me up for breakfast and school. Caught me with my hands in my shorts a few times. Let me know she was displeased about that."

"Is that why you never go into Andy's room to call him for breakfast?"

"You know it, wife. I just thump on his door and tell him to get his butt downstairs to eat. That gives him time to pull his hands out of his shorts, undetected."

"Hungry?" she asked.

"Yeah, but not for food—just you."

"Until the stitches come out, you'll have to content yourself with food, not me."

He pulled her into a tight embrace. "Sure about that?" he asked, massaging her left breast.

"Yes, I am, Kade. I heard the doctor dispense those instructions. No physical or strenuous activity until the stitches come out."

"You're no fun," he said. "Okay, if all you're willing to do is feed me, I could eat a sandwich. Don't know why I need to eat at all. Not to maintain my strength for sure, if I can't engage in . . ."

"I could have easily lost you, so I'm not willing to take that chance by falling into bed with you this soon."

"Guess, if the shoe were on the other foot—if you'd been the one who'd been shot—I'd be cautioning you to be careful, too. We've been through a lot as a couple. I'd rather not lose you, either, so I understand your concern."

"Good. Roast beef or ham sandwich?"

"Beef. I've only been away for a week and you've forgotten my preferences already?"

Abby gave him a look that expressed her annoyance. "Don't take your anger about your sequestration out on me, Kade Andrew Blackburn. I'm not the one who put the anklet around your leg."

He spotted Alli, hanging back before entering the kitchen. "Uh-oh, when Mama resorts to calling me by my whole name, I know to shut my mouth, before she beans me with her cast-iron frying pan."

"When did you get home, Dad?" Alli asked.

"About a half hour ago," he said, wondering how long she's been lurking around the corner. "Did you miss me?"

"Yes. I didn't want to go out and help feed. I was scared the guy might come back and shoot me and Andy."

"He's dead, Alli. He won't be shooting anybody ever again."

"Is that why you have to wear the thing around your ankle?"

"Yes. The police want to be sure they can find me to ask more questions. This device assures them they can find me."

"Do they think you killed him on purpose?"

"I don't know what they think, sweetheart. It takes some time for the officials to work through all their paperwork, and they need me at hand to answer whatever questions they come up with."

"Will you go to jail?"

"I sincerely hope not, pumpkin. But that's not something you should be worried about. Come sit down and eat a sandwich with me."

"Okay, but I want ham, not beef."

*She's like a quiet cat, always lurking around corners. I wonder how long she was there, listening. No wonder she says she can read us like a large-print book. I need to be sure she's out of earshot when I discuss having relations with Abby. Wouldn't want her thinking that's all I care about.*

Alli sat down and laid a hand on his arm. "I'm really glad you're home, Dad. I was so afraid you'd die."

"Why? Because then you'd have to feed the critters every night?" he teased.

She burst into tears, and contrite, he immediately stood up and pulled her into an embrace. He kissed away her tears. "I'm sorry, Alli. I shouldn't have made light of your concerns or fears. I appreciate the fact you love me enough to want to have me around for a few more years."

"We all love you, Dad. We were all so worried."

"I know. But I'm fine, now, so dry your tears and eat your sandwich."

He called in for his evening feeding ritual. Invited everyone to come help him, even Abby. He realized, after Alli's outburst, how scared they'd been, and he hoped he could re-establish their faith in normality by keeping to his usual schedule of chores.

"Da-da," Kory said, "tomorrow can you find some grubs for chickens?"

"Right after we all enjoy one of Mama's pancake breakfasts, I'd be open to hunting up some grubs for the chickens. Your mama didn't take you out to hunt them up while I was gone?"

"No, she didn't take either me or Kathy out to find any grubs."

"Those chickens will stop laying eggs if we don't find them grubs." He ran a hand under one hen and pulled out an egg she'd laid. "Look, she's already laying smaller eggs. If we don't want eggs the size of marbles, we need to find grubs in the mornings for all of the chickens."

"The size of marbles, Dad?" Andy asked. "When have you ever seen an egg the size of a marble?"

"I haven't seen one that size, son. That's because we give all the chickens grubs, otherwise . . ."

When Andy rolled his eyes, Kade was hard pressed not to laugh. Andy had always taken his statements as the gospel truth. "What?" he asked. "I'm gone for a couple of days and you no longer believe me?"

He wrapped an arm around his oldest son and said, "I know none of you wanted to feed the critters or be out here any longer than necessary, because you were scared. It's not as if something that bad happens every day, so I want you to relax again.

"I appreciate the fact you were here to protect our family in my absence, son. Mama said you took over my role while I was in the hospital. You were the one who made sure all the locks were turned and you were the one who looked out to be sure it was safe before you and Alli fed the stock. It's nice to know I have such a responsible son."

"Thanks, Dad. I love you. I never thought about how much I love you, until I saw you lying there, bleeding on the ground."

"I'm a hard man to kill, Andy. I'm sorry you all had to experience such a horrific scene, but I'm almost back to normal, so I'm ready to take my role—as our family's protector—back from your shoulders. You can return to being a teenager, now."

"Dad, what if I volunteered to share those 'protector-of-the-family' duties with you? I think it's too big a job for just you."

"I'd like that a lot, Andy. When I'm not here—when I'm at work—it's always filled me with confidence that you were on the job at home. I'd welcome your assistance—long as it doesn't interfere with your homework."

Andy reached out his hand and Kade shook it then pulled his son into an embrace. He didn't kiss Andy, as he had kissed Alli, but he wanted his child to know how much he loved him.

In the morning, Kade had to make four calls. Before and after he fed. Before and after he set out for work and arrived at the paper's offices.

"Kade, you're back? This soon?" Dean asked as he passed her office. "Why?"

"I'm fine, Ms. Dean. I'm sure Abby is happy I'm back at work, instead of dogging her footsteps all day long."

"How's your wound?" Dean asked, still concerned.

"Not nearly as troubling as having to call the Sheriff's office every time I set foot outside my house or this office."

"You should have taken more time off," Dean said. "Maybe the wound in your leg is better, but I bet there are a few unresolved issues still lingering in your head."

"Nope, there are no mental issues in play," he assured her.

"How could there not be?"

"The police asked me the same question. Did I regret killing him? I told them I had zero regrets. I think that's why I'm currently wearing the anklet. They still aren't sure I didn't shoot him on purpose, before he got another shot off in my direction."

"Surely, they can't believe you'd murder someone like Fred in cold blood."

"I'm not sure exactly how they regard me or the incident—self-defense or plain murder. I'm sure they questioned all of you, so they know there was no love lost between Fred and me. We'd even had that scuffle in the alley behind the press room."

"Yes, they did ask us a lot of questions."

"I hope you answered them all in an honest way."

"None of us thought you'd killed him in other than self-defense."

"How do you know for sure? Maybe I seized my chance to be rid of his troubling presence."

"Kade, please don't say things like that. If they haul you up on charges, those kinds of statements could send you to the gallows."

He grinned. "Well, one thing to be said for hanging, it seems to work better than those methods where they shoot some chemicals into your veins. Me, I'd opt to stand before a shooting squad. Quick, easy, and relatively painless."

"I'm glad you're back, Mr. Blackburn. Diana has done well in your absence, but she's looking a bit frayed around the edges."

"I'll take her out for lunch to thank her for covering for me."

He slid into his chair and looked over the list of current items to be covered this week, which was generated by Ms. Dean every morning.

"Kade, is that you?" Diana asked.

"Yes, ma'am. I'm back in the harness. Come around the corner and fill me in on which items you want to cover. I'll do the rest on the list, or as many as I can before my leg starts protesting."

She came over and pulled up his spare chair to sit at his elbow.

"You aren't going to turn it around and sit on mine backwards, like I sit on yours?"

"A skirt kind of prevents that way of sitting down. How are you, really?"

"I'm fine. I'm a hard man to kill or keep down due to all my Army training."

"Where did he hit you? Nobody would say."

Kade stood up and unfastened his belt, lowered the zipper and pushed his pants down to knee level. "Here," he said, indicating the small patch he still wore over the wound. "I consider myself extremely lucky. Another inch or three to the left and I'd be missing all those male hormones."

"Only you, Kade, would think of a wound in those terms. Which items do you want to cover?" she asked, steering the conversation in a less sexual direction while he yanked up his pants and fastened his belt.

"You choose first. I'll take what's left. Since I have to inform the constabulary of my location at all times, I'd like the items that will take longer to cover, so I don't have to report in so often."

"Okay, if you want the longest, most boring assignment, cover the murder trial in progress at the courthouse. Some dude shot a guy who trashed his opportunity to play poker with the big rollers in Las Vegas. The guy he killed won the last slot in the LV tournament. Now there's a good reason to off someone."

She was looking at him intently. "You'd like to know my reason for offing Fred?" he asked, knowing what her questioning look implied.

"We all wondered. Why did he come to your ranch? Why did you shoot him? When the police questioned all of us, we didn't know what to say. Would what we told them about the ongoing rancor between you and Fred help or harm your case?"

"This is not for dissemination—just for your ears only. Fred followed me home. Passed a bunch of cars on the way to Chino Valley, and fell into line right behind me. I didn't know it was Fred at first, because I didn't know what kind of car he drove, but I had my suspicions. That's why I pulled the rifle down from its rack in my truck and made sure it was loaded.

"When I turned into my driveway, he went past, on up the road. I felt some better, but I couldn't shake the thought it was Fred. My hackles were still standing tall like a dog's hackles when he's on full alert. Fred had been fired, and I knew he probably thought I was the reason for his sudden unemployment. Just as I got out of my truck, he pulled in behind me, and started shooting. I grabbed the rifle when one of his rounds connected with my thigh."

"How could you even function at that point?" Diana asked.

"I knew I was bleeding. I could feel blood running down my leg. I was afraid, if I passed out, he could shoot me to death and maybe kill my family, too. So I took my best shot and nailed him in the heart. And, no, I'm not sorry he's dead, if that was your next question."

"Can you objectively cover a trial where one guy shot another?" she asked.

He grinned. "Sure. In the dark recesses of my mind, I will just compartmentalize what I did to Fred. That will leave all my other gray matter to concentrate on the trial at hand."

"Kade, when you make jokes like that, I know you must feel more dreadful about shooting Fred than you let on."

He shook his head. "No. I have no regrets about killing Fred. Don't plan to lose any sleep over the incident either. I'd like to take you out for lunch all this next week, to thank you for covering all the news while I was gone . . . unless you'd rather not be seen out with a killer."

"You aren't a killer, Kade."

"Oh, but I am—several times over, in fact. The other times, I was sanctioned by the Army to kill. This is the first time I've killed as a civilian, so if you'd rather not be seen out with me, I'll understand your reluctance to go to lunch with me."

"Of course I'll go with you. If you're covering the trial, will there be a lunch break? There are some good restaurants around the courthouse. Give me a call and I'll meet you wherever you name."

"Okay. Even judges need to eat. If my past experience is valid, they usually break about 1:30 for lunch, so they don't run into the noon crowds. Can you be in the vicinity of the courthouse about then? An hour doesn't give us long to eat."

"I'll be in town for this other item, anyhow. A child molester that his neighbors are up in arms about—he's living in an apartment house where small children also reside."

Kade grinned. "Be careful. One of the neighbors may take matters into his or her own hand and dispense with the creep on his or her own. Don't want to have to cover all the items on Dean's list if you get shot."

"How can you make jokes like that? I'm not sure I want to go with you to lunch if you're that blasé about Fred's death."

"You have several hours between now and 1:30 to decide. I'll call and you can give me your decision then."

He put in his call to the sheriff's office. "This is Blackburn. I'm heading out to cover a trial at the courthouse. Then I plan to take my fellow reporter to lunch over the break. Do I need to call when I leave the courthouse, too?"

"Yes, and indicate which restaurant you plan to eat at."

"I didn't realize that was part of my requirements in relation to the anklet. Call when I leave or enter my residence or when I leave or enter the place where I work. Nothing was said about designating the restaurant I plan to eat at. I'm not sure where she'll choose to eat. I'll have to call you once she decides. It's going to cut down on my face-stuffing time if I have to keep phoning you."

"Be sure and call, Blackburn," the officer said before hanging up in his ear.

Kade made copious notes from the trial. He wished he'd brought his colored pencils with him, so he could underline a good lead sentence, and start whipping the article into shape during the down times. At 1:15, the judge halted the proceedings in favor of a lunch break, and Kade called Diana. She told him she'd meet him at the north- side door of the courthouse.

She pulled up and honked, motioning for him to get into her vehicle. She pulled around onto Whiskey Row and found a parking space. As soon as they were seated and had given their orders, Kade pulled out his cell phone. "I'm at the Italian bistro on Whiskey Row, sir. I'll call you when I'm back inside the courthouse."

They'd been barely served, when a man in a deputy sheriff's uniform took a seat at the table next to theirs. Kade leaned across the table to whisper to—warn her about discussing anything he'd shared with her that morning. She nodded her understanding.

"Didn't I just see you at the protest about the sexual predator?" the deputy asked Diana.

"Kade and I are both reporters for the paper, so yes, I was covering the protest."

"He should cover that protest. Maybe he could get out his rifle again and spare the county paying for a lengthy trial. I think he likes blowing people away."

Due to the volume of his voice, by this time half the eaters were taking in the discussion. Kade would have left without eating to spare the eaters any anxiety, but Diana laid a hand on his arm and said, "Disregard the prattle of fools and eat your dinner, Kade. Doubt the judge in the case will want to put up with your stomach growling all afternoon," she teased.

"How can you sit there eating with a guy who gets his kicks out of shooting someone dead?" the deputy asked. "Stand up, sir. I need to pat you down for weapons."

Kade knew better than to create a scene in the bistro. Half the patrons were wearing alarmed looks on their faces. He stood up, keeping both hands in full view on the edge of the table. The deputy did a full body check of his torso, pulling a pocketknife out of his front right pocket. "I wasn't aware you were allowed to carry a weapon, sir," the deputy said.

"That's my toothpick, sir, not a weapon," Kade said, with a grin. "The blade is so short, and with all your adipose tissue, it'd never connect with anything vital. It'd be like when a rattlesnake bites a pig. The pig is so fat, the venom just gets lost in the lard and the pig never experiences any ill effects."

"Are you calling me a 'pig,' sir?"

"Nope, I was just making a comparison as to weapons. The rattler doesn't have fangs long enough to connect with anything vital inside the pig, and my knife doesn't have a blade long enough to be considered a weapon, either."

By this time most of the patrons wore grins, not fear, on their faces. The deputy sat down again at his table, laying the knife he'd confiscated beside his plate. Kade finished his meal then stood up. He walked to the deputy's table, running the tip of his tongue over his teeth.

"I could use my teeth picker back from you, sir. I have meat stuck between several of my molars. Can I please have my knife back?"

Giving him a disgusted look, the deputy handed back Kade's knife. Kade sat down again at his table and opened a short blade. "This is probably going to revise your opinion of me, as a cultured person," he whispered, opening his mouth wide to extract a chunk of meat lodged in his molars.

Diana burst out laughing, as did several of the nearby eaters.

He called as soon as he reached the courthouse again. Sat there until 4:30 when there was a break in the trial.

He followed the judge to his chambers. "Sir, may I ask you a legal question?" he said.

"Not about the trial. I see you're a reporter, and I don't want this case tried in the papers."

"No, sir. About a personal matter."

"Ask away, then."

"I'm Kade Blackburn."

The judge frowned. "The man who shot one Fred Rossman?"

"Yes, sir. The deputies are taking their own sweet time about deciding if it was truly self-defense. In the meantime, I'm required to wear this ankle bracelet and call in to report my location whenever I leave home or the paper."

"You have an objection to wearing it?"

"No, sir. I don't. Nor do I have an objection to calling in to report my locations, either. But today at lunch, a deputy sat down at the table next to Diana and me . . . she's also a reporter for the paper . . . and he started asking Diana how she could eat with a known killer. His loose talk alarmed most of the patrons enjoying their lunches.

"Then he said for me to stand up so he could search me. Confiscated my pocketknife. By that time most of the people were ready to run for the door. I don't mind the anklet, sir, but I sure object to that deputy's overt attempt to embarrass me in public.

"I have not been charged in the case, so for him to label me a killer, I felt was a little over the line. I'd like to prevent a repeat occurrence. Is there some statute I could quote to stop it from happening again?"

"There is, Mr. Blackburn. But it's far too detailed for you to remember the ins-and-outs of what it says. Let me write down the statute number on several note cards. If any of them continue to hassle you, hand them one of the cards and tell them to look it up. Tell them, too, if they don't cease and desist, you're going to take them to civil court and sue their socks off." He scribbled a number on several cards.

"My eternal thanks, sir," Kade said, taking the cards from the judge's hand.

"I read in the paper you shot him in self-defense."

"I did, sir. He shot first. Hit me in the thigh."

"Don't tell me anything more about it. If the case comes up before me in court later, I'd have to recuse myself."

"I appreciate your kindness, sir. I'll get out of your hair so you can get home to dinner."

"How did you lose those fingers?" the judge asked.

"Incoming ordinance in Afghanistan, sir."

"Blackburn? Afghanistan? That name rings a bell."

Kade nodded. "You probably remember the Medal of Honor ceremony. I received one of those medals for saving Joe Biden's life."

"Yes, now it all comes back to me. My respect for you has just taken a quantum leap. Let me know if those deputies continue to harass you and I'll put the fear of God in them. You saved our Vice President's life. Tell me again how it happened."

Once more Kade related the story in its entirety. The hour grew late as the judge asked more and more questions about the situations in the Middle East. Suddenly there was a loud knock on the judge's door and a deputy stepped through it without being invited.

"There you are. Did you forget to call in, Blackburn?"

"No, sir. I haven't left the courthouse yet. I should be getting home. Since you're here, can I avoid another phone call? You know I'm leaving now, isn't that enough?"

"You need to call in. I can't be transferring your oral messages. That's not in the scope of my duties," the deputy said.

"Thank you again, sir," Kade said to the judge. "If you have more questions, I'd be pleased to talk with you again."

"Not about your pending case, Blackburn," the deputy snarled. "Was that why you're still here? Has he been crying on your shoulder, judge?"

"It's none of your business why Mr. Blackburn is here, deputy. I suggest you leave now so Blackburn can comply with your order to call in. I'll be walking him out to his vehicle to be sure you don't hassle him again. Good afternoon, Deputy Fowler."

As he walked Kade to his truck, he said, "Do any of them know about your medal? Might have more respect for you if they knew about it."

"I don't make a point of telling anyone about the medal, sir. I just prefer to do my reporting job, without anyone feeling the need to bow or curtsey when I pass by," Kade said, grinning widely.

He reached his truck and shook hands with the judge, before pulling out his phone to call in. "This is Blackburn. I'm heading for home now. I'll call as soon as I arrive and again after I feed the stock and once more when I go into my home. My cell is about out of juice, so if I'm late reporting in, chalk it up to that fact. I'll have to plug it in on the way home if it's going to work at all. Kade Blackburn, over and out."

The judge stood there shaking his head. "Seems like a lot of nonsense for no good purpose, Kade."

"It lets them feel important, sir. Same as Army orders which make little sense. Lets the upper brass feel important to be giving them out. Gives them a sense of power over the grunts in the field. If they only knew . . ."

"How much the grunts despise them?"

Kade's grin was his only indication that the statement was true.

"What was your highest rank?"

"Second Lieutenant, sir."

"Do you think the grunts despised you?"

"Don't know, sir. I tried to give out orders only when necessary for their safety. I think the men in my platoons knew I wasn't drunk on power. I believe I enjoyed a modicum of respect from the men under my command."

"I'm quite sure you're right, Kade. You strike me as an extremely intelligent man."

"I did graduate magna cum laude from grad school."

"Probably makes it even tougher to knuckle under to some deputy who doesn't have an iota of your smarts."

"It pays to remain polite to those who are in power, sir, regardless of their intelligence."

The judge laughed and clapped Kade on his back. "Now, there's a statement no one would quibble with. Head for home and don't forget all those calls."

"Yes, sir. It was a pleasure to chat with you. Some day you need to come to our ranch and meet the rest of my family."

"I'd look forward to that, Mr. Blackburn. Take care now," he said.

# Chapter Fourteen

Seven calls later, he was seated at his table surrounded by his family. Abby served up a seven-bone roast along with baked potatoes and corn on the cob.

Kade sat quietly, observing his family. Abby mashed the insides of those baked potatoes on the twin's plates, pouring some gravy over the contents. She sliced up some tiny pieces of the roast for them and buttered their ears of corn, adding a sprinkle of salt.

"Dive in," she invited. "I didn't spend all day in the kitchen cooking to have you sit there like dummies."

"Looks good, Abby. I'm surprised your parents didn't smell your efforts all the way to Camp Verde and show up for dinner tonight."

"Sunday is Father's Day," she reminded him. "Would you be open to me inviting Dad and Mom for dinner on Sunday? I picked him up a small gift, but I think I'd like to invite him for dinner, too. He's not getting any younger."

"Long as I can invite my papa, too," Kade said.

"Would he come? It's a long flight."

"Don't know until I call and ask."

"Why now? You've never expressed a wish to include him before."

"He's not getting any younger, either," Kade said.

"You'd like him to be acquainted with our family before he dies?"

Kade nodded, then abruptly got up from the table to call his father. He came back in ten minutes. "He'll come on Saturday, so I can pick him up at the airport. He'll go back on Monday. Now, I need some suggestions about a gift for him for Father's Day. He doesn't wear ties, and he blows his nose on tissues, so that leaves out neckties and handkerchiefs."

"What does he like to do?" Andy asked.

"He likes to make centerpieces out of driftwood. Lamps out of interesting chunks of wood he comes across in the forests. At least he used to enjoy crafts like that."

"In our woodworking class in school, we have these little drills that might be useful for fashioning his wood projects. Dremel drills," Andy said.

"I can get one in Prescott?" Kade asked.

"I'm sure all the hardware stores carry them."

"I think you should get him a camera," Alli suggested. "Then he can take a bunch of pictures of us to take back home with him."

"Another good suggestion," Kade said.

"I think those are both expensive gifts. I only got my father a new set of suspenders. I might need to buy him something expensive, too. If you're going to get your father a camera, pick one up for my dad, too."

Kade tried hard to conceal the smile that turned up the corners of his mouth, by raising his glass of iced tea to his lips, and taking a long swallow.

"I see you smirking, Kade. If you object to getting a camera for my father, just say so. I have money of my own and I'm perfectly capable of getting one for my dad."

"Okay. You get one for your father, and I'll get one for mine. Want to bet the first thing Owen wants to preserve for posterity is the anklet I'm being forced to wear?"

"He doesn't need to know you're wearing one. Keep both feet on the ground and wear those new jeans that have longer legs, because I haven't washed them yet," Abby said.

"Your mother always uses ultra-hot water on my jeans. The legs and the waistline both shrink up, so my ankles are in full view, and I can hardly fasten the button at the top of the zipper, either," he teased.

"You lie like a rug, Kade Andrew Blackburn!" Abby said.

"She's using my whole name again. Guess I'd better eat my dinner and stop talking before she starts throwing plates and glasses in my direction."

"I have a more appropriate punishment in mind," she said.

Dinner over, Abby dished out slices of apple pie for dessert. "You don't get any, Kade. For several reasons, which we'll discuss over our tea at eleven."

"Dad, I don't want my pie," Alli said. "You're welcome to my slice."

"Why don't you want your pie?" he asked. "Mom makes really good pies."

"Someone in my class at school said I was too fat, so I'm not going to eat desserts until I lose some weight."

"Eat your pie, Alli," Kade commanded. "You aren't too fat. In fact, if you were any slimmer you'd blow away in a stiff breeze. I hope you aren't about to turn into one of those anorexic females. Not only do they look like a skeleton walking, but they do damage to their organs, too. Eat your pie."

"But you didn't get a slice. Mom, give Dad a piece of pie," she said.

"Okay, he can have a slice of pie as long as you eat yours. I'll get even for his comments later on."

Kade shot her a look, knowing what she planned to withhold from him later. "Really, wife? I guess you don't need to cut me a slice of pie. I'd rather have the other than the pie."

"Maybe you'll get neither."

"Is Daddy being bad?" Kory asked, observing the mean look Abby gave Kade.

"Yes, he definitely is being perverse," she told him.

"Is perverse like a bad word? Does he need a time out?" Kathy asked. "Are you going to make him sit in the corner until bedtime?"

"It's a definite possibility."

Her comment sent the twins into a spate of giggles. Their amusement also amused Kade. "I think I'm too big to sit in that tiny chair in the corner."

"We could haul a kitchen chair in for you to use," Andy volunteered.

"Or make him kneel on the register as his punishment," Alli said.

"Hey, what is this? Pick on Dad night? Soon as you finish your pie, you're all excused from the table. Andy and Alli will do up the dishes. I'm going to bathe the twins and read them a story. And you, wife, will tackle your bookwork, so when it comes to later, you won't have a ready excuse to deny me . . . a slice of pie," he tacked on, aware that Alli, at least, probably knew what Abby planned to deny him.

"We'll just see about that, Mr. Blackburn."

The older kids soon had the dishes done and retreated to their rooms to tackle their latest fiction books. Kade had announced at one family meeting that reading was the preferred activity for his children. He'd actually banned playing computer games after dinner.

He bathed Kory and Kathy and wrestled them into their pajamas. He chose a book and sat down on the sofa to read it to them. Abby spread out her work on the dining-room table, but didn't pick up her pen to tackle the figures on her spreadsheet.

*He's so good with the children,* she thought, listening to him read. *That's probably the fiftieth time he's read that book to one or another of our kids, yet each time he makes it sound like it's a new and exciting tale to him.* She glanced in his direction to look at the twins. *They're eating up the story, as well as your attention, as they always do.*

"One more story?" Kory asked when Kade finished the first one.

"Okay, bring me another book."

Kory came back with the thickest book he could find. "You wouldn't be trying to postpone your bedtime, would you, son?" Kade asked, grinning over Kory's ploy.

"No," Kory said. "Me and Kathy just like to be close to you and have you read a story to us. What do you want for Father's Day?"

"You don't need to buy me anything. What you just said is the best gift you could ever give me for Father's Day. I like being close to both of you, too. In fact, while I'm buying something for my father, I think I'll get some new books for you and Kathy while I'm out and about."

"Oh, good, Daddy. I saw one about dinosaurs the other day. Can you get me one about them?"

"I'm sure I'll find one on that subject. Kathy, do you have a preference? What do you like your books to be about?"

"I like books about beautiful princesses, like Snow White or Cinderella."

"Yuck!" Kory said. "I don't want to listen to those books."

"Guess I'll have to read to you separately, then. Now it's time for bed. Give Mom and me a kiss and hit the sack. I'll come and tuck you in."

Both kids planted a kiss on his cheek then went to do the same to Abby. He got up and trailed them to their bedroom. Tucked in their sheets and bent down to kiss their cheeks. "Sleep tight, don't let the bedbugs bite," he said.

"What does a bedbug look like?" an alarmed Kathy asked, lifting up her covers.

"They're very tiny, so I don't think you can see them easily. Our house doesn't have bedbugs, so go to sleep."

"How do you know?" Kory asked.

"We've lived here for several years now, and bedbugs leave a lot of red welts on your skin when they bite. I've never seen any of those welts on anyone, so I know this house doesn't have bedbugs."

Even more alarmed, Kathy sat up and pulled up her nightgown. "Look, Daddy. Maybe we do have bedbugs," she said, pointing to a red bump on her thigh.

"That's a mosquito bite because you want to wear shorts in the summer and stay out until nearly dark. If you wore jeans like me, you'd not get bitten by mosquitoes."

"Except around your ankles cause mama washes your jeans in hot water and makes them shrink?" Alli asked, on her way to take her shower before bed.

Kade was still shaking his head in amusement when he came downstairs. Having a couple of hours to kill before the 11 p.m. discussion with his wife, he picked up a magazine and read several articles.

Finally Abby closed up her bookwork and put on the kettle. He closed his magazine and got down their mugs and the tea bags containing chamomile tea.

*This is far and away one of my favorite times of the day,* he thought. *Even if she's loaded for bear and wants to rake me over those coals, it's still something I look forward to every night.*

Abby poured water into both cups and sat down across from him. She launched into her previous bone to pick with him.

"You can't find it in yourself to buy both cameras at the same time?" she asked. "You resent having to buy anything for my father? I've never met your father. I might not like him, either, yet I'd be glad to buy him a gift, just because he's your father."

"No, you've never met my dad so you have no opinions about him—either good or bad. I, on the other hand **have** met your father. He's not my favorite guy, but if you'll fork over the money for his camera, I suppose I could pick one up at the time I get one for my father."

"I'd be willing to get some extra drill bits for that thing you plan to give your father. I'd be willing to spend my money on a gift for him. Why can't you spend part of your money on a gift for my dad?"

"If he learned about my generosity, he'd either feel I had some favor I wanted from him or tell me that such-and-such brand was a lot better camera. I can't win, no matter what I do."

"You poor thing. Tell me some stuff about your father."

"He's kind of taciturn. Not much of a sense of humor. He likes puttering around in his workshop. Enjoys fishing and walking in the woods."

"Why didn't you ever invite him to come visit until now?"

Kade shrugged. "He was upset with me when I couldn't come home for Mom's services because I'd ticked off my commander in Iraq. Since that time, I've only received a few cards from him—only on my birthdays and at Christmas. I always felt like I was a real disappointment to him, so the less I had to do with him—I thought that's what he preferred."

"Why do you think he agreed to come now?"

"I have no idea."

"You need to knock that chip off your shoulder before you go to pick him up in Phoenix. You can't contend with two angry fathers at the same time."

"I know. A piece of your pie would go well with this tea, wife. Do you really intend to withhold it from me—and the other, too?"

She got up and sliced him a big slice of pie. "We'll negotiate the other item, later."

"The other would go a long way to offset a pretty nasty day," he said, licking into his pie.

"What happened?"

He chewed for a bit to give him time to assemble his thoughts. Finally swallowed.

"Diana and I split the items list Dean gave us this morning to be covered. She let me take the court case because it involved sitting, not chasing all over to cover other items on the list. When the judge broke for lunch, I invited her to dine with me, as I appreciated she hadn't left me standing around at various scenes on my newly healed leg.

"She jumped at the chance to eat with you? I see how she looks at you. Did she ask to see where you'd been wounded?

"No, she didn't. She picked me up at the courthouse and we ate at the Italian bistro on Whiskey Row. Just as we were served, a deputy sat down at the next table and asked how Diana could countenance eating with a killer. He actually made me stand up so he could frisk me. Confiscated my pocketknife in addition to scaring most of the patrons half to death.

"After the trial concluded for the day, I asked the presiding judge if I could ask him a personal question. He invited me to his chambers and I outlined what the deputy had done. He gave me several note cards delineating the statute on Arizona books that says I'm not to be humiliated like that in public. Said for me to hand one out to any other deputy who hassles me."

"That must have been very embarrassing."

"Yeah, it was. On Father's Day, I might have to hand one of those cards to your father."

"Kade, if you could remain as mellow as when you read to the twins, he'd probably not pick on you. When you bristle all up, that's what gives him his satisfaction. Try on Sunday not to bristle. Just grin and roll with the punches."

"You're probably right, wife. It's just that he's so adroit at punching the right buttons in me. Makes it very hard to remain calm and pleasant when he starts in punching those buttons."

"We all love you, Kade. I was just reminded of that tonight when Kory said what he did. Can't you concentrate on those family-love

offerings instead of bristling up? Just remember what Kory told you—
'Me and Kathy just like to be close to you.'"

"Yeah, that kind of took some of the stress out of my day, too. I'll
try to keep it in mind on Sunday."

"Let's go to bed, cowboy. Maybe I can delete a bit more stress from
your day. Give you something else to cling onto on Sunday."

"I'm in favor of that."

He rinsed both cups and turned them upside-down on a dishtowel.
As she went up to bed, he locked the doors and hurried up the stairs
before she changed her mind.

On Saturday, Kade got up early and went south to fetch his father.
None of the kids could go, as Abby had instructed them to clean up
their rooms and pick up toys, so she could sweep the rugs.

He got to the airport and parked. Went into the right terminal and
sat down, waiting for the announcement of his father's plane's arrival. It
came right on time, so Kade stood up and walked over to the deplaning
area. His father was at the end of the line. Kade wondered if he'd had
second thoughts about getting off the plane.

"Dad, it's really good to see you," he said, giving his father a big hug.
"It's been so long, I wasn't sure I'd recognize you."

"Whose fault is that?" Ben Blackburn asked. "I suppose by now my
suitcase will be on the carousel."

"Were you way in the back of the plane?" Kade asked.

"No, but there was a mother with a small baby who blocked the
aisle for several minutes, trying to gather up the kid and the diaper bag.
I sat down across from her and told her to wait until all the others were
gone, and I'd help her carry her stuff."

"That was nice of you, Dad. Which bag is yours?" he asked as the
suitcases circled around.

"The green one. It's been forever since you were home if you don't
remember the luggage you gave Mom and me for Christmas."

"You're still using it? It has held up that well?"

"It's Samsonite. Supposed to be sturdy, and I haven't used it but a
couple of times since Mom died."

Kade snagged the bag off the merry-go-round. His father snatched it from his hand. "Right this way, Dad. I'm parked in the closest lot, but if you don't want to walk, I'll get my truck and pick you up."

"There's nothing wrong with my legs, Kade. I walk a mile every day."

"Okay. Let me carry the bag, then."

"There's no reason I can't carry it, either."

Kade closed his eyes and thought of what Kory had told him two nights before. *I wonder if I expressed the same sentiments to you, Dad, if you'd accept the fact I hope to be closer to you, sir, before this mini-vacation is over?*

"I'm really glad you decided to come, Dad. I've missed you more than words can say. I'd love for you to meet my family—show you around the area. I hope you'll decide to stay longer so we can spend more time together."

"I'm going home on Monday. I have responsibilities back in Pennsylvania. I can't spend months out here."

"Okay, Dad. Abby's parents will be coming for the Father's Day dinner, too. Her father is kind of a pistol. Has no use for me at all."

"Why not?"

"Long story. I'll give you the highlights on our trip north."

"How far do we have to go?"

"The trip takes a little more than two hours."

"They don't have a shuttle? If they do, you didn't need to waste your time to come and pick me up."

"I wanted to pick you up, Dad. I've been excited about your arrival since you said you'd come. I couldn't wait to come down to fetch you home."

"Uh-huh, I'll just bet you were excited. Tell me why your wife's father has no use for you."

Kade launched into his spiel about Owen's dislike of him. The telling of the tale took just short of pulling into the ranch's driveway. "That's about all of it, Dad."

They got out of the truck and Kade pulled his father's suitcase from the back seat. The front door opened and Abby came out to greet the pair. The children were nowhere to be seen.

"Mr. Blackburn, welcome to our home. You look so much like Kade, he could have sent me south to pick you up. I'd have recognized you anywhere."

"If you don't mind, I need to use your restroom—or do you still have an outhouse?"

"We have indoor plumbing, Dad Blackburn. Right down the hallway. Second door on your right."

When the bathroom door closed, Abby said, "Was it a fun trip?"

Kade rolled his eyes. "Where is the rest of the crew?"

"The twins are napping. Andy and Alli are out raking up the stalls in the barn. You need to call in."

"Oh, yeah. I almost forgot."

"Would you like something to drink?" Kade asked when his father came out of the restroom. We have lemonade, cola, root beer, or hot coffee."

"Lemonade will be fine. How big is this ranch?" Ben asked.

"We have a little over 14 acres," Kade told him.

"Do you raise anything? Garden?"

"Small plot for summer vegetables, but most of it is sown with grass for the horses and goats."

"Plough horses?"

"No, pleasure horses. The older kids like to ride. They both belong to 4-H. The twins like to ride, too, when Andy and Alli can be persuaded to share the saddles."

"How many goats do you have?"

"Four at present. We keep a buck and a doe generally, but the doe gave us a set of twins at the end of April."

"You said you have twins? What are their names?"

"Kory and Kathy. They're napping presently."

"How old are they?"

"Coming up on their third year, Dad. When we sit down for dinner, I'll make all the introductions. In the meantime, would you like to see the horses and goats, the hens and the roosters?"

"You think I don't know what those animals look like?"

"You don't know what my animals look like."

"I'd like a sandwich. They don't feed you much on the plane," Ben said.

Abby sprang into action to construct a sandwich for Kade's father. "You want a sandwich, too?" she asked.

"Guess I could eat one, but I can make both of them. I think I hear the twins rousing up. Why don't you bring them down for their milk and cookies?"

"*You're* going to make sandwiches? Since when have you ever turned your hand at a domestic chore?" Ben asked.

"With a household of children, Kade often helps out around the place," Abby said, rising to Kade's defense.

"What else does he do to help out?"

"He's been known to do the dishes, the laundry, bathe the twins— even runs the sweeper on occasion."

"He never helped out at home. Never turned a hand to help **my** wife. Couldn't even come home when we buried her."

"Dad . . ." Kade started in to say, before he caught Abby's slight shake of her head. Finally he grinned and said instead, "Mom never took me in hand the way Abby does. If I'm not willing to help around the house, she won't let me make . . ."

"Kade!" Abby warned.

"Okay, wife. I'll shut up and just make sandwiches, but you'll owe me later on."

Abby brought the twins downstairs. "Kory and Kathy, this is your Grandfather Blackburn, your daddy's father.

"You look like Daddy, only more wrinkled," Kory announced.

Ben broke into a huge smile. "Would you like to sit on my lap?" he asked Kory.

"Not unless you bought some books for me. Did you buy me some? I only sit on Dad's lap when he reads to me."

"Kory, what did I tell you about asking for gifts?" Kade said.

"You said I wasn't to ask for them."

"Apologize to your grandfather for asking him that question, son."

"I'm sorry, grandfather. I shouldn't have asked if you bought me a book. Dad promised me one about dinosaurs, and I thought maybe he'd got one for you to give me."

"You like books about dinosaurs?"

"Yes, I love dinosaurs."

"And you, little missy. What's your name again?"

"Kathy," she said, going all shy and hiding behind Abby.

"Do you like dinosaur books, too? Would you like to sit on my other knee?"

"No, I like books about princesses," she said, still hanging back.

"After grandfather eats his sandwich, you might be able to persuade him to sit on the couch and read you the new books I got in Phoenix before I picked my dad up from the plane."

"A dinosaur book, Daddy? Did you find one of those?"

"I found three on dinosaurs and three about princesses, too."

"Oh, Daddy, I love you so much," Kory said. "Hurry up and eat your sandwich, so you can read me those books, Grampa."

Ben dove into his sandwich and ate it at top speed. As Kade cleared the table and drew water to wash the dishes, Kory grabbed Ben's hand and dragged him to the sofa. Kathy still hung back until Kade said, "I think he could be persuaded to read you these three princess books, too, if you'd quit hiding behind your mother and go sit on the sofa."

That was all it took. Kathy and Kory took up their positions, leaving room for Ben to sit between them. Ben read in much the same manner as Kade did. Enthusiastically, like he'd lucked onto a treasure in print. After Ben closed the last book, both twins gave him a hug. Kathy said, "You must like books as much as Daddy does. Thanks for reading all of them."

"Okay, you guys, the time has come for hunting up grubs for the chickens," Abby announced. "Tell Andy and Alli, they need to come meet Grandpa Blackburn, too."

"Are you and Grampa coming out to hunt for grubs with us, Daddy?" Kory asked.

"If Grandpa isn't too tired after his long plane trip."

"I wouldn't miss it for the world. I used to raise chickens and I know how much they enjoy grubs," Ben said, rising from the sofa.

They went to the barn and Kory picked up the bucket to contain the grubs.

"Andy, Alli, put up your rakes and come meet your Grandpa Blackburn."

"We only have one more stall to do, Dad. Then we should wash our hands so Grandpa's hands won't smell like horse apples when we shake his."

"Okay. The twins and Dad and I are going to find some grubs for the chickens."

"If you're hunting for grubs in horse manure, maybe we don't need to wash our hands at all," Alli said. "Hi, Grandpa Blackburn. Welcome to the Ark Ranch."

Andy stuck out his mitt to shake Ben's hand. "Ditto from me, sir. I wish you could stay a longer time. I'd love to hear some of the stories from when Dad was growing up."

"Oh, no you don't, son. You're not going to listen to all those stories about how ornery I was, so you can pull them up to remind me of them when I get on *your* case."

"Was he ornery, Grandpa?" Alli asked.

"A more contrary child never walked the streets of Pennsylvania," Ben said. "He stole the neighbor's apples off their trees, tried to give Mrs. Parker's cat a bath, and mowed over Mrs. Reynolds' prize irises with our mower."

"Dad, I'd as soon you didn't . . ."

"You were no goody two-shoes, Kade. Would you deny me the opportunity to tell them about your childhood, because . . ?"

"No, sir. Spin all the yarns you like about what a handful I was as a child."

"Still are a handful if what you told me on the road up here is any indication."

"I think I'll go find some grubs, so I don't get treated to any more tales. Who's going to come dig for grubs?"

All four children trooped off to the pile where they'd stacked the horse and goat manure. Kade turned over a shovel full of it. Both Kory and Kathy fell to picking out the white grubs. Soon the bucket was full of grubs, so they went to feed the chickens.

"What kind of chickens did you raise, Dad? Must have taken up the practice once I'd enlisted."

"I had a few Rhode Island Reds. They loved grubs so much, when I came out to feed them some, they'd fly up and perch on my arms to peck in the can."

"We haven't taught out chickens that trick," Andy said. "How did you get them to fly up to your arm?"

"First you have to squat down, like this, because Reds are so heavy they can't fly very high. Then you put a grub or two on your shirtsleeve. Go ahead and try it with your chickens."

Andy squatted and placed three grubs on his arm, it being too hot now for long sleeves. Sure enough, a hen leapt into the air, beating her wings furiously, to settle on his arm. The twins dissolved in giggles at the sight of a hen on Andy's arm. They wanted to try it, too, so they both squatted beside Andy and Kade put a grub on each of their arms.

The twins didn't think it was so funny when the hens' talons bit into their arms and the weight of them sent them both sprawling in the dirt.

"I think you twins are still too little for tricks like that with the hens," Kade said, helping them up and dusting them off. "It's getting late. Head into the house and get washed up for dinner. I'll finish the last stall, Andy. You and Alli did the rest so well, we won't need to clean them again until late Monday, after I get back from taking Dad to the airport."

Dinner was full of more tales from childhood. All the children seemed to like listening to the peccadilloes from Kade's growing-up years. Dinner over, Andy and Alli tackled the dishes. Kade bathed the twins and sat down to read to them. Abby checked over the menu for what she wanted to serve on Father's Day.

"If you want to read princess books to Kathy, Daddy, maybe Grampa will read me the dinosaur books again."

"You're bailing out on me, son? I can take turns reading one of each."

"I still love you best, Daddy, but if you both read us the stories, we'll hear more of what we each like before you say it's time for bed."

"Long as you remember to give me and Mom a kiss before bedtime."

"I'd never forget to give both of you a kiss."

"How about me?" Grandpa complained. "I'd like a kiss, too."

"Okay," the twins said in unison. Then they both looked at Kade to see if it was all right to give their Grampa a kiss. "Sure," Kade said. "Kiss away."

"Grampa Blackburn is nicer than Grampa Watkins," Kory announced, "He never sat down and read us a book. I don't think he likes us very much."

"Don't worry about it," Andy chimed in from the kitchen. "He doesn't like Dad much, either."

"Hey, oldest son. Some comments are best left unsaid, especially with these two ragamuffins listening in."

"You said we should always endeavor to tell the truth, Dad. What's not true about what I said?"

"C'mon, kids, it's bedtime." Kade hustled the twins into bed and kissed each goodnight.

By the time he returned to the den, Andy was sitting at the table, still wanting validation for what he'd said. "Didn't you say we needed to always tell the truth, Dad?"

"I did say that, but sometimes discretion if the better part of valor. What if the twins relate what you said to Grandpa Watkins tomorrow? No one, including me, has the right to make him uncomfortable when we invite him to dine with us."

"He sure doesn't mind making you uncomfortable, Dad," Allie said. "I think he looks for reasons to make you angry. He'll ask about your anklet thing. I know he will."

Kade had explained to his father his need to make phone calls and apprise the deputies of his location whenever he left or came back to the house. Had shown Ben his ankle device on the way back from the airport to the ranch.

"So?" Kade asked.

"He's going to try and embarrass you in front of your father," Alli said.

"I explained the situation to Dad on the way up from the airport, so I don't think there's any way for me to be more embarrassed than I already am. Isn't it about time for the both of you to get ready for bed?

We need to do chores and feed early, so we'll be ready for Mom's feast about one in the afternoon."

"Should we wrap the gifts?" Alli asked, "for both our grandfathers?"

"That would be a nice thing to do. Ask your Mom if she has wrapping paper and ribbons, along with two Father's Day cards that I'm sure she bought."

"Okay. Good night, Dad. Night, Grandpa Blackburn."

When both kids vacated the den, Ben spoke in a low voice. "Kade, for a long time I was so angry at you, for not being able to come home when Mom died. I thought you were so irresponsible for mouthing off to your commander.

"In one day here, you've managed to completely turn my head around regarding you. You have a wonderful wife and four children any man would be pleased to claim. They're polite and respectful. They tell the truth—even if you'd rather they didn't on occasion. I think you're very responsible, now.

"I can see you love your whole family. You've done well in your endeavors—both by purchasing this ranch and training up your children so well. It's obvious they all love and respect you."

Kade, uncomfortable with such high praise from his father, said, "If I could just train my wife to love and respect me, I'd be king of my universe."

"I heard that comment, Kade."

"Uh-oh. Are you going to make me sit in the corner?"

"Son, I just want to say, I'm pleased with you and your family. You're a credit to the Blackburn name. But I'm growing weary. It's after 10 p.m. Pennsylvania time. I'd like to go to bed now."

"Yes, sir. Thank you for your kind words, Dad. I wasn't really sure if I should invite you to come out for Father's Day. Now, I'm very glad I extended that invitation."

His father rose from his chair, and Kade rose from his. Spontaneously, they reached for each other, Kade enfolding his dad in a bear hug. Abby could see the tears glistening in Kade's eyes as they came together.

"I see you're still in fighting Army shape, son. Turn loose before you shatter my ribs."

"Dad . . ." Kade said before he choked up.

"Now don't go all maudlin on me, son."

"Yes, sir," Kade said stepping back. "I'll just show you to your room."

"I'd appreciate that more than I can tell you. I'm very weary."

Kade laid an arm around his father's shoulders and took him to his room. "Night, sir."

"What time will you get up to feed?" Ben asked.

"Oh, about 10 a.m. Pennsylvania time. That's seven a.m. here," he said with a chuckle. "Once again, Dad, I appreciate what you said and I sincerely love you to pieces, for being big enough to tell me that."

"Well keep my words in your mind and heart tomorrow if Watkins starts in on you."

"I intend to, sir. It'll be far easier to put up with his diatribes because of what you told me."

"Goodnight, son. I'll be firmly in your corner tomorrow."

Kade gave his father another bear hug. "Sleep tight, Dad."

"I intend to, son."

# Chapter Fifteen

They shared their usual cup of tea at eleven. Kade was all smiles, still reveling in his father's recently voiced approval.

"It was nice of him to say what he did, Kade."

"I know. Maybe he's forgiven me, finally, for not being there to support him when Mom died."

"I think he forgave you long ago. You're both cut from the same stripe—stubborn to the max."

"Hey, don't be giving me grief, telling me negative things right after Dad told me how wonderful I am. I'll get enough of that negativity tomorrow from your father."

"Maybe my dad will take a lesson from yours and treat you lots better."

"Wouldn't count on it, wife. Are you ready for bed? If we have to arise before the cock crows, we ought to get some shuteye."

"I thought you wanted sex."

"Not tonight. I don't want anything to interfere with what Dad said. I want to roll his words around in my head all night—not roll you around in our bed."

"Oh, Kade, were you really that worried about what he thought?"

"Every son desires the approval of his father, Abby. I never thought I had his. Now that I know he approves of me—and our family—it's like he's opened up a whole new outlook for me."

"So, all those times when you were after me to list my good and bad points, you weren't sure your father approved of you, either?"

"I wasn't sure of my post-Iraq status in regards to Dad, not like I was sure of your relationship to the Watkins. Your parents didn't pay much attention to you while you were growing up. I only lost favor with my father when Mom died."

"I'm so glad it all worked out. You're much too nice a guy to have your father still harbor a grudge because you didn't come home when your mom died."

"You don't always think I'm so nice, either."

"That's not true, Kade. We've had our disagreements, but inside, I know you're a really decent guy."

Kade arose at six, to get an early start on the day. Abby got up at the same time to start preparations for their 1 p.m. dinner. "Shall we share a shower, wife?" he asked.

"Sure, Kade. That'll leave more hot water for your father and the kids."

Kade adjusted the water to a warm temperature and held open the shower door for Abby. Once inside, he soaped a sponge and washed her top to bottom. She returned the favor. By that time he was hard, so he boosted her up, bracing her against the wall, and made love to her.

"You didn't want to roll me around in the bed last night, but you wanted to have sex with me in the shower this morning?"

"Best way I know to start off a morning," he said. "I'm both clean and satisfied."

"You couldn't have done that in bed before we took our shower?"

"Variety is the spice of life, so the adage goes," he said. "Got a roll or a donut for my breakfast? I already smell the coffee perking."

"I set the timer last night. I'll make you an omelet."

"You don't need to do that. A donut will leave me room for that feast you've planned for lunch."

He dried her off and then used the same towel on the moisture clinging to his body. Grabbing Abby from behind, he marched her over until they both stood in front of the full-length mirror. "God, you're beautiful in the mornings. All dewy with your hair all tousled up."

She stepped to one side of him. "You're not so bad to look at, either." She ran her hand down his abs. "You've always maintained such a strong body. I appreciate the care you take of yourself. I've felt for a long time, if ever I needed someone to protect me, you'd be there."

"Better believe I would, sweetheart. But I need to call the deputies and go feed the critters."

He went down to the kitchen to use the wall phone to call in. He found his father nursing a cup of coffee. "You beat me up, Dad."

"I usually get up around eight in Pennsylvania. Guess my internal alarm is still set on East Coast time."

Kade pulled the phone down and called the sheriff's office. "This is Blackburn. In another ten minutes I'll be leaving to feed the animals. I'll call you again when I return to the house. Happy Father's Day, sir."

"That has to be a real pain in the keister, calling in whenever you leave the place."

"That it is, Dad, but if I don't call, the device on my ankle emits a scream that California residents can likely hear. It's better not to annoy my neighbors that way. Let's go feed."

Ben pitched in to feed the horses their oats and hay. Kade took care of the goats, pausing to scratch the new kids behind their tiny ears. Mama goat, alarmed because he was touching her babies, stood up and gave him a good butt.

"Be nice, Mama," he said, rubbing his recently healed thigh. He picked up a rake and scooped up the horse apples from both stalls.

"Not going to hunt grubs for the chickens, this morning, son?" Ben asked.

"Nope. I'm just going to fill their feeders. I want to get back inside and call in my location before my father-in-law shows up."

"He'll come this early?"

"He likes to come hours before the meal so he has plenty of time to . . . ah, Dad, the morning started off on such a good note, I'd rather not dwell on how it's likely to end. Thanks again for what you told me last night."

"Abby had something to do with how well the day began?" Ben asked, before breaking into laughter. "You have a very satisfied look on your face, Kade, so I can imagine what put that look on it. Your mother knew how to put the same look on my face. She called it 'my cat with a bowl of cream' face."

"I think that's an apt description of me, this morning. I feel like a cat with a bowl of cream."

"I can tell she loves you a lot, Kade. And your kids adore you, too."

"Yes. I realize every day how blessed I am that I chose Abby. Don't know how she turned out so well, being raised in the Watkins' household, but she's definitely a keeper. You ready for breakfast?"

"Yes."

Abby had fixed bacon, and scrambled eggs. The children, still in robes and pajamas were already seated at the long table. "Don't forget to call in, Kade," she reminded him.

Once more he pulled down the phone and told the men on the other end he had returned to the house. "That's going to be a problem if your father wants me to go out to the barn later today," he told Abby. "He's going to wonder why I have to make a trip to the kitchen before I can leave the house."

"Would they let me call in for you, son?" Ben asked.

"No. I have to be the one to call in."

"I think we sound very alike. How would they know?"

"Don't know, but they might have some instrument that they run the voice through to be sure it's me on the line."

As Kade had predicted, Owen and Corrine showed up at 10:30, three hours previous to the scheduled lunch. Abby made the introductions.

"Mom, Dad, this is Ben Blackburn, Kade's father. He flew all the way out from the East Coast to join us for Father's Day. Ben, these are my parents, Owen and Corrine Watkins."

"I see where Kade gets his good looks, Ben," Corrine said. "I've sketched Kade in the past. I'd love to sketch you, too—maybe Tuesday— if Kade would bring you to my studio in Camp Verde."

"I'll be returning to my home on Monday. Sorry to disappoint."

Kade came into the parlor after introductions had been made. He'd been dressing the twins when he'd heard car doors slamming.

"Kade," Corrine said, moving close to his side. "Would you have a pad or some charcoal pencils? I'd love to sketch your father."

Kade rolled his eyes and whispered in her ear, "In the nude? Doubt he'd be a party to that."

"Of course not. Don't be crude. He looks so much like you and since you won't allow me . . ."

"It's up to Dad, if he wants you to sketch him," Kade said, cutting off the rest of her remark.

"Since we have time prior to dinner, I'd be willing to pose for you," Ben said. "Kory told me I looked like his Daddy, only more wrinkled."

Abby produced a sketchpad and a couple of charcoal pencils. "Here, Mom. These were in the cupboard in the den."

"Thanks. Ben, go sit in the den under the light, so I'll be able to capture you well."

Ben, accompanied by the rest of the adults, trooped into the den. Ben took a seat in the chair, and Corrine put her tablet on a folding wooden table. The kids had scattered to read or play.

"Kade," Owen said, "how's your job going? I see more and more articles by that Diana dame, and less and less stories by you."

"I was on a special project, so Ms. Gardner covered the usual news items."

"What special project? Covering all the whorehouses in town?"

"No, sir. I've been covering a trial in progress. Wish I had your sketching skills, Corrine. No photography is allowed in the courthouse. The emotions flitting over the faces of the folks called to testify tell a better story than anything I can write."

"I'd be willing to go with you and sketch them, Kade," Corrine volunteered.

"I don't think Ms. Dean would go for that. You aren't a reporter, so you aren't covered under our insurance policy."

"Well, think about it. Discuss it with your boss. I'd be happy to go with you to draw them."

All the time she was talking to Kade, she was sketching his father. He hoped she wouldn't offer him a copy of her book.

Ben seemed pleased with her efforts when she sprayed the sketch with fixative that Abby had also located, and turned it around for him to see what she'd rendered.

"You're quite talented, Mrs. Watkins," Ben said.

"Hey, Dad," Andy said, "We have enough big people to get up a softball game outside. I know Mom has to stay in to mind the meal, and the twins are too small to play, so we'd have three on each side. One to catch, one to pitch, and someone to cover the base."

"The twins could cover the outfield," Kade said. "It's not nice to leave them out of the game."

Andy nodded his agreement to include the twins.

"Okay, fetch the bat and ball. How are we going to divide the teams up?"

"Grandma Watkins, Alli and you can be on one side. I'll take Grandpa Watkins and Grandpa Blackburn," Andy said.

"You're giving me two females in the hopes they don't know much about softball?" Kade asked.

"I'm taking the oldsters, so I still think it's fair, Dad."

Kade was so amused by Andy's comments, he went out to the yard to lay out a flat rock for the single base. He had hardly left the porch step when the alarm sounded with a high-pitched shriek."

"Oops," he said, hurrying back inside to call the deputies.

"Sorry," he told them. "We were getting up a softball game and I forgot to call."

"I'll be sending someone out to check on you."

"You don't need to do that. I'm still at the ranch, only I'm giving you notice I'll be outside playing softball until about 1 p.m."

"Don't forget again, Blackburn, or I'll be forced to haul you in."

"I won't forget."

"What the hell was that? Some sort of an alarm?" Owen asked.

"That's exactly what it is," Kade replied, rejoining the teams.

"You're wearing one of those tracking bracelets?" Watkins asked again.

"Yes. Let's play some ball. If we don't get started, we won't get any innings in before we eat," Kade said, hoping to dissuade further questions about the anklet he wore.

They played until 1:15. Abby said for them to come in and wash up for dinner, so they put away the bat and ball. Kade quickly stripped off the twins and gave them a short bath, before putting on clean tees and shorts, as Kory and Kathy had found a damp spot out in the infield to roll around in.

He allowed his father and Owen to occupy the seats on the long axis of the table, and went into the kitchen to help Abby since Corrine was useless in the area of food preparation.

"Kade, you're the head of this household," she said quietly. "You should sit in your regular seat at the head of the table."

"It's not worth stirring up trouble over the seating arrangements. I want you to sit beside me, so you can help me keep a cool head."

"My father made a comment about the alarm?"

"Yes, and I'm sure he has more questions about it. I'll try to contain my temper, give him the bare facts in a toneless voice. Keep your hand on my thigh to remind me to keep a tight rein on my anger.

Sure enough, as soon as Owen filled his plate, he set on Kade, asking question after question.

"Mr. Watkins, if I felt you were mounting this inquisition out of concern for my son's welfare, I'd allow it to continue. Since I ascertain no concern for my son in your questions, may I politely suggest you just eat?"

Kade shot his father an appreciative look and followed it with a grin. Owen persisted with his questions, until Kade finally got up and went to the kitchen. Abby followed on his heels.

"It's not like you to retreat in the face of the enemy," she said. "You march right in and take your seat again. K-dens, let, rye," she reeled off, trying to make a joke of his retreat.

He stood there, shaking his head for another minute. "Don't let him get your goat, Kade. Let! Rye! Let! Rye!

Finally he smiled and lifted his left leg. "Things are so out of control in the dining room, it's probably better if you called, 'K-dens, Rye! Let! There's no way I can keep in step while your father bombards me with his questions."

"Tell him the truth, Kade. It's not your fault you shot the guy and have to wear the anklet."

"Yeah, maybe you're right."

Kade returned to his seat at the table. "Put down your fork, Owen and listen up."

Kade related the whole story in a subdued voice for the whole table's edification. "Now you all know why I'm wearing the anklet, so I hope we can just consume this dinner without more questions."

He glanced at his father and got a nod of approval. He glanced at Owen and realized Watkins had a lot more comments and questions. Even Corrine was frowning.

"You were shot? Where?" Corrine asked.

"Upper left thigh, ma'am," Kade said, keeping his answers Army polite and totally dispassionate.

"That's why the ditz, Diana, had all those articles in the paper? How long were you laid up?" Owen asked.

"Best part of a week, sir."

"The ditz let you cover the trial so you wouldn't have to walk all over town. Why would she do that unless you had more than a passing interest in her?"

"I have no interest in her at all, sir. She just has a kindness to her and realized it would be hard for me to sprint from one scene to another, so she let me cover the trial."

"What's the trial about?"

"It's a murder trial, sir."

"Doesn't it make you nervous to cover that kind of trial? The police have yet to decide if the man you shot doesn't warrant a murder charge against you, too."

"No, they haven't decided my fate yet. Since he shot me first, I hope they decide it was self-defense."

His children looked more and more alarmed. He finally made a joke, telling them, "I think Grandpa Owen went into the wrong business. He sounds more like a prosecuting attorney than a cattleman. Why don't you guys fetch the Father's Day gifts for everyone? Andy, Alli, carry the breakable stuff and let the twins bring down the other gifts."

They came back with all the presents, and piled them up in front of the three men. Kade's gift pile reached higher than the other two Dad's piles. "Open my and Kathy's gift first, Daddy," Kory said.

"I think it would be better to let our older fathers go first," he told them.

Owen ripped into his gifts, saying he needed the suspenders in the worst way. He was less enthusiastic about the camera.

"What do I need with a camera? I don't work for your filthy newspaper. This gift smells like something you'd get me, Kade. Take it back, I don't want it."

"Fine, Dad. It was *my* gift to you, not Kade's, but if you don't want it, I'll return it an get my money back."

"Oh, okay, Abby. If it was your gift, I'll be pleased to keep it."

Grandpa Blackburn went next. He appeared to love both his gifts. "I just hope this little drill or the camera doesn't get stolen from my luggage on the plane. I want to take pictures of all of you, so if you have gravy on your face, please wash it off. I want to see nothing but my angels—my child, his wife and my grandchildren—smiling out of the pictures I plan to take of you."

"Your turn, Daddy," Kathy said.

He slowly opened his gifts. "Wow! You twins got me a new dictionary and a thesaurus, too. They'll come in very handy on my desk at the paper. My old ones are in tatters."

The next gift was long and slim and flat. He tore the paper off, and closed his eyes against the sudden tears he felt threatening. Andy and Alli had given him a laptop computer. "Mom kicked in a bit for that one, too, Dad," Andy said.

"Why? I'm not her father," he teased. "You guys are the best of the best-—three very useful gifts. I love you all so much. This is the best Father's Day ever."

Kory and Kathy clambered onto his lap. Kory asked, "When is Children's Day, Daddy?"

Laughing, Kade hugged them hard, and said, "I think every day is Children's Day."

"You don't give us presents every day, so how can that be true?" Kory asked.

"Maybe not presents wrapped up like presents, but I give you other kinds of gifts."

"Like what, Daddy?" Kathy chimed in.

"Don't I hunt grubs with you? Don't I read books to you? Don't I give a bath and a goodnight kiss to you both? Didn't I teach you how to get worms to come out of their holes? Don't I give you my love every day? Not all gifts come wrapped in paper. Some are gifts I give you from my heart."

"Who's ready for pie?" Abby asked.

A chorus of voices went up around the table. While Abby was in the kitchen slicing up the pie, Owen said, "Maybe if you had a better job, you'd be able to shower some of those real presents on your children. Love and kisses don't really constitute gifts. They don't have any commercial value. If you doubt me, try kissing the woman at the checkout counter at Safeway in lieu of giving her a check."

Owen continued. "If you think love and kisses are a good substitute for presents—well, I always thought you were a parsimonious bastard. You've just proved my thinking correct."

Ben spoke up, "Owen, I've sat here listening to you tear my son down with every statement you've uttered. My son is a reasonable, responsible, upstanding member of society. I wish I could say the same about you. If you think commercial presents count more than his heartfelt gifts, I might remind you that toys are often forgotten, broken or lost, but the time Kade spends with his children will warm their hearts well into their later years—surely until they reach old age and die.

"I understand from my son, that you and your wife were far too busy to pay the kind of attention to Abby that Kade devotes to his children. I'm glad she married my son, as I think she appreciates the fact that Kade is never too busy to show her how much he loves her, too."

***"You're just as mean a bastard as Kade is!*** Owen shouted.

"Kade, this is your home and were I you, I'd be inclined to throw this ingrate out of it," Ben said, in the softest voice.

***"We haven't even had dessert yet,"*** Owen screamed.

"I won't be serving you any, either, Dad. Get up and leave this house right now. Grandpa Blackburn is right. You've done nothing but run Kade down since you arrived."

"How can you agree with *his* father? I'm **your** father!"

"Because he's nailed the truth of the matter, Dad. You, nor Mom, ever had the time to teach me things, or read to me. You never took me out for Halloween candy. Not until I met Kade did I learn the fun of that holiday, after he agreed to dress up and go trick-and-treating with me."

"Abby, it's okay. Let's not end the day on an angry note. Dish up pie to everyone," Kade said.

"It's not okay, Kade. My parents have done nothing but sew discord in our marriage. I'm not going to tolerate any more of that. From this point on, we're going to be a very narrow nuclear family—you, me, our four children, as well as your father if he'd like to be included."

"I definitely want to be included," Ben said.

"You're the one, Kade, who gives and gives to all of us. Dad Blackburn is right. The love you share with all of us, it warms our hearts and strengthens our minds and will last longer than any commercial gift ever will.

"Get up, Dad, and make tracks for Camp Verde. You're not welcome here anymore."

"Fine, Abby. Don't expect to inherit anything when we die, if that's how you feel. C'mon, Corrine, let's go. We'll stop for dessert on the way home. It'll be far tastier than anything we might eat here."

Both of them left.

"I have to apologize for what just occurred. I didn't mean for things to get so far out of hand," Kade said.

"Dad," Andy spoke up. "I think it would be best to do that nuclear-family thing, like Mom suggested. It makes me angry as hell—uh . . . heck . . . when he starts in on you. None of us need to listen to his hateful comments about you. We all love you and Mom is right. You might not have the wherewithal to give us expensive gifts, but you have given us love and understanding. You taught us all kinds of things. You've let us know we're important and smart and you made us respectful. Your gifts *will* last us a lifetime, Dad."

Kade finally couldn't control the tears that flowed over his cheeks.

"Daddy, are you crying?"

"I am, Kory. But they're happy tears, because I'm glad you love me like you do. All of your love has touched my heart so much, I couldn't stop my tears from flowing."

# *Chapter Sixteen*

"How did you ever survive this long under Owen's unrelenting criticisms, Kade?" Ben asked, during breakfast on Monday morning at 6 a.m.

"I just tend to ignore him."

"He's a hard man to ignore."

Kade smiled, "Yes, sir, he is—or maybe I've developed such a tough hide that his jabs no longer puncture it."

"Corrine is one hell of a talented artist."

"Yes, that's true. She is."

"She did a portrait of you, too."

"Yes, in the nude."

"What?"

"I said she painted me in the nude. Included me in the book she wrote about how all the nudes over the centuries were female nudes. She wanted to counterbalance that trend, so she painted many males in their birthday suits, me included."

"Do you have a copy of her book?"

"I think there might be one up in our bedroom. Didn't want it lying about for the kids to find."

"Would you let me see it?"

Kade shrugged. "Why would you want to see it?"

"When she suggested you bring me to her studio, do you think she wanted to paint me that way?"

"Maybe. She also likes to have sex with men she paints. Since you look like me, maybe she wanted to invite you to have some of that sex with her."

"You had sex with your mother-in-law?"

Kade nodded.

"Why?"

"Owen, due to a roping accident, can't perform in bed anymore. He tends to look the other way when she finds her pleasures with other men. When I mustered out of the Army and got fired by the editor of the Payson paper, I hired on at the Watkins' ranch. Corrine required my services to transport her to a show in Phoenix where she was displaying her paintings. She wanted to draw me again in the altogether. One thing led to another, and we ended up having sex. I wasn't married to Abby at the time, and Corrine had threatened me with the loss of my job if I didn't accommodate her desires."

"Oh, what a wicked web we weave when first we . . ."

". . . endeavor to deceive," Kade filled in, finishing the quote. "I've had only one instance of sex with Corrine after I married Abby. Abby ticked me off royally one evening, so I sauntered up to the art studio and Corrine was painting. That time I again posed for her and it's the painting she included in her book. Afterward . . . we had sex, as I was mad at Abby and Corrine was available."

"I'd really like to see the book, son."

"I'll see if I can locate it. We'll need to leave about noon to make your flight."

"It's early yet. You really don't want to show me the book, do you?"

"I'm not keen on tainting your recent acceptance of me, Dad. I do suppose you'll weigh the picture against my current commitment to my wife and family. I just hope you don't revert to your former opinion of me after you lay eyes on what Corrine painted."

"How will I know until I see what she painted?"

"Okay. Might take me some time to find where Abby hid the book."

"Abby saw it?"

"Of course. I don't keep those kinds of secrets from her."

"Did you tell her you'd had sex with Corrine that night?"

"I told her much later. I might be honest to a large extent, but I'm not stupid. If I'd told her I had sex with Corrine after the battle I'd had with Abby, I doubt I'd still be married to my wife."

"Have you cheated on Abby more than once?"

"Yes, one other time. Not since that time, though. I'll fetch the book if you still want to see it."

"I do."

Kade came back a half-hour later with the book in hand. "Bookmark is in the right place," he said, handing the book over to Ben. "I'm going to call in and feed the critters. Don't leave the book lying around for any of the kids to find it."

"I won't."


Kade was feeding the goats when his father came outside and approached the barn.

"She did you justice," Ben said, filling a scoop with oats for the horses. "Are you still in that good of shape?"

"Yes, mostly. I keep up with the Army regimen of exercises, and I try to get in a mile or two of running on the weekends."

"No wonder Corrine wanted to paint you like that. I'd love to have your six-pack abs, not to mention your tight ass."

"And my . . ?"

"Yes, that's impressive, too. It's drawn to scale the footnotes said. True?"

"Yep. She took extensive measurements to be sure she'd captured it correctly in scale. That was one of the reasons I succumbed to having sex with her. It's hard to let a woman take those kind of measurements without becoming turned on."

"Son, you've certainly had an interesting life. Done some things completely beyond the pale."

"So you aren't totally disgusted with me for posing like that?"

"No. I wish there were more time I could spend here. I'd like to take Corrine up on her offer to come to her studio. Maybe she'd paint me like that and measure me, too. I'd like a chance to have sex with someone like her."

Kade burst out laughing. "Dad, if you want her to paint you in the buff, we could change your flight home."

"I'm seriously considering that. Would you be willing to put me up for a few more days?"

"Sure. I'd even show you where to turn into the Watkins' ranch, since I'm not going to be welcome at their door. You'd need to make your own arrangements to pose for Corrine."

"I think I could manage that. Let's call the airline when we go back inside and see if I can go home on Wednesday or Thursday, instead."

At their 11 p.m. tea, Abby said, "What changed his mind about staying?"

"After he looked at Corrine's book, he decided he'd like to pose for her, too."

"Like you did?"

"I get the feeling that's his intention."

"Oh, Kade, it'll be like sending a babe into the woods. You know how she is. Anyone is fair game."

"I think Dad is counting on just such an offer. If he has sex with her, we may have a permanent guest on our hands."

"Surely not. Can he still get it up?"

"I have no idea, and I'm not going to ask him, either. I'm just going to drive him over to the ranch and let him make his own arrangements."

"If Dad sees you anywhere near, he'll call the police. Might do that to your father, too."

"I don't think he'll call them on Dad. He's just mad at me, not him. Corrine has your father wrapped around her finger. If she insists she wants to paint my father, he'll let her."

"Is this a case like son, like father, not the reverse?"

"He's an adult in full control of his faculties, so I'm not going to insert myself into this desire of his to have her paint him."

"I don't think he has any idea what Mom's like."

"He's about to find out. He called her already. The session is scheduled for Tuesday at two."

"Make sure he has some protection with him. Doubt Dad would be willing to raise a child of your father's. He'd harbor the same resentments against Ben's child as he harbors against you."

"Okay, I'll be sure he has protection."

"Kade this is like a really bad nightmare. Can't you talk him out of going through with it?"

189

"Relax, Abby. I'm sure he knows what he's getting into."

"We'd better go to bed if you have to have all your chores done before delivering him into Mom's evil clutches."

"I have to work tomorrow and Tuesday. I think you'll need to deliver him into her clutches."

"No, Kade, I'm not going to get involved in such a harebrained scheme."

"Guess I'll need to take Tuesday off, then."

"You find this amusing, don't you?"

"In a way, yes. He's apparently been lonely since Mom died. Missing the love act, too, if I understand his enthusiasm to pose for Corrine. Since I enjoy engaging in the same act with you, I don't feel it's my right to deny him an equal opportunity. Let's hit the sack, wife."

On Tuesday, Kade went in to work very early, leaving a note for the older children to feed that morning. He told Ms. Dean he was leaving at noon, because he had an appointment at two and he'd be taking the rest of the day off.

"You aren't still suffering after effects from your wound, are you?"

"No, ma'am. I'm fine. It's not a doctor's appointment."

Since he'd covered most of the list of items she'd asked him to write up, she granted him permission to leave at one.

He drove to the ranch and found his father seated on the porch swing. Ben sprinted to Kade's truck. "I thought you weren't coming. Abby has been giving me unhappy looks all morning. I suspected she'd talked you out of taking me to Camp Verde."

"She tried hard to convince me not to transport you there," Kade agreed. "Hey, Dad, you need to be safe. Here are a couple of condoms. Corrine isn't often discriminating about whom she sleeps with, so use these if the opportunity occurs. You don't need a case of the clap to contend with."

Ben tucked both packets in his wallet, making Kade smile. *He's just like a teenager out on his first hot date. Don't think Corrine will have to talk very fast or hard to convince Dad to do the deed with her.*

"Dad, here's an extra cell phone. When you want me to pick you up again, walk down to the end of the lane and call me."

"Where will you be? Home? It's a long drive from home."

"I brought a book. I'll veg out at McDonald's. Eat something and read for a bit. It will take me only a few minutes to drive over to pick you up."

"Kade, thank you."

"Sure, Dad. Don't do anything you wouldn't want me to do," he said with a grin. "Wasn't that your and Mom's usual message when I started dating?"

"I might remind you I'm a long way over 15, Kade. What if I want to spend the night?"

"McDonald's on I-17 is open 24 hours. If you spend the night, I'll still be there."

Ben got out of the truck, and gave Kade two thumbs up. It reminded him of the signal he used to give Abby a hug in the early days. Kade turned around and headed for Mickey D's.

It was long past eight when his phone rang. "Hello," he said.

"Can you pick me up shortly, Kade?"

"Yes, sir. I'll be there in about ten minutes."

His father was at the end of the lane when Kade got there. He jumped into the truck and his face was wreathed in a huge grin.

"I take it the sketching session went well?"

"Boy, did it! Owen was in Las Vegas at some cattle-penning competition. What is a cattle-penning competition?"

"It's where men on horseback try to cut out a few cattle from the herd and hold them behind an imaginary line. It requires a well-trained horse and an agile rider to pen the cattle."

"First, she sketched me with just my shirt gone. She gave me abs like your abs. Then she asked if I had any qualms about being naked. I told her I didn't feel entirely comfortable being in that mode of undress. She offered to give me a massage if I shucked my pants, so I did.

"I never felt so relaxed in my life. When I got up from her table, she pushed off my boxers and started giving me instructions how she wanted me to pose. It seemed so natural to just do what she said, so I stopped being self-conscious and struck up the pose she wanted."

"Once she'd sketched you nude, she measured you, then?"

"Yes. I almost fainted when she took it in hand. She told me I was almost as well endowed as you. She drew it . . ."

". . . to scale?"

"Yes. By that time I was so stiff . . ."

"She invited you to use your rod on her?"

"Yes. I thought about what you said, and rolled on protection. Sex with her was incredible, Kade. I can better understand why you succumbed to her charms, even though you were in love with her daughter."

"I'm glad you enjoyed the experience, Dad. Is she planning to put out a new book of male nudes? Might help you to have some similar experiences in Pennsylvania if you bought a copy."

It was all Kade could do not to roar with amusement. His father had never in his life been so bubbly or so pleased with himself. "So, all-in-all, you enjoyed the experience?"

"Boy, did I."

Kade did laugh then. "Nothing like a little loving from a sexy woman to improve your outlook on life."

"She talked a lot about you. How you were so good with your equipment. I'm half jealous of your relationship with . . ."

"It's not one of my experiences any more, Dad. You don't need to worry you're cutting me out of action with Corrine. I wouldn't screw her if someone offered me a million bucks. Do you still intend to return to the Keystone State on Thursday, or are you planning to move to Arizona?"

"Kade, I enjoyed myself, but I'm no fool. A constant diet of what she offered would have a bad effect on my ticker. While I liked the sex, I'm not ready to give up my life, yet. She's so demanding . . ."

"I know. Good for you, Dad. When you go home, try to find someone your age who still likes to enjoy an occasional tumble in bed—every month or so.

"How about every week or so?" Ben asked, grinning.

"Whatever you feel your ticker can stand, Dad."

Kade delivered his father to the Phoenix Airport on Thursday. Ms. Dean was beginning to complain about his lack of effort at the paper, so he drove directly to the paper to put in his hours after he'd seen his father off, calling in when he got to work and when he left for home.

He arrived in time for their tea session with Abby. Though he was tired to the bone, he called in and still sat down across from her to answer her questions.

"Did he get off okay," she asked.

"He did. The plane was on time and there was no delay in departure. I went from the airport to my job. Ms. Dean was beginning to grumble about my lack of dedication to the news. I worked from two until ten, to give her a full eight hours."

"Was your father still grinning like an old fool?"

"He was still very upbeat about his sketching experience."

"Did he have . . ?"

"I have no idea, since it was a question I didn't feel I should ask him. But given the fact he couldn't quit smiling, I'd be willing to bet something happened of that nature."

"I know you're lying, Kade. You did ask him and you **know** he had sex with Mom."

"What makes you think I'm lying?"

"You get that little frown in your forehead when you lie to me. You're currently wearing it, so I know you're lying."

"Am I going to have to go in for Botox inoculations—smooth out that little frown? Okay, I do know he enjoyed sex with Corrine. Enjoyed it a lot. When she took his cock in hand to measure it, so she could draw it to scale, I don't think even Viagra could have produced such stiffness."

"Please, spare me the graphics, Kade."

"I didn't want to lie about what happened."

"Let's go to bed."

"I'm pretty stiff, too. How about it?" he asked, giving her a grin.

"I don't think so. I don't want you comparing me to my mother. She wants it all the time with anyone she can talk into sex. I'd rather not be a bump off the same log. I think we should limit our sexual activities to twice a week."

"I'd never compare you to your mother."

"Maybe not, but right at the minute, I am comparing you to your father. You'll be 85 and still wanting to hump me every night of the week."

"That's a problem, how? If we are still in love and in good health by that age, why should we forego our pleasures."

"There's something indecent about being old and wrinkled and still wanting sex."

"You're saying my father shouldn't still be interested in such matters?"

"Yes! It's not . . ."

"Forget I asked, Abby. Let me know when you want sex with me, as I won't be asking you for any, ever again."

"Now you're mad?"

"Only dogs, coyotes and skunks get mad."

"But you are angry?"

"No."

"Your forehead is wrinkling up again."

He got up and rinsed out their cups. Went up to their bedroom and undressed, leaving on his boxers and tee shirt. Crawled into bed and turned his back on her side of the bed.

"Kade, don't be like that. I'm sorry."

"Goodnight, wife," he said, refusing to turn over and face her.

Three weeks went by with no bedtime sex between them. Kade got up and fed in the early morning then showered and left for work, so there were no morning sessions of sex, either. He came home late, fed the animals, called in and ate dinner. After dinner, he read steadily until 11 p.m. then consumed his tea without uttering a word. He got up and went to bed, not offering to hug or kiss her.

She spoke in the darkness to him. "Kade, every other time when we had words, you ended up having sex with someone other than me.

This time, too? Is that why you're content to go so long without having relations with me?"

"You know better than that." His voice was as cold as a winter wind. "If you want to cast me in my father's image and you're put off by his behavior in regards to sex, then I'm not willing to force myself on you. The comparisons you were making . . . I think they're grossly unfair. I'm not my father."

"You both seem to have a need for sex, constantly."

"I doubt Dad has had any of that since Mom died. I've refrained from indulging in it for three weeks now. How does that translate into either Dad or me needing sex constantly? Why, exactly, do you care what Dad does? He's not married to you."

"You know how small towns are, Kade. They live on gossip. I'm sure everyone in Camp Verde is buzzing over that old man having sex with my mother."

"Again, Abby, what does that have to do with us?"

"You had a 4.0 GPA, so don't act like you're stupid, Kade. I know you're not. I'd rather not have people think I'd married . . ."

He sat up in bed and shook his head and took up where she left off. "Oh, now I get it. It's your eternal need to have everyone in existence approve of you."

"Yes, I like people to think well of me. You don't seem to care what they think of you or your father."

"You're right, I don't care. I only care what the members of this family think about me."

"Right now . . ."

"Yeah, I know, you're not overwhelmed with praise for me right at the moment. Go to sleep, Abby. You might be a lady of leisure, but I have to work tomorrow."

"That's so unfair, Kade."

"Fair or unfair, I still need to be on the job in the morning. If you're so upset with me, maybe the goats can give you the type of love you seem to want. Their fathers are 'old goats' in the truest sense of the words. Nobody will be gossiping about how the goats' fathers acted, or transferring their condemnations of the old goats to you."

He got home late the next evening, well past eight. Alli met him in the barn. "Dad, did you have another fight with Mom?"

"We had a bit of a disagreement, yes."

"I always know when something is wrong. What did you do to make her sad this time?"

"Is she sad? I thought she was angry."

"Dad! She's been crying all day. Her eyes are red and swollen. She was too upset to read to the twins before their nap. Please, Dad, can you do something so she won't be sad again tomorrow?"

"I'll give it a shot, Dr. Ruth. Go get washed up for dinner."

"We already ate. Mom left a plate in the microwave for you to warm. Said she was going to bed early. If you're almost done feeding, I'll warm your supper."

"Okay, Alli. Please don't concern yourself about your mother or me. Occasionally, every married couple has an argument. Doesn't mean we leave off loving each other. You've had a few fights with Andy and didn't speak to him for a few days. I didn't put my nose into your arguments, and I'd prefer it if you didn't stick your snout into ours."

"Warm your own dinner, Dad!" Alli said, stomping off.

*The older she gets, the more her responses are just like Abby's. Kathy may be the only female in the family who isn't pissed at me tonight.*

He entered the kitchen, washed his hands and sat down to eat his nuked dinner. The house was quiet and he wondered if the twins were already in bed. Usually, they refused to crawl in before he read to them. Finished with his food, he went upstairs and knocked softly on Alli's door, before opening it wide.

"Alli, I'm sorry if I upset you. I know you get concerned when Mom and I fight. I'm glad you exhibit such a sensitive nature . . . maybe when you marry, you'll be so sensitive to your husband's moods, you'll never fight with him."

"Mom isn't sensitive to your moods? That's why you seem to fight so often?"

"Mom and I have a long history. She sometimes brings up things that should have been long ago forgotten. When she mentions those items, right away, I've got a finger on my hair trigger. Only it's my tongue that delivers the bullets, not a gun. I often say things that should remain unspoken. Things, I know will hurt her.

"Often, you're more of an adult than I can claim to be. You're much slower to take offense than I am. Much less inclined to use words to wound people than I am. Maybe it's true, you can't teach and old dog new tricks, but if you keep upbraiding me for my behavior to your mom, I may eventually learn a new trick or two. Can I have a hug from you?"

"Yes," she said, her eyes threatening to overflow. "I love you, Dad," she said wrapping her arms around his waist.

From Alli's room, he went to see about the twins. They were already sound asleep. He checked on Andy, too, who was hunched over his science book. "Night, son," he said.

"Night, Dad."

Abby was huddled in the corner of their bed. Kade sat down next to her and tried to lift her face so he could kiss her. She resisted, not wanting him to see how upset she was.

"It's only a bit after nine, but I'm going to make some tea. I think I may need more time than from 11 p.m. to midnight to right what lies between us, currently. Are you willing to come down for a long discussion?"

"What's the use of talking, Kade? We have the same problems again and again. Maybe Dad was right. I should have divorced you long ago."

"You can't mean that," he said. "I'm going to make tea. I'll leave it up to you to join me or not."

Twenty minutes passed before she came to the kitchen. He poured hot water into her cup containing the chamomile tea bag. Sat down across from her and took her small hand in his—his left hand—the one with the missing fingers.

"How have we arrived at this point?" he asked. "How did we come to the point, where you're willing to say you should have divorced me? No matter how seriously we argue, I've never once entertained that thought."

"Every time we fight, you manage to bring up my need for the approval of others. I know it's a glaring fault in me, but do you have to allude to it each and every time we argue?"

"No, I agree it's unkind to keep reminding you of your need for approval."

"Then why do you do it?"

"My first inclination—when you tell me something that hurts me—is to hurt you in return. I know that's not a very adult reaction, and I'm not sure why that need surfaces in me as often as it does. I just told Alli—who's quite concerned about both of us—that my first inclination is to use words like bullets when you touch some of those hot buttons inside me."

"What hot buttons, Kade? If you'd tell me what they are, I might be able to avoid pushing them."

"When you allude to how much I like to have sex, it dredges up all those times I was willing to have that with other than you. Makes me feel guilty all over again, so that's the biggest button you push.

"Dad just got done, a week ago, telling me he was proud of me—a validation I thought I'd never hear from him. Then you essentially mock him for wanting to be sketched . . . for having sex with Corrine . . . let me know he's not someone I should admire because he enjoyed his session with your mother. That hit me on two levels. It negated my feeling that his validation of me counted, and it again reminded me of my relationship with Corrine.

"I have a few other buttons, too. Alan White is one of them. I realize he's out of the picture since we moved to Chino Valley, but he remains in the wings of my mind as someone who'd be only too glad to take up with you again if we did divorce.

"Your parents are another couple of buttons. Outside of marrying you, I can't think of anything so horrible I ever did to your father that he should have such a negative opinion of me. As to your mother—I don't think I need to explain that one to you."

He smiled across the table at her then averted his eyes. "I once more apologize for my behavior these last few weeks. I still love you, and I hope you didn't mean what you said about divorce."

"Kade, I'm sorry, too. I didn't mean to invalidate your father's new acceptance of you. I knew how much his praise of you as an upstanding family man mattered to you. Can you forgive me for tainting that validation in your mind?"

"Of course I can. How often have you overlooked my indiscretions in the past? You've forgiven me so often, how could I possibly withhold my forgiveness for you from you? Just tell me you didn't really mean what you said about divorce, and my personal ship will right itself in an instant."

"I'm not going to divorce you, Kade. Yes, we've both made some grievous mistakes along the way, but underneath the heated words, I know you love me like I love you. I've known the depth of your love for me since that first breakfast you ate at the ranch table in Camp Verde. You picked up on my loneliness that first day and endeavored to ameliorate it. When things got rough you told me you would have quit, but you couldn't bear to abandon me. That's when I knew your love would be there for a lifetime."

"It has been," he confirmed.

"Kade, I've missed you. Can we kiss and make up. Maybe have a little . . ."

"I've missed you, too. Sure. Nothing I'd love more than to snuggle with you again."

"You don't want to have sex?"

"I don't want you thinking I initiated this discussion because I've missed sex with you. I have missed it, but I'm willing to go without another week or two, to convince you that wasn't my motive in asking you down here to settle our differences."

"You don't need to deprive yourself. I never thought sex was your motive for this discussion. We both needed to clear the air, and now that we have, I'll expect you shower me with and do what we've both been missing."

He came around the table and picked her up. Sat in her chair and held her on his lap. "Abby . . ." he tried to say, but she stilled his words with her kiss. "Don't, Kade. Words are what often get us into an argument. Just love me without words."

"I'll be up as soon as I wash the cups and lock up."

# *Chapter Seventeen*

At breakfast, Abby was all smiles. Kade had on his 'cat-with-a-bowl-of-cream' face. Relief was the emotion that graced Alli's face. "Dad . . ?" she started to say.

He grinned and shook his head up and down, confirming that their fight was over.

Alli heaved a sigh of relief. Before long, the twins were banging their spoons on the table, demanding breakfast. Kade got up to give Abby a hand at the stove. He took the spatula from her hand to turn the eggs in the frying pan, while she fried sausage links in another pan. He gave her a pinch on the butt and she leaned toward him to kiss his ear.

"It's good you and Mom . . ." Alli started to say.

"Hey, Dr. Ruth," he said, again cutting her off. "Please pour the twins' cups full of milk and put some Cheerios on their trays. Might give them something to do beside create that awful din this morning. I didn't get much sleep last night, so I'd appreciate a bit of quiet today," he said, giving Abby a wink.

"Are you blaming me for your short hours of sleep?" she whispered.

"Oh, no, ma'am. I'll never blame you for my insomnia, given the reason I enjoyed my wakefulness so much. May have to come home from the office for a nap about three, though. Are you tired, too? Care to join me for a nap?"

She frowned at the thought. "More? You want more?" she asked.

*Yeah, Abby, you have me pegged correctly. I'm one horny old goat, always wanting sex. But only you will do for that activity anymore. Last night was . . . nothing short of incredible. Maybe, if truth be told, I pick those fights with you on purpose, because the make-up sex is always so . . . intense. I may have to tell you that fact tonight at 11 p.m. Nah! Why spoil a good thing?*

Coming out of her office and closing the door behind her, Dean said, "You seem in better spirits, this morning, Mr. Blackburn."

"Yes, ma'am. I'm sitting on the top of the world today, Ms. Dean."

"There's a detective in my office. He wants to talk to both of us about Fred Rossman's death."

**"Shit!"** he cursed "Why can't at least one day of the year remain uncluttered with problems?"

"Go collect a cup of coffee and join us. Maybe the hot coffee will remind you to keep a civil tongue in your head."

"Sorry, Ms. Dean. I know you don't like us to cuss in your hearing."

Kade slid into a chair in Dean's office and sipped at his coffee, not saying a word until he saw the direction the detective wanted to take.

"Ms. Dean," Palmer said, "you fired Rossman the same morning as the incident occurred at the Blackburn ranch?"

"Yes, that's true. He'd expressed his distaste for my best reporter several times. There was some serious antagonism between Fred and Kade."

"More on Fred's part, or more on Kade's?"

"Definitely more on Fred's part. Kade had already established his credentials here as a good reporter. Fred seemed to harbor some ill will toward Kade from his college classes. When he learned I thought Kade was a top-notch reporter, I think his hatred of Mr. Blackburn increased."

"Blackburn, why did Rossman resent you from his college classes?"

"We both went to the same university. I had to keep up my grades so the Army would continue my stipend. I studied hard because I was afraid of losing that monthly payment. I had a wife and small son to provide for. I studied long into the nights most nights, or got up early to hit the books. I graduated with a 4.0 grade-point average.

"I had earned the respect of my professors, because they knew I had another job and a family to interact with, in addition to my studies. I guess they still tout my study habits to incoming journalism students.

Fred seemed to resent the professors throwing up my GPA in their faces."

"What form did Rossman's resentment take?"

"He challenged Kade to a fight out behind the printing shop," Dean said. "He got the worst of it."

Palmer pulled some papers out of his briefcase. "I have the police reports from that day, when Rossman called the police to say Blackburn tried to kill him. Did you try to kill him that afternoon?"

Kade shrugged. "You have to understand something, Palmer. I was twice deployed to the Middle East during our wars in Iraq and Afghanistan. I'm very well trained in hand-to-hand combat. If I'd wanted to kill Fred that afternoon, I would have simply broken his neck. I didn't do that. I only maintained my chokehold until he passed out. I picked him out of the mud puddle and set him in his chair in his cubicle, believing that might be the end of his challenges to me."

"You stated he followed you home that same evening?"

"No, it was the next evening. If you have the police reports, it's all in there."

"I'd like to hear it in your words from the start."

"Why? You hope to trip me up if anything I tell you now deviates from my previous version?"

"That wasn't my intention."

Kade smiled like he didn't believe Palmer. "Okay, sir, get out your reports. Ms. Dean, lend the detective a red pen so if he can find any inconsistencies, he can mark them in red."

Dean rooted in her desk and found a red pen. Kade started his story for the fifth time.

"I didn't know what kind of car Fred drove, as I arrived most mornings before he did. When I took off that afternoon, I headed for our ranch in Chino Valley. There was some traffic, but I wasn't in a tearing hurry. On a straight stretch of the road, in my rearview mirror I see this car pass several cars behind me. There were a few ahead of me, too, so if the guy was in that much of a rush, I wondered why he didn't go around all of us, as there was no oncoming traffic.

"Instead he dives into line right behind me and proceeds to dog my back bumper until I turn into the driveway to my ranch. He goes on by, but, like often happened in a war zone, I had this hackles-up feeling that something wasn't right. I pulled my rifle from the rack across the back window due to that feeling.

"I just opened my door to go feed the goats and horses, when the same car turned into my drive. Fred had his side window down."

"Wait, just a minute," Palmer said. "You recognized him at the time he pulled into the driveway?"

"Not until he rolled up closer, about 30 yards behind my truck. By that time he had his head and his gun hand out the window. He launched several shots. One hit me in the thigh."

"He was left-handed?" Palmer asked.

Dean pulled out Fred's application. "I think you can see he was a leftie on this application. It has that particular slanted writing that left-handed people use."

"You were shot. What happened then?" Palmer asked.

"My Army training kicked in. I raised the rifle, sighted him in and squeezed off a round."

"And killed him with one shot?"

"Yes, sir. In a war zone you don't often get a second chance, so you'd better make the first one count."

"You told the police you were afraid he'd do harm to your family. If you thought he was dead, how could that happen?"

"I was bleeding a lot. I could feel blood running down my leg. If I'd just tried to wound him, there was no guarantee I wouldn't pass out from lack of blood. That would leave Fred free to kill me, and maybe the members of my family, too."

"You stated you had no remorse for ending his life."

"I didn't, for the above-stated reason. I still don't have remorse. He shot me first."

"The first time I shot a man, I was filled with remorse," Palmer said.

"It wasn't the first time I'd killed a man. Maybe that's the difference," Kade said.

"I don't think it gets any easier, no matter how many times it happens."

"It's obvious you've never served in a war zone, sir. About the second or third time you see women and children blown apart by a market-place bomb, you lose all regard for the bastards who set those bombs off. You want to know how hard those scenes made me? I'll give you an example:

"We used to set up command posts on the roads to check vehicles and men going to the area of the markets. If we found someone wearing a vest full of explosives, we confiscated the vest so we could blow it up out in the desert, not in the market. In addition, we took the vest wearer out into the desert, too. We staked him out on the ground and cut off his family jewels—both of them—without the benefit of anesthesia. We then took him to a triage center, so he could spread the word.

"Once the word got out about our punishment for toting bombs into markets, there were a lot fewer men willing to tote those bombs."

Palmer sat shaking his head. "I think I'd hate to cross a man like you, Blackburn."

"If you don't have mayhem in mind, you'd have nothing to fear from me, sir. Just don't mess with me or mine, and I'd have no reason to take you down. When you come into my drive with your gun blazing, I'm not going to feel any remorse about killing you."

"How are the judicial wheels grinding on Kade's case?" Dean asked. "Is he going to be indicted? I would sure hate to lose my best reporter, for what's clearly a case of self-defense."

"Sounds like that kind of a case to me, too. But after the Trayvon Martin shooting in Florida, police are now unwilling to make hasty decisions in those 'stand-your-ground' cases. That's likely why they're taking so long to decide whether to indict you or not."

"If I promised to not leave the country or the state or the county, could you get them to remove this anklet? I spend half my time phoning in my location. The other night, I was tired, and forgot to call in that I was home. I was having sex with my wife, when the phone rang. It was the deputy wanting to know where I was. Sure spoiled a very intimate moment."

Both Dean and Palmer laughed at his confession.

"I didn't think it was that funny at the time," Kade said.

"I'll see what I can do, Blackburn. I'd hate for you to be angry enough you'd consider removing my family jewels. I think that's all the questions I have for the moment."

"Kade," Dean said, once Palmer left, "you really castrated men without anesthesia?"

"We did. They had no concern how much pain and suffering they caused women or children who had come to shop, so we didn't care a fig how they suffered either."

"You must have a very hard core inside, Kade. I can't imagine any man doing that to another man."

"You never had the urge to kill a husband who beat his wife or smashed his child's head against a wall when you were a reporter?"

"I was content to let the law handle those kinds of punishment."

"You'd rather I'd just wounded Fred? Is that what you're saying?"

"It's best to preserve life whenever possible. Don't you agree?"

"Not always, Ms. Dean. I need to get back to work."

"Do you think you'd ever be incited to that level of rage again? Take justice into your own hands if you came across someone who'd battered a wife or child?"

"I'm sure I'd be tempted, but I'm no longer in the Army. I'm a civilian now, so unless someone is threatening me, or my family, I try to control the rages I feel in those instances. As a civilian, I no longer enjoy the Army's backing for the killing that occurs in a war zone."

"You're saying the Army condones killing?"

"Do you realize what you just said?" Kade asked, beginning to laugh. "I do believe the Army does condone killing. Isn't that why we deployed troops to the Middle East—to kill al Qaeda, or rogue Iraqis and Afghanistan militia?"

"I never thought about. . ."

"Yeah, you and several million other Americans. The troops over there fighting are a hundreds of miles away—in mileage and in your minds as well. You prefer not to concern yourselves about what war does to the young men sent to fight. I have news. It turns all of us into trained, hardened, killing machines. Those deployments tend to remove the last vestiges of our consciences—at least about killing other humans.

"You're over here with your own concerns—your shopping lists, your car repairs, and your businesses. Of course you think the Army is a noble establishment. Couldn't possibly condone killing human beings. Out of sight is out of mind.

"Well, I was sick for a whole week after my commanding officer shot a woman and her two children when he found a bomb maker in her back shed. That's a truer portrait of all the services. The Air Force drops bombs. Navy shells cities from their destroyers. Army men and Marines do their killing up close and more personally. After a bit, you do become hard. It's either become hard or you go crazy, commit suicide, or develop PTSD. I chose to become hard and I don't feel I need to apologize for taking that route. Now, I really need to cover the items on the list you handed out this morning, ma'am."

"I had no idea what war did to you."

"Are you about to fire me, now that you know?"

"No, I'm not. You're still one of my best reporters."

"Good, I'm still heavily in debt for the ranch. I need this job."

"Carry on Mr. Blackburn."

Kade gave her a smart salute and returned to his cubicle. *None of them have any idea what war does to the men and women who are sent to fight,* he thought. *They keep building all those war memorials. Maybe if we produced some memorials to periods of peace we could get beyond the American need to subdue the world.*

"Where were you, Kade?" Diana asked. "It's not like you to come in so late."

"Mind your own business, Gardner. I'm not required to get your approval of my schedule."

"Ooh. You must have had a fight with your wife, snapping at me like that."

Kade came home late, fed the animals and then called in, saying he was home.

"You look weary, Kade," Abby said. "You didn't come home for your 3 p.m. nap, either."

"I'd advise you to tread lightly, wife. It was a long, bad day."

"What happened?"

"Detective Palmer was waiting in Dean's office when I got to work. Wanted me to apprise him about the incident with Rossman all over again. I suspected he was trying to catch me in a lie by making me tell him everything anew. Once I'd regaled him about the facts once more, he kept asking me if I didn't regret killing Fred. Ms. Dean wanted to know the same thing."

"Why would they ask you that? You were already wounded, so of course you shot back."

"I think they thought I should have wounded Fred—not killed him. Let the law provide the punishment, instead of me taking the law into my own hands. At one point, Ms. Dean said I must have a very hard core inside, to have shot with the intention to kill Fred. For a time, I thought she might fire me. I know she's worried if she sends me out to cover a story where someone has beaten or killed a wife or child, I might be have the same degree of rage. She's concerned I might be tempted to kill someone else."

"I don't believe that for a minute, Kade."

"Why not? Obviously I'm capable of doing that. I did shoot to kill Fred, not just wound him."

"I think you were thinking of the safety of our family when you shot him dead. I'm sure you'd think of us again and refrain from killing someone else, because that would result in a very long separation from all of us."

He nodded, "Maybe you know me better than I thought."

"You've often expressed, since your Texas stint in a cell, how you'd hate to be locked away in one again."

"Wasn't the cell I objected to so much, it was being totally cut off from you and Andy. I hated not being able to talk to you both."

"That's why I'm not worried you'd kill anyone else. I know how much you love the children."

"And you, as well. What can I do to speed up dinner? I need to crash right after we eat. Those detectives pussy-footing around the case all the time wear me to a frazzle."

"Sure it wasn't the previous night's activities?" she asked, giving him a grin.

"Yeah, that, too. I was floating on a sea of happiness when I got to work, then Dean announced Palmer's presence. I immediately felt like my ship was caught in a maelstrom and was sinking fast."

"Set the table and get the twins' hands washed up. By then, I'll be ready to serve dinner."

"Yes, ma'am."

He pitched in and helped with the dishes after they ate. When the last plate landed in the cupboard, he said, "I'm going to take a shower and go to bed. Could you slip into bed quietly, whenever you decide to join me? I'd appreciate if you didn't wake me up."

"I won't, Kade. I can see you're almost asleep on your feet. Thanks for a hand with the dishes."

He felt her come to bed after 11 p.m., but she didn't offer to kiss him or touch him, so he didn't wake up entirely. In the wee hours of the night, he remembered he'd forgotten to join her for their usual tea fest. Even that omission didn't linger long in his tired brain.

He was up at six in the morning. Abby heard him call in to say he was going out to feed the animals. She heard him call again when he returned to the house. He didn't come back upstairs hoping to catch another hour of sleep. When she woke up and went down to make breakfast, she found him sound asleep in his recliner, with both twins asleep in his arms.

The books on the chair-side table attested to the fact Kory and Kathy had been read to after Kade fed. She didn't know how he'd convinced them to snuggle in for a nap, as usually when they woke up, it was a whirlwind of activity until their 2 p.m. naptime arrived.

"Kade," she called softly to him. "You need to take a shower, eat something and get to work on time."

He opened one eye and nodded his agreement. "What time is it?"

"Almost 7:30."

"Hey, kids, your old man has to go to work this morning."

The twins roused up. The first thing they did was to wrap their arms around him to hug him and they planted several kisses on his cheeks as well.

"Hey, now there's the way to start my morning off right," he said, giving each of them a squeeze and a kiss in return.

"Daddy, can you stay home and play with us?" Kory asked. "We haven't made worms come out of their holes in a long time."

"Not today, son, but on Sunday, I sure will save some time for that activity."

"Why do you always have go to work?" Kathy asked.

"You know what the elves in Snow White sing?" he asked her.

"They sing, 'Hi-ho, Hi-ho, it's off to work we go,'" she sang.

"I sing a song just like that. 'I owe, I owe, so it's off to work I go.' I owe the mortgage company a payment every month for this house and the ranch. That's why I have to work."

"I have money in my piggy bank, Daddy," Kory offered. "Stay home and I'll give you my pennies."

"I'm afraid, son, that I owe lots of dollars, not pennies. But thanks for your offer."

"You guys run and get dressed if you want to eat breakfast with your daddy before he goes to work," Abby said.

The twins scampered off and came back toting jeans, underpants and tees for Kade to install on them. He then pushed in their chairs at the table.

Across the table at breakfast, Abby gave him several smiles.

"Why do you keep grinning at me like that?" he asked. "You want me to volunteer to dress you, too? I'm willing to take on that chore, but only in the privacy of our bedroom."

Alli and Andy rolled their eyes. He caught their looks. "Hey, guys, wasn't so long ago I was dressing the both of you, as well, so don't be giving me those looks." More eye rolls ensued.

"Those twins—well, Kade, I don't think I count for much in their lives anymore. They always seek you out, for their stories, for dressing them, for a soft place to lie down when they're tired."

"Don't be giving me that 'you don't count in their lives' bit. When I'm not around, they take full advantage of your availability. When I kiss them goodnight, they let me know all the stuff you did with them during the day. I only have their attention for a few hours. You nourish them in so many ways, all day long."

Breakfast over, he ran up to take a shower. Came down clean and smelling good.

"I half thought you might invite me up to dress you, Kade."

"Right. Like I could get to work at a decent hour if that happened."

"You need to comb your hair."

He pulled a comb out of his back pocket and glanced at himself in the glass-fronted cabinets. "I need a haircut in the worst way, but Louie, the guy I like, is only in on Fridays. That's our busiest news day."

"I used to trim the goats with a pair of clippers. Would you trust me to do your hair up?"

"Yes, provided you didn't have one eye on the soaps while you clipped."

She was waiting in the kitchen when he came home from work. He called in to say he was in the house.

"Sit down, Kade, and let me trim your hair."

He grinned at her, before he eased into the chair she pulled out. "Don't you think the porch would be a better place for this? I'd hate to think about clumps of hair in my dinner tonight."

"Okay, let's go to the barn, then. I'll use my old goat stand."

"You're going to put that restraining loop around my neck?"

"Of course not. Call in that you'll be at the barn."

"I'm very tired of calling in. I'm not going to call them. It's going to take less than 30 minutes to trim me up, so let's just go."

Abby had just started his haircut when the alarm went off with a high-pitched shriek. "Don't mind that noise, just finish the haircut."

She'd just finished his trim when two sheriff's vehicles pulled into his driveway. "Should I fetch my rifle?" he asked. "Do you think they're here to do us harm?"

Two deputies marched into the barn. "Afternoon, deputies," Kade said. "As you can see, I'm still home."

"You aren't, however, in the house. Your neighbors are complaining about the alarm."

"I needed a haircut. My wife offered to give me one. Couldn't you guys set the responder-wire around the perimeter of my ranch, instead of on my doorstep? Then I could feed and clean stalls, or play in the yard with my kids without having to call in constantly."

"You know the rules, Blackburn. You need to call each time you leave the house or the newspaper office. Maybe a day or two in a cell would reinforce that need to call in. Put your arms behind your back, sir."

"Is that really necessary?" Kade asked. "I'd like to shower and remove the hair that fell down my neck."

The bigger deputy pulled Kade to his feet. "I believe my buddy asked you to put your hands behind your back. You can do as he asked, or I'll hit you with my stun gun and if I do that, you won't have a choice about obeying us."

"Kade, do as he says," Abby said.

He slowly slid both hands behind his back and felt the deputy tighten the cuffs on his wrists. The anklet was still emitting shrieks, so the bigger deputy called in that Kade was under arrest. Finally the anklet went silent. By that time, some of their neighbors were standing outside the drive to his property. He was roughly shoved in the back of the deputy's Bronco. Several people tried to ask the driver why they were hauling him off. The driver refused to answer any of their questions.

He spent the night in a cell. In the morning, a new set of deputies hauled him into court, charging him with willful disobedience of the rules regarding his required calls. When Kade came before Judge Nickerson, he found it was the same man who'd given him the cards to hand out when deputies harassed him.

"Mr. Blackburn," the judge said.

"Yes, sir," Kade replied.

"You're charged with not calling in when you left the house last evening. How do you plead?"

"Guilty, sir."

"Care to explain why you failed to call in?"

"My wife offered to give me a haircut in the kitchen, in which case I wouldn't have had to call in. But the thought of stray hair all over the place where we eat didn't sit well with me. Abby suggested she could use her old goat-trimming stanchion in the barn. I was amused. Asked her if she intended to make me kneel on the platform and put my head through the leather restraints, like I was a goat. She buzzed out the door and I followed her, still laughing. Wasn't until the alarm started squawking that I remembered I hadn't called in.

"I continued into the barn, so I just ignored the alarm. She was well into my haircut by that time and finished the job about the same time the deputies arrived. I never got to look in a mirror, so I hope my wife didn't take any divots out of my hair."

"Looks like she did a fine job, Mr. Blackburn," Nickerson said, trying to conceal his smile.

"She does the same fine job in all her endeavors, sir."

"Chief Johnson, I think Blackburn made an honest mistake. What are you suggesting as to . . ?"

"He *frequently* makes the same mistake. At least three or four times I've had to send a squad car out to check on his location. I'd suggest two weeks in our custody. Maybe then, he'd be less likely to make another mistake."

"Do you think that's fair, Mr. Blackburn?"

"Long as I can start my time on Monday. I promised my twins I'd help them hunt up some worms and grubs on Sunday. I'd need to make arrangements with Ms. Dean, my boss at the paper, to cover my beat while I'm locked up, too."

"Chief?"

"*No!* He needs to start his time today."

"You are remanded to their custody today, Mr. Blackburn. You will serve two weeks. After that time, Chief Johnson, you will remove the anklet from Mr. Blackburn's leg. After he serves his two weeks, I don't want him having to call in again."

"You can't do that. How will we be able to track him if we remove the tracking device?"

"I remind you, Johnson, that I can so order, and you will comply, or I'll have **you** remanded for custody for two weeks. Might even make you wear one of those devices, so you'd learn how odious it is to have to call in every minute of the day."

Johnson came forward to install cuffs again. Tightened them to the point of pain. Jerked the cuffs to spin Kade around and marched him out of the courtroom. The cuffs played hob with Kade's formerly broken wrist, but he knew better than to complain.

He was locked in a cell. "Do I get my one phone call?" he asked.

"*No!*" Johnson said. "You can rot in here for two weeks. No phone calls. Only one meal per day, and if you give me a hard time, I guarantee you'll regret it."

Kade shrugged, like he didn't care. He stretched out on the bunk and promptly fell asleep, still wearing the cuffs. His hands were numb when he awoke about four that afternoon.

"Unlock this cell," Judge Nickerson said.

"Yes, sir," the deputy replied, unlocking Kade's cell.

"What are you doing here, sir?" Kade asked.

"Chief Johnson was so angry this morning, I wanted to be sure he hadn't found an excuse to smack you around."

"No, he didn't raise a hand to me, but he left the cuffs on. My hands feel like they're about to fall off."

"Turn around, let me see."

Kade pivoted around. His hands were well swollen and slightly purple, too.

"Deputy Short, get in here and take off his cuffs," Judge Nickerson demanded.

"Johnson said for me to leave them on until breakfast. Since that's the only meal he'll be getting for the next two weeks, Johnson said he'd not need his hands to eat dinner."

"Unlock the damn cuffs, Short."

"You need to clear it with Johnson, sir, before I can do that."

"If you don't unlock the cuffs, right this minute, I'll have you arrested."

"On what charge, sir?"

"Try cruel and unusual punishment, Short. He's simply a prisoner, not a terrorist to be tortured like that."

"Yes, sir." Short unlocked the cuffs and Kade experienced several moments of pins-and-needle pains as the blood rushed back to his hands.

Rubbing both wrists, he smiled at the judge. "Thanks. I appreciate the fact you came to check up on me. I need hands to type up the news reports at the paper, and I wasn't sure by breakfast they wouldn't both have to be amputated, like my fingers were."

"I'll come by at random intervals to see about your welfare."

"You don't have to do that. If you'd call my wife and tell her what happened to me, she can, in turn, call my boss and explain the situation."

Johnson was furious about the judge removing Kade's cuffs. He came in late one evening, a week into Kade's sentence. He sent the guard out for coffee and a midnight meal. He then unlocked Blackburn's cell. He snapped a cuff around each of Kade's hands and dragged the half-asleep prisoner over to the bars, fastening each of the cuffs to the cross bars up high.

Johnson then produced an inch-thick rod and proceeded to beat Kade with it, keeping his blows below Kade's face. When Kade continued to grin at Johnson through the beating, Johnson lost it and finally hit Kade across the face, saying, "*I'll guarantee I can wipe that grin off your mug!*"

He finally unlocked the cuffs. Kade slid to the floor. Johnson stepped over him and locked the cell door.

His face was swollen and his lip was cut, to the point he found it hard to eat his one meal for the day. One eye was black. When Nickerson made a routine visit at lunchtime, he closed his eyes. "What happened? Johnson?"

"Yes, sir. He made a midnight visit," Kade said, pulling up the jail top to reveal more bruises.

"Oh, God, Blackburn, I'm so sorry."

"I still have a week to serve, sir, so please don't ruffle Johnson's feathers. Next time he might tell everyone I was trying to escape—explaining that's why he shot me dead."

"Deputy, unlock this cell. We're going to the other side of the mountain. I want Blackburn to spend his remaining week in the Cherry Creek lockup."

Soon Kade was in the back of the deputy's car. They made a quick stop in Dewey at a medical office to have him checked out, before he was transported to the jail between Cottonwood and Camp Verde to spend the rest of his sentence.

"If Chief Johnson comes over here and asks to see Mr. Blackburn, you are not to let him in. Do you understand me?"

"Yes, sir, Judge Nickerson. Did Johnson do this to him? I've heard he has a very vindictive streak."

"Yes. If you think his face looks bad, take a look at his midsection," Nickerson said.

"We'll take good care of him, sir."

"While you're at it, cut that anklet off him. I'd just a soon Johnson couldn't track him via that device."

"Will do, sir. Right this way, Mr. Blackburn. Have you had lunch?"

"No, sir. I was only getting breakfast on the Prescott side."

"Let me see your torso, please."

Kade peeled up his orange shirt, revealing a slew of angry purple welts.

"Do you want me to send in someone to check you out?"

"No, we stopped in Dewey for a checkup and an x-ray. Nothing is broken."

"Bet it's damn tender, though."

"Yes, sir, it is. If you have a mandatory exercise program, I may not be able to do pushups or sit ups for a few more days."

"We don't have any programs like that. I'll bring you some lunch."

Ms. Dean came to see him the next morning. "Let me see your injuries, Kade," she said.

He took off his shirt.

"Oh, that's criminal. I've hired our paper's lawyer. You're going to sue Johnson."

"It might be best to let it go. I'm stuck in here for another four days, which means my family is vulnerable."

"Judge Nickerson has hired a private company to keep your family safe. He finally realized how nasty Johnson is. Said he'd heard some tales like that in the past, but didn't check to see if they were true. He's just furious about what happened to you.

"Some of the men he hired are also guarding the paper, night and day. I got some anonymous threats when I printed up what the judge related to me about Chief Johnson's assault of you. Are you sure you're okay?"

"I am, ma'am. Little tender, still, but it's getting better day-by-day. X-rays showed no broken ribs and the blood test was normal, too. Kidneys and liver seem to be functioning well."

"Will you be able to come back to work once you're released?"

"Yes, ma'am. I plan to take the weekend off to hunt grubs and worms with my twins, but I'll be in bright and early Monday morning."

"Kade, please take all the time you need to heal—a week, two—if you need it."

"I can't meet my mortgage payments if I keep taking time off. I've already spent the most of two weeks in a cell. I need to get back in the harness."

"It goes without saying—I'm paying you for the time you've missed at work."

"Now why would you offer to do that? I know the paper doesn't make that much money."

"You're my best reporter, Kade, and I've come to love you over the years, too. I never have to wonder about you, not like I do with some of the reporters I've hired. You give me the straight-up facts every time."

"Well, I thank you for your generosity, then. I'll make it up to you in the future. I'll work twice as hard and not ask for any more time off until I'm fifty and my mortgage is retired."

"Will it be retired by then?"

"Yes, barring any more unforeseen developments."

"Good."

"Thanks for coming over the mountain to visit. When they said I had a visitor, I half expected my father-in-law. I'm sure he'd just love to give me a hard time about my cell time—again. Have you seen Abby and my kids? Are they okay?"

"Worried about you, but otherwise fine. Oh, Abby sent you this letter. I must be getting old—I nearly forgot to give it to you."

"Thank you for bringing it. You'd better get back to the paper. It's sure to fall apart without you there, riding herd on the printers."

"You're right, Kade. See you on Monday, next, unless you're still under the weather."

"I'll be there. Have me a list of items to cover made up."

"Will do. Take care, Kade."

After she left, Kade sat down to read Abby's letter.

**Dear Kade—**

**I would have come to see you, but Judge Nickerson said it would be easier to keep us safe if we remained on the ranch until Johnson is locked away. I'm so sorry for what Johnson did to you. You didn't deserve all that—not for just forgetting to call in. I understand you don't have to wear the anklet anymore or call in, either. Whoopee!!!**

**We can't wait to have you home again. The twins miss you something fierce. Every day they ask me when you'll be home. Andy and Alli, don't ask me that, but I can tell they're also numbering the days until you return.**

**Once you arrive, you know what I'll want to do with you. I hope you aren't too sore to give me one of those love sessions. I've missed you _and_ those sessions more than I can say.**

**All my love, now and forever,**
**Abby**

# *Chapter Eighteen*

Kade got home Saturday afternoon. Abby had warned the children not to mob him, as he was still a bit sore from the beating.

"My legs aren't sore, so you twins can hug my legs," he said as they swooped in to grab a leg each. "You older kids . . ."

"I want to kiss your cheek," Alli said.

"None of that mushy stuff for me," Andy said. "But if your hand feels okay, I might give you a shake."

After their expressions of love had been taken care of, Kade said, "I need a shower in the worst way. Join me, Abby? Can I count on you older siblings to look after the twins for an hour or two?"

"I know what such a long 'shower' means," Alli said. "It's shorthand for . . ."

"Keep your thoughts to yourself," Kade warned, "and I'll buy you all a banana split after supper."

"C'mon, wife. I need someone to scrub my back."

"And other places," Andy kicked in, giving Kade a wide grin.

"A few more of those comments out of you both, and I'm not going to volunteer to teach either of you how to drive."

"Ha! Dad, I've been driving around the yard in your truck the whole two weeks you were gone."

"You'd better have left me enough gas to get to work on Monday. If you didn't, you're not so big I can't still turn you over my knee and paddle your backside."

That sent the twins into giggles. "Do it, Daddy. Andy is mean to us sometimes. He needs you to paddle him," Kory said.

"Your father still has some sore places and bruises, so any paddling will have to wait for a bit."

"If he's not too sore for sex . . ." Alli said, " . . .why can't he paddle Andy?"

"Daughter, tread lightly, or after I smack Andy's ass, I'd be tempted to do yours, too."

"Daddy said a bad word," Kathy complained. "He has to sit in the corner for two hours."

Amused, Kade asked his wife. "Are you going to make me sit in the corner?"

"Yes, I believe so. You should not be immune from corner sitting if you insist on using bad words. Andy, drag a kitchen chair into the corner for your father to sit in."

"Set the timer, Mom," Kory said. "Daddy, you can't get up until the timer makes its noise."

Kade settled in the chair. "Do I get a magazine to read? Something to drink?"

"No, Daddy. You just have to sit there and think about the bad word you used until the timer goes off," Kathy informed him.

"Okay, that's fair I guess—if Mama makes you all do the same."

The rest of them sat down for dinner. Kade was still in the chair in the corner.

"I'll keep your dinner warm in the oven," Abby told him. "After dinner, Alli, give the kids a bath. Andy, please feed the animals."

Once the children left the kitchen, Abby twisted the timer until the alarm went off.

"Reminds me of the sound of that ankle device," he said, sitting down to eat his dinner. "Thank the powers I'm not forced to wear it anymore."

"Yes, It'll be nice to have sex without it scraping layers of my skin off both legs."

Once the house was quiet, Abby joined him in the shower. She scrubbed his back and all the other parts of him, too. "Must be nice not to smell like a prisoner again. I don't know what they wash their cells with, but it has a very peculiar odor."

219

"Same thing the janitors used to clean up the aisles when a school kid vomited on the floor. It has to have an overpowering scent, or the whole class would be gagging—necessitating much more swabbing of the aisles."

"Kade, how can you turn what happened to you into some kind of a joke?"

"What's the use of crying about it? It happened. Nothing is going to change that fact, so you may as well laugh about it. Are you instituting this philosophical dialog because you don't want to have sex with me?"

"I don't want to hurt you."

"I'll let you know if you hurt me. Get in bed and spread your legs."

"No foreplay? You're going to be like a rabbit tonight?"

She dried off and tried to dry Kade, too. "I'd rather do my own drying," he said.

"Your ribs are still sore, aren't they?"

"A little tender, yes. They'll hurt even worse if I have to tote you into the bedroom, so maybe you could show a bit of mercy to me and walk in there under your own steam."

"How tender, Kade?"

"Not enough for me to postpone what I've been wishing for the last two weeks."

Following a short period of foreplay, he made sweet and tender love to her. She knew then just how sore he was, as usually—after a week's hiatus—he'd be much more aggressive in his lovemaking.

"That was nice, Kade," she said, as he rolled to his back and dragged the sheet over his bruised torso.

"It was nice, wife."

"Why did you let him beat you? I think you're stronger than Johnson is."

"I was very sound asleep, when he entered my cell. He may have drugged my evening coffee—wouldn't put it past him. I didn't feel much of anything until he started hitting me. That woke me up in a hurry. It was only then I realized he'd cuffed my hands to the cell bars over my head. I knew I was in for it at that point."

"How many times did he hit you?"

Kade shrugged. "Don't know for sure. Twenty? Thirty times? I knew he was doing the torso bit, so my face wouldn't show the ravages of the punishment he was dishing out. Once I understood that fact, I started grinning at him, each time he hit me. He finally became so furious over my amusement at his hits, he lost control and forgot to restrict his blows to my torso. He hit me once in the face to 'wipe that stupid grin off my face,' he said."

"Nobody came to help you?"

"I later learned he'd sent the other guy out for coffee and sandwiches. It was good that Judge Nickerson came in early the next morning. Heaven only knows how long my punishment might have gone on if Johnson hadn't hit my face—if he'd kept all the blows down on my torso. Nickerson took one look at my face and . . . well, he transferred me to the other side of the mountain."

"They treated you better?"

"Sure did. No beatings, three square meals a day, no cuffs shutting off circulation to my hands."

"Where are you still sore? Show me."

Kade touched six or eight places over his rib cage. "Still very sore here and here," he said, touching the lower end of his ribs. "Guess because the ribs aren't as stout on the lower end, they were bruised more deeply."

"They need to hang Chief Johnson up, like he hung you up. I'd be willing to take the rod to him—let him feel the burn of all those blows."

"You're into your Sir Lancelot mode, currently? Going to rescue this male maiden in distress?"

"Wouldn't you like to beat him like he beat you?"

"No. I'd rather break his fucking neck. I'll do that if the chance comes along."

"Do you need another time out in the corner?"

"I realize I shouldn't use those words in front of the children. I didn't know you objected to my language, too. Do you want me to sit in the chair again?"

"No, but the more you use those bad words, the more likely they are to slip out of your mouth in front of our children."

"You're absolutely right. I'll try not to use any of my colorful vocabulary in the future. Let's go to sleep. It's nice to be back in my own bed again. The cells weren't too uncomfortable to sleep in, but I didn't have you to cuddle up with."

"You missed me?"

"Every minute of every day. In fact, I'd like an encore before I go to sleep. I need to make up for all those nights alone."

For the second time, he made gentle love to her. "Go to sleep, Kade, or I'll be as sore as you are."

"Did I hurt you?" he asked, concern tinting his question.

"No. You need to rest."


He spent the weekend playing with the kids. Hunted grubs and worms with the twins. Beat Alli and Abby at a game of badminton, and whipped Andy at horseshoes.

"I think you all need to perform some of those Army exercises with me on a daily basis. By this stage in life, you should—save for the twins—be able to win a few of the contests I challenge you to."

"Should we sign up for a tour of duty, too?" Andy asked.

"They could institute the draft at some point. You're of the age they'd call you up, so it might be well if you went off to boot camp in good shape. It's an advantage to be in fighting shape. Nobody picks on you if you're in buff form."

"Do you think . . . is anyone suggesting they have another draft, Kade?" Abby asked, worried he'd heard a rumor from some of his Army buddies.

"No. I think Congress and our citizens have lost the stomach to engage in another war, save for a few diehards, like our Senator from Arizona. If we get into another major conflict, though, the volunteers are so exhausted after serving so many tours of duty, the brass might be forced to reinstate the draft."

"I'd be willing to exercise with you, Dad," Alli said.

"Okay, meet me in the barn tomorrow morning and I'll show you some stuff to keep you in good shape."

"Are you really going to make us exercise?" Abby asked as they got into bed.

"It's a volunteer program, like enlistment in the Army is, wife. I'm not going to force you into doing pushups or sit-ups. I do think some exercise would benefit all the members of this family."

"Do you think I'm that far out of shape, Kade?"

She knew he was grinning in the darkened bedroom. "Do you think you could do ten pushups?" he asked. "If not, you need to join my exercise club."

"I think most of your pushup exercises come during your love-making endeavors. If you let me be on top, I might be as buff as you are."

"Want to give it a try?" he asked, before breaking out in laughter.

"Yes."

He turned over to lie on his back. She straddled him, placing her hands at his armpit level. "I don't think a woman has the right equipment to do the pushup routine on a prone man," Kade teased. "Not unless you use your arms to lift you completely off the bed and lower yourself again and again over my cock."

"Shut up," she said, beginning to rock back and forth.

Whether it was the heat generated by her exertions or her dominant position, she achieved an orgasm in record time. "We'll need to do it this way more often," she said.

"I usually wait for you to have a similar response," he complained.

"You didn't get there? I thought you had."

"Nope, I didn't quite make it, due to the shortness of your efforts."

He rolled her to her back and finished up with his own response.

"You're just mad because I was on top and in charge that time. That's why you didn't have an orgasm."

"Oh, really?"

"Alli is right. We females can read you like a large-print book. You were upset when I took charge, so you decided not to respond until you were in the top-most position."

"Oh, really?"

"Be man enough to admit that you always want to be in charge and on top during lovemaking, Kade. What is it about your ego that demands I be in the submissive position, before you can deliver the goods?"

"Tomorrow morning, you will let me be in the bottom 'submissive' position again. I'll show you that I can deliver the goods just fine from that position. It was only that you erupted so quickly this time around that I didn't quite get there."

"Bull pucky, Kade."

"Are we about to fight about it?"

"No, but I reserve the right to be on top at least 50% of the time. If you can't deliver the goods from your submissive position, that's too bad old man. I never had such a rapid orgasm, so I'd like to enjoy more of those."

He turned his back on her in bed. "Now you're calling me an old man?"

She broke into laughter. "Yes. Old men are totally set in their ways and can't abide any changes to their routines. Does that description fit what just occurred in regards to your failure to ejaculate, Kade?"

He never woke her up for sex in the morning. He was still testy after the exercise session in the barn, which she'd skipped in order to make breakfast. The twins, as well as Alli and Andy were enthusiastic about the exercises Kade had asked them to perform.

"Mom, why didn't you come out and join in?" Alli asked. "I feel so much better when I start off the day with some calisthenics."

"I didn't want to steal any of your father's thunder. He loves to be totally in charge of all those sorts of activities."

"Wife . . !" he warned.

"Well, don't you like to be in charge? How can you deny that after what happened last . . ."

The scalding look he gave her would have curdled the eggs she was scrambling. She turned back to the stove so he wouldn't see the broad smile that graced her face.

He left for work right after taking a shower. He neither kissed her goodbye nor spoke to her before he left. She was doubly amused by his attitude.

He was eating lunch with Diana when Owen entered the same eatery. He ordered a sandwich and joined the couple at their table.

"I thought the restraining order said you needed to keep your distance, Mr. Watkins."

"It's not possible to stay 200 yards away and eat in this establishment. Use your head for something besides a hat rack, Blackburn."

"I'd suggest you move to another table to keep to the spirit of the order, then."

"Do you see another empty seat? I sure don't."

Kade got up at that point and walked out of the restaurant, leaving most of his lunch behind. Diana wasn't sure if he intended her to leave, too, but she was determined to finish her sandwich and fries. Once she'd finished her meal, she asked for a bag. She put Kade's lunch into the bag and exited the restaurant. She found him sitting in his truck. When she handed him the bag containing what remained of his lunch, he got out of the truck and dumped it in a trash barrel.

"What was that all about?" she asked, on the way back to the paper.

He shook his head, not willing to explain. "It's none of your business."

"That's twice you've snapped my head off, Kade. I don't appreciate your attitude. If it doesn't improve, I'll be forced to speak to Ms. Dean. Do you intend to split the items to be covered this afternoon with me, or are you going to maintain your snit and let me cover them all? It might be good to let me cover them. Your current attitude won't likely convince anyone to give you a scoop."

Kade, driving on Gurley Street, grabbed the list out of her hands and took both hands off the wheel to savagely rip it in half. "Choose which half you want," he said, his voice sounding like a snarl from an abused dog. "I don't care which part you want."

She looked over both lists and chose one of them. He dumped her at the paper so she could claim her car and took off as soon as she exited his truck. When she returned at three to write up her reports, he was already hard at work on writing up his columns.

"How did it go?" she asked over the divider between his cubicle and hers.

"Fine," he said. That short answer was all she got from him until their six o'clock quitting time. He left shortly after sending his columns to Ms. Dean.

"What's stuck in Kade's craw?" Diana asked Dean. "He stormed out of the restaurant during lunch when a Mr. Watkins joined us at our table."

"Watkins is his father-in-law. There's no love lost between them. In fact, I think Kade has a restraining order in force against him."

"He seems to be mad at me, too. Did he get up on the wrong side of the bed this morning?"

"I think he's probably worried . . . more than he's willing to admit . . . about the upcoming lawsuit against Chief Johnson. Johnson is a vindictive bastard, who's about to lose his job. If he could beat Kade that hard over a minor situation, Blackburn is likely concerned what he might do if they remove him from his job."

"Why take it out on me? I didn't do anything to him."

"I'll speak to him in the morning. Might be best to avoid him for a day or two. He's undoubtedly worried about his family in regards to Johnson's reaction to the lawsuit."

Dean called him into her office the next morning. "Kade, I'm not going to mince words. Diana is complaining that you're like a bear with a sore paw."

"She should learn to keep her comments to herself. She's always on me about stuff that doesn't concern her."

"Are you worried about the upcoming lawsuit?"

"Wouldn't you be? Johnson is one nasty bastard."

"Your family is protected, and there's a man shadowing you, as well. I don't think he'll try anything. Can you make peace with Gardner this morning?"

Kade shrugged.

"Is that a yes, or a no?" Dean asked.

"I suppose I'll have to if she's taking her bitch to you. If I didn't have this job to keep my mind off Chief Johnson, I'd be twice as tense as I am."

"Tell her you're sorry, then. Try not to worry so much. It's going to turn out just fine."

"Yeah, right. You could talk until midnight and I still wouldn't be convinced of that fact."

He stopped at Diana's cubicle on the way to his own. "Hey," he said, "It's been strongly suggested I ask for your forgiveness for my recent treatment of you."

"You don't intend to apologize on your own recognizance, just because the boss is on your case?"

"Let's have an understanding here. I don't appreciate your comments about issues occurring in my personal life. If you can limit yourself to comments about the items on the list Ms. Dean hands out each day, you will find my comportment easier to deal with."

"You think I'm a nosy busybody, don't you? If I didn't care about you, I wouldn't ask you any questions about your personal life."

"We're business colleagues, nothing more, Gardner. I have a wife to take care of my personal life, so can we just stick to business in the office?"

"If that's the way you want it, that's the way it will be."

"Good." He went into his cubicle and found half the list of items to cover that day on his desk.

"Are we meeting for lunch, per usual?" Diana asked. "Do you have any objections to the half list I gave you?"

"No, to both questions. It doesn't really matter which half of the list I get. It all sucks. Murder, mayhem, and corruption—none of the items ever vary. Sure would be nice to be assigned one of those 'feel good' stories once in a while."

"We aren't eating lunch together? I look forward to that break every day."

"Sorry. I'd rather take off early than spend an hour eating lunch with you."

"Even when you say 'sorry' you still manage to hurt my feelings, Kade."

"Get over it. I don't want a repeat of yesterday's lunch. Now that Watkins knows where I eat, he'll turn up like a bad penny every day.

He lives to make my life miserable, so I'll just go past the drive-through window and eat in my car."

He was eating in his car when his cell phone rang. "Kade Blackburn," he answered.

"Hello, Blackburn, this is Roy Johnson. I understand you're going forward with your lawsuit against me."

"Yes, that's already in the works, so if you're trying to talk me out of it, you can't."

"What if I told you I picked up your wife this morning, along with those cute twins. I have them locked away. I'd be willing to let them go, if you're willing to sign a paper saying the lawsuit is null and void. If you don't want me to ply my wooden dowel on those twins, meet me on the south lawn of the courthouse to sign the paper. Come alone, and unarmed. I, of course, will be armed, as that's my right as an officer of the law, so if you have any intentions of starting something, know I won't hesitate to shoot you."

"What time?" Kade asked, his heart in his throat.

"I think two this afternoon is a fitting time. I'd like to say noon, like what happened in the OK corral, but it's already past that. On the base of the statue of the mounted rider, you will find the document to sign. If you sign it, I'll let your family go as soon as I secure it to my safety-deposit box."

"I'll be there at two," Kade said.

He showed up at two, and scoped out the area until he saw where Johnson was standing. He got out of his truck and started marching in Johnson's direction.

"That's not going to get your family home safely," Johnson shouted, pulling out his gun. "You need to sign the document—over there," he said pointing in the direction of the statue.

Kade kept going in Johnson's direction. Roy raised his gun when Kade was only ten yards in front of him. He fired, hitting Kade in the right shoulder. Johnson was expecting him to drop but Kade kept right on coming. Roy raised his hand to launch another shot, but Kade kicked the gun out of his hand, sending it spiraling. It landed yards away.

By that time, several people had gathered in the windows of the courthouse, watching the scene play out. Two Yavapai deputies, who were about to march a couple of prisoners into the court to stand trial, relocked their van doors and began to converge on Kade and Johnson.

Kade grabbed Johnson's arm and twisted it up behind him with his shot arm. Gritting his teeth against the pain of that wounded shoulder, with his left hand, he reached over Johnson's shoulder, inserted his thumb in Johnson's mouth and gave a hard jerk, ignoring the bite that Johnson gave him.

Johnson gave one shuddering breath and slowly sank to the ground. With his spinal cord severed, he could no longer control his legs.

By that time the deputies had reached the couple. "He shot you?" one of them asked Kade.

"He did, sir."

"Sit down. I'll call it in. Help will soon be on the way."

"Thanks, guys, I appreciate your assistance."

Johnson was moaning loudly on the ground. "Is he hurt, too? What happened to him?" one of the deputies asked.

"I believe he's destined to spend the rest of his life in a wheelchair. He's abducted my wife and my twins to try and force me to rescind the lawsuit I instigated against him for beating me while I was in his custody. The paper he wanted me to sign is on the statue over there."

One of the deputies took off to collect the document.

Kade gathered up Johnson's gun and handed it to the remaining deputy. "I'd suggest you send some of your buddies to Chief Johnson's home to see if my family is held in that location. I'm heading in that direction, myself. If he's hurt my wife or kids, I might come back and deliver a final coup de gràce."

"Whoa, sir. You're wounded. You're also bleeding. You need to go to the hospital, not Johnson's home."

"If you try to detain me, I might be forced to do the same to you as I did to Johnson."

"What exactly did you do to him?"

"I'll let the ER doctor explain it to you. Right now, I have to see to the welfare of my wife and twins. I'll come past your office later to answer all your questions."

Kade took off in his truck. He knew where Johnson lived. As he pulled up in front of the right house, two deputy's vehicles pulled up behind him.

"You think Johnson abducted your wife and twins?" one of the deputies asked.

"I know he did. He told me that on the phone. I'm not sure he's stupid enough to bring them here, but this is the only place I can think of where they might be held."

"Let us go in first, in case he's booby trapped the place, sir."

"Be my guests. I'd suggest you start with the basement."

Kade followed the four men down the cellar steps. There was a thick door at one end of the basement, padlocked with a stout lock.

"Abby?" Kade shouted.

A muffled response ensued. Kade picked up a claw hammer from the workbench and tried to smash the lock. The effort sent a new freshet of blood spiraling down his shirt.

"Let us do it, sir. Sit over there before you bleed to death."

The bigger deputy finally managed to get the lock to disengage. They pulled the door open to find Abby and the kids tied to three chairs with duct tape. The kids looked scared to death.

"Kade, we never lost hope you'd find us. Thank God you did. Are you hurt? What's that on your shirt? Blood?"

"It's nothing Abby, long as I know you and the twins are safe, I'll be okay. I was so worried when Johnson called me to say he'd abducted you."

"My husband needs medical attention," Abby said.

"He wouldn't agree to seek that until he was sure you were safe. Let's go to the hospital, Mac, before you bleed any more."

"Will one of you return my wife and kids to our ranch in Chino Valley? I'll go along peacefully with you if you can guarantee me that they'll get back to the ranch."

"Of course we will, sir."

"Kade, I want to go with you."

"No, Abby. The twins are terrified over what they've been through. They'll need you more than I will. Go home with them. I'll come home as soon as I get treated and answer any questions the deputies have."

She bent over and gave him a kiss. Upset as she was over the situation and Kade's wound, she put on her brave face and said, "Let's go home kids. We need to hunt up some grubs for the chickens.

"Good girl," he said to her. "Try to re-establish a sense of normality by doing normal things. Mix up some mustard and find worms, too."

"Where are you taking Kade?" she asked.

"Yavapai Regional Hospital," one of the deputies said. "If you give me your cell phone number, I'll call you to let you know what happens."

"I don't have my phone with me," Abby said.

"Take mine," Kade offered.

"No, then you won't have any means to call someone or me."

"I may be tied up for a bit. Take the phone and call Ms. Dean to tell her what happened. I doubt I can finish today's list of items this afternoon."

"What if he comes to the ranch and takes us hostage again?"

"I can guarantee he won't be coming to the ranch."

"He's dead? You killed him?"

"No, he's not dead, but I think he's shortly going to wish he were."

After Abby and the twins went off with two deputies in the back of their squad car, Kade finally agreed to go to the hospital.

"Thanks for everything, guys," he said, as they escorted him into the ER. There was a large cadre of other policemen in the hall.

"Blackburn, it was you that had the altercation with Johnson on the courthouse lawn?" Detective Palmer asked.

"It was, Palmer. He called me around one and told me to meet him there or he'd beat my twins like he beat me—he said he'd abducted my wife and the twins."

"What did you do to him?" Palmer asked. "He's in critical shape."

"Mr. Blackburn didn't do anything that the asshole didn't deserve. He shot Blackburn in cold blood. We saw the whole thing from our van. We were delivering some prisoners to the court for their trials when Johnson raised his gun and shot Blackburn."

"Were you also armed, Kade?" Palmer asked.

"I wasn't armed with any weapons, unless you'd like to count my Army training, sir."

"The ER doctors say Johnson has a broken neck. How did you manage to break an armed man's neck?"

"I kicked the gun out of his hand, Palmer. I know 50 or 60 ways to disarm a person, and at least 30 to 40 ways to incapacitate someone. I could demonstrate the method for breaking a neck, but I'd rather not do that demonstration on you. If you have one of those CPR dummies, I can show you on that mannequin as soon as my wound is treated."

"I'm surprised you didn't linger at the courthouse for enough time to deprive Johnson of his family jewels."

"Wasn't any sense of resorting to those measures at the time. Once I'd broken his neck, he wouldn't be able to feel that kind of cutting. It's not so much fun to cut off someone's mountain oysters if he can't feel the pain. The yelling, screaming and begging us to stop are what makes those castrations into such a pleasurable endeavor."

Palmer closed his eyes. "How bad are you wounded?"

"Won't know that until I see the doctor. Entry wound on the front side, but no exit wound in the back. I suppose the bullet is lodged in my shoulder blade in the back. If you choose to hang around, you may get treated to my yelling, screaming and begging the doctor to stop shortly."

"I'd like to be in there when they assess the damages. I'd like to claim the bullet they remove, too."

When Kade was summoned into an exam room, he asked the ER doctor if he'd permit Palmer to observe the procedure in the interest of justice being served.

"I'm sure I don't care as long as he sits in that chair and doesn't interfere in our treatment of you."

"You get your wish, Palmer," Kade said as they cut off his blood-crusted shirt.

They took an x-ray, which determined the bullet was lodged against his right scapula. "You want something for the pain before I try to remove it? It's severed a couple of tiny arteries, but missed any major ones."

"It's kind of numb by now. Just do what you need to do to get it out. Palmer is hot to have the bullet in hand, and I'd rather not be all doped up. I need to get home to my family. Can't drive buzzed on your pain meds."

Using a scalpel, the ER doctor made a couple of cuts to widen the wound. He then used a hemostat to clamp off the bleeders until he could seal them using a cauterizing instrument. Using the hemostat to probe for the bullet, he finally laid it in a metal cup. He irrigated the wound and slapped on a dressing, gave Blackburn a prescription after advising Kade to take it easy for a few days.

Kade looked over to see Palmer shaking his head. "God, you're one tough hombre," the detective said. "Didn't that hurt you? It hurt me and I was only watching the procedure."

"It pinched a bit, but the pain was overridden by my need to get home to the ranch to comfort Abby and the twins. Am I free to go, or are you about to cage me up for crippling Chief Johnson?"

"You're free to go home. Just don't leave the county."

"You aren't going to strap another of those devices on my ankle, are you?"

"No, I'm not. Just stay at the ranch until you recover."

"Will do, Palmer. Thanks for your help this afternoon."

The next morning, when Detective Palmer arrived in his office, he found Kade sitting in a chair on the opposite side of his desk.

"I thought I told you to stay home until you recovered," Palmer said.

"I've recovered, so I thought I'd better come in and explain what happened to Johnson."

"I got the document the Chief wanted you to sign. What sort of pressure did he put on you to make you pen your name to it?"

"He threatened to beat my twins like he beat me. I thought it might be well for me to render him sufficiently incapable to follow up on his threat."

"You knew he was armed?"

"Yes, sir. He told me that on the phone."

"The deputies escorting prisoners to the courthouse said you never hesitated—just marched in Johnson's direction. Even when he pulled his gun you kept on going. Why?"

"In a situation like that, the best thing is to keep on marching forward. Makes your intended target more than a little nervous when they pull a gun and it doesn't seem to phase you."

"They said he shot you when you were about ten feet in front of him. I can't, for the life of me, understand why you didn't fall over at his feet."

"I was marching on pure adrenaline at that point. Don't think he could understand why I didn't fall over, either. When he raised the gun again, I was close enough to kick the gun out of his hand."

"What happened next?"

"When he glanced down at his hand, because I'd kicked it hard enough to maybe break a finger or two, I spun him around and reefed his gun hand up behind his back high enough to cause him additional pain. With my good, unwounded arm I reached over his shoulder, inserted my thumb behind his teeth, and gave a quick jerk. Used enough force to break his neck. He'll be a quadriplegic from the neck down. Only way I could assure myself he'd never get a chance to ply his rod on either of my twins."

"Were you in the Special Forces?"

Kade shook his head. "No, sir, I just paid strict attention when it came to classes on self-defense. Took more than one class on hand-to-hand combat. Learned how to do the ultimate amount of damage, even if I were wounded."

"I'm glad we found your wife and twins, mostly unscathed."

"Kathy joined my wife and me in bed last night about eleven. She'd had more than one nightmare, so I figured it was easier to let her sleep between us, than keep going to her room to comfort her.

"Kory crawled in bed with the three of us about midnight. Course he'd never admit to being scared enough to have a nightmare, but when he pulled my sore arm around him, that told me he was suffering some of his own bad dreams."

"How about your wife? Did she have nightmares, too?"

"She's stronger than she looks, Palmer. She wasn't worried about her own safety, just about the safety of the twins and me."

"I stopped to see Chief Johnson this morning. He swore he'd sue your socks off?"

"Why would he want to sue my socks off? I doubt he's going to need a pair of them until it comes to winter."

"You really don't feel at all bad for what you did to him? He was a vibrant man."

"He was a bully. No, I don't feel bad about his current condition. If he thinks he's going to sue me, I believe there are enough witnesses to what happened, to make a strong case for self-defense."

"If the prosecuting attorney brings up what happened to Rossman—well he's going to paint you as someone who's out of control. It might be best, if it comes to a trial, if you could admit to having a bit of remorse over the fates of both men."

"Doesn't that constitute perjury, sir? Why would you advise me to lie on the stand? I'm not going to shed any crocodile tears over either man. But I need to get to work. You know where to find me if you have more questions."

# *Chapter Nineteen*

Kade arrived at the paper at 9:30. He apologized to Ms. Dean for being late, explaining he had stopped to see Detective Palmer en route to the paper.

"I didn't think you'd be in at all, today, Kade. How's your shoulder?"

"It's just fine, ma'am. I'll stay until 5:30 to give you a full eight hours."

"Diana has the list of what to cover this morning. She already set off to cover the items, as neither of us expected you to show up."

"Okay, I'll give her a call and meet up with her someplace and split the list."

"We were both concerned about you, Kade. Diana left something in your cubicle."

He went to his assigned space and found a box of dark chocolates resting on his desk. Along with a note that said:

**Kade,**

**I'm so glad you're still in the land of the living. I called your wife to ask what I could get you to welcome you back to work, whenever that occurs. She mentioned you had a real sweet tooth, but preferred dark chocolates over the milk-chocolate variety. That's what I got for you, a whole pound of dark chocolates.**

**Diana**

Touched, he pulled out his cell phone and called her number. When she answered, he said, "I was going to catch up with you this morning and split the items list, but now I think I'll just sit here and eat my fill of chocolates. Thanks so much for providing my favorite treats."

"You came in to work? I thought you were wounded."

"I am, but it's not bad enough to take time off. Where are you eating for lunch? The least I can do is split what remains of the list and buy you lunch."

"I know you won't want to eat at the place your father-in-law accosted you. What do you suggest?

"How about El Chaparral? After I consume all this chocolate, I'll need something hot and spicy to counter the sweetness. One o'clock?"

"Okay, Kade, if you're sure you're up to it. What are you going to do between now and one?"

"Ms. Dean wants me to go to the hospital and interview Chief Johnson."

"**What? Surely not!**" Diana said, evidencing dismay that Dean would so assign him.

"I'm teasing. I'm going to work on that story about the crooked garage that I was writing about before Johnson told me to meet him at the courthouse."

"The one that pours stuff like catsup on the engine block and tells women they have a major problem that will necessitate hundreds of dollars in repairs."

"The very one. Tell me you wouldn't fall prey to such malarkey."

"I don't know a whole lot about a car's engine, so I might get taken in."

"Women! If you're going to drive, wouldn't it behoove you to learn some things about the vehicle you're driving?"

"Do you have time to study the workings of the truck you drive? Seems to me you can't even find the time to sweep the mud and gravel out of yours."

"Touché, Ms. Gardner. See you for lunch."

As soon as he hung up the phone with Diana, he checked his phone book and called a florist. Ordered a dozen red roses for her cubicle. *If*

*I send her flowers, maybe she'll be so enraptured over the flowers I've sent to her, she won't come around the divider to eat any of my candy. One can only hope. Hah, fat chance!*

In case the flowers didn't keep her out of his candy, he emptied the rest of the pieces into a plastic container and threw the box away, secreting the candy in his bottom drawer. He went back to the story he'd been working up and completed it at 12:30. Grabbing his laptop, he sprinted to his truck and headed for the restaurant.

She was already there when he arrived.

"Is that some of my chocolates smeared all over your face?" she asked as he sat down.

"No, Abby sent me off with no breakfast this morning. We slept late. The twins are still having nightmares so we didn't get much sleep. Abby did manage to shuffle a chocolate-covered éclair into my hand as I rushed out the door. That's likely what's smeared on my face. I was late into work, so I forgot about it until I got in my truck for lunch."

"A likely story, Kade. What's good to eat here?"

"It's all good. I prefer a shredded-beef chimichanga."

"What is that?"

"Beef wrapped in a flour tortilla. Comes with lettuce, sour cream and guacamole. Protein, bread, vegetables—so it has most of the five food groups in it."

"Okay, I'll have what you're having."

Kade gave their orders to the waiter then said, "Let me see the list of items you were working on."

She dragged it out of her shirt pocket. "I checked off the ones I interviewed, so if you want to split what's left, you need to make your own list."

He dragged out a small notebook from his shirt pocket. "Any preferences you have for me to cover?"

"Yes. I hate going into the cell areas to talk to prisoners. They give me a hard time, with whistles and catcalls. There are two jailed men on the list to interview. Would you mind taking those items?"

"I kind of hate going into the cell areas, too, seeing I've spent a few times in one of those cells. Since you got me the candy, I guess I can spare you those whistles and catcalls." He copied down both names in his notebook. "Anything else you don't want to cover?"

"Commissioner Hunter has a new program concerning the funding for the new racetrack in Prescott Valley. He's such a bore. Drones on and on. I'd really appreciate it if you took that item, too."

"Okay."


After lunch, Kade went to the jail to interview a couple of prisoners. When he walked in the door, the desk sergeant came out from behind his desk.

"I didn't think you'd have the audacity to show up here after you crippled Chief Johnson. Whatever you want, I'm not in the humor to accommodate your wishes."

"I'm here on behalf of Ms. Dean's Prescott paper. I'm supposed to interview Jethro Cline and Bill Comstock. Are you going to deny me access to those men?"

"Yes. Are you planning to break my neck, too, if you can't interview those men?"

"No, sir. I have no such havoc in mind. I'll just put in a call to my editor and tell her you won't let me interview those men. It's not going to look good in the paper that you've prevented me from doing my job, sir."

"Like I give a rat's ass."

The sergeant's response reminded Kade of saying that same word and spending time sitting in the corner. He started to chuckle about how Kathy had called him out for saying a bad word.

"Do you take amusement from the fact you crippled Chief Johnson?"

"No, sir. Your statement just reminded me of some time I spent sitting in a corner when one of my twins caught me voicing a bad word—'ass' in that case."

"I'd like to do a lot more to you than have you sit in a corner."

"You actually liked Johnson? You know he beat me up pretty badly when I spent some time with you last month."

"If you don't get the hell out of my sight, I might be tempted to do likewise."

"Okay. Don't get your knickers in a twist, sir. I'm leaving. I'll leave you to answer to the wrath of my editor for denying me access to Cline and Comstock."

In his truck, he called Dean and reported the desk sergeant wouldn't let him into the jail to interview the prisoners.

"Why not?" Dean asked.

"Guess he's sore about my treatment of Chief Johnson."

"You will wait right there until I arrive, Kade. Do you understand me?"

"Yes, ma'am."

Dean pulled up in twenty minutes. She got out of her car wearing a scowl. Kade had seen that same scowl a few times in the past, and he suddenly felt sorry for the desk sergeant.

"Follow me, Blackburn. I don't know why I have to baby sit such a resourceful guy. Haven't you learned to assert yourself—not take 'no' for an answer?"

"Guess I haven't managed to assert myself like you seem to assert yourself. Maybe the sergeant is just more respectful of women. I couldn't even get to first base with him, myself."

Dean stormed into the jail's office and planted herself square in front of the desk sergeant. "What the hell is your problem, Duran? I've got better things to do than straighten out your thinking. Why did you deny Blackburn entrance? I sent him down here to interview two prisoners and by God, Duran, don't give me any shit about not letting him in to do his job."

"Ms. Dean. After what he did to Chief Johnson, he's blacklisted. He's neither to get any information out of the officers on duty, nor from any of the men in lockup. You can't expect me to let such a violent man into the cell area. What if one of the prisoners ticked him off? Would I be calling for an ambulance because Blackburn here took matters into his own hands and broke another neck?"

"Were you intending to break someone's neck, Kade?"

"No, ma'am."

"Right about now, I'd like to unleash you on the sergeant here. Maybe not to break his neck, but just to convince him you have the right to conduct interviews for the paper. Who's your supervisor, sergeant?"

"We haven't chosen another one yet. We're waiting to see if Chief Johnson can come back in a limited capacity as our supervisor again."

"If you won't let Blackburn in, do you have any objections to me interviewing those men?"

"No, ma'am. I'd let you go back to see both of them, long as Blackburn sits outside in his truck."

"Kade, do you have any other items to cover?"

"Yes, ma'am. Diana asked me to interview Commissioner Hunter about the new racetrack."

"Go do that, then. I'll interview the men here and let you write up your article from my notes—because I fully intend to write a scathing front-page article about how you were denied access."

"One of those fourth-estate articles, with the Voltaire quote?" Kade asked. "*I disapprove of what you say, but I will defend to the death your right to say it.*"

"Something along those lines. It sets a dangerous precedent when reporters are denied access to anyone and everyone."

"He's not being denied because he's a reporter," the desk sergeant protested. "Only because of what he did to Chief Johnson."

"A denial is still a denial, regardless of the reason, Duran. Go on Kade. I'll speak with you later on."

"Yes, ma'am."

Kade went to interview Commissioner Hunter. Diana was right. Hunter was a bore. He talked for an hour without stopping to consult a single note. Finally, Kade said, "I think I have enough information, sir. I'll write up my article and forward it to you so you can make any corrections. What is your e-mail address?"

Hunter rattled it off. Kade copied it down. "Thanks so much for seeing me today, sir."

"Aren't you the guy who put Chief Johnson in a wheelchair?"

"Yes."

"You're so polite. I can't imagine how such a considerate guy could do that to another man."

"He told me he'd taken my wife and my twins hostage to force me to drop my lawsuit against him. Told me to meet him on the courthouse square. Said if I didn't sign the paper he'd generated, he would take the same wooden rod he'd used on me to both of my twins. I had no intention of letting him follow through on that threat, nor did I have any intention of signing his paper. Sometimes you have to do what you have to do."

"Are your family members safe?"

"They are, sir. Twins have had some lingering nightmares about being trussed up in Johnson's basement, but my wife and I are working on restoring some normalcy to our family. I believe the children are beginning to have less nightmares due to our efforts."

"Chief Johnson beat you with a wooden rod?"

"Yes, he did, while I was in custody at his jail."

"That's why you're going to sue him?"

"It is, sir."

"Even now? Even after you put him in the wheelchair?"

"Yes. There are only a few things that impress a bully like Johnson. One is to render the bully incapable of bullying anyone else and two, to sue his socks off, so he has no means to support his bullying habits."

"You don't think he's suffered enough?"

"If he were threatening to beat your children like he beat me, would you feel the same degree of empathy for him? It took me weeks to recover from his caning, so I had no intention of letting him do that to my twins. They're only four."

"I didn't realize . . ."

Kade smiled at that remark from Hunter. "Don't think anyone realized the man had such a cruel streak. He managed to mask his anger fairly well."

"Okay, send me your report when you get it written."

"Will do, sir."

When Dean came back from her interviews, she still had steam erupting from both ears. "That Duran is a piece of work," she said, inviting Kade into her office and slamming the door.

"He continued to give you a hard time?" Kade asked.

"Yes. I went from those two interviews directly to the mayor's office to complain about you not being let in to do the interviews. It seems like they've closed ranks around Chief Johnson. The mayor didn't want to extend you the right to interview prisoners, either."

"My usefulness to you is curtailed? If I can't interview any Prescott officials, it's going to be hard to do my job."

"I agree, Kade. How did your interview go with Hunter?"

"Fine. He's very talkative, also kind of a bore. Hardly takes a breath between paragraphs once he gets on a roll. No wonder Diana gave me him to interview."

Dean laughed. "Well at least he **let** you interview him."

"What do you intend to do with me—if I'm not welcome at the police station or in the mayor's circles?"

"Wait until I write my article about the press not being allowed to cover the news. I expect we'll get some strong response from our readers. Let's just see how much pressure those readers put on the guys like Duran and our mayor."

"Will you let me read what you write up before it hits the newsstands?"

"You want to edit my piece—like you edit Gardner's?"

"I'd just like the chance to see what you write. Make sure you have all the facts straight in regards to what happened to Johnson. I intend to sue him, so I'd rather you didn't include anything in your article that isn't completely factual."

"I suggest you go to your cubicle and write up your interview with Hunter. I don't need you to look over my articles. I was in this business before you even thought about being a reporter. I was writing articles when you were still standing on a stool to get your dick over the edge of the toilet."

"Have it your way, then, Ms. Dean."

"I intend to, Mr. Blackburn."

Kade returned to his cubicle and began his article on the new racetrack. He was still worried about what Dean might write up, but knew he'd pushed her as far as he dared by asking to see her article before it hit the streets.

"You're awfully quiet over there, Kade," came Diana's voice. "Were you so overwhelmed by Hunter's output you can't speak again while you write up the bore's report?"

"He does tend to go on and on," Kade said.

"How did your interviews go at the jail?"

"I wasn't allowed in. Sergeant Duran wouldn't allow me back to interview the men. I called Ms. Dean. Even after she ripped Duran a new asshole, he wouldn't let me in, because of what I'd done to Chief Johnson."

"Wow! That's going to play havoc with your ability to cover crimes in this fair city."

"I know. Dean may decide to put me on a permanent vacation. I may have to ship out for another city and write articles for some other paper. Or, re-up in the Army and become one of those imbedded reporters covering the war zones again."

"Cool it, Kade. Wait until you see what becomes of the article Dean plans to write. Don't do anything stupid until we see how that plays out."

"Doubt it will change the mind of Sgt. Duran or the mayor of Prescott."

"You don't know that. Thanks for those dozen roses. They smell heavenly. You're such a nice guy."

"Not everyone thinks so, Diana. I would have gotten you a box of chocolates, but I know women like flowers more, since blooms don't add any weight to their waistlines."

"Good choice. You're right. Women do like flowers better than candy for that very reason."

"Well, I need to write a very long article about a racetrack."

# Chapter Twenty

Kade was still working on the racetrack article after everyone else had departed, but Dean.

"Kade," she called.

He saved his article and shut down his computer, going to her office as soon as he felt none of his writing would be lost. "Yes, ma'am," he said, sticking his head inside her door.

"I need to apologize to you. I was just so angry about how everyone had closed ranks to deny you access, that I . . ."

"You don't owe me any apology. I was out of line to suggest you let me edit what you wrote."

"Go home, Kade."

"Permanently?" he asked.

"No. I know you're as upset about the situation as I am. I realize you could be in for a hard time if Johnson counter sues you. Take my piece with you tonight and let me know in the morning if you feel anything I wrote would jeopardize your suit."

"I respectfully decline to do that, Ms. Dean. You wrote what you wanted to write, so I'll just have to let the chips fall where they will. I'll read your article in the paper on Friday, same as everyone else does."

When he got home, the twins came barreling out the door. He scooped each one up in opposite arms, glad for their enthusiastic embraces. "Hey, guys, what has you so happy this evening?"

"Mama baked a big cake and let us put candles on it for your birthday, Daddy."

"It's my birthday?"

"Yes, today is your birthday. You don't know when your birthday is?"

"Of course I know when my birthday is, I just didn't realize this was the 10th of August. Good thing Mama keeps tabs on the calendar better than I do."

"We put 43 candles on the cake. It's going to take a long time to light all of them," Kory announced.

"If you light all of them, one of two things will happen."

"What will happen, Daddy?" Kathy asked.

"Either the light from all those candles will be brighter than the sun and you'll need to put on sun screen to slice a piece to eat, or the heat from all those candles will melt the icing from the cake and we'll have to scoop it up using some big spoons."

"Ah, Dad. Mom will make you sit in the corner again, for telling such a big lie to the twins," Alli announced. "Dinner is ready, so go and sit down. Mom fixed all your favorites. Roast beef, yams with maple syrup, green beans in mushroom sauce."

"Gee, and I had my mouth all watered up for ham, baked beans and a tossed salad."

"You hate ham, Dad," Andy said. "You might enjoy baked beans, but the rest of us hate when you eat them. All that gas . . ." Andy pinched his nose shut.

"Okay. Let's sit down to what your mama made for dinner. Unless you eat everything on your plate, you don't get any cake tonight," he said, knowing the kids preferred potatoes with gravy to yams.

Abby came in bearing bowls and platters full of the feast she'd prepared. "You really didn't realize it was your birthday, Kade?"

"Nope. So much happened at work today, I completely forgot the calendar had arrived at my birthday."

"Happened good or happened bad?" Abby asked.

"Tell you later during our tea break. No use casting a pall over the birthday festivities. Pass me the bowl with the yams, please."

They ate for an hour then Abby produced the cake. It did sport 43 candles. "I'll need to use my furnace lighter to light so many candles. A match will never last long enough to get the job done," Kade teased.

Kade went to the basement and got the lighter he used to light the pilot light of the furnace. That instrument made short work of lighting all the candles.

"Where are my sunglasses?" he asked. "The light from all those candles really is brighter than the sun. Look, the icing is melting."

"Take a big gulp of air in, and try to blow them all out," Kory said. "If you can do it with one breath, all your wishes for the year will come true."

"Don't think I can do it in one big breath. Might need to get the fire extinguisher from the kitchen to blow them all out. But let's see how many I can manage on a single lungful of air."

He sucked in enough air to make his ribs hurt and managed to blow out all 43 candles without resorting to a second intake of air.

"What did you wish for, Daddy?" Kathy asked.

"If I tell, then the wish won't come true. I'm not going to tell anyone what I wished for."

Both twins looked unhappy because he wouldn't reveal what he'd wished for, until Abby pulled the melted candles from the cake and started slicing large pieces of it. "I want the piece with the K on it, Mama," Kory announced. "That's the same letter as my name starts with."

"Yours and mine and Kathy's. Since it's my birthday, I think I should get the slice with my whole name on it. If you take the K, then I'd be left with only 'ade.'"

"Okay, Daddy. Take the piece with all your name on it," Kory said.

"You know the letters in your name now?" Kade asked.

"Yes. Mama has been teaching Kathy and me our letters. Every morning she puts another letter on the door of the refrigerator."

Kade caught Abby's eye over the length of the table. "I must be spending ***way too much time*** at the paper. Not only do I forget today is my birthday, but the twins are learning to read their letters without me knowing that. I suppose you guys will be reading books to me shortly, instead of me reading to you. Makes me regret the clip job. No more babies to read to and bathe."

"Kade!" Abby admonished him. "Do you need to sit in the corner?"

"You'd make me sit in the chair on my birthday? UH-UH, not until I eat my cake and ice cream."

They showered him with gifts, too. Kathy and Kory had given him neon bootlaces in both green and orange. Alli had provided him with a book of Robert Burns' poems. Andy gave him a new strap for his digital camera. Abby promised him her gift for later.

After dinner, he played a couple of board games with the family, then bathed both twins and tucked them into bed. He beat Alli and Andy at a few games of checkers, before both of them said they wanted to watch CSI before going to bed.

"You up for a game of checkers, wife?"

"No, I'm up for a sink full of dishes. I used almost every bowl and plate in the house to provide you with your birthday treats."

"I'd like to help you restore the kitchen to order," he volunteered.

"It's your birthday. You shouldn't have to do KP on your birthday."

"Didn't realize it was my birthday, so I don't think I'm absolved from KP. Thanks to you and the kids for making the day so special."

"Do you really regret your vasectomy? I know how much you like to have a small one underfoot, but aren't your ready to give up dandling babies?"

"In my job, so much horrible stuff happens, that I have come to cherish the innocence of small children. I've loved bathing them and reading to them and tucking them into bed. I miss those duties once the kids get older."

"Well, I'm ready for a cessation of the chores associated with kids under kindergarten age."

"Has it really been so awful?" he asked.

"No, of course not. But those twins ask me dozens of questions every hour of the day. Sometimes I just yearn for an adult to talk to."

"Trade you jobs. You go work for the paper and I'll stay home and teach the twins their letters."

"Really? You'd be willing to trade me jobs?"

"Days like today, yes, I'd swap occupations with you in a nanosecond."

"What was so bad about today?"

"What did you get me for my birthday? Is it something related to the bedroom?"

"Are you avoiding my question? My gift is up in the bedroom. I was just too tired to hike up and bring them down this evening."

"Go sit down and read. I'll take care of the kitchen," Kade said. "No, don't give me that look. Looking around at the disaster this kitchen is, you have to be tired. Go sit down while I make 'neatness counts' in here."

"Bless you, between running to the store with twins in tow, cooking and making the cake, I am very tired. I just don't feel right about letting you clean up my mess. I should have managed to do that before you came home."

He had the kitchen cleared before the 10 p.m. news came on, so he joined Abby on the couch to watch it. During all the political ads and commercial ads, he muted the sound while he hugged her and planted a few kisses on her cheeks.

"Are we having tea at eleven? Or are you too tired for that, too?"

"Yes, we can have tea and I'll give you my gift at that point."

"It's not sex? When you said you'd give it to me later, I assumed you . . ."

"I believe you'll be well past the century age when you finally stop thinking about that subject."

"I'll be six feet under before I want to stop having sex with you. But if you're too tired this evening, I can forego it for one night."

When the news went off, Abby went to the kitchen and set the kettle on to boil. "While it heats, I'll go fetch your gift," she told him.

She returned with a large box. He untied the ribbons and unfolded the paper. Inside the box was a new pair of hiking boots, same size and variety as the ones he loved—ones that were about to disintegrate from constant wear.

"Wow! I love these boots. I know I'll appreciate them more than sex the next time I go hiking. Last time I took the kids for a walk, I felt every pebble on the path because my soles were so thin. Where are those laces the twins got me? I will have to put one green one and one orange one in each of the boots."

He sat down again at the table and sipped his chamomile tea, while opening both packages of laces. "If I installed green in both boots, Kathy would think I loved Kory more, so, even if it looks weird, I'd better put green lace in the left one and an orange lace in the right one."

Abby shook her head. "You're right. It'll look very strange, but those twins do compete for your attention—enough so that one or the other would be hurt if you just used one color in both boots."

"How many letters do they now recognize?" he asked.

"They're up to M. Are you going to tell me what happened at work today to have your forehead all rumpled up?"

"Why spoil a birthday?"

"Kade . . ."

"Okay. Diana and I split Ms. Dean's list of items to be covered, same as always. She wanted me to interview Commissioner Hunter about the new racetrack in Prescott Valley. Said he was a real bore. Also asked me to interview two prisoners being held in the local jail, so she could avoid all the name-calling and whistles she gets when she goes into the cell area. I agreed to take on those items.

"When I got to the jail, the desk sergeant, Duran, said he wouldn't let me in. Told me no one could talk to me after what I did to Chief Johnson. I called Dean and she came down and yelled at Duran, but he still wouldn't let me into the cell area. Said the mayor of Prescott had put out a notice that I wasn't welcome to cover anything in the city due to breaking Johnson's neck.

"That left me only Hunter to interview. If it's all shut down to me, there's no way I can hold up my value to the paper. Dean said she was writing a front-page article about me being denied the right to interview anyone connected to the city. I asked to read what she was going to publish and she told me in no uncertain terms she didn't need me to edit what she was going to write.

"Later she apologized, telling me she was just so angry about the way the city was circling the wagons around Johnson. She offered to let me read the article, but I declined. I felt if I wanted to change a single word of it, she'd be as huffy as she was when I asked to see it in the first place."

"It may be time to move again, Kade."

"Nah! With only Gardner to write up the items, half of them won't get covered. Pretty soon, this commissioner or that mayor will want to get re-elected and when his article doesn't appear in the paper in time to inform the voters, he'll raise holy hell. That's when Dean will tell him or her that with all the news items being closed to one of her reporters, they can't expect the one remaining reporter to cover all the items. I'll be invited back to the inner circles at that point."

"How is your suit against Johnson coming along?"

"Slowly. I would assume that my lawyer is running into the same brick wall as I ran into today. With no witnesses—law-side witnesses—being willing to share what they saw, he's having a tough time building his case."

"I hate small provincial towns for that very reason. Everyone is in everyone else's pocket. Let's go to bed."

"Yeah, let's do that. I'll wash up the cups and lock the doors and be up in a few."

"I'll try to stay awake long enough for . . ."

"You don't need to do that. Go to sleep. Just because it's my birthday, you don't need to feel obligated to provide me with . . ."

"We've been married so long, we don't either one need to complete our sentences. I'll still be awake when you come to bed, Kade."

She was still awake and she proceeded to provide him with such wonderful . . . well, it more than made up for the rotten day he'd had. It became the highlight of his entire day—overcoming all the negative aspects his August 10th birthday had contained.

"I love you, wife. Tired as you were . . . you still . . ."

As his eyes slid shut. Abby wished she'd brought the digital camera to the bedroom, to capture the beatific smile that graced his face.

Kade came in early and went to his cubicle at the paper the morning after Ms. Dean's article appeared. He was in long before anyone else had arrived. He buried himself in the crooked-garage story to take his mind off what he'd read in Dean's article.

At the ten o'clock coffee break, Dean sat down across the table from him. "Well, did you read it? What did you think of my article?"

He failed to smile or wink or joke, or do any of the things she was used to seeing or hearing as his response to her questions. Instead he just said, "No comment," before getting up to go back to his station.

Dean followed him to his cubicle. "No comment? Come to my office and explain that response."

He saved what he'd been working on, and got up to trail her to her office. He sat down, after he'd pulled her article from the folder he carried.

"What was wrong with what I said in the article? Something must have been seriously wrong if you don't care to discuss what I wrote."

Kade unfolded the article atop her desk. Several passages had been circled in red, with the word 'dele' written in big red letters above the circled sections. Dean skimmed the parts he'd circled. "What do you object to in these red-marked passages?"

"No comment. I'd like to return to the story I was writing, if it's all the same to you."

"You aren't going anywhere until you explain why you believe I shouldn't have included what you circled."

"You want it straight up and honest?"

"Of course."

"Okay, here goes. You know several things about me that aren't known to the general public."

"Like what?"

"Like I didn't regret killing Rossman or putting Chief Johnson in a wheelchair. You told me you thought I was very hard inside to have no regrets about either of those incidents. Now, everyone that reads your article will have the same impression—that I'm a man without a conscience—who can kill or cripple without remorse. Some of those same readers will sit on the jury when Johnson sues me. If their sympathies lie with Johnson, the penalty for assault is between eight and twelve years."

"You did say that you had no regrets. Am I supposed to lie to our readers?"

"No, ma'am. But some of what you heard in this office when Detective Palmer questioned me, should have been considered like a private conversation—the same as one between me and my lawyer—not something to be broadcast to the entire county due to your snit about me not being allowed to interview anyone at the jail."

"You think I did it to enhance my reputation? I did it so maybe the readers would put enough pressure on the high and mighty they'd let you cover whatever stories I assigned you again."

"Be hard to cover any stories if I'm in jail."

"I think you're making far too much of my article. If you're that angry at me, are you planning to do me bodily harm, too?"

"The thought briefly crossed my mind, Ms. Dean, but I rejected it because I'm not in the habit of laying my hands on females."

"You considered slapping me around? Breaking my neck? Shooting me?"

"Briefly, yes. All of the above. If your article taints the jury against me and they incarcerate me for that many years, it'd do irreparable harm to my children and wife. I'm quite sure you know how I treat those that would harm my family—you've had two recent examples."

"I suggest you go back to your story about the garage. If you weren't the best reporter I ever hired, I'd be tempted to fire you after what you just told me. Know this, Kade Blackburn, if you ever lift so much as a finger to me . . ."

Kade smiled at her. "You'd do what? I know a hundred ways to kill a man. How many do you know? None—that I'm aware of—unless you include the article you wrote. That might be the one way it's possible for you to kill me. If I end up in prison, it will kill me, to have no congress with my family for that many years."

He got up and carefully pushed his chair in under the edge of her desk. The whole time he was pushing it in, she wondered if he were **briefly** considering bashing her head in with it.

The story of the crooked garage was on her screen by the time he left the building. Despite his apparent anger over her article, the facts were all there to support his accusations. Unlike Diana, Kade made it nearly impossible for anyone to sue the paper, so complete and accurate were his articles. She made a note on her calendar to give him some praise for the article he'd written.

Dean met him the moment he stepped into the paper's offices in the morning. "Kade, another word?" she asked.

"Sure, Boss. Planning to write another article? Need to plumb me for more information of a personal nature. Maybe you'd like to write about how Abby and I make love. Those warm-fuzzy disclosures might counter the readers' impression that I'm just a hard-hearted bastard who kills and cripples without remorse."

Dean pointed to her office and after he'd entered her door, she shut it none too gently. "I didn't intend to take up where we left off yesterday, Mr. Blackburn. I just wanted to tell you your article about the garage was a top-notch accounting."

"Thank you. If that's all you wanted from me, I'd better discuss with Diana which articles I can cover without having another door slammed in my face—or behind my back."

"I had a call from the mayor. Guess he's feeling some heat from the citizens from what I wrote. He's called me in to discuss the situation with you—you not being able to cover all the news. I'd like you to go with me. Let him see for himself what a good reporter you are."

"Yesterday, you were this close to firing me," Kade said, holding his thumb and index finger very close together. "Why the change of heart?"

"You remember our former discussion about how I need the admiration of my reporters or I fire them?"

"Yes. You discussed that very personal item with me a long time ago. Don't think you ever saw a reference to it in any of the articles I wrote, did you?"

"Kade, I'd print a retraction of my article if I thought it would do any good. It would likely just cement their opinions of you more in their minds if I did that."

"I agree. No retractions."

"I'd like to apologize for creating that negative impression of you in readers' minds in the first place."

Kade shrugged. "It's water under the bridge now. I got a notice yesterday that my trial on the assault charges is scheduled for the second week of September. Finally, I guess, the Johnson lawyers have a hook to hang their hats on."

"Because of my article?"

Again he shrugged. "That might have let them line up their ducks in a row. Won't know until we all sit down in the courtroom if the article is responsible for their sudden flurry of activities and filings."

"Kade . . ."

He shook his head. "I need to go to work. What time is the meeting with the mayor?"

"It's at one. Can I take you to lunch at 11:30 and then we'll go to the meeting?"

"No, I'm meeting Abby for lunch. There are some private things I need to talk to her about. Can't do that at home. Alli is always skulking around one doorway or another, listening in. I think that child is destined to become a CIA agent."

"Will you be back in time we can go to the meeting together?"

"I'll be back by one. Is that in enough time?"

"Yes. Enjoy your lunch with Abby."

He came back to the paper at 12:45. Dean was in Diana's cubicle letting her know she didn't approve of Diana's latest article. He went quietly to his own station and sat down to read what Diana had written. Gardner always sent him her articles before she sent them to Dean. He'd been so upset about Dean's article, he hadn't felt his head was together enough to edit Diana's.

"You've been doing so much better, Gardner," Dean said. "This time you've opened the paper to a lawsuit because you didn't support your assertions with facts and proof. Kade always has enough facts and proof included in his article to not lay us open to a suit."

"I always shoot him my article before I send it to you or the printers. He usually catches me on the errors of omission, but this time he never came back to me with a single suggestion."

"Kade has enough work to do without having to edit—or make suggestions—on your articles. How long have you been relying on him to critique what you write?"

"Ever since you hired me. He's gracious about looking over what I write . . . at least he's never complained."

"I'm going to have a meeting with both of you, but right now I am due at a meeting with the mayor. I'm taking Kade with me. If you have some facts to back up this article, they'd better be in your report before I get back."

"Yes, ma'am."

"Kade are you ready to go?"

"Two minutes, then I'll be ready."

"Make that one minute. It's best not to be late when you're going hat-in-hand asking for a big favor."

"Yes, ma'am, one minute it is."

# Chapter Twenty-one

They arrived at Mayor Hoffman's office and took side-by-side seats in the reception area.

The secretary said, "I set the appointment up for just you, Ms. Dean. Were you intending to invite him to meet with the mayor, too?" she asked, nodding at Kade.

"This is Mr. Blackburn. He's the reporter that everyone has deemed persona non grata. So I brought him along to assure the mayor he's not the devil incarnate."

"The man who broke Chief Johnson's neck?"

Kade smiled and nodded, "Yes, ma'am."

"I'm not sure the mayor will want you in attendance. Not while he speaks to Ms. Dean."

"That's fine. I'll just keep you company if Hoffman wants to talk to my boss alone."

She paled at his suggestion. "I don't want to seem inhospitable, but . . ."

"You'd rather not be left alone with me?"

"Well, yes . . . I'd be afraid . . ."

"Mr. Blackburn was very angry with me a couple of days ago, but he assured me he's never raised an angry hand against a woman. I think you'll be perfectly safe if I leave him here."

"Let me check with Mayor Hoffman, perhaps he can see you both at the same time."

She picked up the phone and called back to the mayor's office. "Ms. Dean is here for her 1 p.m. meeting and she's brought Mr. Blackburn with her. Can you meet with both of them at the same time?"

She finally hung up the phone. "He wants to see Ms. Dean first."

"Behave yourself, Kade."

"Yes, ma'am."

Dean disappeared into the hallway going to Hoffman's office, leaving Kade alone with the secretary. She kept looking at him with questions apparent in both eyes.

"You're curious why I did what I did to Chief Johnson?" he asked.

"Yes," she said in a very shaky voice.

"Okay, brief explanation. I was wearing one of those tracking anklets because I'd shot Fred Rossman. My wife offered to give me a haircut at the barn. I never thought about calling in when I left the house, until the anklet went off with a scream. I let Abby finish my haircut.

"When she was done, two deputies showed up. I was hauled to jail for not reporting in when I left the house. While I was in custody, I stood before Judge Nickerson. He gave me two weeks as a sentence. I asked to start my incarceration on Monday as I'd promised my twins I'd hunt up worms and grubs for the chickens on Sunday.

"Johnson insisted I begin my sentence Saturday. While I was in his jail, he came in at midnight, sent the guard out for eats, and proceeded to beat me with a wooden cane. Later, I indicated I intended to sue him for that beating."

"Did you file a complaint about the beating?" she asked.

"Yes. Both Ms. Dean and I filed a lawsuit. Then I get a call at lunch from Johnson, saying he's abducted my wife and the twins. Told me to meet him on the courthouse lawn and sign a paper dropping the lawsuit or he'd take the same wooden cane to my twins."

"What did you do?"

"I drove to the courthouse and saw where he was located. He directed me to the paper he wanted me to sign, but instead of heading off to sign it, I started in his direction. He pulled his gun and shot me through the right shoulder. I was so angry by that point, I kept on coming anyway. Kicked the gun out of his hand and put him in a half-nelson hold. To protect my twins from any canings by Johnson's hand, I reached over his shoulder with my left hand, inserted my thumb behind his molars and broke his neck."

"How?"

"I'm Army trained. I'm a veritable killing machine. I know a lot of ways to kill a man, which came in handy in Iraq and Afghanistan. Killing is officially sanctioned in a war zone, but if someone threatens my wife or children, I find it hard to turn off those impulses, now that I'm a civilian.

"I knew I didn't want Johnson taking his wooden rod to my twins, so I decided I would incapacitate him permanently, so he couldn't do that."

"Have you ever killed a woman over there in the Middle East?"

"No."

She seemed to visibly relax after he'd related his reason for putting Johnson in a wheelchair.

"His beating hurt you a lot?"

"Yes, ma'am. He kept his blows down off my face, so no one would know he'd taken his rod to me. Each time he hit me, and he hit me some 30 times, I'd grin like it wasn't all that painful—even though it was. Finally he hit me across the face, ostensibly to wipe my grin from it. Otherwise, without the cut lip and black eye, Judge Nickerson wouldn't have known about the beating."

"You couldn't imagine putting your twins through a similar experience?"

"I wasn't willing to take that chance, that's why I broke his neck."

"Maybe you're not such a horrid fellow after all. Just listening to everyone talk about poor Chief Johnson, all their chatter colored my feelings about you. Thanks for telling me why you really did that to him."

Her phone rang at that point. "The mayor said for you to come in now. I think I'd tell him what you just told me."

He walked into Hoffman's office, unsure of the reception he'd get. Stuck out his hand to shake the mayor's extended mitt.

"Have a seat, Mr. Blackburn. Ms. Dean has explained in detail why you felt the need to break Chief Johnson's neck. I went to visit him several times in the hospital and he's come to see me here in my office. Not once did he mention his threat against your family, or allude to what he'd done to you in jail."

"I suspect I wasn't the only one he'd applied his cane to, sir. I think he put something in my drink that night. The cell monitor, Burt . . . likely against orders . . . brought me a glass of water at ten most nights, since I only got one meal each day. I believe Johnson knew Burt had broken the rules, so that made it easy to dose my water and send Burt packing so Johnson could beat me."

"You will, of course, be allowed to continue to report on all phases of the news without further restrictions."

"Thank you, sir. Not sure if your edict to that effect will have much influence on the guys at the police station. They seemed to stand firmly in Chief Johnson's corner."

"I suspect Johnson has something on all of them, making them afraid he'd spill the beans if they let you in for your interviews. I'll assure them that any information the Chief holds against them will not influence me as to their continued employment."

"That might just do the trick, sir. We'll see in the next few weeks if they'll loosen up enough to again give me information for the paper."

"Kade, I'd like to apologize on behalf of the City of Prescott for what you endured under Johnson's hand—both the beating and the shooting."

"No permanent harm done, sir."

"Ms. Dean says your court date is scheduled for September. I'd be willing to come and testify on your behalf if you think I could do you some good."

"I appreciate that offer, sir. Since you weren't there, I'm sure your testimony would be dubbed 'hearsay' and would likely be thrown out. Might be of greater use to get some of the cops at the jail to testify to what they'd actually seen of the Chief's transgressions."

"I'll see what I can do in that regard. If you have no further questions, I'll let you get back to producing that wonderful paper you both put out."

Kade and Ms. Dean left the mayor's office, just as an orderly was wheeling Chief Johnson in.

"**You! Why are you here?**" Johnson shouted. "They should never let you into city hall. Did you break the mayor's neck?"

"No, sir, since he never stole my children or threatened to beat my twins."

"Kade, let's go," Dean said, noticing Johnson still wore his gun. Though she knew he couldn't access it, she wasn't sure the orderly wasn't one of his toadies.

"Yes, ma'am."

"I'll eventually convince Ms. Dean to evict you from your job, since you'll have no more access to any crime reports. He won't be much use to you if he can't cover the police station's beat, will he?"

"I'm sure I can find enough other news to keep Mr. Blackburn busy, Chief Johnson."

"Maybe I'll make sure no one from the paper, including you, has access to any news from the police station. Ralph, wheel me into the mayor's office, then wait outside until I need to leave."

"Of course, Chief Johnson."

As they approached Ms. Dean's vehicle, she said, "He's one nasty piece of work. Even in a wheelchair, he still thinks he can lord it over the general population. Thanks for keeping your cool, Kade."

"What did you think I was going to do? Upset his chair and send him sprawling?"

"He's still wearing his sidearm. Wasn't sure if he could lift it, or if the guy pushing him around might be tempted to shoot you with it."

"Wait until the mayor tells Johnson that his ban is off. We might need to sit here in your car for a few to see if the guy is mad enough to instruct his valet to shoot the mayor."

"You think his valet is in Johnson's pocket? Willing to do anything the Chief demands?"

Kade shrugged. "I have no idea if the orderly is on Johnson's payroll or how far his loyalty extends."

"Let's leave. I have stuff to do at the paper."

"Okay. I have stuff to do there, too."

The trial Chief Johnson filed about Blackburn's assault came up on September 10th. The one Dean and Blackburn had filed for Kade's beating got lumped in with Johnson's suit.

Abby and all four children sat in the row behind the table where Kade sat with his lawyer. Johnson sat at the table to Kade's right with his lawyer. That promoted some nervousness in the twins.

*Just seeing him again is going to rev up more nightmares,* Kade thought. *I was hoping to spare them this ordeal, but my lawyer said the jury needed to see the twins that Johnson abducted.*

Chief Johnson's lawyer called Ms. Dean to the stand. She took her seat after being sworn in. Crossed her legs and gave Kade a wink.

"Ms. Dean, what kind of man do you think Kade Blackburn is? Is he a responsible employee?"

"More than a responsible employee. Kade works long hours. He's a very good writer. He knows how to put together an article better than any other reporter I ever hired."

"Is he honest?"

"Yes, very honest."

"So when you wrote in your article that Mr. Blackburn has a hard core inside, what did you mean by that?"

Dean could see Kade's grin. She frowned at the finger he used to scratch a point in the air related to Dean's article, the article he'd asked to edit before it hit the streets.

"I meant he doesn't nourish much sympathy for those who'd do his family harm."

"He evidenced no regrets for having killed Fred Rossman?"

"No, since Fred showed up with the intent . . ."

"A simple 'yes' or 'no' will suffice, Ms. Dean. He didn't feel at all bad about killing Rossman?"

"No."

"What was his reaction to breaking Chief Johnson's neck? Again he advanced no regrets?"

"No, he seemed to have no regrets in that instance, either."

"He's admitted to you that he knows several ways to kill or incapacitate a person, has he not?"

"Yes. He served in Iraq and Afghanistan. It was part of his Army training."

"Did that make you afraid of him?"

"No. He told me he'd never raised a hand in anger toward a woman."

"He has been angry with you a few times, hasn't he? Did you ever worry that he might make an exception for you?"

"When Kade's been angry with me, I never worried about that sort of retaliation."

"Why not?"

"I don't believe it's in him to harm a woman. It's not in his code of ethics."

"You think he has ethics?"

"I do."

"Was it ethical to break Chief Johnson's neck and put him in a wheelchair?"

"Maybe not, but under the circumstances . . ."

"Questions of this witness?" Johnson's lawyer asked Kade's legal beagle."

"One or two. When Fred Rossman came to the Blackburn ranch, who fired the first shot?"

"The sheriff determined Rossman had fired first."

"Why didn't Blackburn try to just wound Rossman?"

"Kade was shot through the thigh. He said he could feel the blood running down his leg. He said if he just shot to wound Rossman, he couldn't be sure that Fred wouldn't take advantage of him if he passed out from pain and loss of blood. Said he couldn't take the chance that Rossman wouldn't kill him and his family if he passed out, so he shot to kill to prevent that from happening."

"Redirect? No? Then, you're excused, Ms. Dean. I call Kade Blackburn to the stand," Kade's lawyer said.

Kade came forward, took the oath and seated himself in the witness chair.

"What led up to the fiasco on the courthouse lawn, Mr. Blackburn?"

"Because the deputies weren't sure how to assess the fact I'd killed Rossman, I was required to wear a tracking anklet on my leg. I was supposed to call in each time I left or returned to the house, or the paper."

"Were you faithful in meeting that requirement."

"Mostly. A couple of times I forgot to call in."

"What happened when you forgot?"

"Deputies showed up at my door, to ascertain I hadn't taken a powder."

"How many times did they come to ascertain that?"

"Two or three times. Once when I'd gone out to feed the stock. Once when Abby, my wife, wanted to give me a haircut in the barn."

"Why not give you one in the house?"

"She wanted to do it at the kitchen table. I didn't want to be eating shorn hair mixed in with my dinner, so she suggested I kneel down on the stanchion she uses to trim her goat's hair. Her suggestion made me laugh, so I forgot to call in. She'd just finished my haircut when the deputies rolled in. Cuffed me and hauled me to jail.

"Chief Johnson dragged me before Judge Nickerson the next morning. Told him he was tired of sending out his men to check on my whereabouts. I said I'd be willing to start my two weeks in jail for my transgressions, if I could start my sentence on Monday. On Sunday I had told my twins I'd hunt up grubs and worms with them to feed to the chickens. The Chief took exception to that. Said he wanted my jail time to start right then. So I was incarcerated that very day."

"What happened while you were jailed?"

"I got breakfast, but no other meals. The chief left my hands cuffed tightly until I lost all feeling in them. Judge Nickerson came by and insisted the guard take off the cuffs. I think that made Chief Johnson even angrier."

"What occurred at midnight?"

"The guard always gave me a glass of water about 10 p.m. I drank it, then fell asleep. Next thing I knew I was cuffed with both my hands over my head to the bars of the cell. I wasn't aware of much until Chief Johnson plied his rod to me. That woke me up in a hurry."

"How often did he hit you?"

"Didn't keep count, maybe 25-30 times. He kept all of them down on my torso, so that told me he didn't want any blows to be seen. I started grinning at him each time he hit me. My grin made him angry enough to hit me once in the face. When Nickerson came to see me, it was apparent I'd been beaten, so Nickerson shipped me over the mountain to serve my remaining days at the Verde Valley jail."

"Tell me about the phone call you got at lunch once you were free again."

"Chief Johnson said he'd taken my wife and children—abducted them. Told me to meet him at the courthouse and sign a paper that said I'd be willing to dismiss the lawsuit for the beating he'd given me. Told me if I didn't sign, he'd use the same rod he used on me on my twins."

"Those twins sitting behind our defense table?"

"Yes, sir. They're only five. I knew they'd never be able to abide even a couple of licks from Johnson's rod."

"Go on."

"Instead of heading over to the paper he wanted me to sign, negating the lawsuit, I started marching in his direction. He pulled his gun and shot me in the right shoulder. I think he thought I was all out of fight, but I kept right on coming. I grabbed him by the arm and pulled it up into a half-nelson lock behind his back with my bad arm. I reached across his shoulder with my left arm, inserted my thumb behind his molars, ignored his biting, and gave a jerk, breaking his neck."

"Judge Mitchell, I'd like to enter into evidence the paper Chief Johnson wanted Mr. Blackburn to sign."

"So entered."

"Cross?" Kade's lawyer asked the other lawyer.

"Of course I want to cross him. Mr. Blackburn you never entertained the idea of signing the paper Chief Johnson wanted you to sign?"

"No, sir. I had no idea where he might have sequestered my wife and children. Because I was afraid he might ply his rod on the twins, I knew I had to negate his ability to do so. Due to my Army training, I knew exactly what I had to do to prevent him from raising his rod and hitting my children."

"A good man will never walk again. You have no regrets about that?"

"No, sir. When we located my wife and the twins in the basement of Johnson's home, they were trussed up with duct tape and the twins looked absolutely petrified. They still have nightmares about that experience."

"You may step down, Mr. Blackburn."

"I call the twins to the stand."

Abby stood up and took Kory and Kathy by their hands, to lead them to the witness chair.

Judge Mitchell spoke to both twins. "You do know what it is to tell the truth, don't you?"

"Yes, sir. That means we can't tell any lies," Kory said. "Me and Kathy know how to tell the truth. Our daddy taught us the difference between truth and lies."

"Good. You can both sit together in the seat and tell the truth."

Kory and Kathy climbed on the witness seat and looked anywhere but at Chief Johnson. The chief's lawyer went first.

"Children, did your father tell you anything about testifying today? Did he tell you what to say or not to say?"

"We didn't know until this morning after he left for work we had to come here, so Daddy didn't have a chance to tell us anything."

"He didn't say anything to you?"

Both kids shook their heads.

"Move on, sir," Judge Mitchell said.

"Who took you and your mother to somewhere you didn't want to go?"

"He did," both twins said, pointing at Johnson.

"What did he say to you when he put you in his car?"

"He didn't say anything, just told Mom that he'd shoot both of us if she didn't go along with his plan."

"Did she go along with his plan?"

"Yes, I could tell she was scared, but she tried to be brave so as not to scare us."

"What did Chief Johnson do when he got to his house?"

"He made us go down to the cellar. Told us he was going to lock us in so he could scare the shit out of our daddy to get him sign a paper to drop his lawsuit."

"Kory Alan Blackburn, I don't think we use language like that in our household," Kade admonished his son.

"Daddy, aren't we supposed to tell the truth—the whole truth? How can I tell him what that man said," Kory cried, pointing at Johnson, "if I can't say it the way he said it?"

"Okay, son. I'll overlook your bad language this time."

"Then what did he do?"

"He tied up Mom first, then made me and Kathy sit in chairs and he tied our arms and legs to the chair using that gray tape."

"Were you frightened?"

"Yes, I think it's fair to say he scared the shit out of me, too," Kory said, pressing his advantage.

Kade saw Mitchell was trying hard not to laugh.

"What happened next?"

"I tried to be brave for Mom and Kathy, but I was really frightened. He had that gun in his holster and I was scared he'd shoot Daddy and maybe all of us, too."

"What happened then?"

"He turned out the lights and it was very dark. He went out the door and I thought I heard him lock it from the outside. I was really scared then. Not as much as Kathy, because she saw a spider before he turned off the lights and she hates spiders. But Mama began to sing some songs and that took my mind off how scared I was."

"Your witness," Johnson's lawyer said.

"Did Chief Johnson threaten you in words? Did he say he was going to beat you, or shoot you?"

Kory shook his head. "No, but he had a very mean look on his face, so I wasn't sure what he'd do if Daddy wouldn't sign the paper."

"I'd like to recall Kade Blackburn to the stand, your Honor."

Kade hugged Kory and Kathy as he traded seats with them.

"It was implied he'd beat your twins if you refused to sign the paper?"

"Yes, sir. It was more than implied. It was a direct statement over the phone when he told me to meet him at the courthouse."

"It's obvious you love your children, so you didn't want that to happen?"

"No, sir. I'd have gone to any lengths on earth to prevent him from harming my wife or the twins."

"That's why you chose to break his neck?"

"Yes, sir. I knew if he couldn't use his arms or his legs, he wouldn't be able to use his wooden cane on my children."

"You have no regrets for placing Chief Johnson in a wheelchair?"

"No, sir. My twins are still having nightmares about being snatched off the street and tied up. If he'd succeeded in beating the twins, you wouldn't have been able to find any two inches of him to put back together. He'd be like Humpty Dumpty and none of the king's horses or none of the king's men could reassemble Johnson. He should consider himself lucky he's not in Humpty Dumpty pieces."

"How would you have accomplished that deed, Mr. Blackburn?"

"I'd have caught him. Tied him up, used a stick of dynamite. Placed it inside his ass and lit the fuse."

"Daddy, you said a bad word again. When we go home, you need to sit in the corner for two hours," Kathy told him.

This time Mitchell couldn't contain his laughter. Finally he regained control, and asked, "Is that the standard punishment for saying a bad word in the Blackburn household?"

"Yes, sir, it is. Kory and I may be sharing the corner later on."

"I believe I've heard enough. I'm going to retire to my office and consider my judgment in this case. I don't believe it will take me very long."

Judge Mitchell was back inside an hour. Kade grabbed Abby's hand and crossed his fingers in hopes of a good verdict.

"After reviewing all the testimony as well as the input of the jailers about Chief Johnson's treatment of others incarcerated in his jail, it is my considered judgment that Chief Johnson's actions warranted what befell him. If he'd threatened my family members, I might have contemplated a like punishment. Judgment in favor of Kade Blackburn."

*"Jesus Christ! You're just going to let him off after what he did to me? I might be in a wheelchair, but I have friends. You'll rue the day you let him off."*

"Are you threatening me, Mr. Johnson?"

"That's still Chief Johnson to you, asshole."

"Wrong. I have it on good authority, that the mayor will be firing you in the morning. You'll never again hold a position of command in the city of Prescott."

"I'll sue Blackburn in civil court. He's going to pay for what he's done to me in one way or another."

"Doubt you'll win in that court, either, Mr. Johnson. You may as well admit defeat. Even your friends want nothing to do with you anymore."

*"I'll never admit defeat!"*

"Then I'd advise you to keep your nose clean and stop making threats, sir."

Kade and his family, along with Ms. Dean went to celebrate the verdict that night.

"I see what you meant about my column giving Johnson's lawyer a lot of fodder to question you about," Dean said.

"It's all water under the bridge, now, ma'am. I'd just as soon not dwell on any more aspects of the trial. I want to eat my steak and join my son in the corner as soon as we both get home."

"Aw, Dad, are you really going to make me sit in the corner with you? I was just telling the truth about what that man said."

"It might be something we can negotiate about, Kory."

"What's 'negotiate' mean, Daddy?"

"It means we can talk about it and work out a solution that makes us both happy."

"I think you'll only be happy with me sharing the corner with you."

"I would have been okay with you telling what Chief Johnson said, in the first instance, but you just had to go and test my limits by saying 'shit' twice, didn't you? That's why I think you deserve to share the corner later tonight with me."

"Aw, Dad. How come it's okay for you to say that word, and not me?"

"I suppose Mama will make me sit in the corner for four hours for using two bad words in a row."

"Can I come over and get a photo of that?" Dean asked.

"Oh, no you don't. If I see you lurking around any corners hoping for a candid shot, I'm going to start writing my articles just like Diana does."

"Oh, for the love of God. Spare me the grief," Dean wailed.

"Daddy, she said a bad word, too," Kathy said.

"What bad word?" Dean asked.

"You said 'God' in a disrespectful way," Kathy said. "Mama says we need to be respectful of the person many in the community worship."

"Think we should be three in the corner after dinner?" Kade asked, grinning.

"Yes, Daddy."

"Are you game?" Kade asked Dean.

"Of course. Far be it of me to be dismissive of the Blackburn family rules. Course tomorrow you'll get the worst half of the list I generate."

"Deal. Give me the worst assignments you can think up. After the court decision, there's no assignment that can possibly rankle me."

Once back on the ranch, Dean and Kory joined Kade in the corner. Abby laid out the rules. "No talking, no eating, no anything. Just contemplate your bad words and vow to let them never pass your lips again. Kade you have to sit for four hours. Kory and Ms. Dean will do two each."

"Aw, Mom," Kade whined in his best Kory voice. "Can't I just do two, as well?"

"Nope. You have to do all four."

"Okay. I may be late arriving tomorrow at the paper if she makes me sit up until midnight. By the time I get done making whoopee with her . . ."

"**Kade!** One more word out of you and you won't make it to work at all tomorrow, or you'll be in with two eyes so black you can't see out of them well enough to work."

"Better shut up while you're still ahead," Ms. Dean said, before bursting into laughter.

Dean went home at ten, and Kory went to bed at the same hour. Kade continued to sit in the corner.

"Sometimes I wish the judge had sentenced you to a few months behind bars. You can never just let well enough alone. You always have to embarrass me in front of a total stranger."

"Ms. Dean is a stranger?" he asked.

"To me she is. Making whoopee? Is that something you'd appreciate me saying about you in front of my friends?"

"Come here and share the corner with me for a moment." Abby came over and sat on his lap. "I should be more circumspect when it comes to embarrassing you. I will try to accord you more respect in regards to that in the future."

"I know how much you enjoy sex with me, Kade. No wonder it becomes the topic of conversation so often. Whatever happened to those family secrets that tend to glue us together? You don't mind voicing those secrets to anyone and everyone."

"You're right, Abby. I shouldn't be talking about sex with anyone but you. Can you forgive me?"

"I could if you didn't feel the need to joke about our bed relationships so often. You've made the same promise at least a dozen times, and every time you have an audience, you feel the need to amuse them by alluding to our sexual romps."

"No more, then. If you feel I'm heading off in that direction, just say, 'STOP' and I'll clam right up. Are my four hours up yet? Are we having tea and talk?"

"It's nearly midnight, so I guess you can get up five minutes early. Do you want tea and talk? You'll be dead at work tomorrow if we do tea and talk and sex besides."

"I'm willing to skip the sex. Let's have a cup of tea. We've already had our talk, so maybe I won't be totally dead at work tomorrow."

"Do you think there's any validity in Johnson's threat to make you pay in one way or another?"

"He's one angry camper, but he's going to need his money to hire attendants to take him places. That won't leave him much for hiring a hit man to take me out."

"Kade, please promise you'll be alert and not take any chances."

"I'm always alert and I seldom take chances. No use fretting about what may never occur."

"You always blow off my fears. Come sit down for tea and let's discuss that tendency of yours to make light of all my concerns."

"Sweetheart, several times now I've come out on the upside of some nasty situations. I don't want you to worry. It wrinkles up your brow and makes you look ten years older than you are."

"Oh, Kade, can't you be serious for once in your life?"

"Abby, I have plenty of insurance. If someone does me in, you'll be a lot better off than you are currently."

"Maybe in the money sense, but there are other things I like about you more than your insurance."

"I know. I still don't want you to keep fretting. What's going to happen will happen, so you don't need to worry about it in the present or the future. All that worry will not prevent anything from occurring. In the meantime, though, it tends to eat you up inside. Gives you ulcers. So stop worrying. I forbid you to worry."

"Let's go to bed. That's the one place where I can stop worrying. When you make love to me, I can't think of anything else besides what you're doing to me."

"I'll never turn down an invitation like that," he said, taking her by her hand and heading for the stairs.

# Chapter Twenty-two

He was late getting to work in the morning. Ms. Dean teased him about his tardiness, asking if he'd gotten some of that promised whoopee.

"I promised Abby not to allude to those family matters in front of strangers any more."

"I'm a stranger, now?"

"Abby said she didn't know you as well as I do, so I shouldn't be making sexual comments in front of you."

"Your son was just darling on the witness stand, and your daughter is no slouch about pointing out our adult transgressions, either. We get into such a bad habit of letting fly with bad words, or disrespectful ones that it's good she called us on our language."

"Mistress Morality, I call her. And my son thought he'd gotten permission from the judge to keep saying 'shit' several times. That kid takes advantage of every opportunity."

"Sort of like you do, Kade? I saw you wink and draw a point in the air when the Johnson lawyer referenced my column as a way to start casting you in a bad light."

"Have you given me the dregs on my half of the assignment list for drawing that air point?"

"You and Diana can split it however you please. These are the items I think should be covered. I, of course, will write up what happened at the trial, as I believe you could be a tad prejudiced about that article."

"I get to edit what you write this time, so if it comes to another trial I won't have to draw another point in the air?"

"Are you trying to take advantage of this specific opportunity, Mr. Blackburn?"

"No, ma'am. I need to get on with the day, seeing I'm getting a late start on it."

He stopped at Diana's cubicle to split the items for the day with her. Diana was in a bad humor he quickly realized.

"Does it give you inordinate pleasure when Dean rakes me over the coals? She's always holding you up as the end-all and be-all of reporting."

"I'm sorry I didn't get to edit that piece she was yelling about, but I had other more pressing matters on my mind."

"How did the trial go?" she asked.

"Judgment in my favor, for once in my life. Course, that doesn't prevent Johnson from suing me in civil court. I still have that to look forward to."

"Do you think they'll allow you to cover the jail matters?"

"I don't know. All I can do is try them out down there. See if they're willing to fill me in on the recent cases."

"Well, I'll give you that half then. I still hate all the prisoners yelling at me and whistling, calling me a dumb broad. I know you think I'm one of those, too, since I can't seem to write anything that merits Dean's approval."

Kade didn't comment on her statement, so she handed him part of the list to be covered.

"Are we meeting up for lunch, Kade?"

"I don't think so. I like sharing lunches with smart women, not dumb broads," he teased.

"Well, don't you think I'm one of those? I noticed you didn't leap in to deny my earlier statement."

"I'm rather tired this morning, Diana. No matter what I'd say, you'd take it wrong. It's obvious to me you aren't in the best of humors this morning."

"Because of you—your expertise at reporting is always being thrown in my face."

"Not by me. If you have a bitch with Dean, she's the one you should be discussing your unhappiness with."

"Right. You'd like it if she fired me, wouldn't you? Then you wouldn't have to edit everything I write. It would decrease your load here by half."

Kade pivoted and beat a rapid retreat to his own cubicle, thinking, *Sweetheart, if you'd learn to write some decent articles—ones where you didn't leave the paper open to a lawsuit, I sure would like that to happen. You're right, it would decrease my load by a lot here if you learned to put all the facts in your pieces. Ah, hell, Kade. No use tilting at windmills. Long as you keep editing her pieces, she'll never learn to do them right. I should let Dean kick you in the ass as often as she kicked me there when I started. That might make more of an impression on you than me editing your articles.*

About three that afternoon, she sent Kade her articles to edit. He continued to work on the pieces he was writing. When it came to quitting time and he still hadn't offered to comment on her articles, she marched into his cubicle.

"Are you going to put your imprint on my articles, or not?"

"Didn't think I would. Maybe if Dean applies the toe of her shoe to your posterior as often as she kicked mine when I hired on, you'll finally learn to do the articles right. I'm not willing to be the crutch you lean on anymore."

He could tell she was furious. She raised her middle digit in his direction and muttered something under her breath before returning to her small area with the intention of sending Dean her unedited columns. After she'd forwarded what she'd written, she left the building.

Dean came to his cubicle first thing the next morning. "Blackburn, why didn't you clean up her copy yesterday afternoon, like you always do?"

"I'm tired of doing that. I get a lot of grief on both sides of the issue—from you if I don't edit her stuff, and from her if I do. From now on, if you aren't happy, you should take it up with Diana personally. Pound some sense into her like you once pounded it into me. Don't put me in the middle anymore."

"Kade . . ."

"No, I'm serious. She, and you, count on me to clean up her copy. She needs to learn to stand on her own two feet. She suggested I think she's a 'dumb broad' then railed at me when I didn't contradict her statement.

"It never took me the better part of two years to learn the ropes, maybe because you rode me hard for the first six months. She might benefit from being ridden that hard by someone who has the power to fire her. She certainly isn't learning much from the fact that I'm editing her articles. I didn't contradict her statement, because I'm coming to think she *is* a dumb broad."

"Kade, that's by far the unkindest statement you ever made about a fellow journalist. Yes, you were quicker to pick up on my methods for writing articles, but she doesn't have your brilliant mind. It's not that she's a dumb broad, but she's not magna- cum-laude graduate in journalism, either. She'll get it eventually."

"Not by my hand or editing. I think she needs your hoof implanted in her panties as often as you planted it in my boxers."

"You're no longer willing to look over what she writes?"

"No, I'm not. It's doubled my workload. I get home later and later at night. The twins are about ready for bed, too tired for me to even read to them. I intend to quit at five from now on, not be hanging around until seven to edit her work. I'd like to eat at a decent hour and be able to spend some time with my family before they forget I'm a part of it."

"Will you be done with your assignments for the day by three, as usual?"

"Yes, ma'am."

"What do you intend to do between three and your 5 p.m. departure?"

Kade shrugged.

"I'll tell you what you're going to do. Edit Diana's work."

"If I refuse to do so?"

"I'd be forced to give you a sabbatical for a month or more, without pay. I need you to remember that I'm the editor here and you serve at my pleasure, Mr. Blackburn. Now are you willing to work with Diana's articles?"

He sat there a long time, not saying either 'yes' or 'no.'

"If you aren't willing to edit what she writes, you need to hand in your resignation. I'll not have employees who balk at following my orders. Is that clear, Mr. Blackburn?"

"Very clear, Ms. Dean. Since you hold all the aces, tomorrow morning, tell her to send me what she wrote so I can rewrite it in its entirety. May as well give me the whole list every morning and let me tackle it all. That way, I might still get home for dinner at a decent hour."

"You really are impressed with yourself, aren't you, Kade?"

"Yes, at least in the realm of journalism, I think I have good reason to be impressed with myself. You must be impressed with me, too, since you want to make me rewrite all Diana's articles."

"Not one word more, Mr. Blackburn, or I'll arrange for you to have a week off with no pay. That'd put a real crimp in your ranch payments."

He left at six, having rewritten all Diana's articles before forwarding them to Dean. Abby could tell, when he walked through the doorway into the kitchen, it had not been a good day at the paper.

"Tired?" she asked.

"Mad as he . . ." He cut off what he was about to say, not wanting to merit a couple of hours sitting in the corner. "I'll share the problem after all the kids are deep into dreamland and can't hear me cussing. Two hours in the corner would be the icing on a rather disastrous day."

He didn't say much to the children during dinner, which told Abby, more than anything how bad his day had been. He did bathe the twins and read to them, which to Abby seemed to unwind Kade a bit.

*No matter what a bitch of a day you endure, interacting with the twins seems to mellow out those problems. It almost makes me sad we won't have any more children. Once they get older it's hard for them to function as your stress reducers.*

At eleven, she fixed tea for their discussion session. "Tell me what went wrong today? Still not allowed to cover the crime scene?"

"No. The mayor seemed to have solved that problem. It's Diana. She still counts on me staying long into the evening to edit what she writes.

I told Dean I was not willing to do so anymore. I wanted to leave by five each afternoon to have time to spend with my family."

"How did Dean react?"

"Told me in no uncertain terms she was the editor and I served at her pleasure. Threatened me with a couple of months of leave with no pay if I stopped editing Diana's articles."

"I hope you agreed to pull in your horns and edit them. Two months without your income? We'd be out on the street in short order."

"It was only that vision, that made me knuckle under. I wanted in the worst way to tell Dean to 'shove it' and walk out—after I'd filled out my resignation. It may still come to me quitting, but not until I find another paper to work for."

"You weren't tempted to break her neck, were you?"

"I was sorely tempted, but I managed to throttle that desire. Got any more of those cookies? I could use something to sweeten up my disposition."

"Would a hot and steamy sexual encounter allow you to end the day on a better note?"

"Don't think I want to take you up on that. As angry as I am, you might get bruised up a bit."

She came back to the table bringing him four more cookies. She sat down on his lap and fed him the first one. "Kade, I know you'd never deliberately hurt me."

"No, not deliberately, but when I'm this angry, my mind isn't always in control."

"Would a back rub help?"

He grinned. "One of yours, not Corrine's? Sure, it might help."

He stretched out on the bed and she sat on his rump. She poured musky oil between his shoulders and began her massage. "Ummm. That sure feels good, wife."

She knew she'd succeeded in reducing the stress of his day when he started to softly snore. She snuggled in beside him and pulled up the comforter. *If you weren't burdened with all the members of this family and so many responsibilities, you could quit that job. I'm so sorry, Kade, that we add to your burdens.*

He came in to the paper the next morning in no better humor than he'd left the night before. Only Abby's massage let him eschew cursing at everyone he met. *I need to do something special for my very special wife,* he thought. *It's only because of her I might be able to keep my raging temper in check today.*

He called a florist and ordered her a dozen pink roses. That obligation done, he picked up his half of the list, and set out to cover the news. On the way out the door, he encountered Diana, who asked, "Are we meeting for lunch? Do you have any objections to the items you were assigned this morning?"

"I'm not allowed to object to anything at the paper, and no, I won't be meeting you for lunch. I need to skip lunch and get my articles written so I'll have time to edit yours before it comes to the witching hour of midnight."

"Are you angry about something this morning, Kade?"

"No, I'm not allowed to be angry, either. Try to get your stuff to me before three this afternoon. That way, I might not fall asleep with my face in my potatoes at dinner around ten tonight."

As Kade went to cover his items on the list, Diana went directly to Dean's office.

"What's up with Blackburn? He practically snapped my head off this morning."

"Kade told me last night he no longer wished to edit your articles. I told him I could arrange for a couple of month's sabbatical without pay if he was refusing to help you out. For a few seconds, he looked so furious with me, I thought he might do the same to me as he did to Chief Johnson."

"He shouldn't have to edit what I write."

"You still don't seem to have a complete idea about what has to be included. Kade knows instinctively what's missing. I'd as soon we weren't sued because you left out a critical fact, that's why I insisted he keep on editing your articles."

"So he's as furious with me for not knowing what has to be included as he is with you? Is it safe to sit in the next cubicle to his if he's that angry."

"I'll speak to him again when he gets back."

Kade returned at 11:30 and went to his computer to write up his articles. Dean summoned him to her office at noon. He'd completed three articles in that half hour, so he sent them to her before heading off to her office for what he surmised would be another tongue lashing.

Once he'd settled in the chair across from Dean, she said, "Diana said you bit her head off this morning. If you're angry at me, I'd as soon you didn't take it out on her."

"Is that all you wanted? I have to finish my articles so I'll be free this afternoon to edit hers."

"I don't like your current attitude. Take the next week off without pay. Let's see if that will improve your outlook."

"Starting now? Who will edit her articles if I'm enjoying an unpaid vacation at the ranch?"

"Leave now, Mr. Blackburn, before I'm tempted to fire you for good."

"Yes, ma'am."

When he came home at one, Abby knew he'd been given an unplanned vacation, even before he slammed the door hard enough to break one of the tiny panes of glass.

"Sorry. I'd better go get a replacement for that glass, since it's the one right above the lock. Anyone could reach in and turn the lock. If we were sleeping, no one would be the wiser."

"You still think the Chief is out to get even with you? She fired you?"

"No. Kind of wished she had. I'd have time to look for another job without having to return to my job to give her the standard two-week's notice. I'm not sure I want to go back to that particular paper."

"Kade, the twins are getting older. This fall they'll be in kindergarten. If you have to stay overtime to edit her articles, they can stay up a bit longer to enjoy dinner and some stories with you."

"You want me to pull in my horns? Put up with all the nonsense Dean thinks up?"

"Isn't that better than losing everything you've worked so hard for?"

He shook his head. "Yeah, I guess. Maybe after a week of Dean editing Diana's disasters, she'll have more sympathy for me. Is there something for lunch?"

"Of course. I'll fix you a sandwich."

"Where are the munchkins?"

"Up in their room, playing house. Kathy has her doll for their baby and Kory is hard at work on his toy computer, earning their pseudo family a living."

"Lord forbid he should go into journalism. But enough of this—I don't mean to infect you all with my bad humor."

With that, he plastered on a grin and poured himself a cup of coffee. "Nice to have some extra time to spend with all of you, I guess. Might get a few of those 'honey-do' chores accomplished in the next week."

"Kade, you don't need to work yourself to death in the next week. You've gotten up early and stayed up late to look after the animals, so there's not a herd of tasks awaiting your attention."

"We may be twisting a few more goats on the spit to have something to eat in the near future."

"Please, Kade, don't remind me of that time. It makes me sad all over again."

"Sorry. Didn't mean to dredge up painful memories."

She laid a sandwich on the table and he sat down to eat it. His appetite was at a low ebb, so he took a long time to consume her contribution. Before he'd eaten half of it, the twins arrived in the kitchen.

"Daddy, why are you home?" Kory asked.

"I got fired this morning. I may need a loan from your piggy bank. I was so angry, I slammed the door too hard and broke one of the small panes of glass. You both want to go with me to the hardware store and get a new piece of glass?"

"Yes," Kory said.

"No," Kathy told him. "Mama said I could help her make a cake for supper. She even said I could use the mixer to beat the batter for it."

"Okay, the women will take care of the domestic duties and we men will hie to the hardware store. We need to get some putty to hold the new pane in place, too. Kory, can I put you in charge of mixing up the putty?"

"Is it hard to mix the putty?" his son asked.

"No, I don't think so. If it turns out to be hard, maybe we could borrow mama's mixer to mix it up."

"*NO!*" Kathy wailed. "You can't use the mixer. It'd be all yucky for making the cake."

Kade rolled his eyes and said, "Are all females opposed to anything us males suggest?"

With the twins underfoot, with their endless questions, Abby saw that Kade had again relaxed and seemed less angry, too. *They're better than a session on the psychiatrist's couch for loosening you up, Kade. I hate to see them grow to adulthood. Who will temper your anger then?*

"Okay, we men are off to the hardware store. Do you need anything while we're gone?"

"I know you like walnuts on the cake, so if you pass a store, bring some of those home."

He nodded his willingness to fetch the walnuts. She waited until his truck had cleared the driveway before she sat down at the phone. For weeks, she'd intended to call Ms. Dean and tell her Kade was at the end of his tether because he had to spend extra hours editing Diana's articles. She wanted to apprise his boss of how early he got up to manage all the chores before he even arrived at the paper. He was putting in 16-hour days and not sleeping well because of all the items on his plate to accomplish.

She phoned the number and asked for Ms. Dean before she lost her courage.

"This is Dean," the voice said.

"Ms. Dean, this is Abby Blackburn. Kade didn't ask me to call you, nor do I want him to know I've called you. You've put him in an untenable position, asking him to edit or rewrite Ms. Gardner's articles. I don't know if you realize it, but he gets up at dawn to work around the ranch and feed all the stock. He often goes in early to the paper to do his own work. Then, when you require him to edit Diana's work, he gets home late and still has to do all the evening chores.

"He's putting in 16- to 18-hour days, and because of all the stress, he's not sleeping well, either. He was so angry when he came home . . ."

"He put you in a head lock and tried to break your neck?" Dean asked, chuckling.

"No, but he slammed the kitchen door hard enough to break a pane of glass."

"Shall I send the deputies out? Are you afraid for your life?"

"No, but I am afraid for Kade's life if the stress on him at work doesn't abate."

"I don't believe he didn't put you up to this call."

"I assure you he didn't ask me to call. He just left to get more glass to replace the broken pane, so I took this opportunity to call while he was gone. I can see that my call will have no effect on his stress levels, so just forget I called. When Kade drops over with a heart attack due to you requiring he do his work and Gardner's work, too, then whom will you get to edit her articles? I think he's been a damn good sport about that, and should have been paid extra for his efforts. Maybe . . . no, enough said."

"Maybe what? He'll look for another job? Fat chance—with his background, nobody in their right mind would hire him. Good afternoon, Mrs. Blackburn."

Abby's hand shook as she replaced the receiver. Kade would be furious with her when he learned she'd interceded on his behalf with Dean. She knew Dean would tell him at the first opportunity—unless, Kade found another job and never went back.

"Mama, when are we going to start the cake?" came Kathy's plaintive voice.

"Soon as your father gets back with the walnuts."

"Can't we bake the cake now? It has to cool before you can frost it and put on the walnuts."

"You're right. Let me get down the cake mix and a bowl and we'll start on the cake immediately."

Both of them were busy constructing a cake when Kade returned. Kathy was using the mixer to homogenize the mixture. Abby wasn't sure, from the look on his face, that Dean hadn't called him on his cell phone, to apprise him of her call.

"Kade . . ." she started to say.

"Later, wife. I need to trim this glass and get it in the right place. Kory, I'm going to put this putty into a plastic bag. You need to keep mixing it so it's soft when I need it to cement the pane into the hole."

She was sure he'd heard from Dean, when he said, "Later, wife," in what sounded like a growl to her. She was also sure that her insides would be roiling until their 11 p.m. tea, waiting to see how he viewed her intrusion into his work situation.

All through dinner he kept giving her glances. She knew that his raised-eyebrow questioning look didn't bode well for a quiet discussion at tea. He did help her with the dishes, in spite of his obvious displeasure. She was on pins and needles until all the children had gone to bed. She jumped when he laid a hand on her shoulder once he returned to the kitchen where she was putting a cover over the leftover cake.

"We need to talk, Abby," he said in a deadly quiet voice, like he was trying very hard not to give expression to his anger.

"I'll make the tea. Do you want another slice of cake?"

"I don't want tea or cake. Sit down, please."

"She called you?" Abby asked.

"Yes. Right in the middle of the hardware store she was shouting like a banshee over my phone. Accusing me of putting you up to calling her. Told me you said I put in some incredibly long days between ranch chores and work."

"You do put in incredibly long days. You shouldn't have to do Gardner's work in addition to your own."

"It wasn't up to you to plead my case to Dean, Abby. I didn't appreciate getting that call in the hardware store. I'm asking you to not make any more calls like that—not to anyone."

"Why not? I hate what she's done to you. Hate it when you come home so angry you break stuff. It makes me afraid when I see you that upset."

"That I might shoot you or break your neck?"

"Yes, you lose all reason when that kind of anger overtakes you."

"Have I ever lifted a hand to you in anger, no matter how angry I was?"

"No, but there's always a first time. I remember you snatching a book from my hand and hurling it so hard at the wall, a picture dropped down and broke."

He was quiet for a long time after she said that. "Abby," he finally said, "I'll never hurt you, but you've got to quit trying to protect me. It will be a thousand times more difficult to go back to work once my sabbatical is over."

"I just thought she should be aware of the long hours you put in without having to tackle Diana's articles, too."

"I appreciate your concern, but I don't appreciate you inserting yourself into my work situation. That's all I'm going to say about the matter, save for asking you not to ever call Dean again. Now I'd like some tea and cake."

She jumped up to cut him some cake and fill his cup with tea, thankful it had been a very quiet discussion.

# *Chapter Twenty-three*

His week off work came to an end. In the space of the week, he'd picked all the ripe fruit and vegetables, plowed up the garden, washed up the storm windows, and reseeded the lawn, getting ready for the long slide into an Arizona Indian summer.

Sunday night, before he was due to return to his job, he was very quiet at their 11 p.m. tea session.

"Will it be very hard to go back?" Abby asked as the silence continued.

Kade shrugged. "Yes, I suppose so. Both Diana and Dean have likely been chortling about your call all week. It's hard on my ego when they give me those Mona- Lisa smiles, alluding to the 'poor Kade' secret they've shared for the last seven days. Harder yet, when the printers have been told how you called to beg Dean for mercy about my duties—interceded on my behalf—like I was unable to address the problem myself."

"Would it help to have some very soothing sex? Maybe then you could smile your own Mona-Lisa grin."

"Yeah, that might help."

"Kade, I'm terribly sorry for calling Dean."

"Too late now to do anything about that call. I should have held the cell phone away from my ear in the hardware store, so everyone in existence would know what a harridan she can be."

"Let's go up to bed."

Once in bed, she thought he'd still be nourishing enough anger about the call to be rough with her. Instead, he was so gentle it surprised her.

"Kade, that was so sweet of you. Why were you so gentle this time?"

"Nothing I've said to you has convinced you that I'll never raise my hand in anger to you. You thought I'd take the last vestige of my anger out in our sex tonight, didn't you? That's why I was determined to keep it gentle. You don't remember how I walked you up to the big house the night I was so angry over your words that I threw your book against the wall?

"This gentle sex was the same as me walking you up to the big house that night. My way of telling you that you don't ever need to fear me, because even when I'm furious, I'll not be doing you any physical harm."

Abby started to cry at his admission. "Kade, I could never have picked a man who suits me more than you do," she sobbed. "So many times you have been so very angry . . .and mostly for a good reason . . . yet you have never . . ."

". . . and I never will, wife. Let's go to sleep. I need a good six hours if I'm expected to bear up under all those Mona-Lisa smiles tomorrow."

"Just remember how much we all love you, Kade, and you should be able to sail through all their grins."

"I'll try to keep that in mind tomorrow."

He arrived at eight and went directly to his cubicle. Diana came in at nine.

"Oh, look who's returned from his unintended vacation."

Kade didn't say a word in response. At ten, Dean invited both of them to her office. Kade kept the sex with Abby firmly in mind as he sat down across from the boss in her bailiwick.

"Have you learned your lesson?" Dean asked. "Are you going to continue to give me grief about me asking you to edit Diana's articles?"

"Yes, I've learned my lesson about that subject."

"Your wife won't be calling me up to weep on my shoulder again, will she?"

"I don't believe so, Ms. Dean."

"You had a discussion with her about that subject, I take it?"

"Yes, ma'am."

He could see Diana smirking to his right.

They were finally dismissed, Dean handing each a separate list to follow for articles to cover for the day.

"You might want to remove that grin from your face, Ms. Gardner," Kade said sotto voce as they walked down the hallway. "I still know at least 30 ways . . . I might not be inclined to use any of those ways on a female . . . unless she kept provoking me."

"Are you threatening me, Kade?"

He shrugged. "Construe my statement anyway you wish."

Kade had his articles written up by three, anger having lent speed to his fingers on the computer. He forwarded them to Dean. She arrived at his cubicle shortly after she'd received them.

"These articles are not up to your usual excellence this afternoon, Kade. Care to give me a reason why you've adopted Diana's style?"

"No, ma'am."

"This is your form of payback for your week off?"

"No, ma'am."

"You'll rewrite the articles and I'd better not get any more bullshit out of you, Mr. Blackburn."

"Yes, ma'am."

His endeavors were interrupted late in the afternoon by a cell phone call from Pennsylvania. "Mr. Kade Blackburn?" the caller asked.

"That's me. To whom do I have the pleasure of talking to?" he asked.

"This is Brandon Gilkey. I was your father's lawyer."

"Was? He fired you?" Kade asked, smiling while thinking about his father's visit.

"No, he died yesterday. He called me before he passed on and, per his instructions, I'm taking care of his affairs from this end."

Kade again smiled. *If you only knew how much he enjoyed his Arizona affair.* "Then, I'm supposed to come back there to take care of the things you can't bill him for?"

"No, he made it clear that you're not to come east for any reason. He asked that no services be held because he wanted to be cremated. He's to be buried in the same plot with your mother. His housekeeper, according to Ben, is charged with cleaning out his clothes and other items. Then an auction company will come in to auction off his furniture and sell the house. He left only a large mailing tube with me to be forwarded to you. All other instructions were written to me.

"I'm very sorry to be the one to transmit such bad news, Mr. Blackburn. There is one piece of good news, however. There was a $100,000 insurance policy that Ben had. He wanted you to be the beneficiary of that amount of money."

"Less what you're charging for taking care of all the other matters?" Kade asked.

"No, Ben put aside enough to cover those other matters. The whole check will be sent to you as soon as the insurance company forwards it to me. It should go to The Ark Ranch in Chino Valley, Arizona. Do you have a box number?"

"Yes, it's box 425, highway 89 north. Thanks so much for taking care of things on Dad's end, Mr. Gilkey."

"Ben was my friend. When the house sells, I'll forward the check for those funds to you, too."

Saddened by the news of the death of his father, it was five in the afternoon before his articles approached his usual standards. Instead of going home, he had to edit Diana's articles. That took him until well after nine. Abby called once on his cell phone, and he explained he was still editing Diana's work. He punched out at ten, copied his time card on the Xerox machine and stuffed the copy in his pocket. He saved telling Abby about Gilkey's news of Ben's death for their tea session.

*I think I know what's in the big tube Dad left with you, Gilkey. It's got to be the painting of you that Corrine did. I wonder if she'd be willing to put some pants and a shirt over your naked body, so I could hang the painting up in our home to remember you by. I'll call her and ask her about altering the portrait once it arrives.*

Each day that week, his quitting time approached nine in the evening. Each day, he carefully copied his time card.

*Ms. Dean, now due to Dad's insurance policy and the possible sale of his home, I intend to hire a consultant who concerns himself with overtime pay—or the lack of it. I'm not going to say anything for the next six months or a year, then I'm going to hit you up for all my overtime hours. Let's see you laugh with Diana about that extra pay you'll owe me.*

After apprising Abby of his father's death and the benefits Ben had left for his only son, Kade kept his head down for the next six months, before he filed a complaint with the Board or Adjustments over his unpaid extra hours. Two weeks later a representative from the board showed up and demanded to see everyone's time cards—those of all eighteen paper employees for the last year or two. He also confiscated Dean's financial records so he could tally the hours employees had worked against the pay she was paying to those who had worked more than eight hours.

"Ms. Dean, you have several employees at the paper who have not been afforded overtime pay for their long hours. Care to explain that lack?" the agent asked.

After a long-winded explanation, which didn't satisfy Agent Coburn in the least, he asked her to summon Kade Blackburn to her office.

"Was he the one who filed a complaint?" she asked.

"I'm not at liberty to divulge who filed the complaint," he explained, "but Mr. Blackburn seems to have more reason to complain, though I'm not saying he filed the formal complaint. Last week, Blackburn put in 72 hours and was paid for only 40 of them, according to his time card and your records. I suggest you invite him to join our discussions."

Kade came at her summons and took a seat in the chair beside Coburn.

"This is your most recent time card?" Coburn asked, laying it out on the desk.

"Yes, it is, sir."

"This is the amount you were paid, for this week's work?" he asked consulting Dean's checkbook.

"Yes, sir."

"You owe Mr. Blackburn for 32 hours of overtime."

"No, I don't. It's not my fault he's so slow about writing up the news items I send him out to cover," Dean said.

"That can't be true. I took the liberty of accessing Mr. Blackburn's recent evaluations, for which he had saved copies. He keeps his evaluations in his desk. It says here in his photocopied personnel file that he's your best reporter. I doubt you'd have given him that sort of praise if he were such a slacker. What time are your articles usually written up each day, Mr. Blackburn?"

"Mine are always done by 3:15 or 3:30, sir, forwarded to Ms. Dean no later than 4 p. m."

"What holds you so long past the quitting hour then?"

"Ms. Dean has asked me to edit another reporter's articles. I essentially have to rewrite them, which holds me over until a much later quitting time. All articles have to be on Ms. Dean's computer by eight the following morning, so she can check them before they go to the printers for their run."

"Why have you asked him to edit another reporter's articles?"

"I asked him to mentor her. He's dogging that editing if he's staying that late. He should be done with her stuff by six."

"That's still an hour past his eight-hour quitting time. I believe you'll need to show up before our board and explain the discrepancies. You'll also need to arrange to pay all the overtime due to all your employees."

"This is a small paper. I can't afford that much overtime pay. Certainly not for slackers like Mr. Blackburn here."

"Then you need to make sure each of them goes home after their eight hours of work."

The Board of Adjustments scheduled her hearing for the first week in November. Kade, who had yet to see an overtime check, was summoned to be there, along with several of the printers who had worked overtime, too, and not been paid.

The Board assessed Ms. Dean a sum of $85,604 in overtime pay, a sum due her employees for the past three years.

"Who filed the initial report?" Dean asked the Board. "I have a right to know the name of my primary accuser."

"We're not allowed to give out that information, or no one would report any wrongdoing to us," the chairman said.

"I know who turned me in. He'll be lucky to have a job—any job, anywhere—after I get done blacklisting his name."

"I would suggest you not follow through on your threat. That would give the reporting person grounds to sue you."

"Let him sue me. You've essentially killed the paper I put out by insisting I compensate my employees for their overtime. Neither you nor he will be able to get blood out of a turnip if the paper folds."

"If you can't pay what this board assesses, I'm sure some time in jail could be arranged," Agent Coburn advised her.

"Can this board set up some monthly payments until the $85,000 is cleared? I can't pay that all at once."

"Yes, we can set up payments, but unless you stop asking your employees to stay past their quitting hour, you'll never get done paying out money."

"Once the politicians don't get their re-election coverage in the paper, because I have to send everyone home at five, I'm sure this board will enjoy some rather large repercussions. I'll be sure to let them know how you operate. Why I can no longer send out a reporter to interview them during the evening hours."

"This meeting is adjourned. If you'll call the board office next week, I'll see you have a schedule for the amount and times your payments are due, Ms. Dean."

Kade came in at nine the next morning, intending to work until five. He was sitting in his cubicle when she hit him in the back of his head with a rolled-up newspaper.

"I know it was you that turned me into the board, Blackburn. This may be the last paper I can ever print, due to your perfidy. I should fire you on the spot."

"Why bother? If the paper is going belly up, I'll be out of a job anyhow. Might save yourself another lawsuit by just letting the paper run its course."

"If you entertain any thoughts about me giving you a recommendation, as they say in New York, 'fugetaboutit.'"

"I entertained no such thoughts. Don't think a recommendation from you would carry much weight anyhow. I prefer to take my chances on my own recognizance."

"Yeah, like you have such a sterling reputation."

"Tomorrow, I'd like to kick an idea around with you, if you're willing to come in at seven."

"Like I'd discuss anything with you, you turncoat."

"Okay, don't come in at seven. It might save the paper if you were willing to listen to my idea."

"Hah! Listen to you? Why should I? You're worse than Judas."

"I'll be in at seven, regardless. Come if you're of a mind to."

He arrived at 6:45 the next morning. Sat down and began writing up an article on how containers at grocery stores were decreasing in size while the price kept going up. He had been keeping track of those prices and smaller containers for a good two years, so he had no qualms about comparing sizes and prices, knowing he could prove everything he wrote.

Dean arrived at seven. Invited him to her office and asked Diana to join them. *She must have called Ms. Gardner for her to be in this early. Wanted a witness to what I'm about to propose?*

"Let's have it, Mr. Blackburn. I don't have the time to waste on loony proposals. I have fines to pay, so I need to get on with the authentic news—not some cockamamie scheme you've hatched up."

"What if I offered to pay that $85,000 fine?"

Both Diana and Dean broke into sustained laughter.

"How do you propose to pay that much?" Dean said after she stopped cackling.

"I'll write you a check for the entire amount. I'm prepared to do that this morning. But there will be some adjustments made if I'm to bail your butt, Ms. Dean."

"What adjustments?" Dean asked.

"I would need to be made a co-owner of the paper. I've had my lawyer draw up an agreement of that nature."

"We'd be co-editors? I don't think that would work. Who'd have the final decisions about what got printed?"

"I'd make those decisions until you paid me back what I'm willing to lend you for your fines. After you retire the entire debt owed to me, then I'd be willing to let you make more of the critical decisions."

"Where did you come by $85,000? Did you steal it?"

"No, ma'am. I came by the money honestly. My wife says I should put it all aside for our children's education, but I figure, even if you pay me small amounts over several years, I'll be able to swing college for all four kids."

"What if you pay the fine and then I refuse to refund your money?"

"You've had a few examples of how I regard . . . know what happens to those who try to harm my family members. I'd consider your refusal to reimburse me as doing harm to my kid's education. Might be tempted to find a dark cave or mine and sequester you in it until you decided to repay me. I know a couple such holes in the earth. Mostly they serve as den sites for rattlesnakes in the winter. Do you enjoy keeping company with snakes, Ms. Dean?"

Kade saw her shudder. "I'll give you a couple of days to think over my proposal. If you decide in my favor, I'd like the paper's financial records to be kept by my wife, so all the overtime pay is paid out weekly. Abby is a certified CPA, so she's quite adept at bookkeeping."

"What do you envision me doing in regard to your proposal? Seems to me you want to be the head honcho in both the editorial slot and the financial end of things, too. What does that leave for me to do?"

"You could get out of the office and cover some news. You could edit Diana's articles, as long as you were quick about it and leave by five."

"You intend to replace me . . . totally?"

"No, ma'am. I'm willing to share duties. Come prepared to discuss what it is you'd like to do, and if we both agree it's a good plan, I'd have no problem implementing your ideas."

"You'll never agree any of my plans are valid."

"I think you'll find me much fairer in that regard than I've found you."

"When do you intend to pay off the debt?"

"Soon as you have a chance to read my proposal and sign on the bottom line, saying I own half the paper."

"Only until I pay you off?"

"We can discuss that ownership once the money is all paid back to me."

"I still think you're full of hot air."

"You're willing to take the chance of the paper folding because you think I'm lying to you?"

"Give me the agreement. It may take me a couple of days to sign it. I want to have it vetted by a corporate lawyer."

"Sure, take the agreement. I want you to check it out. Say we meet again a week from today. If you'll call me at home and say you'll sign the agreement, I'll cut you a check for the entire fine and deliver it the next morning."

# Chapter Twenty-four

"Kade," Abby said when he walked in the door after work, "this long tube came for you today. The postman brought it to the door because it wouldn't fit in the mailbox."

"I've been expecting it. Dad, I believe, sent me the portrait your mother did of him. I intend to have it framed so I can hang it up to remember him."

"It's a **nude** portrait, Kade. You can't hang it up . . . well, maybe in our bedroom," she amended when she saw the determined look on his face.

"Thought I'd see if Corrine would be willing to paint some pants on Dad, then I can hang it over the fireplace."

"How can she paint pants over it? If it's anything like your nude, she'd have to paint such a bulge in his trousers, it'd still be something I'd not be willing to hang in a public place."

"It's just a flat canvas, wife. It's the perspective that makes it stand tall. She'd have no problem putting pants on Dad, sans the bulge in them."

"Oh. I guess you're right, Kade. Do you want me to come with you when you ask her to paint on his pants? The very sight of him nude, might make her want you in the same condition—use that to demand you have sex with her before she'd put pants on your father."

"I think I can handle your mother, but you're welcome to come along if you don't trust me."

Kade opened the tube and found it was indeed the portrait Corrine had done of his father. There also dropped out a sealed envelope addressed to him. He slit it open with his penknife and saw it was a letter from his father.

**Dear Kade,**

> **My time on earth grows short. Since you never made it home for your mother's funeral, I don't think there's any reason to return for mine. Your family needs you to be there for them—to feed the animals, hunt up grubs, read them stories and make love to your sweet wife, Abby.**
>
> **Once more, since my visit, I want to say how very proud of you I am. You've become a good husband, a better father, and a credit to your community. Since my visit to Arizona, I thought you might like my portrait to remember me by. I only wished I'd known Corrine before your mother died, so you'd have her to grace your walls as well—well maybe NOT grace your walls in my current rendition. I've included a late photo of your mother. Maybe Corrine would be willing to put some clothes on mine and do up one of Mom, too, so you could display them both.**
>
> **Again, son, you've turned into the man I always hoped you'd become. Continue to raise those sweet grandchildren and love your wife.**
>
> **See you on the other side, Kade—**

**Love always,**
**Ben**

Kade laid the letter on the table and said, "I wish I'd had a lot more time with him than his one brief visit."

"It was nice of him to send along the note," Abby said, reading Ben's letter.

"Yeah. He made it possible for me to remain here with my family. Took care of everything through his lawyer. I can't help but think . . . if he's met up with Mom on the other side . . . that's why he didn't want me at his services, so he could keep it even. I didn't make it to Mom's services, therefore he didn't want me at his."

"I don't think that was the reason. He knew, from his visit here, what a hole your absence would leave in all our hearts, so he didn't want you to be missing."

"Maybe. Tomorrow, after lunch, I'll take his portrait and Mom's picture over to see if Corrine is willing to make Dad decent and render up Mom from the photo. We could all make the trek and after I dicker with your mother, take the seniors out to eat at Manzanita Inn. It's getting chilly enough in the evenings now, I could wear my sweats."

Abby broke out in laughter. "Okay, let's do it."

Owen met the group at the front gate, which he now kept locked. "You have an order of protection against me, but you feel free to visit here whenever it suits you?" Owen growled.

"I need a favor from your wife. Are you going to let us in or not?" Kade asked.

"I think she's done you enough favors of that nature."

"Dad, let us in. Kade's father has died and he'd like Mom to put some clothes on the portrait she did of his father and maybe paint up a portrait of his mother, so we could hang them in our home."

"What's this, Kade? You want to commission a portrait? It'll cost you," Corrine said, joining Owen at the gate.

"I'm willing to fork over $5000 to $6000 if you'll install some pants, at least, on Dad and do up a portrait of Mom. I'd like to hang both portraits in our home, but I can't in Dad's current condition."

"I don't want money, Kade."

"That's all I'm willing to pay. If you decline to do it, I'll find another artist who can do what I'm asking."

"You'd hire someone else to mess with one of my renditions?"

"I would. I'd like to hire you, because I know what a good artist you are, but not if the asking price is other than money."

Corrine pouted. "Oh, all right. I want the whole $6000, then."

"You'll have it once the dual portraits are done. Dad sent the most recent photo of my mother along with your rendition of him. Can you work from a photo?"

"Can you write a decent article? Of course I can work from a photo."

"Would you both like to go eat at the Manzanita Inn for dinner? I'll pay for everyone."

"You have a pair of sweats in the car?" Corrine asked.

"I'm wearing what I intend to eat in. Will my slacks and a sports coat suffice not to embarrass you this time around?"

"Do you want to go eat with Abby and this man she calls her husband, Owen?"

"No, I don't think so. He's dressed okay, but I'm pretty sure he'd do something else to embarrass us. Get into a food fight with the twins or something else just as crass."

Turning around to get in the truck again Kade said, "Guess we're dining without your parents, Abby. Let's go, I'm hungry."

His curiosity whetted, Owen asked, "Where did you come by $6000? Last I heard, you were up against it rather hard."

"I don't believe I need to explain my finances to you, Mr. Watkins."

"How does Corrine know you'll pay her if she paints those portraits?"

"Wait here, Corrine, and I'll write you a check on the spot. You can take it to the bank in the morning before you lift a single paintbrush. All you have to do is sign this agreement, so I know you won't pocket the money and refuse to paint the portraits."

"You don't trust me, Kade?"

"Since Owen doesn't trust me, we need to have all the legalities covered." Kade went to his truck and got the agreement. Brought her a pen to sign with.

"This is ridiculous, Kade," Corrine said, handing back the signed agreement. "Give me the canvas and your mother's photo. I'll call you when I'm done painting both of them."

Kade put his checkbook on the mailbox to pen her the check for $6000. He ripped the check out and handed it through the gate to her, along with the canvas of his father and the photo of his mother.

The entire arrangement was concluded without the gate being opened. Kade had to laugh about that once they were again on the road to the Inn. "Your father sure doesn't trust me as far as he can see me," Kade said.

"Well, he's not allowed within a hundred yards of our place, so maybe turn about is his idea of fair play."

"Would you like me to rescind the order of protection, wife?"

"I don't know, Kade. If my father were as pleasant and as supportive as your father, I'd say 'yes' to that notion. Since he isn't, I think I'd let the order stand."

"You wish our relationship was better, though, don't you?"

"Yes, my father is getting up in years and I do wish he'd let go of his anger toward you so we could all enjoy a better relationship."

Kade nodded his agreement.

On the road back to Chino Valley and their ranch, the twins were asleep and Alli and Andy had on their earphones listening to music. Kade said, "What do you think it would take to get your father past his hatred of me?"

"I have no idea. Divorce me?" Abby said, grinning up at him and laying her hand on his thigh to let him know she wasn't serious.

"Don't think I'd be willing to go to those lengths, love, but maybe I'll rescind the order of protection and invite the pair of them for Sunday dinners once a month."

"I remind you how often sparks fly when we eat with them."

"I know. Maybe if I didn't take offense at his words, we could get through a Sunday dinner without rancor."

"You'd be willing to do that, Kade?"

"When I think how much my father's renewed faith in me meant to me, I'm not willing to deny you the same relationship with your parents, Abby."

"Okay. We'll give it a try, but if Dad still continues to grind your gears, the experiment is off."

A week later, Kade met with Dean.

"I don't know why you're willing to go to these lengths, Kade Blackburn, but my lawyer said he doesn't find any hidden agendas in this contract, so I'm willing to sign on the dotted line this morning."

"Good. I brought my checkbook, so once you sign, I'll give you my check for the agreed-on amount."

"Then can we discuss how this is going to work?" Dean asked.

"Sure, I have some ideas, and I think you'll have some suggestions, too."

She picked up her pen and signed each of three copies—one for Kade, one for her files and one for Kade's lawyer to file away.

"Lay your demands on me, Blackburn," she said, evidently expecting the worst once she'd signed.

"No demands, Ms. Dean. I think we should meet at eight each morning and decide what's important to cover for the day. Monday, Wednesday and Friday, I'd be willing to help Diana put her articles in shape. Would you be willing to cover Tuesday, Thursday and Saturday in that capacity?"

Dean rolled her eyes at him across the desk. "That's really what lies behind your offer to pay my fine? Editing Gardner's articles? You hate that so much you're willing to lay out $85,000 to get some relief?"

"I enjoy eating dinner, at least a few days of the week, before 10 p.m. More, I enjoy reading to the twins and interacting with my family members before they go to bed. This arrangement will mean I can do so a bit more often than I've enjoyed lately."

"All right. What else?"

"I'd like my name on the editorial page of the paper as a co-owner. We can discuss that situation again once you have paid me back the entire amount I'm loaning you."

"I'm not sure I want you as a co-owner."

"I'd like to hear your reasons why you're opposed to that."

"Not many women head up papers. I like being in charge. Men tend to go totally arrogant when given that kind of power. I can imagine, if I acceded to your demand, you'd be one of those arrogant males."

"I didn't plan to ride roughshod over you, Ms. Dean. I'd just like the chance to discuss the direction the paper should take with you—maybe once a month. I'm perfectly content to cover the news as a reporter, but I have a few ideas I'd like to run under your nose on occasion. How we could increase circulation. Better ways to arrange the articles, for instance."

"What's wrong with the article arrangements now?" she asked.

"I hate having to turn to page five or six to finish the headline story. We should find a way to complete the most important news on the most important page."

"Then we'd have no place for other eye-catching news on that same front page. If readers weren't as into the headline story, they might just put the paper down, unread."

"What if we put the inside stories in a box in dark print, to entice them to read the inside pages. That wouldn't take up so much space as having a couple of paragraphs of the less-important stories on page one."

"You'd want me, as co-owner, to get out of this office and cover some of the news, too?"

"Yes, occasionally. You tend to lose touch when you're isolated in an office."

"But you don't know anything about how to line up the press runs. Those runs require me to be here in case of problems."

"I'm willing to learn, if you're willing to teach me. I envision this period as one of mutual respect, where we're both able to toss around ideas."

"Mutual respect? Like I'd believe that in a . . ."

"Okay. If you want to be totally in charge, give me back the check."

"Let's not be hasty, Blackburn. I'm willing to give it a six-month try, but at the end of that time, we'll renegotiate the contract."

"Fair enough."

At tea that night around 11 p.m. he announced the news to Abby. "I'm now a co-owner of the Prescott Frontiersman. You'll see the proof of that in Saturday's edition."

"Ms. Dean agreed to that?"

"Not willingly, I don't believe, but with her owing so much money for overtime pay to the Board of Adjustments, she didn't have much choice."

"Once she pays the fine, the Board will return the monies to me, as the new bookkeeper of the paper, and I'll figure up what each employee is to get in overtime pay?" Abby asked.

"I believe that's how the system operates. The printers have been there for many years and they'll get the biggest windfall. That should make them happy as meadowlarks in springtime."

"You're due a lot of overtime pay, too."

"Yes. That kind of takes the sting out of using Dad's insurance to pay off Dean's debt. Plus she's agreed to pay me $5000 per year on the loan."

"She'll be long gone to her grave before you get back the $85,000, Kade."

"She's not that old. She should last another 17 years. I plan to hang around that long. Maybe during that amount of time, she'll get over thinking I'm about to screw her out of the paper."

"She suggested that?"

"Told me men tend to get arrogant if they are accorded the power that accrues to owners of papers."

"Like she's not arrogant?"

"She's about to learn to be less that way. I negotiated her into editing Gardner's columns three days a week."

# *Epilog*

The next dozen years proved to be good ones for the Blackburn family. Andy and Alli went off to college on the payment Kade inherited from the sale of his father's home. Dean continued her payments each year in August, assuring Kade there'd be monies available for the twin's education, too.

All the denizens of the Ark Ranch continued to prosper. They had enough hens that they supplied a dozen eggs to about twenty families who stopped by for fresh eggs each week. Abby also supplied baby goats to 4-H members wanting to raise them as a project. She was still sad to think her baby goats would be auctioned off at the end of those projects, but she realized they'd be slaughtered in a humane way, and would add to the 4-H member's college funds. The horses grew old and fat because the twins were involved more with school and friends than spending time riding them. Kade occasionally saddled one or the other of the horses to ride out into the hills.

Corrine's redone rendition of Kade's father and the portrait of his mother now hung over the fireplace at the ranch. Kade often teased Abby that, despite the pants her mother had painted over Ben's erection, he could still see a bulge in his Levis.

As Corrine grew older and felt her age more, she'd stopped propositioning Kade for sex. Owen had mellowed a bit as he grew older, too, and he was finally able to give Kade his due—as a good husband to Abby, as a good father to his and Abby's children, and as an astute businessman, because the paper had prospered under Kade's co-ownership. As a consequence, Kade rescinded the order of protection and the Watkins now came once a month to dine with the Blackburn family.

With Ms. Dean, he'd also achieved a measure of respect. The paper's circulation was up three-fold. People stopped by the office to say they liked the new format where the main story was completed on the front page.

Kade was still reporting the news, including the crime scene, and editing Diana's columns three days each week. He'd discussed firing Gardner with Dean, but Dean was singularly unwilling to fire a female journalist, no matter how long Diana remained under his and her tutelage.

She'd told him, "I need Diana to remain on the paper's staff. I need another female who's willing to agree with me when you advance one of your lame-brained schemes, Kade."

"Which schemes are those, Ms. Dean? Seems to me that we work well together now and the paper is a lot higher in circulation, assuring its continued existence. Not all my schemes have missed their mark."

"You suggested adding a puzzle to the paper, and the Astrograph, too. The puzzle was a good idea, but giving Prescott loonies their predictions for the day was less of a good idea. Do you know how many people are unwilling to undertake any tasks if their horoscope is unfavorable for the day?"

"I don't undertake anything of a serious nature if my horoscope is unfavorable," Kade teased. "Tell me you don't pay attention to it. I see you looking at it every day. Why look if you think it's so hokey?"

"I read everything in the paper we produce. Why should that be the only thing I skip?"

"You read even the hokey pieces?"

"That's what an editor worth his or her salt does. There could be an error in that section as there could be in any other section."

"It's a canned column. It's been vetted before it ever comes to us, Ms. Dean. I think you're looking at it to see if fortune will smile on you that day."

"I'll be so glad when I finally pay off the last of my indebtedness to you, Mr. Blackburn. Then I can claim my undiluted editor's position and not have to put up with any more of your smart remarks."

"You plan to reclaim your sole ownership of the paper, too?" he asked, knowing only five or six years remained until her debt to him was paid. "I've kind of enjoyed being a co-owner of the paper. After the debt is repaid in full, will you regard me as just another journalistic flunky for the remaining years until I retire?"

"That will remain to be seen, Mr. Blackburn. I suggest you return to your station and begin editing Diana's columns if you want to remain a co-owner of the paper. I don't want any slackers on my team after the debt is retired."

Giving her a grin that stretched nearly ear-to-ear, he said, "Yes, ma'am."

"That's another annoying thing about you, Kade. You've been out of the Army so long, I'd think you wouldn't still be saying that."

"I'll be saying 'Yes, ma'am' or 'No, sir' until they plant me in the ground. Doesn't have anything to do with my service years. It's just a term of respect."

"Like you ever respected me, Kade Blackburn."

"Much as you'd like to believe otherwise, Ms. Dean, I really do hold you in great respect. You know almost as many ways to kill my ego, as I know how to kill a man. I'll get to Diana's columns now so you'll have no reason to rescind my co-ownership of the paper."

*—the end—*